"Do you not know to have a chaperon with you at all times? 'Tis not meet for a lady to have assignations alone with a man in the stable of all places!"

Maris's eyes snapped. "And here I stand with you, then! Alone in a stable, with no chaperon...and my virtue has never been safer!"

He dropped the bridle, grabbing for her as his patience broke. "I would not say that your virtue is safe with me, my dear lady," he said, pulling her to his long body. "In fact, Maris, I should say that you are treading upon very thin ice...once again." He looked down at her and saw no fear in her eyes, only surprise, and he felt the warmth of her breath touch his face. His hands on her shoulders, he eased her backward until she felt the wall behind her and he imprisoned her there, holding her with his muscled legs.

Dirick let his breath out slowly as his hands ran through her hair. She was not afraid, he noted, although if she had any sense, she would be. It was all he could do to keep from tearing off her clothes and tossing her onto the bed of hay in the next room. It was madness!

"Maris," he said softly as their gazes met. He would never see her again; and she was not yet betrothed. "I cannot leave without kissing you once more." He did not wait for a response, but dragged her up against him.

A Whisper of Rosemary

by

Colleen Gleason

Avid Press, LLC

Published by
Avid Press, LLC
http://www.avidpress.com
1-888-AVIDBKS

A Whisper of Rosemary
ISBN 1-929613-42-3

Cover illustration donated by Chris Dodge

All royalties from this publication will be donated to the
Cystic Fibrosis Foundation.

To Linda, Lauren, and Mom and Kate....
Thanks for being there for the journey.

Prologue ᔑ

1137 London, England
The Court of Stephen of Blois

*T*he chamber was as cold as her hands…as cold as
her heart.
 Allegra stood, passive, as her maid Maella fussed with her
intricate coiffure and its covering wimple. Her gown was beautiful—His Majesty would not have his ward marry in tatters—a
soft blue velvet undertunic that fell to the stone floor, covered by
a busily-embroidered tunic of yellow and green.

Her hands were so cold!

"I cannot do this." The words issued from her lips like the
hiss of breath from a dying man. "Michael…."

Maella paused in her ministrations, looking up at her mistress from where she knelt to tie her slippers. "My lady…you
cannot fight the king's will."

"I cannot marry this Merle Lareux!" A tear appeared in the
corner of one hazel eye, threatening to spill onto a tear-streaked
cheek. "I will not forsake my love!"

"My lady, Lord Michael left London early this morn," Maella
smoothed her mistress's hair under the wimple.

"He could not bear to see me given to another," Allegra
sighed, painful tears glistening in her eyes.

"Or, some say, wanted to be reunited with his wife."

"Nay! He has no wife!" Allegra cried angrily. "What evil lives in this court that the tongues wag of such nonsense!"

Maella started and looked fearfully over her shoulder. They were in the ladies' chamber alone, but the walls always had the ears of greedy courtiers eager to find favor with the king. "Hush, my lady!" She smoothed her hand down the soft velvet of Allegra's tightly-laced sleeve. "Hush. 'Tis enough that you will appear at your wedding with tear stains on your face to show your mislike of the king's will!"

A wave of nausea engulfed the bride and, covering her mouth, she groped for a bowl. Maella was quicker and managed to save the beautiful tunic from being soiled. When Allegra finished emptying her churning belly of that morning's bread, her maid carefully wiped her mouth.

"The babe must have a father. You cannot wed with Lord Michael, my lady. The king has given his orders! His majesty favors you with this marriage—Lord Lareux is a wealthy man. No one need know that the ward of the king goes to her marriage-bed less her innocence."

Allegra let the tears pour forth. "He will kill me!" she breathed. "He will kill me if I come bearing the babe of another man! Why did Michael not come for me this morn?"

Maella snorted, "'Tis not as if he were foolish enough to take the maidenhead of the king's ward and then come steal the prize away from his man!" She turned to dampen a cloth to wipe her mistress's face and muttered to herself, "He is a fool in many ways…but not foolish enough to be run through for wife-stealing. He may pluck the fruit, but then leaves it damaged on the ground for the farmer to retrieve later." Then she added in a mumbling undertone, "That strange light that glows in his eyes is enough to make ye cross yerself thrice in his presence."

Fortunately, Allegra did not hear her maid's dire opinion, or 'twould likely have meant a hard slap across the face for the outspoken servant. Instead, she was bewailing her fate once again. "What know you of this Merle Lareux?" she demanded tearfully. "What say his lackeys, what is the gossip?"

"The lord is fair and just," Maella invented as she adjusted the bejeweled girdle around Allegra's waist. "He fights like a true warrior. He is close to the king." That last was true—King Stephen would not bestow the well-landed Allegra Branwen, Lady of Cleonis and Firmain, upon an unimportant vassal. "He is very proud."

"He will kill me if I bear the babe of another man!" She looked as though she would burst into tears again. She smoothed her hand over her flat middle, knowing it would be a girl-baby. She would never make her daughter–Maris, she would call her–marry a man she did not know.

"He need not know of the babe!" Maella whispered fiercely, again casting about to see if anyone listened. She, too, was fearful of the wrath of the great Lord Lareux. He was as lief to throw them out of the keep as he was to toss them into the dark dungeons of Langumont if he was dissatisfied with his wife. "You must be brave, my love." Maella's voice was a comfort to Allegra, as it had been for most of her short life. "I have the calf's bladder—I will be there when you come to prepare for him tonight. We will secret it under the bed, and you will use its blood to show proof of your innocence whilst he snores through the night. Use it well—smear the blood over you and onto the bed, and there will be no questions that the babe born six months hence is but proof of my lord's virility. You must flinch and scream when he joins with you, as if 'twas your maidenhead that he breaks."

Tears crept down Allegra's cheeks, but she nodded. It was her only hope. She had to be brave.

She shivered at the thought of a strange man's hands on her body and wanted to scream. Why did Michael leave her? Why did he not take her with him? She sighed, thinking of his oddly-colored eyes that seemed to delve right through her, and the heat that flared in them when they were together.

"My lady, we must to the chapel," Maella draped a light cloak around Allegra's shoulder and they swept out of the room.

The long hallway through the keep seemed darker and more damp than usual. Although it was early summer, the stone walls kept out much warmth and Allegra found herself drawing the cloak still closer about her as if protection from the chil, as well as the man whom she was to wed.

Uncontrollable shivers wracked her as she entered the chapel and caught sight of the tall man at the altar. He was dressed in royal blue and grey. She could not make out his features from this distance, and his face was half-hidden by a full, dark beard. Allegra caught a glimpse of the king, who sat complaisantly near the altar in his specially-carved armchair. One of the royal men-at-arms appeared to take her elbow and prod her leaden feet down the aisle toward her fate.

The walk to the altar seemed to take forever…and at the same time, it was over much too soon. Suddenly Allegra was standing next to the man who, by whim of Stephen of Blois, and by virtue of politics alone, would be her husband.

Her hand was placed in a large warm one, and, at last, she raised her chin to find herself the object of curious study by surprisingly warm eyes. The man gave her a small smile that perhaps belied the fact that he was as unsettled as she about the speed of this marriage…and then he turned to the priest, nodding for their wedding to commence.

Part I ❧

One ✌

*T*he coffin lay in the center of a dark, damp room. Flickering candlelight threw shadows across the long, oak-hewn box and along all sides of the room. A bunch of rosemary had been placed on the red-garbed coffin by the grief-stricken widow, though she had quit the room to weep in her chambers long before. Only her son—the youngest—knelt nearby, offering prayers to the Heavenly Father, and vows of revenge to the murderer of Harold Derkland.

The pain of kneeling on the cold stone floor registered in the back of his mind—yet the discomfort was naught compared to the anger in his heart. He still wore the heavy hauberk of battle, still had a sword belted to his waist, still knelt into the chain mail of his chausses. The tears of grief had long dried in rivulets down his grimy face, yet his hands clasped still in impeachments to the Father Above. A thick hank of dark hair fell upon his forehead; more wavy locks clung in sweat to the back of his neck. His grey eyes were hooded in prayer, his jaw clenched in anger, and the stubble that grew upon his face from three days nearly hid a ragged scar along his left jawline.

A soft clunk behind him went unnoticed until his squire knelt beside him.

"Sir Dirick," the boy said in a low voice, "you've eaten aught, and slept little—"

"Leave me," he interrupted tonelessly.

"My Lady Rosamunde sent me 'ere—"

"My mother of all would understand. Leave me." His gaze had not flickered from the carved wooden cross on the prie-dieu. When the boy would speak again, Dirick began yet another paternoster and the squire was forced to adhere to his commands.

The night was the blackest then, and as the tallow candles burned lower and began to flicker, drowning in their own wax, the room slipped into murk. Still, Dirick did not move.

Dawn began to light the east and the room took on a greyish cast. The walls were dull grey stone, covered with tapestries woven by his mother's sewing women. Two narrow windows near the eastern end of the long chamber captured the pale glow of dawn and allowed it to leak into the room of sorrow. He was once again able to make out the ornate cross he had focused his prayers upon through the vigil. As light colored the cold room, warming it, the thick red bolt that covered the coffin turned from a shadowy grey to the color of his father's blood. A presence beside Dirick at last drew his attention; the scent of his mother and the rustle of her skirts against the rushes announced her. Though he did not turn, he knew her face, as it was as dear to him as the one now swathed in burial clothing. Pale golden hair covered demurely by a heavy wimple and the same grey eyes that he had been blessed with, along with a smiling mouth: those were the images he kept of his mother in his heart.

She spoke, her voice raw with grief, "Come, Dirick. We must to the chapel."

"Nay, Mother, I'll come with Father." He at last turned from his vigil to look at her. Rosamunde's face was wan and drawn, yet the tears had dried and she was resolute.

"Mother...." He took her small hands in his and pressed a kiss to her palms, doffing his face against the softness. "I am sorry."

The doors were opened to the room, and Lady Rosamunde's two other sons entered, and behind them, the pall-bearers and a tiny blond woman.

"Dirick!" Bernard, now Lord of Derkland through this horrible twist of fate, embraced his younger brother. "We feared you would not come in time." The small blond woman, the wife Dirick had yet to meet, came to stand beside her husband.

"Lady Joanna." Dirick gave her a small bow. "'Tis sorry that we should meet under these circumstances." He responded, then, to Bernard. "His Majesty bade me leave when the news came." Rising stiffly to his feet, he turned to his tonsured sibling. "Thomas, please take Mother. I'll come."

Father Thomas and Lady Joanna led the weeping woman from the chamber as Dirick and Bernard hoisted the heavy coffin to their shoulders. They and the other four pall-bearers led the procession through the keep and out into the biting November air. The chapel, of the same square-cut, grey stone as the keep, was nearby and packed with mourners. Lady Rosamunde knelt at the altar next to Lady Joanna, clutching more rosemary tied around dried roses from her garden. She watched the procession inch up the short aisle and her gaze did not move from the box that held her husband. Light streamed in from the round, stained-glass window above the altar, casting blue and red shapes upon her face.

Father Thomas of Derkland led the ceremony, and needed to be assisted more than once by the village priest when words failed him. Harold Derkland had been much loved by his family and the people who knew him, and would have long remained so had not someone helped him to a violent, early death.

࿓

It wasn't until the coffin had been covered with the brown, clay-like soil of Derkland, and Lady Rosamunde had been led solicitously to her solar by her daughter by law, that Dirick made his way to a different abovestairs chamber. His squire, Ivan, was there to disarm and disrobe him, then disappeared to fetch some food while Fennel, the chambermaid, prepared a steaming bath.

With a groan of pain and exhaustion, Dirick slid his sticky, filthy body into the water. Three hard days of riding and twenty hours of vigil at his father's side had taken their toll. He hadn't taken the time to speak with his brothers since his arrival; but now, despite his complete physical depletion, Dirick's mind reeled with the question of how his father had died so suddenly—and so violently—during a peace-time.

But he was so tired that he could do naught but close his eyes and rest his head on the side of the tub, and wait for his brothers to join him. He hadn't even the strength to ask for a cloth to wipe his face; and was thus heartened when the maid began to pour water over his shoulders.

Fennel was just rinsing the soap from his hair when the chamber door opened.

"Dirick."

At the sound of his name, Dirick opened his eyes just as a bucket of water was emptied on to his soapy hair. Blowing out of his nose and mouth, he shook his head and opened his eyes to see both of his brothers, along with Ivan, who carried a tray of food.

"How did it happen?" he demanded immediately, disregarding the too-long hair that dripped down his face.

Bernard sighed, running a huge, hamlike hand through his hair, but seemed unable to find the words to speak.

Dirick rose from the tub, water cascading down his long, lean body. Stuffing a chunk of bread in his mouth, he took a long gulp of wine, then stilled so Fennel could rub him dry. She worked quickly in the ensuing silence, as if knowing they would not speak whilst she was there.

"Looks belike you've seen some battle," commented Thomas, his bald pate gleaming in the candle light.

Dirick glanced down carelessly at his naked body, which was battered with bruises and several fresh wounds. "Aye," he replied from around a thick hunk of cheese. "The king seeks to subdue his own brother and keep all of Anjou for himself." He gulped three swallows of wine, wiping his mouth with the back of his hand as he finished the last bite of cheese. "Geoffrey will soon learn the wrath of Henry the Angevin and leave his brother's lands as if they are full of plague. He must needs be content with what his father left for him."

"Some say Geoffrey has rightful claim to Anjou now that Henry has been crowned King of England." None of the brothers, including Bernard, feared to speak what some would consider treasonous words in their own company. "They say 'twas his father's will."

"Aye," Dirick said as he pushed a crust of bread into his mouth. "Yet the king is not one of them. He will have all of Anjou, all of England, and, aye, all of the lands brought him by Eleanor of Aquitaine."

"And you will help him get there," Thomas said dryly.

Nodding, Dirick relieved Fennel of her cloth and briskly rubbed his thick, tousled hair, impatient to get to that which ate away at his mind. "Aye. Whither King Henry goes, so I go. He's been on English soil nary a year and already seeks to gobble up lands in France. He won't have an easy time of it without the queen's blessings—at least in Aquitaine."

Dirick looked out from under the towel and found his squire through the strings of hair obscuring his vision. The boy stood ready with a clean undertunic of white linen and handed it to his master. "You may go," he told Fennel. "Send Clive for the tub anon."

"Aye, my lord."

As soon as she disappeared from the room, Dirick rounded on his brother. "What happened?"

Bernard leaned forward as Dirick sat on a nearby stool. "Father left a fortnight ago for Maitland to see about subduing a band of thieves." Bernard looked grey for a moment. "Had I gone, as I wished, 'twouldn't have been a tragedy."

"Father has always done his own will," broke in Thomas. "And it was God's will that He call him then."

"Then God's will was helped by someone's knife!" snarled Dirick with sudden venom, furious and sickened at the loss.

Thomas gave his brother a quelling glance. "We don't question how God goes about His will—"

"Aye; but I will know who helped Father to an early grave— God's will or nay!" He slammed a clenched fist onto his thigh.

Bernard broke in, "'Twas on Father's trip to Maitland he was murdered." The last word came out bitterly. "No one of Father's escort survived. There seemed not to be even a battle—they were set upon and murdered by men hidden in the wood."

"They were relieved of all gold and valuables," Thomas added, his grey eyes troubled. "Yet, since there were no survivors, it bespeaks of something rotten. It would seem that it was no mere robbery."

"There is one other thing." Bernard's eyes took on an intensity and his face became grim as he leaned toward Dirick. "I mislike speaking of it…yet you must know. Merle Lareux, Lord of Langumont—know you of him?"

"Nay. I've been on the king's business in Anjou for five years—I know little of his vassals here. Is he the culprit?"

Bernard shook his head firmly. "Nay…. Lord Lareux came upon the bloody scene and rode to inform the castellan at Maitland."

"The bearer of bad news is not absolved of suspicion," Dirick reminded him. "'T may be that he wishes to appear the innocent." Although Bernard was the older brother, Dirick's years of spying for the man who was now King of England had stripped him of all naiveté, and the result was a crust of cynicism he was unable—mayhaps unwilling—to shed.

"Merle Lareux is not a murderer." Bernard shredded Dirick's suggestion with a black look. "He is a man of honor. Father wished to betrothe me to his daughter, and 'twas Lord Lareaux who witnessed at my wedding with Joanna." When Dirick opened his mouth to speak, Bernard's anger flared and he knocked the stool out from under him with one swift kick. He stood, glaring down at him, "Be still! What else I must tell you is not an easy thing to say, yet you try my patience!"

"Do you not speak to me like a woman!" Dirick raged, bolting to his feet as weariness and impatience got the better of him.

"Bernard! Sit!" Thomas stepped in before yet another royal fight erupted between the two tempered brothers. "Dirick! Close your mouth and listen! I will tell the tale since I have more sense than you both!"

Dirick sank back onto the stool, an unsettling feeling swimming in him. When Thomas's face tightened as it had, 'twas bad news.

"Lord Merle noted an unusual thing about the scene whence he came upon it. Father was dead from a lance in his back, yet...." Thomas's swallow was audible. "'Twas as if he'd been...arranged. Father was sprawled on his face, his arms were bent, reaching out for aught...and Sir Gregor was laid the same, and their hands were touching."

Dirick choked back a grimace. Before he could speak, Thomas raised a hand to still his tongue.

"And Father's neck was broken—it looked to be smashed by the boot of an angry man...or, more like, by that of his destrier.

Merle Lareux said he was on his stomach, having bled all he could bleed, and it was as if someone drove his heavy foot onto his neck. His head was tilted back to look up at the sky as the bones of his neck pressed into the ground. As was Gregor's. The other bodies were left untouched in this manner."

There was silence for a moment as Dirick digested the scene. Nausea swirled in his stomach and he fought the urge to let his recently-eaten meal surge back up. A seething anger swept through him and he bolted to his feet. Thomas and Bernard were ready for him—they understood what he was experiencing—and they caught his arms, steadying him back onto his stool. "God's blood!" Dirick groaned in pain. "I will kill him. I will hunt the man down and kill him." His voice was deathly cold and filled with bloodlust.

"We will find him," Bernard promised his brother. "We will avenge Father."

༄

Maris stabbed herself with her embroidery needle for the third time and bolted from her chair. "Mama, I can no longer sit, waiting for news of Papa!"

Allegra, Lady of Langumont Keep, as well as Firmain and Cleonis, looked up from her tiny, perfect stitches. "What would you have done? We can merely wait till he is sighted from the tower. The messenger of two days ago rode hard and told us of his delay—"

"But Mama, he must be near to the edge of the village by now! May I ride to the village to see what news?" Just as it was typical of her mother to sit staidly and wait for what would come, it was in Maris's nature to rush headlong to meet her future when it did not move quickly enough to suit her.

"Nay, my dearling, we shall have news soon enough. Rushing to the village won't bring your papa any more quickly." She looked firmly at her only child. "Christ's Mass is almost upon us, and you must finish your embroidery soon."

Maris frowned down at the intricate blue and silvery grey design she had wrought into a fine cream-colored linen. 'Twas true: she much preferred galloping across the meadows of Langumont Village to neatly stitching a border for her father's surcoat. The stitches were done well enough—though not as perfect as her mother's—but the whole length of the tunic stretched out in front of her, and she could see naught but hours and hours and days and days of embroidering royal blue falcons among grey swords. There were so many other things to do than sit in the solar with her mother and the castle seamstresses and ply needle to fabric!

A great lady must know how to sew, her mother always reminded her—and how to play the lute, and how to mix the right herbs to treat the ailments of the castle-folk and villagers. But a great lady would not be a great lady if she did not know how to run her household, or ride well enough to visit all of her lands, or how to mete out justice when it was needed. When Lord Merle was in residence, Maris spent her time with him, learning all there was to know of the lands. But the moment he left, Lady Allegra jealously guarded her daughter and kept her busy with ladylike occupations; leaving the steward to run the household, and the master-at-arms to watch the keep walls.

With a sigh of defeat, Maris plunged the needle into the fine wool of her father's surcoat. The ladies sewed in silence for a few moments, and Maris tried desperately to keep her mind on her stitching. When she jabbed herself again on her already scarred and pin-pricked finger, Maris shot to her feet and stalked over to the narrow window of the woman's solar room. Her shoulders relaxed in disappointment when she realized what she thought may have been dust from the pounding of her father's horses was the sway of trees in the distance.

"Why do I not speak with Gustave about the meal for Christ's Mass. I do not recall giving him a number for special loaves of bread for the serfs as yet." Maris suggested, turning back to her mother, who had continued to stitch without pause. It was a contrived excuse—Gustave, the seneschal of Langumont Keep, had been running the household and overseeing the meals since the day Allegra had been brought there as Merle Lareux's wife.

Allegra glanced up, giving her a defeated smile. "Be off with you, then, Maris. I trow you'll be stitching on that surcoat on the eve of Christ's Mass to finish it on time."

Pressing a kiss to her mother's cheek, Maris fled from the room—lest her mother change her mind and guilt her into continuing work on her Papa's gift.

On her way down the steep, stone stairs, Maris passed Maella, who trudged up to see Allegra. "A guest belowstairs wishes to speak with your mother," explained Maella as the old woman puffed her way up the steps.

"I shall greet him for a moment while you announce him to Mother," Maris offered. "Who is he?"

Maella shrugged against the harsh wall, "I know not; 'twas Gustave 'at sent for Lady Allegra. The man asked expressly to see her."

Maris frowned at the irregularity of the situation. Guests were announced to the lord of the manor, and if he was absent, the castellan—the man-at-arms in charge in her father's absence—greeted the visitor. When she became lady of the keep, guests would be announced to her. Allegra rarely became involved in these matters except as the wife of the host: she was too timid and shy to wish to appear as lady of the manor, particularly since Maris had reached an age where it was her pleasure to do so.

As Maris came around the corner of the stairway, she entered the large, busy room of the Great Hall. Serfs hurried about in preparation for the evening meal. The ceiling of the hall loomed high above, and across the room, a fire roared in its place. It was tended carefully by one of the cook's sons all the day, and by another son all the night. A bulky man stood warming his hands at another fire crackling at the north end of the hall—the end at which large chairs and benches were gathered for the lord and his family to sit.

Trestle tables lined the rest of the hall, radiating from the dais at which the high table was placed. The dais was built off the wall adjacent to the fireplace so that Lord Merle and his guests had warm, comfortable seats during meals.

The man seemed to be alone; no squire or page was in attendance. Maris swept her skirts and crossed the hall, noting as she did so that the rushes that covered the floor would need to be replaced before her father arrived home.

"Sir, you are well come to Langumont," she greeted, hurrying toward him.

The man turned in surprise and his stare locked on her. He was not a tall man—Merle would top him by a hand or two—but he was well-built and muscular. A neatly-trimmed black beard and moustache covered the bottom of his face beneath a hawklike nose with a distinct hump on its ridge. His lips were a thin line among the black hairs that grew there, and his deeply-set, hooded eyes studied Maris as she drew closer. "My lady Maris," he greeted her.

Maris was slightly discomfited that he seemed to know her when he had asked for her mother; but her confusion grew to discomfort when he did not offer an introduction. Instead, he instead continued to look at her with shiny black eyes as if he'd never seen a woman before.

"Aye, sir knight?" she responded, hoping to prod some sort of identification from him. It wasn't as if he were staring at her like a love-struck swain, but as if he were searching for something in her visage.

When he still did not speak, Maris was set to demand an introduction and a reason for his invasion of her keep, when the strange, dark man spoke. "Ah, you do favor your father."

She frowned in spite of herself, unease trickling down her spine. Shaking it off, she replied sharply, "Sir knight, I know not what game you play—if 'tis to gain my father's favor by odd compliments, you play alone, for he is not within. 'Tis well-known that 'tis my mother that I favor—as I have her eyes and the set of her mouth."

He burst into a rough laughter. "Aye, my lady, and you gain the jut of your chin and the cast of your fair skin from none other than your father." He seemed to find this increasingly amusing, and Maris, having been dissuaded from her purpose long enough, was just turning to the castellan to have the man cast out of Langumont Keep when Lady Allegra made her appearance.

Maris turned to her mother, speaking, "Mama, 'tis no need for you to be bothered with this traveling knight. We shall offer him a evening meal, and a pallet in the stable, then he shall be on his way after breaking his fast in the morn."

Allegra froze halfway across the hall. She stifled a small gasp and stared as if she could not believe her eyes.

"My Lady Allegra," the man was sweeping her a mocking bow.

"You—are well come," she said haltingly. Then, turning to the others that gaped at her—the least of which was her own daughter—she commanded with the strong tone of voice usually heard only when the sewing ladies laxed on their duties, "I will speak with our guest. Maris, continue about your task. The rest of you, go back to your duties."

She turned from them, carriage rigid, and paced toward the blazing fire. Her orders were obeyed, though she knew that Maris was the last to leave the room.

"What a lovely daughter," spoke the man musingly, turning slowly to face the woman who had not seen him in years.

"I...Bon! 'Twas thought you were dead!" she sank onto a stool next to the fire, staring at him.

"I've come back to life, so it seems." His dark eyes taunted her.

She forced a smile over her frozen features. "You are then well come to the home of my Lord Lareux and myself."

A soft, cruel laugh rumbled from deep in his throat. "Aye, Allegra, I am so well come that you did not greet your brother with open arms in view of your serfs and daughter! Are you so certain I am well come?"

"Half-brother," she reminded him angrily.

"Aye," his laughter stopped abruptly. "Son of a lord and his lady, I am...unlike my sister—" he bit the word out, "who was spawned by a whore!"

Allegra flinched as if she'd been slapped. "Why come you here?"

"Your daughter is lovely," he said, his attention boring into the orange flames. "The beauty of the fair Maris...The fair maid with the same look of her mother...eyes that change with her mood...." He taunted her further, "The daughter of Lady Allegra and Lord Merle...."

She felt her head lighten as he speared her with his gaze, his last words floating in the air between them. A cool hand fluttered in her lap, digging into the material of her gown. "Aye...." her voice was a mere whisper.

"...Or not?"

Her eyes widened in horror. "What...do you say?" she

breathed.

Lord Bon de Savrille stepped back from his trembling half-sister, turning to look across the empty hall. There was a cold confidence in his movements and words; the proprietary sweep of his gaze. "Thither is the beautiful maiden, heiress to the vast lands of Merle Lareux. She must be near a ripe age to be wed…. It has been seventeen years, has it not?" He turned slowly to look at Allegra. "'Twould be a shame if the truth were found out, aye? Were the great Lord Lareux to learn that the daughter he adores is not of his—"

"Enough!" Allegra cried violently, whirling from the fire to cast her gaze fearfully about the room. Her heart was in her throat, choking her so that she could barely speak. "Do you not speak such lies in my home!"

"Lies," Bon rumbled from deep in his throat, "that have such truth to them that the walls of Langumont Keep could come crumbling down about you." He looked at her calmly, seeming to enjoy the fear that ate into her. "Lady sister, I have returned…from the dead, if you wish…for my rightful inheritance."

The numbness of fear was so great that she did not comprehend his words.

"What…?"

"Cleonis, Firmain…and now, thanks to your marriage to Merle Lareux…Langumont, Edena, and Damona." His eyes took on a fanatical gleam. "I am the rightful heir to Father's lands!"

"Nay! He disowned you, you disappeared when he wed with Mother! You cannot claim Cleonis!" Though she knew little of the ways lands were enfeofed and distributed, Allegra felt certainty sweep over her like a cool storm.

Bon was upon her in a quick stride, wrapping a hand around each of her upper arms, leaning into her face so that she could not get away from the stench of his wine-sodden breath. "I cannot claim Cleonis…as a son," he said softly, "but perhaps as a husband.…"

"A husband?" she breathed, the fear stifling her as the meaning of his words penetrated. He would claim Maris as his wife? His own niece?

He stood back, a nasty smile easing over his face. "'Twould be such a shame for Merle to learn of the truth of his daughter…and his wife. However," he stroked his beard with menacing slowness, "that unpleasantness could easily be avoided were the beautiful heiress of Langumont entrusted to the right husband.…"

"Never!" She turned away in a rush of fear and anger. "Never!" she spat again. "I will never give Maris to a dog such as you!"

His face was angry, but he merely looked down at her with cold eyes. "In time, you will come to see the advantage of my offer. I wed Maris, inherit Langumont and Cleonis, and you remain the healthy wife of Merle Lareux. If not…ach…I fear 'twould be a convent for you…or worse."

His eyes were sharp as they raked over her still form. "This is not the last you will hear from me." Without another word, Bon turned and strode from the hall to be escorted to the gate.

Allegra eased herself slowly onto the stool, her head light, the room a spiral. An icy hand crept to her forehead and she stared blankly into the bright flames as tears strolled slowly down her cheek.

ॐ

Upon receiving word that his favorite personal knight was back at court, Henry Plantagenet summoned him immediately to his presence.

He paced in his private bedchamber, indulging in a jewel-encrusted goblet of one of the finer wines fermented in the homeland of his wife, Eleanor. As he tipped the last swallow of the contents into his mouth, a squire was there to refill the goblet. Henry pulled a hand across his mouth to catch a drizzle of blood-red wine as a firm knock came at the door.

A man-at-arms poked his head around the heavy oaken door and announced, "Your majesty, Sir Dirick of Derkland."

The king waved his attending squire and the man-at-arms out of the room and prepared to greet his man.

Dirick strode into the king's chamber—where he'd had the privilege of many such private audiences in the past—with a flutter of flowing cape and tunic. The sword that was normally removed in the presence of the king clattered onto the stone floor when he knelt hastily and pressed the king's outstretched hand to his forehead.

"Get the hell off your knees!" Henry demanded jovially. "Have I not told you the next time you come into my presence armed, you will be permanently unarmed?"

"Aye, sire," Dirick stood at his full height, looking down at his shorter king and liege. "Shall you do it personally, or require a man-at-arms to disarm me on the field of battle?" A wicked, easy smile crossed his face, "Surely even your majesty could unarm a travel-weary knight—even the best fighter in the realm!"

Henry roared at his man's audacity, slopping more wine into his goblet. "'Twould be your own comeuppance were I to bite that challenge!" If the truth were to be told, both men knew that Henry was a champion jouster and fencer and he and Dirick would be well-matched if set against the other. In fact, 'twas Dirick's prowess—evenly matched with his king's—that caused Henry's eyes to cast his way many years ago when Henry was but a well-landed lord. The king chuckled into his goblet as Dirick waited expectantly: though they had an easy relationship and threw irreverent barbs between them in private, both men knew who was the king and lord of the realm.

"Sit yourself down!" Henry growled, continuing to pace. "Your height offends me!"

Dirick sank onto a stool near the crackling fire and tried to warm his hands. Henry's sharp eyes surely did not miss the weariness and pain that lined his man's face, but he said nothing save, "Your father is laid to rest?"

Dirick swivelled toward his liege lord, surprised at the personal tone of his voice. Though Henry relied upon him to keep him apprised of the mumblings and grumblings across the channel, the king normally remained exactly that: the king—uninterested and uncaring about the personal lives of his men—even to the point of demanding the immediate presence of a travel-weary knight that had been ahorse for two long, cold days; even to the point of having him met at the gate of the keep to be ushered into his presence before he'd been able to divest himself of cloak and sword. Dirick answered, "Aye. He is laid to rest— yet I will not rest until I lay hand and sword upon the man who helped him to an early grave."

"What is this?" He stilled, facing Dirick suddenly.

His face set and hands clenched, Dirick told him of the scene upon which his father's body was found. "'Twas without a doubt a mercenary, conscionless man—and I will meet him."

"And you say Merle Lareux of Langumont found the body?" asked Henry, his handsome, ruddy face serious.

"Aye. My brothers discount him as the guilty party; yet I am not as certain. If he had aught to do with my father's death—"

Henry shook his head wisely, "Nay, Dirick, here you bark up the wrong tree. Langumont is as just as any man in my kingdom—aye, I would be the happiest of lieges were half the men of England and Aquitaine of his ilk. 'Tis a fact—you have been among the French courtiers for too long and see evil where there is none." He began his incessant pacing once again.

Dirick inclined his head, politely, but remained unconvinced. He would not discount Lord Merle Lareux at the least until meeting the man. "My brothers assured me of the same, sire. I am gratified to hear it from you as well." *And I will make my own decision upon the matter.*

"You may have cause to speak with Langumont in the near future…and I do not wish to see my best man step in cow dung because of his suspicious nature." Henry took a sip of wine, watching Dirick over the rim of his goblet. "I have no more need of you in Paris for the time."

"My lord?" Dirick tried to keep the relief from his voice, but did not quite succeed. Not to be sent back to France was more than he'd hoped—indeed, he'd expected to plead for a short release from the king's service to accommodate his need for revenge. "You have another charge for me?"

"Know you of Bon de Savrille? Lord of Dreakskil—by the fault of whom, I do not know." Henry rolled his eyes in disgust, then his sharp stare pinned Dirick as he waited for a response.

Dirick shook his head slowly, remaining outwardly patient; but chafing inside to learn how he could be free to find his father's killer. "Nay, my lord, I've not heard even the name."

Henry tapped a long finger thoughtfully against his upper lip. "'Tis just as well." He was silent for a moment, and Dirick waited for him to speak, content to let the feeling creep back into his frozen fingers.

"I have heard rumblings concerning Bon de Savrille," Henry began. "'Tis said he is not as fond of the new King of England as he should be—yet he has done nothing yet to alarm us. Still…he has yet to pledge fealty since my coronation. 'Tis always a plausible excuse…first 'twas an uprising of bandits that had to be put down…then he was ill with the ague…another time he was unable to come for the harvest was coming in." Henry cocked an eyebrow at his companion, "As you see, 'tis nothing that which I should have excuse to call arms…yet it does not sit right. De Savrille vexes me."

Dirick helped himself to a goblet of wine, wondering how this bit of information was to help him in his quest. "As I have not heard of de Savrille, 'tis likely he has not heard my name. Were I to use the false name that served me well in Paris, I could root around to find out if 'tis aught but his feet that smell."

Henry chuckled. "Aye. 'Twould work well were the itinerant knight Dirick de Arlande, lately come from Anjou, to befriend the possibly disloyal Lord of Dreakskil."

"If Bon de Savrille seeks evil against my lord, I will find him out."

"Very good." Henry nodded. "On your journey to Dreakskil—'tis near the Welsh border, if you do not know—you will pass through the lands of Merle Lareux—Langumont, Cleonis, and Firmain. 'Twould befit you to avail yourself of his hospitality, and you have my permission to reveal your true purpose to Langumont so that you may pursue your own trail. He may also know something of de Savrille. I shall have a letter with my seal as proof of your mission to be shared with his eyes only."

"Thank you, my lord," Dirick felt the weariness ease away, to be replaced by an invigorating energy. "I am gratified at your generosity."

Upon speaking with the Lord of Langumont, Dirick would, at the least, learn more about his father's death…and at the most, he would catch a murderer.

Two ᔰ

It was a cold, clear day, and the sun was high in the sky. Maris shielded her eyes from the brilliance of the snow as she picked her way to the herb garden next to the keep. A thin veneer of ice gave the ankle-deep snow a glassy look but it did not hold her weight, so that when she stepped, there was a soft crunch on the ice, then a *whoosh* as the ice gave way and her foot sank into the soft snow.

Crunch—*whoosh!* Crunch—*whoosh!*

Maris walked like Good Venny, the old man who'd taught her of the healing herbs—plodding along slowly, one foot higher than the other until it *whooshed!* into the snow. She carefully waded into what would be a lush, green garden in the summer…but what was now a patch of straggly-looking bushes scattered with footsteps from other herb-gathering ventures since the last snow.

Using a stick to poke through the crusty snow, Maris uttered a sound of satisfaction when she spotted some bruisewort leaves still clinging to their branches. In another fortnight, there wouldn't be any left, and she'd have to resort to the dried ones—or even the roots—but until then, Maris didn't mind the walk outside to pick fresh leaves. Although the dried leaves would do, the fresh ones would make a better poultice, and she wanted to be certain that Hickory's foreleg healed properly.

Having gathered the last handful of the season, Maris clumped back to the keep. Inside, she went to her herbalry, a small room near the kitchen, and, using a knife she kept expressly for that purpose, chopped the leaves into a pot. Maris poured boiling water onto the herb, stirred them briefly, then strained the excess water from the mixture.

Gathering the mass of soaking leaves into a clean cloth, Maris returned outside, heading quickly to the stables. Her mare, Hickory, nickered softly from the last stall on the left. Maris crooned gently to her, petting the soft black nose that rooted about the folds of her cape for the dried apple hidden therein. She offered the treat to her, then knelt in the stall to look at the injured leg.

Yesterday's poultice was long dried, and Maris peeled the strips of cloth away. Gingerly feeling the length of the mare's foreleg, she noted Hickory's start when she pressed on the muscle that had been strained a week earlier. The swelling from an abrasion against a rough stone had gone down; but the mare was still in too much pain to walk easily.

Before the bruisewort poultice got cold, Maris pressed the cloth that held the herb onto the tender spot on Hickory's leg. The horse nickered softly and butted her nose against the top of her mistress's head. Holding the herbal mass firmly in place, she wrapped clean strips of cloth around it and bound it firmly to the injured leg.

Just as she straightened up from her task, Maris heard excited shouts from the courtyard.

"Papa!" she exclaimed, having been attuned to his imminent arrival for days. With one last pat on Hickory's nose, she grabbed up the old bandages and rushed out of the stable.

It was, indeed, Merle Lareux's arrival that had sent the entire bailey into an uproar. Nearly half a year had elapsed since he'd left to answer King Henry's call to arms—not in Aquitaine, with his majesty himself; but up in the north, where the Welsh were sampling away at the border.

Maris stopped right outside the stable and stood impatiently as the marshal rushed to take the reins of her father's mount. She knew well enough to stand back from the war-trained destrier her father rode—the horse went mad at the smell of blood, and it was only her father's voice that could calm the steed. Even outside of battle, the horse was high-spirited and mistrustful of strangers. That in itself was the ultimate security—it would take a brave man to get near enough to the steed to take him from Merle's stables.

"Papa!" Maris exclaimed as soon as his feet hit the ground.

"Daughter!" he exclaimed, sweeping her into a warm bear hug.

"Papa, I am so happy you are here at last, and in time for Christ's Mass!" Maris kissed him on his bearded cheek, her hands wrapped around one of his sturdy arms.

"Look at you, lass!" He set her away from him to get a good look at her, then pulled her back to plant a kiss on her forehead. "You should not be out in the cold, little girl," he reprimanded. "See you how red your nose is! Come, let us to the hall. How fares your mama?"

"Mama is well," Maris kept her grip on his arm as they walked together toward the keep. "She has seen me in the solar, plying the needle without rest, it seems, since you have left."

"Ah, so that is why you are so glad of my arrival," Merle teased, "so that you do not have to sit like a lady and do the things that ladies do!"

"Nay, Papa!" Maris's outraged denial shook the rafters of the Great Hall as they burst in. "I have missed you sorely! And there are many things that great ladies must do to keep their lands in order—things that cannot be done whilst sitting in a solar!"

He chuckled. "Aye, my love, I but like to see your nettle up." Their attention was drawn to the frail, fluttery figure of Lady Allegra as she glided across the room to greet her husband.

"My lord," she raised her cheek to receive his kiss, "you are well come! It is glad I am to have you home for Christ's Mass."

"My lady Allegra," he returned, taking her long fingers in his large hand. He tucked them under his arm and led the two women to a warm seat by the blazing fire. He took his place in a carved oaken chair whilst Allegra chose the smaller chair next to him.

Maris sank to her knees, gathering her skirts about her in the fresh rushes, and curled up at his feet. "Tell us of the new king!" she insisted, gesturing for a maidservant to bring mulled wine for her father.

"He seems a fair man," Merle replied with a fond smile at her. He reached out to smooth a hand over her thick hair, then turned to accept the wine offered him by the maid. "'Tis glad I am to swear homage to him than one of Stephen of Blois's ilk."

"And Queen Eleanor?" asked Maris. "The news we have received, scanty as 'tis, says much of her."

Merle nodded his silvery grey head. "Aye, she is fit to be queen. Her lands number almost those of Henry's. She holds her own court, and sits in with the king. She is a shrewd, beautiful woman. 'Tis said she took up the cross when her first husband, Louis of France, went to Jerusalem."

"She went on crusade?" Maris was so astounded she nearly pulled to her feet. "Queen Eleanor? How did that come to be? The king allowed it? What did she wear? I should love to meet such a woman! What tales she must have!"

Merle took a piece of bread from a tray and chuckled. "I am not surprised to hear you say thus, Maris. Her majesty brought her own legion of women with her," he replied. "And I shall not relate to you the manner of clothing, for 'twas scandalous to even the French—and I fear you may get your own ideas from it!"

Maris pouted, and was just about to ask another question when a light hand rested on her arm. "Milady."

She turned to find Widow Maggie, the lines that creased her face deeper than usual. "Aye?" she dropped her voice so as not to interrupt the conversation that continued around her—already turning from talk of the queen to battlefield stories.

"Milady, you must come at once. Thomas the Cooper's wife—she be strainin' to deliver her babe an' she ain't comin'. I done all I kin," Widow Maggie—who wasn't nearly as old as the lines on her face made her look—pleaded in earnest.

"Of course." Maris rose with a sweep of her skirts. Merle looked up at her questioningly and she leaned to plant a kiss by his ear. "Papa, I must go. There is trouble with a birthing in the village."

He nodded permission. "If it is dark when you finish, be certain to send for a guard to escort you home. I wish to speak with you this evening, if I am not too weary and have found my bed before you return. Else, I shall see you on the morrow, daughter."

Maris hurried to follow Widow Maggie, stopping only to retrieve her pouch of herbs and her cloak.

Outside the keep, a chill wind had kicked up and flurries of snow blew raucously about her cape and Widow Maggie's three layers of wrap. Maris knew the way to Thomas the Cooper's home, and trudged along as quickly as she could. She wondered briefly what her father wished to speak with her on—for his face had seemed overly serious, and mayhaps a bit uncomfortable. But, she could not think on that now, for upon reaching the dank, dark hut, she could hear the screams of the woman inside.

Drawing a deep breath—as much to calm her nerves as to dispell the stench of blood, urine and other waste—she ducked her head and, pushing aside the heavy door, entered the hut.

In one corner of the dwelling was a bed, with a prone woman

twisting agonizingly on it. Her huge belly swelled up from under the old blankets. Thomas sat next to her on a three-legged stool and held her hand. A block of wood was clamped tightly between her teeth, but did nothing to stifle the moans and shrieks of pain.

The windows were shrouded, and smoke from the firepit choked her vision. Within moments, Maris had Thomas and Maggie opening the windows and chimney to let the stagnant air out of the room.

"Good Venny says darkness is not good for the humors," she explained, pushing the blankets up over the woman's abdomen. Dried blood smeared her legs, but Maris could see the crown of a babe erupting from her womb. "Bring water," she ordered. "And, Maggie, some of that lye soap. Good Venny says to wash before touching aught."

The leeches and physicians of England did not always agree with the tenets of Good Venny's homeland, Jerusalem, but Maris had been taught by him and rarely veered from his wisdom. She washed her hands quickly, then wiped the legs of the woman so she could see better. "'Tis crowning," she offered to Maggie, who stood next to her. "We must get her up. Can you help me?"

When Maggie nodded, Maris made her way to the side of the bed and spoke to the woman, "Mistress, the babe is near come. We will help you to stand for a moment, and can you push? I know you are weary, but 'tis almost here."

"Aye, lady," she breathed. "Thank you, lady."

Thomas watched in horror as Maris and Maggie lifted his exhausted wife to her feet, and, holding each arm, urged her to push.

"The pull of the earth," Maris explained between gasps of air. "The pull helps the babe to come."

After a long push, which ended in a keening moan from the woman, Maris felt a huge movement in the stomach. "It comes!"

She and Maggie eased the woman back onto the bed. The babe's head was well out, and Maris carefully helped pull from its shoulders. Suddenly, it was all over and the squall of a newborn filled the hut.

"'Tis a son," Maris announced, handing the babe to Maggie. "Now, mistress, one more push to rid you of the afterbirth and you may rest." She looked at the woman's stomach that was still huge and realized something was wrong. The long, low keen of pain from Thomas's wife attested to that. "Push!" Maris ordered, replacing the block of wood between her teeth.

She saw a foot crest at the woman's womb and exclaimed to herself, "Aye! 'Tis as Good Venny said." Back to Thomas and his wife, she said, "Push, mistress! Comes another babe!"

It took the rest of the woman's strength to rid herself of her second son, and the afterbirth, mercifully, came immediately after.

"She will sleep," Maris told Thomas. "'Tis like the babes were tangled in the womb and could not come." She gave him a packet of herbs with instructions to boil them with water and have her drink it as often as she would. "Send Widow Maggie if aught else happens. She will bleed some, but not overmuch." Turning to Maggie, she asked, "Is there not a wet nurse in the village? She cannot see to suckle the babes for some time; cannot the smith's daughter, whose babe did not, come wet-nurse?"

"Aye. I will fetch her."

"My lady, we thank'ee for coming." Thomas tugged profusely at his forelock. "My lady, thank'ee for my sons."

"It is glad I am that they came. Your wife will be poorly for some time—do you not work her until Maggie gives the word. Keep the smith's daughter for a wet nurse as long as you need."

Then, because the room was closing in on her, Maris had to get out. She said her last farewells and slipped from the close, smoky hut.

It was dark—Maris looked up in surprise at the moon and stars. She'd spent nearly the whole day in that tiny room! Weariness washed over her, followed by a burst of exhilaration at the realization that she had helped two new babes into the world.

Her feet crunched in the snow as, exhausted and hungry, she trudged along. She clutched her pouch in one cold hand, and tucked the other inside her cloak. The moon was bright in the clear sky, lighting her way as if it were day, and despite her father's suggestion, she saw no need to have a guard escort her through the village to the keep.

The gate was just ahead, lit invitingly with torches. Her papa would likely be in bed; she would have to wait to speak with him on the morrow. She hoped he wasn't angry that she missed supper. Her stomach gnawed at her in reminder that she'd barely tasted her midday meal when Maggie called her away. Mayhaps Gustave had saved some bread and cheese for her when she didn't return for supper.

Suddenly, she was jolted from her thoughts as a huge horse appeared from nowhere. He was coming too fast down the narrow street for her to move, and Maris shrieked, holding up a hand to shield her face.

"'Sblood, wench!" cried the rider, jerking back frantically on the reins of his mount as soon as he saw her shadowed figure. "Foolish woman, do you not open your eyes when wandering at night?"

She turned her face indignantly up to meet the eyes of the rider. He was a stranger to her, but obviously a man of high rank, as he wore chain mail and rode a horse as valuable as her father's. Even in her anger and fright, she took in the details of his appearance: he was tall and dark, with thick black hair curling wildly at the nape of his neck. One big hand waved his helm angrily at her while the other fought to keep his mount under control.

"'Twas your good fortune that I could stop Nick in time!"

Dirick snapped, noting the dirt-streaked face hooded by a thick cloak. In the bright moonlight, he could see her eyes flashing green sparks at him—rather like an angry cat, he thought fleetingly—and with an indignance that did not befit a simple peasant wench. A comely wench, she would be, however, if she were cleaned up a bit, he thought suddenly, allowing his gaze to do a leisurely sweep over her from head to toe. Before he could voice his thoughts, she snapped back at him.

"'Twas no fault of mine!" she told him haughtily. "I did not leap into your pathway! Do you not open your eyes when ahorse? If not, sir knight, 'twould befit you to do so, else in battle, you may find yourself in a more telling situation than nearly trampling a woman!"

Annoyance flashed through him at her scornful response, and he jerked Nick nearly on top of her, glaring right down into her face. She did not back away, but glared back: her burning golden-green eyes an incongruity in the dirty face. A cuff would serve this saucy wench well, he thought angrily, his palm itching to lay across her face. At the same time, he found himself wanting to cover those saucy lips with his own, and soften that firm, cleft chin with his fingers.

"I can think of much better things to do with a woman than trample her," he replied harshly, wheeling Nick in front of her to cut off her escape. Marry, the girl was beautiful!

The wench drew her breath in sharply, obviously understanding his meaning all too well. "Sir, you overspeak yourself!" she told him, backing away.

Dirick lunged for her arm from his saddle, but she was too quick and dodged into the shadows. He sat back and, after a moment, laughed at himself. 'Twas just as well. He was wound so tightly 'twas unlikely he'd pleasure her much; and 'twould be a pity to spoil such comely goods. How his blood had boiled at her sassiness! he thought, smothering a grin. His brothers would have laughed to see him in a sparring match with a spitfire maiden!

With a frustrated shake of his head, he gathered up Nick's reins and urged him on down the street toward the center of the village. He expected to find an inn where he could sleep this night, and then present himself to Lord Merle Lareux on the morrow.

Dirick frowned as he looked about him. The streets of Langumont were lit only by the moon and stars, but clearly showed well-built houses and a relatively clean center square. When he'd passed some men-at-arms at the edge of the village, they'd taken notice of him—a single rider on a good mount—but did not attempt to stop him from entering the town. 'Twas obvious that, although they were sharp-eyed enough to notice a stranger, they did not deem a single knight to be a threat.

He shifted in the saddle, peering into the darkness in search of an inn, and realized he was annoyed. Although the wench had fueled his short temper, his foul mood truly stemmed from the fact that Dirick had seen nothing abnormal about the town or its inhabitants—nothing that might indicate that its liege lord was a maniac who mutilated the body of Harold Derkland. In sooth, Dirick *wanted* Merle of Langumont to be the man who killed his father. He wanted him to be the murderer so that his vengeance could be had and he could put the pain and ugliness behind him.

But Dirick was very afraid that it was not so, and that he had just begun his journey of revenge.

༄

Maris ran the last bit to the gateway of the keep. The hood flew off her head and her long braid bounced along her shoulder as she hurried into the safety of the keep. What a mule's behind! she thought irreverently of the man who'd accosted her. A handsome mule, she admitted, with good taste in horseflesh...but much too overspoken; and nearly blind to boot.

Had he laid a hand on her, she would have called the guards down on him so quickly he wouldn't know what happened.

Suddenly, she was embarrassed. The Lady of Langumont Keep had only been challenged because she looked like a wench—in a simple cloak, without a wimple; her face dirty and her hair straggling about, trudging the village streets at night.... What was he to think?

He'd thought exactly what he should have thought: that only whores walk the streets at night.

A blush suffused her face as she hoped profusely that this man was not a visitor of her father's, that she would never face him again; for she would certainly be recognized as the lady that walked the streets at night, filthy as an urchin.

Maris let herself into the Great Hall and was surprised to find her father seated in his chair by a blazing fire. The serf who tended the fire during the night slept curled on his pallet in the corner, near enough to tell if the flames lowered.

"Papa!" she exclaimed softly, aware of the pallets for the men-at-arms that lay just on the other side of a screen of blankets.

"Daughter," he looked up from a chessboard. "You are here at last! I'd begun to worry, but Father Abraham's servant sent to me that the birthing was difficult."

Maris lowered herself into her mother's chair and gratefully took the chunk of bread her father offered her. "Aye—'twas two babes. Two boys. They are well and squalling, and overjoyed to be in this world!"

"With much help from you, I trow. 'Tis good work you do, Maris. You are good to the people here."

She felt herself swell with pride at her father's words, and tears glinted at the corners of her eyes when she saw the smile on his face. "Thank you, Papa. You know that I love Langumont, and its people, above all—save you, of course."

Merle shifted in his heavy chair, seeming uncomfortable. He darted a look at the fire, which still burned happily in its grate, then filled his lungs with a long, steady breath. "Maris, I nearly did not live to see you again," he told her, returning his gaze to her. "I was sorely injured in battle, and were it not for the grace of God and the assistance of another man, I should have been left on the field to die. 'Tis why my return was delayed so long."

Maris stared at him in shock. "But Papa, why did you not send word? I would have come—"

He smiled fondly, patting her hand. "I know you would have, daughter, and I could not have had a better one to nurse me back to wellness than you. I did not send word because I did not wish to worry your mother. And I did not wish you to leave Langumont." He sighed, stroking his beard, and was silent, as if struggling to find the right words. "As I lay there, determined to live, I realized that had I perished, I should have left you and your mother alone and unprotected. And Langumont unprotected."

Maris felt an unease creep over her. What was he trying to say? It did not bode well, if the expression on his face was any indication. "We would not be unprotected, Papa. Sir Raymond is here, and…." She trailed off and folded her hands in her lap, looking at her herb-stained hands and scratched fingers—the fingers of a maidservant, not a great lady.

"'Tis time you were wed," he told her quietly, but with a firmness in his voice that brooked no disobedience.

Her gaze snapped up to him as horror shot through her. "But I do not wish to wed, Papa!"

"I know that," he responded, his words steady, "but wed you will, Maris. And by Christ's Mass next."

"Nay!" The denial sprang from her lips in a whisper.

He appeared not to hear her. "I have sifted through the many suitors that have inquired for your hand—"

"You misspeak yourself, Papa, they inquire for my lands! Nothing more!" Maris said wryly. "Would that you had heirs other than me, that I could choose my husband!"

He gave a short laugh. "If you were to choose your husband, the occasion would never happen!"

Merle's bushy eyebrows furrowed, "You are heiress to Langumont, Maris Lareux! You are Lady of Firmain and Cleonis—and one of the most powerful titles in the land! You cannot disown your heritage. Your husband must be worthy of your lands and be well able to protect your rights." He leaned toward her, his blue eyes serious. "You are lady of the lands in your own right—I would not wish to see you lose that power, Maris. You will rule in your own right, yet a man is needed to ensure that you remain able to do so."

"Papa, have you not allowed me to learn to ride and hunt as well as a man? Have you not insisted that I learn to read and write so I can keep my own accounts? Yet you feel that I am not able to retain hold of my own lands without a husband!" She looked imploringly at her father, her small hand resting over his big one. "Do not force me to marry yet!"

He was shaking his head slowly. "Aye, Maris, I insisted that you be as able to rule your lands as a man, yet never did I disallow the fact that you must marry. It is the best for Langumont, too, daughter—Langumont, which you purport to love as much as you do me! The people cannot be left without a strong liege to protect them, and, intelligent and brave as you are, my dearling, you cannot ride into battle and defend the lands."

Maris opened her mouth to argue, then closed it as she realized he spoke the truth. "Papa, at the least, do not force me to wed with a man I do not know!"

"Maris, I am not fond of the word 'force.' Yet, I cannot let this linger any longer. If aught should happen to me, Maris, dearling, I could not protect you from the wolves out there. They are there, my love, and I would that you do not have to meet with them." He paused for a sip of his own wine. "The son of the man who saved my life in battle rides to Langumont," he told her suggestively. "Do you not startle him away as you've done your other suitors by flaunting your horsemanship and archery skills."

"The son of whom?" she asked suspiciously, fearing her fate had already been sealed.

"You shall meet him," he promised.

Maris's heart sank. Merle's admonishments were enough to place the suspicion in her heart that her husband had been well and fairly picked for her. "Aye, Papa," she said, staring studiously at the hands in her lap.

"Good girl, Maris." He put his arm around her, pulling her shoulder to his. "Know I want only what is best for you."

"Aye, Papa," she said again, struggling to keep the sadness from her voice.

After a few moments of silence, she rose slowly. "I'll to bed now, my lord." She kissed his cheek gently.

"Sleep well, child," he said quietly, brushing her face.

༈

Merle hoisted himself carefully into bed. He'd not slept for two days in his haste to get home, and he was more than ready to close his eyes. His muscles ached, not to mention the wound in his side that was barely healed enough to sit ahorse.

Allegra sat in the bed next to him. She had dismissed Maella after the maid brushed out her long hair and braided it in its customary plait. Curls framed her face as her wide gaze fastened on her husband. He sensed her tension and, not understanding the reason for it, reached to take her cold fingers.

"'Tis glad I am to be home," he told her, bringing them to his mouth for a soft kiss.

"And I too," she murmured, pulling her hand away as she reached over to drag the draperies about the bed.

"Maris is grown to a beautiful lady," he said, staring at the velvet draperies as she drew them together. "'Tis well past time for her to be wed."

Allegra froze. "My lord?"

"Aye. She will be wed within the year. 'Tis not safe for her otherwise."

"My lord, have you—know you—my lord, you may not find a worthy man in the year."

"Aye, yet I have found one. One that is worthy of my Maris's hand, worthy to have Langumont." He scratched his belly and looked at her slim form with interest. It had been a long while since he'd bedded his wife, and though she wasn't the most receptive woman he'd coupled with, she was his wife, and she was there.

"But, my lord—who?" she croaked.

"'Tis the son of a dear friend." He struggled under the blankets to twist and show her the ugly wound in his side. Allegra gasped and covered her face at the sight of the red, swollen gash. "A dear friend that caused this not to be my last wound."

"Maris must see to it," she managed to say, pointing at the pus that oozed from it.

"Aye. On the morrow," he told her. "She was late in the village tonight, and it can wait another day."

"But, my lord, do not make the decision to betrothe Maris in haste," she said, reaching out to touch the grey-speckled hair on his scarred chest. "Mayhaps there is another—"

"Nay. Lady, know you this—Maris will wed with Victor d'Arcy on Christ's Mass next. He is well suited for her. He rides as we speak to sign the betrothal agreement."

"So soon?"

"Aye. 'Tis tired I am of fending off the offers for her; and tired I am of her scaring off every available suitor. Even Bernard of Derkland, giant that he is, was dissuaded by her manliness. She talks like a man and they turn tail and run. She will marry Victor—'tis for her own well-being."

She twisted her fingers into the heavy fur that covered their bed. "But my lord, surely there are others—"

"Woman, do you not hear me?" Merle was irritated. "She will marry Victor d'Arcy and that is the end of it."

"Aye, my lord." Her voice was choked and her attention was turned away, fixed on the inside of the curtains near the bed.

Merle thought of one other thing, "Allegra. Do you not let Maris bathe Raymond Vermille any longer. He looks at her too admiringly; and 'twould not be good to inflate his infatuation. Send Maella or Verna to take care of him."

"Aye."

Weary of waiting, and in no mood to coax, he closed his hand softly over her breast and drew her close. "Come, woman, 't has been nigh long."

Three ✍

Bon de Savrille opened his swollen eyes slowly. Too much wine and wenching to celebrate Christ's Mass, he thought wryly. His head pounded and the daylight streaming into the inn's room was too bright. Verna stirred next to him and he swatted her hard enough to force a squeal as she started awake. She rolled over leisurely and gave him a long, tonguing kiss.

His hand grasped her large breast and squeezed until she emitted a moan of pleasured pain, then his teeth bit at her nipple. Verna purred as Bon's large hand swept over her body. She closed her own work-roughened fingers over his erection and proceeded to torment him until he threw her onto her back and drove fiercely into her body.

Rough nails scored his back and the pain and smell of blood only served to heighten his pleasure. The pounding in his head receded and passion ruled him now. Verna was quite the best lay he'd had for years; 'twas good fortune that had led him to her on the threshold of Merle Lareux's keep.

In the afterglow of their angry, violent mating, he lay staring at the low, dark ceiling. He'd watched from a distance as Merle Lareux returned to his home; seen how the people greeted him—and, especially, how his daughter Maris attached herself to his side. 'Twas obvious that the man adored her—and that made

Bon's scheme all the more brilliant. Allegra, his stupid sister, would not dare chance driving a wedge between her husband and daughter…not if she wanted to continue as Lady of Langumont Keep.

A sigh of satisfaction gleamed over him as his thoughts wandered to having the beautiful heiress of Langumont in his bed. He'd watched her follow the old lady into the village two days earlier and spend the better part of the afternoon in a tiny, filthy hut ministering to some peasants. They would be good partners—she the figurehead, the healer…he, the great lord, the meter of justice. And in bed…. He felt himself become aroused at the thought of her face screwed up in passion, her hazel eyes smoky with pleasure.

Verna felt him stir against her and lazily turned to face him. "My lord, you are randy this morn," she murmured, pressing her buttocks into his erection.

He said nothing, but when his hand felt between her legs, he found her ready for him as well. Bon thrust into her from behind, catching her off guard. She writhed with pleasure, and he pounded himself inside Maris of Langumont over and over until he filled her with his seed.

"Soon, my lady," he promised softly, knowing he would ride from the gates of Langumont Keep this day. "Soon."

৵

Merle Lareux sat opposite a stranger knight, listening to his story. The young man, Dirick de Arlande, had come to the keep early that morning, requesting a private audience with him in the name of the king, and Merle had no choice but to take the time to meet with him.

He was glad he'd done so.

When he was handed a missive sealed by the king, he was

even more impressed. This was no mere messenger of his majesty. Merle's gaze raked over the figure dressed in black and blue that stood confidently before him. His standard, which Merle did not recognize, was a shield with a sword on the backdrop of a blazing yellow flame. Lord Merle felt himself being studied by the pair of cool grey eyes, and sensed an underlying impatience and restlessness from the man.

"To account for my words," Dirick concluded his explanation, gesturing to a thick parchment packet, "I bring a missive from His Majesty."

Merle turned the parchment over in his hands, noting the red-waxed seal of his sovereign. Breaking the seal and unfolding the creased missive, he perused the king's words carefully.

"The king speaks highly of you, Sir Dirick," he said, refolding the parchment. Something niggled at the back of his mind, and it took a moment before he realized what it was. "You are Dirick of Derkland—Harold's son? Bernard's brother?"

"Aye." Dirick's gaze bored into him and he shifted his stance into a more imposing position.

"Good men; 'twas an honor to know your father. Eh…you are aware that I…came upon his death-scene." He tightened his fingers on the parchment, remembering the depravity that pervaded the glen where he'd found Harold's mutilated body. It was like nothing he'd ever seen, even on the worst battlefield. A maniac had been there…and even as he'd attempted to see if there were any survivors, he felt the weight of the evil suffocating the small, still glen.

"Aye." The word was a short, snapped one, and still the grey eyes did not waver.

"My deepest sympathies are with you," Merle told him somberly, recognizing the hurt and anger in Dirick's face, but uncertain as to why he sensed defiance emanating from him.

"Thank you."

"The king writes that you are in search of the murderer of your father," Merle continued, gesturing with the parchment. "I would be happy to be of assistance in any way I can." His offer was sincere, although he did not have any urge to relive the experience of coming upon that bloody scene.

Dirick looked at him directly. "I should like to know every detail."

"We traveled along what must have been the border of Maitland and the king's forest—my man-at-arms, Raymond, my squires, and several other arms-bearing men rode with me. 'Twas late in the day—twilight—and we were weary, seeking the Keep of Maitland for succor. As we rode, a shrill, horrible cry met my ears. 'Twas the cry of a horse in pain. My mount reacted as if itself were in danger; but once given his head, he thrashed through the brush to the glen."

Dirick took a drink from his wine. "There were no survivors?" he asked after a moment.

"Nay. We put the horse out of her misery—she was tied to a tree with three broken legs," he swallowed. "'Twas a waste."

"My father?"

Merle took a deep breath, remembering the scene...and recalling the last time he'd seen Lord Harold hale and hearty—at the wedding of Bernard and Lady Joanna Swerthmore, nearly a year ago. "I would it had not been your father. We had talked on betrothing your brother to my Maris—the marriage of Langumont and Derkland would have been a fine one. Alas, 'twas not to be—Maris and Bernard did not suit, and he was busy rescuing Joanna of Swerthmore from her brute of a husband. However, your father did favor the match."

He sipped from his wine to moisten his parched throat and continued his description of the scene. "Your father was dead from stab wounds, yet the bastard slit his throat. Very little blood drenched the ground; so'twas clear he was already dead when his throat was cut. And then…" He rubbed his temples with a fore-finger and thumb. "…the madman drove a horse's hoof into the back of his neck; snapping it; driving his neck into the ground even as his face looked up at the tree. He was arranged opposite another man, their hands joined at the wrist."

Dirick swallowed heavily, unable to thrust the vision from his mind. His body hummed with fury as he realized, faintly, that his suspicions of Lord Merle were beginning to dissolve in the wake of Merle's obvious difficulty in reliving the horrific experience. "By God, I will find him." His vow was soft and hard and reverberated certainty. "For my father to die unshriven…in such an unspeakable manner.…"

"Nay, he was not unshriven, lad," Merle told him. "A priest was in my party and gave last rites to your father and his companions."

"Praise God for that, at the least," Dirick said quietly. "Is there aught else; aught that will help in my quest?"

Merle was silent for a moment. "I can think of naught. The men were divested of coin and weapons, some horses were missing…yet, I believe 'twas no mere robbery."

"Nay. Slaughter is more like," Dirick agreed harshly. "God help the man who did this."

"I questioned the nearby villages for news of a roaming party of bandits, but either they were too frightened to tell me, or they saw no one. That is all I can tell you, I am sorry."

Dirick nodded, and at that moment, there was a knock on the door of Merle's private chamber.

"Aye, come," he called.

The door opened and a page entered, bearing a folded parchment. "My lord, this arrived by messenger. He was told not to await your reply."

"Thank you," Merle took the missive, and, glancing at the seal, smiled in satisfaction. "Ah, good, 'tis from Victor." When

Merle looked up, Dirick returned his attention from taking in the details of the small, wood-furnished room and met his gaze. "'Tis a message from the man with whom I hope to betrothe Maris," he explained. "He rides with his father, Lord d'Arcy, and should arrive within a se'ennight."

Dirick raised his brows, remembering that his own father had considered matching Bernard with Langumont's daughter. "Hope to betrothe?" he repeated, wondering what it was about the woman that kept his brother—and, obviously, numerous other suitors—from laying claim to her many lands through her hand. Mayhaps she was impossibly ugly—still, few men would turn away the chance to hold as many lands as the Lord of Langumont regardless of what the woman looked like.

"Maris is rather...unusual," Merle confided with an indulgent smile. "She is well nigh over seventeen summers, and to date I have not found a suitable man for her. 'Tis nearly done—just the papers need to be signed upon Victor d'Arcy's arrival."

"Unusual?" Dirick's suspicions were heightened. She must be incredibly ugly, or deformed in some way...or, perhaps, mad? Nay, surely Bernard would have mentioned such a detail.

Merle chuckled to himself, and, smiling at Dirick, dismissed his question. "You will join us at the high table anight?"

"Aye. Yet, my lord, please remember that outside of this room, I am Dirick de Arlande—lately come from France, an itinerant knight in search of work. I do not know Bon de Savrille at all; but I cannot chance that word might get to him about me before I arrive at Dreakskil."

"Aye, of course, Dirick. I do not know him well, yet I know of him. He was slated to be at my side in the battles in the north; he showed himself for a mere three days. He kept to himself, and eventually left his men to return to Dreakskil—presumably to handle some goings-on there. Methinks the man is merely a coward; yet, I would not be too surprised were he to turn up as a supporter of the Welsh uprisings."

"I will not leave immediately for Dreakskil, if I may intrude upon your hospitality for a time. I must be sure he is there before I make the journey; and 'twould do me some good to be nearby if you remember aught else of my father's demise." *And to ascertain that you are, in sooth, the honorable man you seem.*

"But of course—stay as long as you like. 'Twould be my pleasure to put some work your way, if 'twould help your tale?"

Dirick smiled. "Aye. That would be helpful. Thank you, Lord Merle. I will sit at table with you this eve and be most pleased to make the acquaintance of your daughter." *Most pleased indeed.* Dirick tucked a grin into his cheek as he imagined telling his brother Bernard of his meal with the lady who had rejected his suit.

ॐ

When she heard the news that a man had arrived to see her father, Maris made her escape from the keep. Wishing to put off meeting her betrothed, she grabbed two apples and a hunk of cheese and went out to the village. There were several people she should visit—including Thomas the Cooper and his wife—and she wanted to gather the last of the bruisewort leaves from her garden. It was her intention to be scarce for the entire day.

And so it was nearing dusk when she finally returned to the keep. Managing to avoid her father, mother, and probable suitor, she sneaked up the huge stone steps that led to the women's quarters above the Great Hall. Verna was awaiting her in her own chamber, ready to help her dress for dinner.

"'Tis late, my lady. My lord will soon be voicing his displeasure if you are to miss a third evening meal," Verna commented as she helped Maris out of her work tunic.

"Aye." Maris's teeth chattered as she stood in the chill room clothed only in her shift. "I could not find a reason to miss this meal as I have the last two. Nay, I think the gold bliaut, Verna."

Her maid dutifully pulled the gold-colored undertunic from her lady's wardrobe. It was shot through with gold thread, making the tight-fitting garment look like the ocean under a sunny sky. Verna laced up the sides so that it fit like a second skin.

"The green tunic, my lady?" she asked, pulling on a brilliant overgarment trimmed with gold thread.

"Aye." Maris refused to give thought to why she would dress her finest when a man she should detest sat below, waiting to slather all over her hand and her lands.

Verna pulled the long, loose-fitting tunic over Maris's head. There were no sides to the tunic; merely a hole for her head with a deep neckline to show off the golden bliaut underneath. A gold girdle wrought in the shape of loose flowers and leaves cinched the tunic in place at her waist.

She was strangely nervous at the thought of descending the stairs to dinner. She knew that her father's mind had been made up, and that most likely the man she was to marry awaited her below. As much as she might abhor—and fear—the idea of marriage, Maris had come to realize that 'twas for the good of Langumont that she must wed…and that it would do her little benefit to anger her father by rebuffing her intended betrothed. At the least she knew her father would not wed her to a man as brutish as her friend Joanna of Derkland's first husband.

There was no time to redo her hair, so Verna left it in the heavy plait that hung down her back. Flyaway wisps of rich, dark brown had sprung from the braid, framing her face. Verna tucked them under the sheer, gold-shot wimple that was draped over Maris's head and neck. A thin filigreed headdress held the wimple in place, and Maris was dressed for dinner.

She inched her way along the hall and toward the steps that would bring her to her father's table for dinner. Reluctantly, she started down the stairs, enjoying her vantage point of the hall.

The cacophony of readying for the evening meal drifted up to her. Serfs bustled about, men-at-arms pulled the long trestle tables together and settled benches along each one. Female serfs stood aside, ready with trenchers and crudely-carved wooden cups to place on the tables. The three dogs that were allowed in the hall slept next to the fire, knowing that their scraps would come much later. Maris allowed those three hounds in the hall only because they were her father's favorite hunting dogs—or had been before one was blinded, one lost a leg, and the third got so old he couldn't run any longer.

A group of men-at-arms sat in front of the blazing fire— some were engrossed in games of chess or chance; others were drinking ale and sharing jests. Still others were flirting with the female servants, hoping to find one to share their bed, no doubt.

Maris's feet brought her closer to the bottom of the stairs— directly across the room from her father's table. She wove her way carefully between the tables, serfs, and men-at-arms, toward the dais…and noticed with a sinking heart that indeed her father was engrossed in conversation with the man who was undoubt-edly her unwanted suitor. He suddenly looked in her direction, catching her by surprise and causing her heart to leap awkwardly into her throat.

His dark gaze, that was suddenly, embarrassingly familiar, caught hers and held from across the hall. She nearly stopped walking; but with effort managed to continue on, willing herself to act undeterred. Instead, her own gaze traveled over the thick, dark hair that tousled about his face, less wildly than it had in the breeze the night before. As she drew closer, she saw that his eyes were grey—not the angry black that she remembered flashing their fury at her in the starry night. His nose was straight and angular; below it, a firm, generous mouth stilled as he broke from his conversation with Merle.

Dirick had happened to look up as one of the most beautiful women he'd ever seen entered the room in a swirl of green and gold. He lost track of what he'd been saying to Lord Merle, and could not keep from staring as she made her way closer to the dais.

She sparkled gold: from the gossamer veil on her head to the long, wrist-length sleeves of her gown. It wasn't until their gazes locked that the shock of recognition flashed through him. Those were the same, thick-lashed, green-gold eyes that had spit fire at him the night before!

As she drew closer, he scrutinized her closely—his voice automatically rejoining the conversation with Merle while he studied her, trying to determine that he was mistaken. But, no, the nearer she came the more clear his error was. A warm flush began to settle over his features as he recalled the rude and angry words he'd shouted at her the night before.

His next question—who was she?—was soon answered; but not before he privately agonized over whether he'd insulted his lord's wife, his mistress, or—but quite improbably—his daughter, Maris.

When she reached the dais, her gaze flitted over him and then turned to her father. "Ah, my love," Merle stood to take her hand.

Dirick rose stiffly beside him, trying desperately to think of something to say in defense of himself. After all, what the hell had a noble lady been doing dressed in peasant clothes, wandering through the town—alone!—in the middle of the night?

"Sir Dirick de Arlande, may I present you with my daughter, Maris Lareux, Lady of Langumont," Merle said proudly.

His daughter! Dirick felt himself go numb as the only clear thought that remained in his mind was why had his brother rejected her! "'Tis a pleasure, my lady," he managed to say, pressing a light kiss to her fingertips. He noticed the stains and scratches on what should have been a lily-white hand with interest and wondered what she did other than embroidery.

Maris refused to look up at him when he took her hand. His fingers were firm and warm when they closed over hers, and she noticed the strength evident in the veins and tendons that molded the back of his hand. The feel of his skin against hers jarred Maris and she slipped her fingertips out of his grip, moving away from his unsettling presence. "Good eve, Sir Dirick," she said steadily, refusing to meet his gaze, and took her seat next to Merle. Allegra would sit on the other side of him, with Dirick next to her—for which Maris was supremely grateful. The last thing she needed was to be seated next to the overbearing man who had not only threatened her, but propositioned her as well.

With good reason, she reminded herself. She'd been dressed like a serf, and looked like one with her dirty face and straggly hair. She hoped he would not share the story with her father—particularly because she'd disobeyed Papa and walked back to the keep unescorted.

Merle was speaking to her. "Sir Dirick is lately arrived from France—Paris, I believe. I knew his father quite well, and he will be staying with us for some time."

Maris's stomach clenched. So it was he. "Yes, Papa," was all she could bring herself to say. And, thankfully, Allegra's arrival distracted Merle from noticing her discomfort.

Dirick shared a bread trencher with Lady Allegra, and as his mind raced, he occupied his hands by serving her as elegantly as the fine courtier he was. No sooner had she sipped from her wine than he refilled it. Her meat was cut swiftly into bite-sized chunks with the knife that he kept at his waist. She had the choicest pieces of bread, the sweetest-smelling pieces of fish. And she had charming conversation.

He didn't realize until near halfway through the meal that he'd been holding his breath, waiting to hear the roar of fury from Merle as Maris told him of their encounter. When it didn't come, he began to relax, finding Allegra's empty-headed company simple to handle. Though she didn't talk much, she asked several questions and giggled like a girl at his jests.

Dirick was well adept at carrying on a conversation with half a mind, and following his own trail of thoughts—or eavesdropping on another conversation—at the same time. When he realized that Maris wasn't going to share the story of their first meeting with her father, he had to wonder why. Mayhaps Merle did not know of his daughter's midnight sojourns…and perhaps she was just as desperate for him not to know. That would account for her downcast eyes, and why she would not meet his gaze even now.

Merle turned to him, wresting Dirick's full attention from Allegra. "'Tis said the king will cross the channel to deal with Geoffrey now that Christ's Mass has passed."

Dirick nodded, chewing his bread slowly. While he had to take care what he said—after all, he was newly come from Paris, not from the king's side at Westminster—much of what they spoke of would only be heard between the four of them. 'Twas unlikely that Allegra or Maris would take much from his words. "Aye. Rumors come over the channel that Geoffrey is stocking his estates for war—claiming that Old Henry meant for his son to relinquish Anjou to Geoffrey when he succeeded the throne of England."

"Matilda is at Westminster with Henry?" asked Merle.

"Aye. 'Twas she that kept him from heading off to Ireland to conquer the lands for his brother William. With Geoffrey stirring the pot in Anjou, the king has trouble enough over the channel. It is said the queen's vassals do not like him overmuch."

Merle tsked into his cup of wine as he took a long draught. "He has his hands full," he wiped his mouth with the back of his hand.

"Aye. Aquitaine seethes for her mistress, Eleanor; Anjou is about to be gobbled up by Geoffrey—the king has much on his plate." Dirick wiped his hands on a damp cloth proffered by a page. "The queen is enceinte once again," he offered in a low voice.

"Then she will not accompany her husband across the channel?" asked Maris.

Dirick started, assuming that his conversation had been between himself and Merle; but he recovered quickly. "Nay, lady. She stays at Winchester—so the rumors say—because of her condition." He leaned forward so that he could see her on the other side of Merle, and was struck again by her beauty.

Maris quirked an eyebrow in a most becoming manner. "'T might be worthwhile for the king if she visited Aquitaine if 'tis in the uproar you tell us of."

"'Tis not so bad as that...and Henry has enough with Geoffrey in Anjou. Methinks there is more than that. The king will leave Richard of Luci as official administrator of England— yet the queen will still be here."

Maris was nodding. "Aye, the king would want someone he trusted to remain in his stead. He must needs appoint Luci officially; yet, Queen Eleanor is certain to hold her own. Aye, I agree with his purpose."

Dirick almost choked on a chunk of bread, taken by surprise at her grasp of the situation, and shocked that she sounded as if her approval of the king's actions was of great import. Women didn't talk politics—at least, women other than Matilda and Eleanor—and they were queens, for God's sake! "Aye, my lady." His silvery gaze flicked to her, to his trencher, and once more upon her.

Dirick recovered from his surprise at Maris's opinions and turned back to her father. "Tell, my lord, how fares the king's chancellor? 'Tis said he takes the court by storm."

"Aye, Thomas à Becket is the king's friend as well as his chancellor. To think that it was the Archbishop who forced Henry to take him on as chancellor…now the two are nearly inseparable."

"'Tis said the chancellor holds court rather than the king," volunteered Maris. "The king goes to Becket's court, rather than the chancellor coming to his. Even the diplomats attend Becket, rather than the queen. He dresses in all frippery and serves the most gluttonous meals…'tis said the king even rode his horse into Becket's hall one eve for dinner!" She paused to wipe daintily at her mouth, and Dirick's attention followed her hand as it brushed over those soft, plump lips. She lifted a goblet to sip from her wine and he watched the long smooth lines of her ivory throat as she swallowed. When she pulled the goblet away, a drop of wine glistened at the center of her bottom lip.

"Is that so?" was all Dirick was able to choke from his dry mouth. An unaccountable urge to kiss the droplet away surged through him, heat sweeping over him at the thought of taking that mouth. Closing his eyes firmly, he turned to his trencher and took a long swallow of wine. He had obviously been too long without a woman—a state he would rectify tonight. Until then, he would firmly steer his thoughts away from the daughter of his host.

"Maris, do you not carry tales," Merle was admonishing her good-naturedly.

"Aye, Papa," she conceded with a grin. "Though 'twas only yourself who told me the same story last even."

Merle chuckled and changed the subject. "How fare the cooper's wife and babes?"

"The woman is a bit weak, for she has lost much blood," she said. "The babes thrive, and I have sent Bernice, the smith's daughter, to wet-nurse for them whilst Thomas's wife recovers. Her own babe died this se'ennight past, and she was glad to do it."

Merle turned to Dirick, "Maris has the gift of healing and she spends much of her time in the village, caring for the people."

Dirick nodded in understanding. "The cooper's wife bore two babes?"

"Aye. Both hale and hearty boys, 'though 'twas a horrific birthing."

"You have done all you can for the cooper; and with the smith's daughter to keep the babes, verily the mill will continue to function. I will visit him on the morrow to express my own felicitations," Merle offered.

Dirick remembered how much it meant for him when his lord showed sympathy for his recent loss; it bespoke well of Merle Lareux that he would do the same for a lowly peasant. A sudden yawn cracked over his face, and he muffled it with a large hand. "Pardon, ladies," he said immediately. "'Tis not the company, I vow! I'd a long journey, and the day was even longer."

"Of course," Merle agreed. "I am near ready for bed myself. Maris, will you not show Sir Dirick where the men-at-arms lay their pallets? And any other comforts he may need? Come, Allegra, let us go abovestairs."

Maris stood reluctantly, clenching her teeth at her father's innocent command. The last thing she wanted was to be alone with this man. She'd felt his attention returning to her again and again during the evening. Did he truly think of her as the soiled, loose wench he'd met last even? "Of course, Papa," she said in a voice that disguised her discomfort.

Obviously, Dirick did not miss her mislike of the situation, for as soon as Merle and Allegra were out of earshot, he said, "Lady Maris, I am perfectly able to find my own pallet."

"Nay, 'tis my father's wish. I should not put a guest out," she smiled at him, swallowing the resentment she felt for being pressed into a marriage she did not want. In all honesty, 'twas not this man's fault—and he seemed pleasant enough now that he was not ahorse. "Have you bathed?"

"N-nay," he shook his head, surprised.

"May I offer you a warm bath before I direct you to your pallet?" she asked. "Gustave will bring the water. I won't take long, and you will soon be for bed."

His eyes turned on her with a sudden intensity, and the lids sank half-closed as he looked at her for a moment, as though contemplating more than her simple offer. A faint smile hovered at the corners of his mouth. Maris's throat went dry and she nearly stepped away from him and the unexpected stirrings in her middle.

"Nay," he rumbled at last in his smooth, low voice. It carried easily to her ears, even over the noise of the servants as they cleared off the tables and stacked the benches. "I do not believe I should put myself through such torture."

Her heart in her throat and her mind whirling, Maris spun away to hide her discomfiture. "Then if you would follow me," she murmured and blindly began to make her way between the nearly-empty tables, anxious to be rid of her charge.

As they approached a group of rowdy knights, Maris paused, resting her hand on the shoulder of a burly, red-headed one. They quietened. "Sir Raymond, how fares your shoulder? Is the pain lessening?"

The man's face nearly matched the color of his hair when he turned it up to look at her. "Aye, my lady. 'Tis a wonder that the pain is near gone!" He moved his arm as if to demonstrate.

"You will let me see it again on the morrow," she ordered in her firmest voice. It would not do for her father's best man to have an injured arm. "On the last I dressed a wound for you, 'twas only once that you came to me—and look what has happened to it because of your carelessness!"

He grinned up at her. "Aye, my lady. On the morrow, I will allow you to torture me yet again! 'Tis only that your touch is so sweet that I sit through the pain!"

She pushed at his shoulder playfully as the other men laughed. "Do you keep that sweetness on your tongue, or I am like to put you through more tortures if you spread tales!"

She obviously had no concept of what she did to a man, with those teasing golden-green eyes and pretty smile, Dirick thought as he watched her interact with the men-at-arms. His body still jumped at the memory of her innocent offer to bathe him. Desire shot through him at the thought of her scratched and stained hands soaping his body…but he thrust the thought away immediately. He *must* find a woman anight! Mayhaps one of the maidservants would oblige him.

Not for the first time that evening, he wondered why he'd heard nothing of the beautiful heiress of Langumont—from either his brother or the court. Certainly a well-landed maid as comely as Maris Lareux would not escape the notice of some of the greedy barons he'd had dealings with.

Her voice broke into his thoughts as she led him around into the area reserved for the men-at-arms and other important visitors. It was a large room, cordoned off from the rest of the hall by a heavy oaken door—much nicer than many of the men's quarters he'd slept in throughout England and France. A fire roared in the corner, and a serf slumped against the wall, snoring, with a stack of wood within reach.

"Sir Dirick, you may place your pallet anywhere you like," Maris offered. She handed him a pile of blankets, quite generous enough to keep one warm—especially with a blazing fire in the same room.

"Thank you, my lady." He took the bundle.

She paused for a moment as if contemplating her next words, and when she spoke, a small grin bowed her innocent, plump mouth. Her speech, however, when it came, eliminated any hint of innocence. "Papa bade me see to your comforts—if your need is as great as 'twas yestereve, I will send a woman to you."

Dirick felt his face flush hot as he ground his teeth together in an attempt to maintain his dignity. Words escaped him, and before he could gather his wits, the little spitfire took his silence for dissent and whirled away down the dark corridor. He could only stare after her, trying to decide whether he wanted to murder her or kiss her.

Four ❧

Maris dressed without Verna's assistance the next morning. She'd wakened earlier than usual and found too many thoughts scattering her mind to make more sleep likely, so she rose. It was a frigid morn, and the sun had not even begun to peek over the edge of the earth to warm it.

Down the stone steps she went, breezing through the hall where several men-at-arms were sprawled in a corner. Obviously, they had not made it to the knights' quarters where she'd left a dumbfounded Sir Dirick the night before. A bemused smile quirked her face at the remembrance of his shocked expression; and, engrossed as she was, Maris misstepped and trod upon the cat's tail. The tabby emitted a yowl of protest—the men still did not stir—and stalked off through the matted rushes, refusing to accept Maris's apologies.

She tsked at herself, fearing that the cat's reaction was merely a foreshadowing of what her father would say if he heard of her unladylike gibe at Sir Dirick. She could not keep from glancing again toward the common sleeping area, where Sir Dirick was likely sprawled out on his pallet. For a moment, she imagined his thick dark hair tufted and curling where he rested his head, his face lax and smooth in his rest. Mayhaps an arm would be thrown out, away from his blanketed body…or a leg, lying atop the woolen blanket whilst the rest of him slumbered in comfort. His disturbing grey eyes would be closed in sleep—those eyes that looked at her with such intensity that her heart dodged about in her chest. Yet, when they were not focused on her, she'd noticed that they were a soft, cloud-like grey, the color of Langumont Bay on a winter day, fringed with the longest, darkest lashes she'd ever seen—or noticed—on a man.

Maris started, realizing in confusion that she had paused in the hall and stood, staring toward the sleeping area as these thoughts danced through her mind. Though no one was about to see her actions, her cheeks warmed and she turned resolutely away. Although there was no harm in mooning over one's betrothed, she had balked against marriage for so long that it felt odd that she should begin to relish the thought of knowing all aspects of a man's body. Maris gathered up her heavy wool tunic and draped it over her arm as she stepped over an up-ended bench.

The kitchen was deserted except for Bit, the daughter of the cook, who slept in the corner on empty flour sacks. One large blue eye opened as Maris approached, and a yawn cracked across the pudgy, dirty face.

"Milady!" she started awake and jerked to her feet.

"Go back to your bed, Bit," Maris told her. "'Tis well before matins, and all are sleeping soundly but myself and the cat."

She turned to root about in an apple barrel, and, finding a barely-bruised one, she polished it against the soft blue wool still draped over her wrist. She broke her fast with a piece of day-old bread, found wrapped in cloth under a board, and a large swallow of watered-down ale.

She made her way out into the bitter morning, crunching the apple. It was nearly as dark as the night she'd trudged home from Thomas the cooper's wretched home. Stars lit the dark blue heavens, and a large moon still hung in their midst. Despite the cold, Maris stopped for a moment to look up. She drew her squirrel-lined cloak tighter about her shoulders as she stood in the center of the silent bailey. The only other creatures stirring were her father's midnight watch, posted on the north and south walls of the bailey. Richard, on the north wall, saw Maris and waved in greeting and recognition.

She waved back, and, finishing the last of her apple, pocketed the core for Hickory. A shiver took her by surprise, and she hurried on her way to the stable.

It was warmer in the old building, but much darker. It took a moment for her eyes to adjust, but then she could just make out the moving grey shapes of the horses. Maris clicked her tongue hello and moved down the length of the stable to where her mare nickered in greeting.

She buried her hands in Hickory's warm brown mane, to warm them as much as to say hello. Stroking her neck, she spoke soothingly to her as the horse poked her velvety nose into the folds of Maris's cloak. Her mistress never visited without a treat, and the rest of her apple was quickly munched down.

"How is your leg?" Maris asked softly, kneeling in the stall. She pushed the hood of her cloak back from her face and ran her hands along Hickory's foreleg. The mare didn't wince, and she unwrapped the bindings to find the swelling nearly gone.

"Ah, you are feeling much better!" she crooned. "We'll be off to hunt the wild boar on the morrow, sweet Hickory!" Maris whispered as she stood to caress the velvety nose that bumped her head. "We'll tear the beast into little pieces, aye, will we not?"

"Does your father approve of this hare-brained plan to snare the wild boar?" The voice from behind startled her and she whirled about.

"Sir Dirick, that was not very nice," she told him indignantly as she tried to slow her thumping heart. "I could have been talking about you!"

Dirick looked down at her, barely able to distinguish her features in the pale light. He'd noticed her crossing the bailey in the greying dawn and followed her into the stable, as there were several things he was of a mind to say to her. "It seems much too early for a lady to be about her business—whatever that may be," he said, squinting in the dim light.

"Aye," she replied. "But 'tis the quietest part of the day, and I wished to see about Hickory's foreleg."

"And the night?" he asked pointedly. "Is that also a quiet time for a noble lady to go about her business?"

It was starting to get lighter, and the dark grey shadows began to take on muted colors and details as they stood in the stable. He could see that her hair was uncovered, hanging in a fat braid over one shoulder. He felt a strange intimacy with her, seeing her hair; for although many maids at court disdained the covering wimples, it was obvious that in Merle's household they were standard ware. He couldn't tell what color her braid was, though, and for some reason, he needed to know.

Maris cocked her head like a falcon, as if trying to read the second meaning in his words. "Aye, there are times my business takes me out in the night."

"And what business is it that brings the Lady of Langumont to walk the streets—alone—in the darkness?" He held her gaze steadily in the dimness, determined to receive an answer as to what she'd been doing on her own in the village in the middle of the night.

To his surprise, she laughed. "Ah, Sir Dirick, are you so protective of your betrothed's reputation that you do not even go to Papa with your evil suspicions? Aye, I trow you do not wish your lady to be seen wandering the streets at night!" Her hand rested lightly on his arm as she became serious. "My lord, do you not fear for my reputation. I but came from the bedside of a woman after a day-long battle to birth her two sons. 'Twas a long, wearying day, and I fear I was not in the best of tempers when you bore down on me."

The dawn broke over Dirick so that he almost missed the import of one of her comments. "Please accept my apologies for my rude behavior," he said, flustered; then, nearly choking, repeated, "Betrothed?"

Maris had returned to stroking Hickory's nose, turning her back to him as if to hide her expression. "Aye, sir, 'tis not a secret that you are here to speak on my hand. 'Tis—"

"Nay!" Dirick flushed, shocked. By God's bones, the lady presumed much of herself! To speak of a marriage contract only the day after meeting Lord Merle and his daughter was, to the least, embarrassingly rude. Beside that, marriage was the last thing on his mind—he had no lands to bring a wife, nor any wish to be saddled with one woman when God had put so many beautiful ones on His earth. "My lady—"

"Forgive me," Maris broke in, relief and mortification in her voice. "I meant not to be—'tis only I bethought you were the man to which Papa means to bind me."

"Your Papa did say you are not yet betrothed," he told her, regaining his faculties; embarrassed himself at his outburst. 'Twas an honest mistake she made.

"Nay—nor am I desirous of having my person bartered over," Maris replied tartly. She looked up at him, and he was surprised to be able to make out the shape and shade of her eyes in the dawning light. "Papa has stopped urging me to find a man to my liking, and he vows he will choose one for me." Her face fell, and she returned to stroking Hickory's velvet nose, "'Though 'tis the truth he has already chosen my husband."

Dirick was taken aback by her forthright words and well-expressed opinions. Most maids were at the least betrothed by age fifteen—a good majority of them wed—and before him stood a woman of more than seventeen summers calmly declaring she had not found a man to her liking and was unlikely to do so.

Maris continued, interrupting his thoughts, asking, "What, then, do you here at Langumont if not to look me over and set a dower price?"

Dirick tried not to flinch at her words, which callously described something that he'd never thought much on; and, instead, tried to ignore them. "I am lately come from Paris and travel through the area, looking to work for a lord such as your father."

"Aye?" she asked, "It seems you have much knowledge of Henry's court for one come so newly from France."

"King Louis keeps many eyes on the court of the man who stole his wife," Dirick replied smoothly, chagrined that she seemed to have seen what she shouldn't.

"What beautiful horseflesh you have for an itinerant knight!"

Dirick stared at her, certain that the innocence in her voice was feigned, but unwilling to believe that she could be suspicious of him. What did a woman know of horseflesh? He decided to divert her attention. "Aye, I have an eye for good horseflesh...among other pleasures."

Maris flushed and turned away. "Did you partake of such pleasures last night?" she threw back without looking at him.

Dirick choked on his astonishment, speechless at her blunt question. "Lady—" A noise behind them drew his attention. "Who goes there?" he called, stepping in front of her with a sudden, graceful movement, hand going to the sword buckled at his waist.

"'Tis Peter the Marshal," replied a voice. "An' who be ye?"

Maris brushed past Dirick, and the scent of her—fresh and lemony—filled his nostrils as she stepped into the walkway. "Peter, good morrow to you! Hickory's leg is near healed," she greeted her father's stablemaster; glad for the distraction. "'Tis Sir

Dirick de Arlande with me," she explained as the stooped old man peered behind her shoulder. "Peter has been Langumont's marshal for near three score years—and his sons and grandsons after him."

"Aye, I see the same look as the young man who took Nick's reins upon my arrival. The young burly man with bright red hair, and nearly as many freckles as stars in the sky? He had a gentle touch with my stallion, a definite way with horses," he said, knowing 'twas not oft that the gentry noticed the man who took their horse; let alone complimented him.

Peter nodded his head with pleasure. "Aye, my lord, 'twas my oldest grandson, Percival. I vow, 'e 'as 'orseblood in 'is own veins!"

Dirick chuckled, and his attention turned back to Maris when she knelt to show Peter the mare's foreleg. By now the stable was fairly light, and the shades of grey had turned to muted color. The fat braid that roused his curiosity had been flipped back over her shoulder when she stooped and he nearly reached out to touch its glossy darkness. Brown hair. Rich, chestnut hair and green- and gold-flecked eyes and full pink lips.

Dirick jerked his thoughts back from impropriety just as Maris stood. They were nearly on top of each other—her nose almost bumped his chest when she turned quickly. Dirick took a step back and crossed his arms over his chest, attempting to appear forbidding and unmoved.

She ignored him. Peter had her full attention and her eyes snapped golden while her cheeks flushed pink as she explained the healing process of Hickory's leg as proudly as if the mare's steps were her own child's first ones.

When at last the marshal turned to go about his business, Maris turned to Dirick. "Well, sir, do you intend to stand there supporting the stable wall all the day? I assure you, my Papa would not allow any building on his lands to come to that state in which a well-paid man should hold it up!"

He could not help but grin at her saucy tongue. "Nay, lady. I but wait for you to finish trilling with the marshal and leave to go about your business."

"Trilling, indeed!" She stamped her foot indignantly, and even in the soft dirt floor he could hear the thud.

"God's bones, lady, you sound like my destrier when he seeks a mare in season!" He cocked an eyebrow and widened his grin.

Maris turned in a huff and began to stalk out of the stable. Dirick followed behind, hands clasped innocently behind his back. His long legs gave him the speed to catch up with her, and he stepped into her stride just as they came out of the stable. "Why do you nip at my heels like a starving pup?" she threw up at him.

"I am interested, 'tis all," he said with all sincerity. "'Tis the truth, I was intrigued by your story this morrow about the cooper and his wife...and your gift of healing."

Maris stopped and turned to face him full in the bailey. The huge ball of the sun peered over the wall of the courtyard, nearly blinding her. Her squint was most unladylike as she looked up at him. "Interested, you say?" she asked.

"Aye. I know many noble ladies, and many well-landed ones such as yourself, and I have yet to meet one that stays out till all hours of the night to midwife a cooper's woman. 'Tis true, my lady mother will see to the ills of her people, aye, and I've met others that do the same—but, all too often, 'tis only at their convenience."

"People do not become ill to convenience their healers," Maris said with disdain, her lips pinching together. "'Twas near the first thing I was taught—after which plant is deadly hemlock, of course," she smiled at him. Her nose was red with cold and her cheeks soon to follow and she looked quite lovely as she jested with him.

He grinned down at her, suddenly light-hearted for the first time since he heard the news of his father. "'Twas, I'm certain, an informative bit of knowledge."

"Aye, yet not as important as creating a draught to rid oneself of pompous knights that tear down upon you like a demon in the dark of night," she said dryly, turning away and pulling up her hood to cover shiny dark hair.

In so doing, she missed the spark of humor quirked his mouth and was privy only to his words, "Aye, well, I would make the woman rich that could create a draught to whittle away at the tartness of a certain Lady of Langumont. I trow, my mouth is like to pucker less at the taste of a lemon than at her wit."

"You dare to speak of my mother in such a manner?" A little giggle escaped from her lips, and she looked up at him, her eyes dancing. "I should toss you out on your ear for taking such liberties!" A thick strand of hair blew in her face and caught at the corner of her mouth. She brushed it away and sobered. "In truth, Sir Dirick, your interest is an unfamiliar state for me. More oft than not, men of your ilk turn tail and hie themselves away rather than hear the extent of my duties at Langumont." She brushed her heavy cloak over her torso. "And, now, 'tis well past time for me to tend to those duties. I have kept you from your own work long enough."

"Nay, my lady, you have kept me from naught," Dirick was quick to respond, clenching his hands deeply into the warmth of his tunic. It was quite frigid on this side of the bailey where the slightest breeze seemed to catch and swirl brazenly about.

Maris smiled. "Then, sir, I am off to Mass and then about my duties." She turned to make her way toward Langumont's tiny chapel.

"My lady," he was in her footsteps as if he were pulled by a rope. She turned and he suddenly felt foolish. "I—Lady Maris, I do not know where the chapel is and I am in need of absolution," he said.

She gestured him forward, "Come, then, to Mass and Father Abraham will see you after."

"Aye, my lady, and thank you."

‿୭

Maris had an audience as she peeled the dressing off Raymond of Vermille's shoulder. Her father's squires watched closely, hoping for a sign of the gore they'd been told they'd see. Unfortunately for them—and quite happily for Sir Raymond— the green pus that had oozed from his wound a mere two days earlier was gone, and the swelling had decreased greatly.

It had been no May Day when Maris first saw the ugly, puss-infested cut and been forced to expel all of the evil humors that festered inside—not only was the pain excrutiating, but it was nothing compared to the ringing in his ears when she finished lecturing him.

"See you, Sir Raymond," she began again, this time with the intent of teaching the young boys as well, "'tis no great feat to keep soil from an open cut and 'tis much easier on the skin, so it heals nicely. Do you keep mashing dirt and wool and lice from your tunic in the cut, and it swells greatly as the humors grow." She was finishing with a clean wrap around his shoulder.

"My thanks, my lady," Raymond told her, winking at the squires.

"I saw that!" she remonstrated, pulling the binding tighter. At his exaggerated grunt of pain, she released it slightly. "Do you not listen to me, Sir Raymond, and you will soon be without your sword arm!" Then she smiled and patted his good shoulder. "You shall be wielding a lance in a week's time."

"Thank you, my lady," he said again, this time seriously.

She urged him off the stool on which he'd perched. "On the

next you ride with Papa, I will send some of my green salve with you to put on a cut such as this until you are home for me to treat."

She gathered up the rest of her medicines, packing some dried leaves and berries into a pouch to carry in her basket. "Off with you before cook puts you to work," she shooed the young boys out of her corner of the kitchen. Maisie, the cook, grumbled in agreement as she leaned over a steaming kettle of water and Maris brushed by.

Outside, the air was just as brittle as it had been early that morning. The sun was so bright that Maris found herself blinded at the change from the dark kitchen, and walked full-faced into a warm body.

"Do you not watch where you are going," came a deep, amused voice, "Lady Maris?"

"Sir Dirick." She was beginning to make out shapes now. She looked up where his face would be and her eyes immediately watered from the brightness of the sun. Blinking the tears back, she looked back down and saw his scuffed brown boots in the compressed snow of the bailey. "I am sorry, 'twas so dark in the herbalry and the sun is so magnificently bright, I could not see for a moment. I trust your confession was well-received?"

He laughed. "Aye, my lady, and well-deserved, also."

"I had not expected to see you emerge from the chapel so quickly," she returned, now able to look up at the face that blocked the sun. "Father Abraham is not known for his simple penances—and with a confession such as yours, I should think you'd be saying paternosters until Judgement Day and selling your fine Nick to pay for all your pardons."

"Nay, lady, my penance is much heavier than you could think." His eyes twinkled like the brilliant snow. "Father Abraham bade me accompany a headstrong lady healer on her visits to keep her from getting under the hooves of any more destriers such as my fine Nick." Before she could react, he relieved her arm of the herb-filled basket and said, "And since I have nearly been flattened by one lady healer, 'tis fitting that I take up my penance now. Where are you off to, Lady Maris?"

"Do you not have aught to do but dog along my footsteps?" she asked, barely able to keep back a smile. "Does not Papa have work for you?"

Dirick grinned, "Aye, lady, 'twas he who sent me to find you—and ensure that you are back to the keep for this evening's meal. He says you have missed too many suppers as of late. Now, again, where are we off to?"

"To visit the cooper," she told him automatically. Her father had sent a strange knight to be her chaperon? A chaperon in Langumont?

"Ah, the cooper." Dirick sobered, "Have you heard any news?"

"Nay. Widow Maggie—the village healer—would have sent to me if there were cause for concern. Yet, I still wish to see how the babes fare, and see that Bernice, the smith's daughter, is still wet-nursing them."

They trudged along the well-packed snow through the gate of the bailey, over the drawbridge and into Langumont Village. Dirick watched in amazement as Maris greeted every person they encountered—by name yet!—and even ventured into the smoky, dark houses to see to a child with the ague, or show a woman how to make a draught for pain. Well-accustomed to accepting the hospitality of the peasants that dwelled on his father's lands, Dirick was still quite surprised at the ease with which a great lady did the same.

He plodded along in her wake as a mere fixture to Maris. This was the first he'd seen of Langumont Village in the light of day, and he took note of its condition with a watchful eye.

There was one main throughway that led up to the iron

portcullis of the bailey of Langumont Keep, and through the length of the generous village. Small structures of roughly-hewn logs lined the road. The homes of the villagers were topped with thick thatching, and curls of smoke drifted up from crude chimneys. Most structures had at least one small window that was covered with well-greased linen to keep the wind out while letting the light in. All of the doors seemed sturdy enough that they wouldn't blow open in even the fiercest wind.

Dirick noted a smithy, a weaver, a baker, a prosperous-looking silversmith, the inn he'd lodged in two nights earlier, and various other merchants and workshops. He picked out a butcher and a shoemaker, and his nose eventually pointed out the mart where the fishermen brought their wares. Outside of the village, he knew, were acres and acres of farmland—some belonging to the villagers; but a good portion belonging to Merle Lareux and worked to produce the barrels and barrels of food that fed his household and his guests.

As he noted the prosperity of the village, Dirick could not help a twinge of envy. Such would never be his, he knew. He was destined to a life of travel and war, with no lands or title of his own. Though he was well-regarded by the king—even so well thought of as to be Henry's confidante and advisor—the most he could expect or even aspire to was the fortune of marrying an unimportant heiress with a single fief and a liege lord of such greatness as Merle of Langumont…or, mayhaps, even to be himself awarded the position of castellan at a small fief. As the youngest son, such was his fate—and 'twould only be altered should his brother Bernard, Lord of Derkland, die without issue. And even in his deepest heart, in his most private thoughts, Dirick did not wish for that to come to pass.

He sighed. Ah, but he had ever known that this would be his destiny…and never before had he questioned it. He turned a covert glance onto the woman who walked next to him, suddenly forced to subdue a pang of regret. The man who was to wed her was fortunate indeed!

Dirick returned his thoughts to the scenery and peasants as they continued through the village. 'Twas to the credit of Lord Merle—and, most certainly, his daughter as well—that the peasants did not lower their eyes and slink into their homes as the nobility progressed through their village. Instead, they invited Maris and her companion into the well-maintained, albeit dark and smoky, huts. In fact, Dirick noted that the buildings of the village seemed extremely well kept up. The streets were even reasonably clean of refuse and animal waste—his nose wrinkled at the memory of London's offal-strewn streets and the stench that accompanied one's carefully-placed steps.

At last they reached a structure near the south side of the village. A man whom Dirick assumed was the cooper greeted them at the door, his face full of hope. "My lady, you have come!"

As soon as he saw the scene within, Dirick knew the man's hope was in vain.

Five ♫

*M*aris brushed past Dirick, pushing her way into the hut. Anger shot through her at the scene: the windows had been resheathed, and old smoke clung to the air. Two babies squalled in the corner; but the woman was silent.

"Uncover the windows," Maris snapped, moving quickly to the bedside of the patient. Widow Maggie, who had been tending to her with a damp cloth on her forehead, stepped away, looking abashed at her lady's entrance.

"But, my lady, the leech said—"

"Leech?" she exclaimed, turning on Maggie. "What said the leech?"

Thomas spoke helpfully, "The leech said the humors need darkness and heat from the fire. He said Mary's blood should be let to rid her of the poison that draws her life."

"Nay!" Maris clenched her fingers to keep from screaming in frustration. Maggie knew that as far as she was concerned, leeches were banned from the village of Langumont. She threw back the blankets to reveal the pitiful figure of Mary, knowing by the amount of blood that it was too late. "Good Venny says leeches have little use—and oft cause more damage! God's teeth, what have you done?"

"'Twas Thomas, my lady," Maggie whispered. "She bled the

night through after the birth, and he did not know what to do. We did not wish to spoil your Christ's Mass celebration and your father's homecoming. The leech promised to save her."

Maris looked at the shocked cooper and swallowed her anger as well as she could. He could not have known—leeches were famous for promising the moon if they were paid enough. Vaguely, she noticed that Dirick, who had been standing in the doorway, had moved quickly to tear the heavy, cloying blankets from the windows. Oiled cloth covered the openings, and he made a slit in the top of one near the fire so that the smoke would wend its way out of the hut.

Grateful for his help, she transferred her gaze to the seven black slugs that sucked away the lifeblood of her patient. "Remove the leeches," she told Maggie shortly, then turned to Thomas. "Leeches do not come into Langumont Village. I do not know how he came, but if you see this leech again, you will send for me immediately."

"Aye, lady," he whispered. "My lady, my Mary…will she…?"

Maris spared a look at the grey-faced woman, and her fears were confirmed. She hadn't stirred since her arrival. Blood soaked the bed beneath her as the leeches drew even more from her arms and legs. "I will do what I can, but mayhaps 'twill not be enough."

The babies were screaming in the corner. "Where is the smith's daughter?" Maris asked, gritting her teeth at the sound.

"She went home last night," Thomas told her. "The leech thought Mary would suckle the babes this night."

"Fetch her," she said tightly. "She is not to leave until I say."

Thomas scurried for the door as Maggie pulled the last reluctant leech from the woman's flesh. Again, Maris noted out of the corner of her eye that Dirick had moved silently to where the babes lay. Suddenly, silence reigned and she breathed a deep sigh.

She worked quickly to mix a paste from dried yarrow to lay

over the open wounds from the slugs, and ordered Maggie about
to steep a decoction of peppermint and clove to dribble down
the woman's throat.

Maris lost track of time. She vaguely remembered Thomas
returning with Bernice, the smith's daughter; and sensed more
than once when Dirick stepped over to assist her or Maggie. The
silence that hovered as she worked became monotonous and
hung like death over the small, bleak house.

Time blurred. Maggie brewed a draught from herbs meant to
ease the pain, and Maris helped her choke it down Mary's
parched throat. The woman breathed ever so slowly, her hands
remained cold and clammy, while her face suffused with heat.
Groans of pain emitted from her dried and cracked lips. The
other women bathed her and found too much blood still coming
from between her legs.

At last, she had no choice. "Sir Dirick...." Maris turned to
him, brushing the hair from her eyes. He looked down at her,
knowledge flaring in his eyes. "Go you to seek Father Abraham."

Thomas's eyes widened, then his stare dropped to the dirt
floor of the hut. "My lady," he whispered, moving to the bed to
grasp his wife's lax hand.

Maris did not know what time it was when Mary finally
stopped breathing. With a muffled exclamation, she fell on the
bed next to her patient, frantically feeling her chest for the beat
of a heart; then put her hand near Mary's mouth in hopes of
feeling the soft, labored breath that had kept the woman alive.
Nothing. She looked slowly up at Maggie, struggling to keep her
tears in check.

Dirick arrived with the priest moments later. Maris stood
wearily and stepped back from the bed to allow Father Abraham
to shrive the woman. She leaned against the wall of the hut, passing a grimy hand over her cheek, and her gaze was caught by
Dirick's. His face was grim and his eyes soft as they looked at her

with admiration and regret.

She shook her head in discouragement, turning away, feeling as though she'd failed miserably in front of him. Had she or Maggie been aware of Mary's condition before the leech was brought in, perhaps she could have prevented the bleeding that most assuredly cost her her life. The struggle to give birth to two large boys, and the subsequent loss of blood was simply exacerbated by the bloodletting.

What did it matter now? she thought, wiping away a tear that suddenly appeared. She had done what she could and the woman had died. Good Venny told her that when God called someone there was naught she could do to prevent that person from going. There would be many times when she would succeed, but she could not work against God's will.

"'Twill be a hard lesson to learn, Maris," he'd told her somberly. "You may learn it early, you may take years to learn it. You must never question your gift of healing, though. You are blessed to be chosen to save God's people when ill befalls them. Use your gift, but do not seek to play God."

She wished he were here now.

Tears of frustration welled in her eyes, and she blinked them back before Dirick saw them. Plucking at Maggie's sleeve, she whispered, so as not to disturb the prayers of the priest, "I must go."

With that, she slipped quickly from the hut.

శు

Dirick found her not far from the cooper's hovel, leaning against a tree, staring at the ground. He approached without speaking, knowing that the sound of his boots crunching through the icy snow would announce his presence.

Standing to the side, he took a moment to observe her, allowing his gaze the leisure of absorbing every detail about her. The hood of her brilliant blue cloak had fallen back, leaving her head bare and thick strands of hair fluttering in the breeze. Her nose and cheeks were red—whether from the chill, or from weeping, he did not know—and she stood motionless, like a tree herself, her chest rising and falling under the heavy cape.

Dirick felt a strange warmth seep through his limps, warming him even in the coldness, as he watched her. She had been magnificent in that desperate hovel, and he had been able to do naught but stand back and watch. Doubtless she had known from the instant she stepped foot within that the woman would perish, but Maris had worked urgently to save her.

Even now, he could see the results of her efforts in a rusty streak of blood across her cheek, and the disheveled wisps of her braid and shiny dampness of her face. He had never seen a noblewoman look so unkempt…so work-roughened…so noble.

Maris turned suddenly, surprising him in his study of her. Her eyes were red-rimmed and faintly bloodshot, and the tip of her nose quite scarlet. She looked at him with a mixture of resignation and embarrassment, and Dirick struggled to find something to say. Words of comfort usually sprang easily to his lips when he was faced with consoling a woman whose gown had been stained, or one whose feelings had been hurt by another…and suddenly, those moments seemed as superficial as the veneer of ice over snow when faced with a woman such as Maris of Langumont.

"You have a great gift," he spoke finally, his words rumbling roughly from a throat tight with emotion.

She sighed. "'Twas not enough of a gift this day, I fear." She stepped away from the tree and started toward him. The faintest trace of a wry smile quirked her mouth, and a small dimple echoed in her chin. "I have yet to learn, as my mentor tried to teach me, that despite many lives saved, there are others that I cannot turn from God's will." The smile saddened and her eyes took on a faint sheen. She blinked quickly and brusquely turned to pick up her pouch of medicinals, starting off past him, toward the keep's walls.

Feeling clumsy and inarticulate, Dirick was moved to action. He took her arm, stopping her, and propelled her so that she looked up at him. For a moment, he froze, looking down into her beautiful, dirty face, streaked with tears and blood, her chin quivering as she valiantly tried to hold back her emotions. Her eyes seemed to beg for him to speak, and he groped mentally for something that would cause the pain to melt away.

"'Tis amazing to me, Lady Maris, that I—and all men— should spend our lives seeking war, when you should work so hard to save a simple life. The wars are fought for lands and riches, yet you would spend all of the day slaving to save the life of a simple peasant. It shames me, and at the same time, I am filled with admiration for you."

Snow drifted lightly down from a greying sky. Maris tilted her face up to catch one of the filigree flakes on her pink cheek and blinked quickly. "Thank you, Sir Dirick."

"Aye, and I know the pain of losing a loved one," he added, his sensitivity allowing the grief of the loss of his father to bubble to the surface.

She looked at him. "Praise God, I cannot say the same. 'Though 'tis nearly as bad if a patient dies," she added. "Your loss was recent?"

He nodded but remained silent, looking at her and then needing to tear his eyes away. "Come, we shall return anon."

With a short nod, she slipped the strap of her pouch over her shoulder and gestured toward the river. "I must search for something before we return," she told him apologetically. "'Tis for my father."

"Of course." With an effort, Dirick threw off the heaviness of grief and sobriety that had cast a pall over them and summoned a smile. "Lead on, my lady."

They were nearing the edge of the village and the huge stone wall of Langumont Keep loomed ahead of them when she stopped and crouched on the ground.

Dirick watched as she knelt to dig in the icy snow with a stick. Thick locks of hair had fallen from her braid during the day, and now light wisps of it blew about her face, dancing against a pink cheek and catching at the corner of her mouth. Her hair, he realized, was not a simple brown, but a deep, chestnut color with the glints and depth of her eyes. She made a comely picture—squatting near the snow, her deep blue cloak a swirl on the brilliant white, her dark head silhouetted against a nearby drift. When she looked up at him, she caught him by surprise and he blinked to recover his normal expression. Maris did not seem to notice, and she gestured to the patch she'd cleared away.

"Look you here," she pulled at his cloak, and he knelt down next to her. Brilliant, dark green leaves clustered under the snow, cluttered with dried leaves and branches. "See, 'tis the bearberry," she told him, clearing more icy crystals away. A few red berries still clung tenaciously to the sturdy mahogany stems; but she ignored those and began to pluck the leaves.

"Bearberry?" he asked.

"Aye," Maris explained, stuffing the leaves into a leather pouch that she'd pulled from the folds of her cloak. "'Tis a wonder the leaves are still here under all this snow," she remarked.

Dirick started to pull some of the berries from the plant. "Need you the berries as well?" he asked, proffering a small handful.

"Nay, Sir Dirick," she told him with a smile. "'Tis only the leaves are good for steeping in a draught. They help fluids pass easily from the body."

"Ah, I see," he tossed the dark red berries onto the snow where they scattered like drops of blood. He turned to clearing away more ice while she picked as many fresh leaves as they could find. Their heads were bent together and he was close enough that, once, a light lock of her hair tossed daintily against his cheek. The fresh scent of lemon and another smell he could not identify reached his nose above the crisp cold of winter.

"'Tis pretty," he said without thinking, sniffing lightly.

Maris turned and the smell became stronger. "Pardon?" she asked, her green-and-gold-flecked eyes so close that he could count the thick lashes that framed them.

"'Tis lemons—I smell lemons and—another scent," he said quickly, moving away from her.

Dirick felt her smile all the way to the pit of his stomach. "'Tis on my hair," she told him, "'t cleans it well and makes it smell fresh. Lemon verbena and mint and rosemary," she explained.

"'Tis unusual," he commented. Every other noble lady that he knew—or had been close enough to to notice—wore either the cloying scent of roses or gillyflowers.

The tiny dimple on the left corner of her chin appeared. "Ah, Sir Dirick, 'tis quite the diplomat you are," she brushed the errant lock of hair behind her ear. "'Tis unfashionable, as my mama tells me. I should not smell of utilitarian herbs, and I should be embarrassed ere 'tis noticed."

"Nay," he told her forcefully, "'tis but uncommon—as you are, my lady. After all," he said, trying to ignore the heaviness singing through his veins, "'t has never happened before that a lady has me digging in the snows for shiny green leaves!"

Maris jerked back so that she almost lost her balance. "Marry, Sir Dirick, I did not think–! What you must think that I have involved you in the tasks of an old midwife!" The tinge of pink from the cold flared into a darker, rosy flush over her face. Maris began to struggle to her feet, but her cloak had become wrapped around her foot and she lost her balance, tilting backward into the damp snow.

"Nay, my lady," Dirick grasped her hand to help her regain her balance. "Never think that," he faced her, squatting in the ankle-deep snow. He took both of her hands and steadied her as they faced each other. His breath misted in the chilling air, and he noticed the sun was rapidly disappearing behind the keep. "My lady Maris," he said quietly, looking into her eyes. Her lips parted slightly. "My lady," he began again, having been distracted by her mouth, "'t has been a pleasure to be in your company all the day long—throughout the time at the cooper's as much as assisting you in this simple task. 'Twas only as a compliment that I say you are uncommon…and uncommonly beautiful as well." Those last words came as a surprise to him, and he found himself caught in a very warm, trusting, golden gaze.

Dirick swallowed heavily, knowing that he was going to kiss her and fearing that her reaction might be a heavy hand across his cheek. Pushing that aside, he tugged gently on her hands and she came forward—easily—and he met her lips halfway.

They were sweet lips…so sweet….

His mouth was tentative at first, but when she did not pull back, he pressed more firmly against her lips. They were chilled from the winter air, but melted warmly, softly against him. One of his hands freed her fingers and slid to cover the back of her head, digging into her braid. He fingered the thick rope of hair, touching its fat smoothness, his rough skin snagging it as he slid his hand down its length. A charge of desire swept through him with such force that he groaned at the back of his throat, surprised, wanting more. The scent of lemon verbena and rosemary caught in his nostrils, mingling with the crispness of the cold air, dancing through his being with the nearness and the taste of Maris.

She was responsive, warm; taking him into her mouth and

kissing him back with ardor. He felt a tiny shiver race through her body and knew it was not the cold. Nevertheless, he slipped his mantle over her shoulders, pulling her closer and into his arms. She was small and delicate under his fingers and he sighed, sliding his hands down her waist and over her hips.

At last—though it seemed like hours, 'twas a mere few seconds—Dirick regained his senses and pulled away quite suddenly. His breath was coming in faster, whiter puffs now and he forced himself to set Maris away from him. He was heavy and hard with arousal, and when she looked up at him with glazed hazel eyes and swollen pink lips, he nearly reached for her again.

Instead, he pulled away from the temptation, resting his hand against the smooth bark of a birch tree as if to keep it from doing any further damage. "My lady," he said, trying to speak coherently when all he wanted to do was pull her to him again, "that was unforgivable. I hope you will find it in your heart to allow my escort back to the keep. I will return you to your father's care and you need not be bothered with my presence again."

"Nay, Sir Dirick," she said, struggling to her feet with a dazed look on her face. "Think you not of it." She brushed her fingers lightly over her full mouth. "I allowed you leave to kiss me only in order to have some questions of my own answered."

He quirked an eyebrow at her, ignoring the throbbing between his legs and trying to act as cool as she. "And did you have your questions answered?" he replied.

"Aye," she breathed, still touching her mouth unconsciously, "aye, that I did."

Six ✣

At dinner that evening, Maris avoided looking at Dirick de Arlande

He sat on the far side of Merle, sharing a trencher with Lady Allegra. The two men, seated next to each other, were engrossed in conversation regarding the latest news that had come in from Westminster—the king's call to arms for his battle to subdue Geoffrey of Anjou.

Though he sat away from her, and she could not see him unless she leaned around her father, Maris was as aware of Dirick's presence as if he'd brushed against her. His hands, serving Allegra and himself, moved in and out of her view…and she found herself watching them, noticing their tanness, the short, clean fingernails, the molding of muscle and tendon and sprinkling of dark hair, the way the sleeve of his tunic fell back to expose a narrow, tanned wrist.

She heard him laugh; a low, masculine, husky laugh that heightened her awareness of him. His conversation carried over the noise of the meal, collecting in her consciousness, as close to her as if he whispered in her ear. The cadence of his voice, rising and falling as he alternately admired and charmed Allegra, and debated and argued with Merle, was soothing and exciting and haunting.

A simple kiss…a simple kiss had made her as aware of him as she'd become of herself when his lips touched hers.

Even now, her fingers trembled when she remembered the heat, the shock of pleasure that took her by surprise and made her body come alive. Warm, demanding lips and the hard strength of his body were enough to steal her breath and pool desire into the center of her being.

Even now, she felt the stirring of desire, the flutter of arousal in her middle.

The memory of his lips still burned on her mouth as she sipped from her wine. She wanted to taste him again. She wanted to know if the kiss they had shared could be duplicated, if it would be the same charge of energy should it happen again.

Casting a covert look in his direction, she saw him leaning flirtatiously toward her mother, a smirk curling his mouth, and realized suddenly that he was most likely well-accustomed to kissing maidens in the wood. That knowledge settled in her middle like a large chunk of bread and she turned away to sip from her goblet.

'Twas her own doing, she reprimanded herself, for she had wanted to kiss him—had known he wanted to kiss her when he helped to pull her to her feet—and welcomed the chance to see if kissing was any better now that she was older than when her father's squire Raymond had stolen a kiss from her years ago.

It was.

"Daughter, are you ill?" her father asked suddenly, turning his attention to her and startling her from her own thoughts. "You are so quiet tonight."

"Nay, Papa." She gave him a soft smile. "'Twas a long and wretched day, for I could not save the cooper's wife."

His face sobered. "Ah, aye, Father Abraham's servant sent to me that aught was not well. I did not hear that she had perished, though."

Maris pushed back the sadness that threatened to bring tears back to her eyes and replied, "There was naught I could do."

He smoothed a comforting hand over her arm. "I know you did all you could, dearling."

"They had a leech in!" she said, her grief being replaced by anger. "'Twas the cause, I vow!"

He shook his head. "Maris, I know Venny taught you well, and he knows many things, but there are others—leeches—that know medicine as well. They are not always bad."

"I have yet to meet one that has not worsened the situation," she told him defiantly.

Her father shook his head and changed the subject, obviously knowing that neither of them would win the argument. "I am sorry that she died. I will send three chickens to the cooper on the morrow, and visit on Justice Day. Is the smith's daughter still wet-nursing the babes?"

"Aye. She will do a fine job, and mayhaps the cooper and she will marry. She is of an age, and lost her own husband to the fever several moons ago." She flickered a glance at Dirick, who was mooning over her mother's slim hand, then looked back at her father.

"I have brewed some fresh tea from the bearberry bush for you this night." She patted his arm lightly. "I know you are in need of it, for Mama told me this morn in Mass. The leaves are fresh and the tea is strong. I will have Maella bring it to your chamber when you retire."

༄

Verna crept up the dim, cold steps that led to the upper chambers of the keep. The sounds of pleasantries from below drifted up to her keen ears; she even heard the light laughter of her mistress.

On the floor above the Great Hall, several chambers were set into the tall stone walls: Lady Allegra's solar, where the seam-stresses worked; the private chamber of the lord and lady; several smaller chambers for important guests; and, finally, Verna's destination.

Lady Maris's chamber was the last along the narrow, dimly-lit hallway. Attached was an antechamber where Verna slept when she was not with a man; Maris did not require that she attend her every night as Lady Allegra would. She passed silently through the small antechamber, skirting the small pallet piled generously with three pillows, and opened the heavy door into the main chamber.

A large bed sat in one corner, its curtains drawn back to show a thick fur coverlet and many more pillows than Verna's meager pallet. To the left of the bed, along the wall, was a narrow slit of a window—just wide enough to pass a hand through. A second window was staggered at the other end of the room. Both slits were covered with heavy tapestries to keep the harsh winter from entering the chamber.

The fireplace carved itself into the corner opposite the windows, and a small blaze crackled within. One of Verna's tasks was to build the sparks to a roar just as her mistress mounted the steps to her chamber. A large trunk rested at the foot of the bed, and a second one acted as a table near the fireplace. A stool and a straight-backed chair completed the room's furnishings.

Verna padded across the chamber, her feet rustling through the soft rushes that covered the stone floor. She poked briefly at the fire, adding two small logs to the protesting flames, then turned to the trunk at the foot of the bed.

Resting her candle on the table behind her, Verna kneeled and lifted the lid of the heavy wooden trunk. Inside rested piles of silks and velvets, wools and linens, of the brightest colors and the most intricate embroideries. She passed a hand slowly over them, crushing an emerald silk bliaut in her fingers. A strange curl moved her mouth and she stood, pulling the bliaut with her. It fell in a cascade of silk to her feet…she knew the green would complement her pale blonde hair and catlike green eyes.

For a moment, she stood thus, smoothing the silk down the front of her body, imagining how she would look garbed in the riches of Lady Maris of Langumont. Then, the curl of her mouth deepening, she carefully refolded the garment and replaced it in the trunk.

Verna dug carefully through the piles of clothing, to the very bottom of the trunk, and rummaged gingerly there. Pulling the candle closer, she peered into the depths of the clothing, mindful of dripping wax, and at last extracted the object of her search.

It was a headdress, woven of cloth of gold, which oft confined the thick locks of Lady Maris during the summer months. Verna examined the snood closely in the candlelight and was pleased to find several strands of rich brown hair trapped in the intricacies of the headdress. With a small sound of satisfaction, she folded the cloth carefully and pushed it up into her sleeve.

༄

Dirick could see the object of his thoughts from around her father's broad shoulder, even as he carried on a light-hearted conversation with Allegra. He'd been alternately cursing and congratulating himself for seizing the opportunity to taste her; and now desire curled and unfurled itself in his belly as he tried to tamp it down.

Whatever had possessed him to kiss the naive, headstrong daughter of Lord Merle still lurked in his gut, since he was unable to keep his attention from returning again and again to that mouth. Dirick was not an impulsive man when it came to women. He took his time, wooing and flattering, teasing and titillating a woman until she was like a ripe peach falling into his hand. There were plenty of willing women—ladies and whores alike—that made themselves available to him and did not give him cause to take chase. That was the way he preferred it.

Nevertheless, not only had he enjoyed his day at Maris's side, but he knew he would kiss her again—betrothed or not betrothed.

He was able to look at her openly for the first time that evening when she stood to bid them good evening. "I must see to Maisie's daughter, for she is not feeling well, and then I shall go abovestairs," she explained, carefully avoiding his glance. "Good night, Sir Dirick, good night, Mama." She bent over to kiss her father on his cheek, then, with a quick glance at Dirick, she turned to walk from the hall.

She had just disappeared into the kitchen and the hall was beginning to quiet down when the messenger made his appearance. Most of the men-at-arms had retired from bawdy conversation and raucous story-telling to the beds of whores, chess and dice games, or the night watch. Dirick himself was becoming ready to find his own pallet when the messenger was announced quietly to Merle.

"My lord, a messenger at the gate brings tidings to our guest, Sir Dirick de Arlande." The seneschal stood primly, awaiting permission to call the messenger within.

Dirick's face froze as his heart nearly stopped pumping in his chest. The news must be bad indeed for a messenger to track him whilst on a secret mission for the king. Fresh from the experience of having news of his father's death brought in the same way, he felt his stomach clench into iron.

Merle nodded his assent to the seneschal, who disappeared to retrieve the messenger. The moments that passed until his reappearance seemed an age to Dirick as he forced nonchalance, sipping more ale. At last the messenger appeared, and Dirick's concern was heightened when he recognized the man-at-arms of his brother Bernard.

"Sir Dirick de Arlande?" he asked of Merle, as if to confirm his identity—and to let the recipient of his message know that his true identity was still safe.

"This is Sir Dirick," Merle gestured expansively to his guest.

"The message I bear is best given in private," the messenger said as he swung to face Dirick.

"Then let us step to a private corner," Dirick stood, his mouth compressed and his middle roiling.

The man followed him to a dark, chilly corner of the room and Dirick rounded on him as soon as they were out of earshot of the others. "What is news, Sir Ivan?"

"Lord Bernard sent me thus—"

"He is well then? Bernard is well? Is it Thomas? Speak, man!"

"Aye, they are well, and—"

"Mother! 'Tis not Mother?"

"Nay, nay Sir Dirick—all is well."

The breath expelled from Dirick in relief. "Well, man, you nearly affrighted me into an earlier grave than I should wish! What news is it that Bernard should send you to find me whilst on the king's business?" He held his hand out for the missive.

"'Tis not writ," Ivan told him. "Lord Bernard did not wish to chance the wrong eyes to see it and alert them of your assumed identity. He learned a story from a traveling knight who stopped at Derkland for succor en route to the king. Upon hearing the details of your good father's murder," Ivan crossed himself, "this Samuel of Lederwyrth told the tale of another murder thus:

"He came upon a terrible scene near London—nearly two leagues south of the city. 'Twas obviously the scene of a robbery—there were two men dead and picked bare of their valuables. Both lay on the ground, facedown, in the most odd position: with their arms positioned as if their hands were joined.

One of the men—knights they were both," Ivan crossed himself again, "had been stabbed so as to leak blood for hours, and his throat cut. He was placed in the ground with his face in the dirt—"

"And his neck broken by the hoof of a horse so that his forehead touched the sky?" Dirick felt his heavy meal surge in his stomach.

Ivan shook his head. "Nay, though a horse's hoofprint tore into his back."

"Bastard!"

"My lord Bernard bade me also tell you of the horse found on the scene—a fine horse with two legs broken and hobbled to a tree. The horse had died thus." Ivan's face mirrored the horror that Dirick felt—but there was still more to tell. He drew forth a small bundle from the deepest folds of his cloak and offered it to Dirick. "The knight hied himself to the king's court and stopped in Derkland for rest. He showed Lord Bernard this, which was found embedded in a tree above the horse."

Dirick's hands trembled slightly as he held them out to catch the object rolling from the cloth.

The item was a wicked-looking dagger. Dirick caught it easily in his hands, measuring the blade against the length of his hand from wrist to the tip of his longest finger.

The blade was silver, and the tip had been nicked off so that instead of a perfect point, it ended in a jagged edge. The dagger's handle was such that Dirick had seen naught like it. Silver filigreed roses entertwined with serpents, the blooms as true to life as the sharp thorns, as wicked as the slithering serpents. A small crystal was set in the end of the handle and it glittered in the light of the blazing fire.

Dirick gazed at the dagger for a long moment, turning it over and over in his hands as if willing it to speak. "'Tis beautiful yet murderous," he murmured to himself. Looking up at Ivan, he asked, "What said my brother—shall I send this back with you to go to the king?"

Ivan shook his head. "Nay, my lord—Lord Bernard wished you to keep the dagger if you thought it of use to you."

"Good." Dirick wrapped the knife in its cloth and tucked it into his tunic. "This Samuel of Lederwyth—where did he come from? I should like to speak with him."

"He hails from the southern lands—near to London. He left Derkland for his home in the stead of continuing to the king. Lord Bernard explained that he would inform the king."

Dirick was nodding. "Aye. 'Twill do me more good than his majesty, and mayhaps soon I will have an identity to this mad killer."

"Aye, my lord. I will send word to Lord Bernard of your response."

"Do you tell Bernard of my thanks for this message. I would like to hear of any further events." He turned and pulled Ivan in his wake as they headed back toward the dais. "Lord Merle sets a good table and offers soft pallets. Do you stay a night or two before your journey back to Derkland."

Seven ❧

irick arose from his pallet after a fitful sleep. Most of the other men-at-arms that shared the sleeping area had already vacated their blankets and were, no doubt, going about their day's business. He couldn't remember the last time he'd awakened to an empty sleeping chamber!

With a stifled groan, he pulled on his heavy woolen chausses and slowly wrapped the cross-garters about them from ankle to knee. An undertunic followed, over a thin cotton shift, and then a sleeveless tunic that laced loosely from mid-torso to the neckline. It was a dark red wool that favored him well, as his mother Rosamunde oft told him, and the edges were simply embroidered with black clover.

Dirick found a barrel of water near the entrance to the sleeping area and splashed his face with the chill water, hoping to startle himself awake. It didn't work; his thick hair hung dripping onto his face, but his eyes still felt gritty.

With a gusty sigh, he flipped his head so that droplets of water flung in all directions, and his long bangs were whipped out of his eyes. It had been a miserable night.

Dirick groped under the meager pillow at the head of his pallet and withdrew the broken dagger, still wrapped in its old cloth. Between racing thoughts of tracking down his father's murderer, and memories of Maris's sweet lips, it had taken much of the night for him to drift to sleep. Yet, he'd wakened shortly thereafter—sweating and shaking—as nightmarish visions of his father's broken neck and anguished face swam in his dreams. Maris showed up in the midst of the evil, her beautiful hair swirling about his body, tangling him helplessly, as he reached out to his father. A hobbled horse with bared teeth and garishly-twisted legs screamed in his nightmare, pulling Dirick's attention from his father and Maris. When he turned back, his father was gone, but a naked, bleeding Maris lay sprawled in his place, her vacant eyes gazing up at him.

When Dirick truly awoke from that black dream, his heart raced and it took him moments to realize that the visions were twisted remnants of the day's activities. Still, those memories did not invite sleep.

It seemed he did not find peaceful rest until the keep lightened with dawn and the serfs began to stir. When he awoke the last time, it was embarrassingly late; yet he had to pry his eyes open.

Now, since he had certainly missed the bread and cheese to break his fast, he would have to try to sweet-talk Maisie into finding him something in the kitchen. Stuffing the broken dagger into the pouch that hung from a belt around his undertunic, he folded his pallet and left the room, heading for the kitchen in search of aught to break his fast.

Once there, he hailed the cook and gave her the charming smile he used when wooing a woman for any reason. "Might a crust of bread be found for a late-sleeping man?"

The plump, sweating cook snorted heavily, but a smile crept at the edges of her mouth. "Aye, an' a piece of cheese, too, my lord," she told him; beckoning for another girl to bring the wares forward.

Dirick thanked both of them and allowed himself to be

shooed out of the kitchen as he stuffed the heel of day-old bread in his mouth. After a quick dip of water from a barrel to wash it down, he exited the kitchen by a different door than that from which he'd come, out into the courtyard.

After wandering about the courtyard and past the herbalry, he realized he was searching for Maris. Dirick could not explain why he felt compelled to seek her out—aside of the fact that she had not only kept him awake most of the night, but also showed up in his nightmares as well, she really had no place in his mind right now. He should be concentrating on the king's business and revenge for his father's death—not the nearly-betrothed, well-landed daughter of his host.

Nevertheless, he trudged through the snow that had fallen during the night. The new drifts reached halfway to his knees and were soft, so that he sunk easily into the light flakes. The stables were empty with the exception of Peter the marshal and three mares. Hickory, Maris's mount, was not in her stall and Dirick found himself requesting a saddle and bridle for Nick.

༄

Verna pulled her mantle more closely about her face, pushing back the hank of blond hair that threatened to obscure her vision. She trudged through the drifts, stepping carefully over the branches of the deepest part of the wood bordering Langumont Village. Her burden was secured tightly at her waist with a heavy cord, and she patted it several times to assure herself of its continued presence.

After a very long walk, Verna at last came upon a tiny hut nearly hidden in the trees. She shivered, but, gathering her courage up with her mantle, she approached the hovel. The wood was deathly still—even the birds were silent. She glanced over her shoulder as if expecting a red-eyed wolf to be watching.

Something touched her leg through the long cloak that caught in the snow, and she nearly choked on her heart. She leapt back before she could catch herself and nearly tripped over a huge black cat.

It hissed at her, then eased through a crack into the hut as Verna watched in frozen trepidation. Her eyes wide, she stared at the hut, wondering if that had been the old crone herself.

Her fears were justified when, moments later, without her even raising her hand to knock, the door swung silently open. No one was there. She didn't move except to clutch at her throat.

At last she took a hesitant step forward, and then another, until she could see into the dark, cavern-like interior. The only light came from a blazing fire in the far corner.

"Are ye comin' in er not?" a voice suddenly shrieked.

Verna started, but was galvanized to move forward. "Dame Marthe," she whispered, crossing the threshold into the meager hovel.

Inside, she found a room filled with an assortment of tables and stools, and each stick of furniture was cluttered with crude wooden bowls and utensils. A heavy odor pervaded the room, and she saw what looked like the remains of several animals on a nearby table. The huge black cat was not to be found.

At first, Verna didn't see the tiny, wizened lady ensconced in a corner chair. When her eyes rested on Dame Marthe, they were fastened and held by a cold, rheumy blue pair. The crone's face had more lines in it than a linen altar cloth, and her mouth was yet one more deep line. Spidery wrinkles radiated from the place her lips would be, and when she opened the lipless orifice to speak, Verna caught a glimpse of one stump of a tooth.

"My, my! A pretty lady has come to call!" the hag cackled with poorly concealed distaste. "And who might ye be?"

Verna swallowed, but forced herself to speak with confidence. "Verna of Langumont," she answered. "Lady of Langumont."

Overcome with mirth, Dame Marthe nearly fell off her rickety stool. "Lady of Langumont in a pig's eye, ye are!" she returned harshly. "Ye're no more The Lady than I am the Blessed Virgin!"

Verna nearly winced at the blasphemy; but caught herself before she responded. She'd deviated too much to devote any thought to such mundane cares as blasphemes. "I shall be Lady of Langumont, old woman—my time will come. My time will come with help from you."

The hag contained her laughter; then her runny eyes narrowed. Mucus spilled out of them, running into the deep crevices in her cheeks. "Verna, ye say? Verna of the smith, might ye be?"

The maidservant nodded slowly, "Aye, dame. If you know of me…then you know of my plight. I have brought something to you. I am in need of assistance, old woman. You will be well-rewarded upon completion of this deed."

She pulled from her waist a cloth-wrapped package. With a swift flick of her wrist, she opened it and a cloth of gold snood tumbled onto the dirty table. "And when we are through today," she looked expectantly at Dame Marthe, "you shall tell my future."

క్ర

Maris breathed deeply of the cold winter air. 'Twas always a pleasure to smell snow and ice and cold after the cloying smokiness of the Great Hall. She nudged Hickory forward with a click of her tongue, then gave the mare her head. Maris nearly laughed aloud at the exhilaration she felt as the trees whizzed by—and, certainly, Hickory shared in the feeling of recently-gained freedom as she bounded through the forest.

This was the first time since the mare had strained her leg

that her mistress gave her the thorough exercising she craved. They went along the river, well past the village, skirting the farm-land that lay untouched during the winter months. The keep rose in the distance behind the woman and her mare, far enough away that, upon looking back, Maris was newly awed by the structure.

Built in the recent years after The Conquerer made England his, Langumont Keep had begun as a smallish, round stone structure. It had replaced the daub-and-wattle home of a Saxon land-owner who was beheaded during the Battle of Hastings. Merle Lareux's great-great-grandfather, Gilbert, had been awarded the lands of Langumont and Shawdon for his service to William. Merle's family had done fealty for the lands ever since; often adding to its fiefdom over the centuries.

The simple keep had been added to in the same manner as had the Lareux holdings. At one point, the roof of the old keep had been razed and the upper chambers added—a huge under-taking, and one that stripped the village of any extra coin in the coffers for half a decade. Side buildings had been added to what came to be known as the manor house: a kitchen that was attached to the keep by a narrow hallway, along with the herbalry that had originally been manned by Maris's grandmother; an armory and smithy; and larger stables. A chapel was built during the reign of Henry I, and, at the same time, a gaol to hold pris-oners.

Now, the great walled structure of Langumont Keep glared down at passersby from its high perch. A river that ran nearby had been redirected one year—with the help of hundreds of serfs and men-at-arms—and now curved around the base of the hill. The waters ran deeply and roughly, and had assisted in staving off more than one siege over the decades. The walls of the bailey enclosed all of the buildings and were capped at each corner by a guardsman. The crennelated walls served as shields for men-at-arms as they strove to protect Langumont.

Maris shivered. There had only been one siege upon Langumont during her lifetime—but it had been enough for her to learn to hate war. She'd been a mere seven years and even now, she recalled the panic of her mother as flaming arrows were shot over the walls in an attempt to set people and buildings on fire. She and Allegra had remained in the innermost part of the keep for three days until reinforcements came from Shawdon and Damona to rout the besiegers.

A victorious end to the siege had not lessed her hate of battle.

Maris, who'd been lost in thought as she stared back at the looming keep, was suddenly jerked out of her thoughts as a scream echoed in the distance. She whirled Hickory back toward the sound—toward the keep and toward the river—and dug her heels into the mare's sides.

The scream came again, and as she rounded a bend in the river she saw its source.

A villager, Ingretta, stood at the edge of the river, her hands out in supplication, her mouth moving in a shriek. "My Peter!" she cried. "My lady, my baby!"

Several other villagers had gathered and stood at the edge of the river, stunned and unmoving. Maris at once comprehended the situation and she leapt off her horse, quickly doffing her cloak.

The ice had begun to thaw slightly as the weather was a little warmer than it had been. Obviously, young Peter was well used to crossing the river on the ice and did not pay heed to the center of the river, where the ice had broken free and rushed along with the current.

A tiny head floated amidst pieces of ice. He appeared to be jammed among several of them; that was the only thing keeping five-year-old Peter from being sent rapidly downriver. His head bobbed under the water twice as Maris pushed her way between the gawking villagers and gingerly out onto the ice.

"My lady!" one of them exclaimed in fright as she moved out toward the center.

Most of the peasants were not only deathly afraid of the water, but few could swim enough to battle the angry current of Langumont River.

"Nay, stay as you are!" Maris shouted. She was, by far, the lightest of all the peasants staring from the edge, and had the best chance of reaching the child. She moved quickly, carefully out onto the ice.

She'd made it halfway to the child when a loud crack rent the air. Maris felt the ice move under her feet and froze. Everything was silent for a moment; the only sound was the rushing water.

"Fetch a large branch," she called back to the group on the shore. One of the men dashed to obey, and she turned back to the quickly tiring child.

As she turned, another crack sounded and a shift in the ice set Peter free from his moorings and he was pushed into the current. With a scream from Ingretta as her backdrop, Maris forgot all care and dashed lightly along the snow-covered ice in the child's wake, running closer to the center as she hurried along the length of the river.

At last, the child caught himself among the floatsam and she was able to draw nearer. The ice was not much more than a shell, and she held her breath as she moved toward the child.

"Peter!" she called, dropping slowly to her knees, her gown a pool of gold on the whiteness. "Peter!"

There seemed to be no response from the boy, and she inched closer, screaming backward over her shoulder, "The branch! Be quick!"

She was just at the edge of the ice. Reaching a careful hand out, she called to the boy. "Peter, can you grasp my hand?" She leaned forward, nearly touching the boy's shoulder. She was inches away, and the boy was not moving. His face was blue and he bobbed helplessly in the icy water. Tears of frustration coursed down her face as she leaned infinitesimally closer.

A sudden shout from the shore, followed by a bellow that sounded like her name, distracted her for the merest second—but she could not glance that way. She was almost there.

༄

Dirick had heard the screams minutes before and hurried Nick toward them. When they stopped for a time, he lost track of the direction and it was only after Ingretta's last cry that he was able to burst from the forest upon the scene at the river.

"Maris!" he shouted in anger and astonishment when he finally recognized the daft woman out on the ice. "God's teeth!" He gritted his own teeth in fury and alarm. He started toward the river without thinking; but one step on the ice, followed by a loud crack, was enough to stop him in his tracks. He would endanger her even more if he continued.

A voice from the crowd caught his attention, and there stood one of the burliest villagers with a long, stout branch. "Aye, thank you, my man," Dirick said, grabbing the branch.

He turned back the river just in time to see Maris tumble face first into the water. "No! Maris!" he bellowed, starting out onto the ice, his heart leaping into his throat.

༄

The water was the worst shock she'd ever had. She couldn't move, and the heaviness of her woolen gown made her arms and legs ironweight. Her hair was plastered to her face, blinding her.

As she struggled in the frigid water, she at last felt something soft and somewhat warm—Peter! With a heavy arm, she brushed the hair from her face and forced her freezing limbs to move. She was able to close one hand over the boy's waist and with a sudden, earthshattering movement, propelled him from the water onto the ice. The force of her movement sent her under the water, and when she came up, her head hit something.

She was under the ice!

Lights flashed in front of her eyes, and then blackness, as panic overtook her. Maris floundered in the water, her gown paralyzing her legs and her arms exhausted from the cold so that she could hardly move them. At last, she broke free and her head sprang up from the water, several feet down the river from where she'd gone under.

Dimly, she heard cheers; and then, more closely, a shout. She tried to turn about in the water to find the source, but her body would not move. She felt the water close over her again, and panic shot through her leaden muscles—but, mercifully, she rose again into the cold air. She was able to stop her flow with the current by latching onto a piece of ice.

"Maris!" The shout was closer and more intelligible. "Godammit, Maris!" Dirick's voice was desperate.

Maris was vaguely aware of him inching slowly along the ice with the branch in his hand. Just as she slipped under the ice, she heard him cry her name.

The icy water swallowed her again, and she floundered, her movements slowing as her limbs grew more frigid. Suddenly, she bobbed back up to the surface, and as her head broke from the water, Maris heard cheers from the people onshore. When she heard Dirick call her name, she turned her head to face him. The branch was almost within her reach.…

"Grab it, Maris!" he shouted. The ice was protesting and, while he'd jump in to save her, it may not help the situation. "Grab the branch!"

Maris opened her mouth to yell and swallowed water. Choking, she splashed in the water, her movements sluggish as fatigue crept over her.

Dirick inched closer, sticking the branch into the water next to her. "Grab the branch, Maris!" he pleaded, desperation crowding his voice.

She raised her iron-weight arm and it fell back into the water, onto the foreign object of the life-saving branch. Galvanized, she pushed herself and wrapped both arms around it.

Not daring to make the sound of relief that rose in his throat, Dirick began to ease the branch back.

The ice cracked.

He stopped.

"Hold on, Maris, hold on!"

He inched the branch slightly more. Ice broke away under her heavy body as she was dragged closer to safety.

Dirick swore in frustration. It wasn't going to work—he'd be in the water with her if he kept pulling.

He took a deep breath. "Hold on, Maris, I'm going to pull hard. Just don't let go!"

With a swift prayer, he grasped the branch with all his might and lunged back with one swift, strong movement. Maris popped out of the water and slid across the ice several feet before she lost her grip. Dirick was at her side in a moment, and, sweeping her up in his arms, dashed off the deadly ice. A crack followed them back to the shore where each of his feet landed, and he barely made it before water showed between them.

He eased her lightly onto solid ground, and, turning to grab the cloak he'd tossed over Nick, whirled back to wrap her in it. When he turned, she was gone—standing over by Ingretta.

He could see that Maris was shivering so hard, and was so exhausted from her bout in the icy water, that she could barely stand—and, in fact, was leaning against a tree. Even in this state, however, she was giving orders. Peter had choked up the water from his lungs and was breathing and shivering violently. At her demand, he had been wrapped in her cloak, and now she stood over him, water dripping from her sodden gown and her tangled hair.

Dirick was at her side with two quick strides, and threw his cloak over her head. "You daft woman!" he shouted, his temper raised along with the fear that she might drown. He hauled her up against him, wrapping his arms firmly around her body, and started away. "I'm taking you back to the keep, you foolish woman!"

She struggled for a brief second, and her shivery voice could be heard bleating from the insides of his wrap, "Call Widow Maggie—she'll care for Peter."

Dirick strode angrily to Nick with his burden. He set her on her feet next to the destrier and unwrapped her. "You are the veriest fool of a woman!" he shouted, then, before she could react, he yanked her body full-length to his, and—ignoring the wide eyes of the bystanders—slammed his mouth onto hers, covering cold, trembling lips with his own. "Damn fool woman," he muttered, pulling away after the brief, fierce kiss.

Then he set her back from him and roughly placed the heavy, fur-lined cloak around her shoulders, wrapping her, and hoisted her onto Nick. That was the last bit of tenderness she received from him. Dirick swung up behind her and, gathering her against his warm body, took off at a gallop back to the keep, cursing her foolishness all the way.

Merle and several men-at-arms met them at the portcullis to the bailey. One of the villagers had rushed to tell the tale, and the lord of Langumont had rushed forth from the keep.

"Dearling!" he cried, scooping Maris from Dirick's mount. With nary a backward glance, he rushed his violently shivering daughter into the keep, leaving her rescuer to follow.

Dirick swung off his destrier, tossing the reins to Peter the marshal, and followed in Lord Merle's wake. Maris was quickly taken to her chambers, Allegra giving unusually firm orders for warm draughts and heated bricks to be brought abovestairs. Dirick, of course, could not follow to the upper chambers. The only men allowed abovestairs were specially-invited guests and members of the family.

ॐ

Maris of Langumont lay in a fever for three days.

When it broke at last, her mother Allegra was at her side, and Merle had stepped away just long enough to use the garderobe.

Dirick received the news in the Great Hall.

A portly, red-headed man by the name of Edwin Baegot dispatched a messenger to Dreakskill to notify Bon de Savrille of her recovery.

Verna cursed the old crone.

Eight ⟋

Edwin Baegot returned to Dreakskil after Maris's recovery.

He entered the Great Hall of the keep to find his friend, Bon de Savrille, in quite an uproar.

"Ah, at last he deigns to grace us with his presence!" Bon erupted drunkenly. He was sprawled on a heavy oaken chair that would have rivaled Henry Plantagenet's throne had someone the urge to move them side by side. His buff-colored tunic, embroidered with red stags and stallions, was stained and hung haphazardly over his broad shoulders. The cross-garters that should have kept the hose fitted to his legs had drooped into a pile just above his ankles.

"Greetings, my lord." Edwin gave a short little bow, then turned to help himself to a cup of ale.

"And what news of my bride?" demanded Bon, sitting straighter in his chair.

"The fair Lady of Langumont has risen from her chambers and rejoins the workings of the castle...or so Verna reports to me." Edwin nearly smacked his lips. "And a hot little piece she is—"

Bon leapt out of his chair, his fingers wrapping around Edwin's throat in an instant. "What say you!" he raged in his henchman's face, instantly sober. "If you have touched my lady, I shall dig out your fingernails and feed them to you with your entrails!"

Edwin gurgled helplessly behind the iron fingers that lifted his stocky figure off the floor. He pulled futilely at Bon's arm, and just when his struggles were weakening, the hand released him and he fell to the floor. Bon glared around at the curious faces of the men-at-arms. "And the same or worse to anyone that lays a finger—a *breath*!—on Lady Maris!"

"My lord, Bon," Edwin croaked, "'twas not of your intended that I so spoke!" Hastening to defend himself, he continued, "'Twas the maidservant, Verna, that kept me apprised of my lady's actions…and tended willingly to my other needs!"

"Ah…yes, Verna.…" Bon's eyes softened, glinting with lust-ful remembrance. "Aye, she is a hot little box! You are not injured." His anger disintegrated, he waved away his violent attack on Edwin. "Here, drink up! A toast to the next Lord of Langumont!" He raised his glass and declined to drink to his future as the others downed full cups of ale.

"*Á Langumont!*"

"My lord," Edwin claimed his attention once more. "There is talk—from the wench Verna—of a candidate for betrothal to the Lady Maris to arrive in the next se'ennight."

Bon froze from adding ruby wine to his goblet. His hand went to the stiff black hairs that bristled about his lips, clenching them. "Ah.…" A long sigh hissed from his thin lips, and he pulled his hand slowly away to stare at the signet ring that adorned the middle finger. "Allegra…the bitch must needs have a reminder of her daughter's husband.…" The ring, slick with grease from a roasted pheasant on which he'd feasted earlier, slid off easily.

Bon weighed the heavy circle in his palm, looking at the bat-tered gold that still held etched the arms of his father. He tossed it into the air, catching it, tossed it again, and caught it once more. "Berkle!" he bellowed, his decision made.

A tall, thin man nearly dropped the skin of ale he'd been pulling a draught from. "Aye, my lord." He rose to his feet and stumbled clumsily through a group of men-at-arms to approach the dais.

"Berkle, see that Allegra of Langumont holds this trinket in her hand by the day after next." He tossed the signet heedlessly into the air, watching as his messenger caught it neatly. As the thin man turned to make his way to the stable, a loud cough stopped him still. "And, Berkle, no one but Allegra is to lay eyes upon it or 'twill be your death."

"Aye, my lord," Berkle grinned an evil smile. He paused again nearly halfway across the hall. "And where might I find this other piece of fluff—Verna?" His smile, specked with black where two teeth were missing, turned lascivious.

"Ask at the Boar's Meat," Edwin told him. "The innkeeper will be pleased to provide entertainment for the right price."

Berkle gave a funny salute and darted out of the keep and into the chill night.

Bon gave a huge belch, and, rubbing his belly in satisfaction, shouted another order. "My lute, Agnes, fetch me my lute!"

A curvaceous young woman with a long purple scar on her face hurried to do his bidding. She brought the instrument forward and knelt at his feet.

"Ah, my lady love…" Bon sighed, "how I pine for thee! Edwin, by my troth, I cannot wait for much longer." He strummed a chord on the lute, a sad expression covering his face. "'Twas, at the first, her lands—my lands—that I wished to regain…. But now," another chord accompanied his wistful words, "'tis more." There was silence as he took another long gulp of wine, taking care not to spill any on the beautifully carved lute. "My lust for material goods has grown to full, mature love, Edwin," Bon told him earnestly. "I cannot live without her...."

His red-headed companion rolled his eyes and finished off more ale. God's bones, his master was a pussy when he imbibed in too much wine! He would have to ask the castellan to stop importing that red wine from Bordeaux—it made Bon impossible to live with! God's teeth, he was glad English-brewed ale did not affect his master in that way!

"Do ye hear what I say, Edwin," Bon slurred. "Listen you, I have written a song for my beloved. I shall play it on my wedding night." Drunk as he was, his short fingers stumbled agilely over the strings of the lute and the resulting melody was surprisingly moving. He sang in a slurry, off-key voice, obviously making up the words as he went along:

O, Lady of the Fairest, I praise thy beauty... The clouds will cry for thee, for they see not such grace in heav'n... Thy face, thy voice make my heart swell with joy, and on thy wedding day, thee shall have my love for'er more...

"She would make more than my *heart* swell," Edwin mumbled into his ale. Fortunately, Bon did not hear him, for he was well into his second pitiful verse.

As Bon continued his tribute to his intended, the men-at-arms crept one by one from the hall. His verses became more and more redundant, and of the worst poetry, and Edwin was forced to be subjected to the poor musicality of his master. Once, he dared to rise from his seat, hoping to follow suit of the other cowards that had since left him alone in the room; but a look from Bon froze him in his tracks. Edwin sank onto a cushioned chair, and, refilling his ale cup yet again, prepared himself for a long night.

༄

"Check and mate, sirrah!" Dirick announced with pleasure as he moved his bishop for the last time.

"God's bones, de Arlande! 'Tis thrice too oft I have heard those words from your mouth! Methinks I shall give you a rest!" Raymond of Vermille pushed his stool away from the table. He paused and extended his hand. "'Tis a pleasure to face a man of your skill."

Dirick shook the proffered hand and smilingly waved the man away. Out of habit, he began to realign the chess pieces when a quiet voice startled him.

"Have you then wearied the entire keep of facing you across the chessboard? I should like to match against you."

His head snapped up and he saw Maris. "My lady," he rose to his feet. He had not seen her since Merle had taken her from his arms after her near drowning. "I—'tis glad I am to see you. You feel well?"

She smiled, and, though her face was drawn and rather more pale than usual, she did look fully recovered. "Aye. Widow Maggie and Mama would not let me rise from the solar even yesterday when I was screeching of my boredom." Her smile became wry. "An' yet I feel not as strong as I should, I am well recovered." She gestured to the chessboard, her long sleeve nearly knocking the pieces awry. "If there is not another challenger, I should like to play." Her eyes twinkled in the dim light of the Great Hall. "My mind has had little exercise in the last days."

"But of course, my lady." Dirick swept his hand toward the other stool.

As she sat, her hand reached across the table and rested lightly on the warmth of his sturdy wrist. "Sir Dirick," her gaze dropped, then rose to his again, "I am indebted to you for fishing me out of the river. I should—I should like to make reparation in some manner, some day. My life," her lips twisted wryly again, "is of the greatest value…and I thank you deeply for giving it to me."

He swallowed and raised her hand to press his lips gently to it, inhaling her familiar scent of lemons and rosemary. "My lady, your thanks and your presence still are the only reparation I should wish. Indeed, your father has expressed his gratitude many times over as well."

His mouth thinned in remembrance of Merle's overzealous thanks and offers of coin or position within his household. The man even offered him a small fief from his vast holdings—one whose income would allow him to garner enough to collect the brides-price for a decently-landed maid. Dirick had put him off, explaining as delicately as possible that his work for Henry Plantagenet kept him in more of a comfort than Merle could imagine, and forced himself to not consider the possibility of holding his own lands. 'Twould never happen.

"If there is ever aught that I can do for you...." Her voice trailed off as their gazes locked.

Dirick saw the uncertainty in her eyes and watched as the tip of her tongue brushed over her beautiful lips. He knew that his desire for her showed in his face, and he knew it would do no good to try and hide it. If she were not a maiden, he thought, resisting the urge to brush his fingers over the delicate skin of her hand, he'd find some way for her to make reparation...and it would definitely involve those incredibly sensual lips.

She ducked her head, breaking their eye contact, and turned her attention to the chessboard. "Do not look at me like that," she whispered.

"Lady Maris, your betrothed is a very fortunate man," Dirick forced himself to say lightly. Then he raked his attention to the game and suggested, "You may make the first move, my lady."

❧

Merle sighed and settled more easily in his chair.

Allegra turned to him. "Husband, may I pour thee more ale? Thy cup is near empty." She was seated in the chair next to him, working on her embroidery. The dais on which they sat was near the fire; yet not near enough to be well-lit. Merle had had torches and candles on tall stands set about so that his wife did not have to strain her eyes.

"Aye, love, more ale. And mayhaps some cheese?"

"Of course, my lord husband." Allegra provided him with his wishes as he watched Maris and Dirick thoughtfully.

Just settling back in her chair, Allegra was startled by a quiet voice in her ear. "My lady Allegra." Turning, she found Maris's maidservant, Verna.

"Aye, Verna?"

"You are needed in the kitchen," Verna whispered, tugging at her mistress's sleeve.

"I am needed in the kitchen?" she repeated.

As they walked away from Merle, Verna spoke in a humble voice, "Aye, my lady, there is someone that has asked to speak with you. He did not wish Lord Merle to know of it."

Fear gripped Allegra's chest and she felt her heart thumping uncontrollably behind her ribs. She had hoped and prayed that Bon had forgotten his threat, or had given up when she had not responded. In sooth, she had not had the courage to broach Merle on the subject of Maris's betrothed, for she could not fathom a solution to the problem. If Maris married as her husband wished, Bon would make good on his threat to expose her true parentage. But Allegra could not allow her daughter to wed with her own half-uncle—most especially to a man such as Bon de Savrille.

Allegra was taken back to the day of her own wedding, and the memory of her vow that her daughter should never marry against her will as she herself had. In all these years, she had not forgotten Michael; nor had her love for the man she remembered dimmed. Someday, she vowed, she would be with him again, may God strike her dead. She had never grown to love Merle as she should—although she'd been a good wife to him, and served him well, she did not feel the passion and blind love that she still harbored for Lord Michael. She oft fantasized about the day that Michael would ride to Langumont Keep, and whisk her away to be with him forever.

She was pulled from her thoughts by a plucking at her sleeve. Allegra swallowed her fear and followed as Verna turned toward the kitchen. The maid stopped just near the door, gesturing to the entrance to the bailey. "My lady, the man awaits near the stables. I did not wish to alarm Lord Merle to his presence."

The wind was cold and Allegra had not pulled a cloak around her. Her dread grew, causing her stomach to churn, and she forced herself to walk across the courtyard, head bent. She shivered and stumbled to the stables, suddenly aware that Verna was no longer in her wake.

Stepping hesitantly inside, she breathed a sigh at the inherent warmth of the building of whuffling horses. The stable was dark, but she saw a shadowy figure stood near the rear.

"What do you wish?" she asked in a quavery voice.

"My Lady Allegra…." A slight, bent man stepped forward so that she could make out the barest of his features. "I bring you a token from my master." He reached forward, and she stepped back in alarm. He was, however, too quick for her reaction, and his fingers closed around her hand. Something heavy was pressed into her palm, then he closed her fingers tightly around it. Metal pressed into her tender palm and Allegra cried out at the pain.

The man laughed with a low rumble, showing gaps where his teeth had been, and, leaning forward, breathed into her face, "My master insists that if you do not heed his warning, you will be in much more pain. Good eve, my lady." He pushed roughly past her and suddenly she was alone.

Allegra stumbled out of the dim stable moments later, still clutching the heavy metal object. The light of the moon led her through ankle deep snow to the chapel. Leaning on the heavy door, she nearly fell into the haven.

Candles flickered along the altar and at each corner of the chapel. Allegra slowly unfurled her clenched fingers. Even in the varying light, she was able to make out the signet on the ring. If she'd had any doubt that Bon de Savrille still intended to marry her daughter, that doubt was now gone.

و

The next day was unusually fair for January. The sun glared high in the sky, and the serfs and men-at-arms disdained cloaks and gloves alike as they went about their business.

Merle stood in the bailey, watching his men practice their swordplay, when visitors arrived. Dirick, who had just put his own sword down, looked up curiously when Gustave approached.

"My lord," announced the seneschal, "the Lords d'Arcy have identified themselves at the portcullis. I shall show them to the Great Hall and have them take their ease, but you wished to be informed upon their arrival."

Merle's rugged face broke into a smile, and he clapped a hand upon Dirick's shoulder. "Aye, Gustave, and Dirick and I shall soon follow."

The younger man's eyebrows rose. "Merle, 'tis not meet that I join you in greeting your guests. I am sure you have much to discuss that does not concern me; I can most certainly occupy myself until the evening meal." He wiped an arm across the sweat that trickled down his forehead, brushing his hair back in one slick motion.

"Nay, nay," Merle said heartily—and so firmly that Dirick did not argue. "Come you with me and meet my dear friend and his son. Verily, they shall have much news, as they come from south of London Town, and will bring the latest from there."

Eagerly, Merle led the way to the huge entrance of the keep, beckoning for Dirick to follow. Resigned, he pulled on his tunic and followed, wondering why Merle was so insistent that he meet his guests.

Inside the hall, Dirick sheathed his sword and rested it on one of the heavy oaken benches that lined a trestle table. Merle had already greeted the two men that were settled on stools in front of a blazing fire. Dirick approached more slowly than necessary, scrutinizing the Lords d'Arcy. The elder—presumably the father—was comfortably sprawled on a three-legged stool that he tilted backward so that his back rested against a nearby table. Pale, wheat-colored hair hung in a cap just to his ears, cut straight across his forehead, and looking like a silvered helm. Pale blue eyes darted quickly to Dirick as he approached, then to Merle, then back to Dirick.

As Dirick extended his hand to the father, he felt the gaze of the younger d'Arcy boring into him. An unaccountable sense of mislike swept over him.

"Sir Dirick de Arlande, please meet my dear friend, Lord Michael d'Arcy of Gladwythe; and his son, Sir Victor."

"You are well met." Dirick clasped the proffered wrist of Michael d'Arcy, feeling a trickle of unease at the strange light in his pale eyes. Dismissing it, he turned to greet the son. "Sir Victor," he said, taking his time to observe the other man while he tried to place the familiar name. He was definitely Michael's son: he had the same pale blue eyes that were colorless as ice, and thin wheat-colored hair hung raggedly to his shoulders. He was a fairly large man—easily as tall as Dirick—with a tanned, square face and full lips.

"Sir Dirick de Arlande," mused Lord Michael, running a finger slowly over his full lower lip. "I do not believe I have heard mention of you at court."

"Nay," Dirick's lips thinned in a cool smile, "'tis not likely. I am late come from Paris, an' have not spent time in the court of your Plantagenet." His words twisted with an authentic Parisian accent.

Merle stepped in, "Sir Dirick has pleaded succor during his journey through England. I have kept him quite busy at Langumont for the past fortnight."

Michael gratefully drank from a warmed goblet of wine, then, daintily wiping his lips and the tips of his fingers, glanced around the hall. "And where might the fair Lady Maris be? I am well keen to meet her. As, I am certain, is Victor."

It was not clear to Dirick until just then who these visitors were. He nearly slapped his forehead in disgust. Merle had mentioned Sir Victor's imminent betrothal to Maris on the day Dirick had arrived in Langumont; but somehow he'd managed to forget the man's name. 'Twas no wonder Victor stared at him so coldly—most likely, the man thought he had designs on his betrothed. Dirick rolled his eyes as he took a swig from his own ale mug. The lady was not hard on the eyes, but he'd no other interest in her…but mayhaps to kiss her once again.

Foolish! Dirick gave his head a little shake as if to clear the thought. Nay, she was comely and pleasant, and quick-witted, but he'd no desire for anything but a tumble in the hay from any woman. Nor, he reminded himself flatly, did he have aught but that to offer a woman.

Dirick was just replacing his mug on a nearby stool when Merle called across the room, "Allegra, wife, come attend our guests!"

The frail woman had just entered the hall, having been drawn from her solar at the arrival of the honored guests. She glided across the rush-strewn floor, her eyes humbly downcast.

Merle reached out for her hand and drew her into the circle of men around the fire as she looked up. "Wife, do you meet Sir Victor d'Arcy and his father, Lord Michael of Gladwythe."

Dirick's attention was on Allegra as she curtsied and nodded to her future son-by-law. She turned to Michael, and Dirick saw her eyes go wide, her mouth open in a silent gasp, and he watched as she crumpled slowly to the floor.

Instantly, the room was astir. Merle leapt to his feet, bellowing, staring down helplessly at the small heap at his feet. Michael's face had registered no shock, and, in fact, Dirick noticed that he was the calmest of the bunch, leaning forward to ease Allegra by loosening the ties of her bliaut. Victor frowned and turned questioningly to his father.

By the time Dirick had taken in these jumbled facts, Widow Maggie and Maella had scurried to their mistress's side. The healer waved a small bouquet of herbs in front of Allegra's nose, and Dirick was gratified to see her stir.

Allegra's eyes fluttered open and her gaze rested upon the face that was nearest hers, one that was bent over her in concern. "Michael," she breathed between stiff lips, so quietly that no one but the man to whom she spoke heard. She blinked again, rapidly, then saw her husband looking down at her. Allegra closed her eyes against the pain that suddenly exploded in her head. "Merciful God," she squeezed her lids shut in silent prayer. But when she opened them again, the faces that looked down at her had not changed.

Merle reached over to assist her to her feet, and she sagged heavily against him. "I am sorry, my lord," she breathed softly. "I am sorry to cause you embarrassment."

"Nay, wife." Merle hugged her lightly. "Are you feeling unwell? Is there aught can be done?"

"Nay," she brushed away his concern, "nay, my lord, I—'twas

just a spell of dizziness." She drew a shuddering breath and pulled herself to her full height, stiltedly keeping her eyes from Lord Michael.

She noted Maella's stricken face, and that Widow Maggie was pressing a steaming draught upon her. "Shall I call for Lady Maris to attend our guests?" asked Maella, smoothing Allegra's arm familiarly.

"Nay! Nay." Allegra forced herself to sound calm, forced the spots that danced before her eyes to disappear. She could not bring Maris into this mess until she thought how to handle it. "Maris is in the village," she explained, "and the ache in my head has gone." She made a smile of her lips, and bravely turned to look at Michael. "May I offer my lord to bathe? You are likely weary from your long journey."

Michael's gaze had not moved from the woman in front of him. "Aye, a bath would be more than I could hope for!"

"Sir Victor?" Allegra turned to the younger man. "I cannot attend thee myself, but a bath will be prepared for you as well."

"'Twould be most welcome. Mayhaps Lady Maris could attend me," Victor suggested.

Chill swept through Dirick at the scene *that* comment evoked, and he stepped away from the group, trying to control the sudden rage he felt. Verily, Maris would do more than bathe Victor d'Arcy after they were wed, and it should mean naught to him. It *must* mean naught to him!

Merle spoke. "Maris is in the village, tending to the sick. I have sent a man-at-arms to fetch her; but 'tis most like she will not return until the evening meal. You'll likely not meet her until then, but 'twill be time for you to bathe and change your clothes."

"Very well," Victor replied, his disappointment obvious.

His tension fading, Dirick suddenly felt like an outsider—excluded from the glances passing from Allegra to Michael, and

from the way Victor continued to look at him with undisguised
dislike. He watched as everyone dispersed, leaving him alone
with Merle and a full cup of mead.

༄

Allegra could not stop her fingers from shaking as she
unlaced Michael's cross-garters. She had to force her attention to
the task, else her fingers would travel up the curve of his calves to
relearn their strength.

How can this be? How can this be? Her mind chanted the
phrase, echoing the incredulity that swept through her each time
she looked at the man she had pined for, fantasized about, and
begged God for since marrying Lord Merle seventeen years ago.
*How could he come here, be here…and plan to marry his son to his
own daughter?*

Allegra tamped back her panic. But of course—Michael did
not know that Maris was his daughter! She would tell him and
then all would be well. And then, mayhaps she could find some
way to suggest Bon as a husband…. Nay! That she could not do.
There would be another solution—Michael would see to it.

A maidservant bustled about the small chamber, laying out a
tunic and hose from Merle's trunks to clothe Michael after his
bath. Boys from the kitchen came and went with buckets of
steaming water. Maella sprinkled dried lavendar over the steaming tub. The room was busy and crowded, so much so that it
played upon Allegra's nerves and it was all she could do to keep
from screaming at them all to leave…to leave her alone with
Michael.

"Maella, go you to see that Verna has found the tub and is
serving Sir Victor," she said at last, uncaring of the shrewd look
her maidservant flashed at her.

"Aye, my lady." Maella reluctantly turned to leave; noting

that two other maidservants still assisted her mistress.

No sooner had Maella brushed out the doorway than Allegra had found two other contrived excuses to send the others away and at last she found herself alone with Michael.

He rested comfortably in the tub that had been fashioned to hold a body as large as Merle's, eyes closed restfully. A wad of soft linen propped his neck up from the rough wooden edge of the oval tub. Allegra knelt, folding his tunic, and watched as the steam rose from the water. Blond hair was plastered to his neck and his fine features were flushed with the heat. He breathed easily, and she allowed herself the luxury of remembering the warmth of his smooth, muscular chest.

As she watched, one ice-blue eye slowly opened and his gaze rested knowingly upon her. "At last." A smile quirked his generous mouth. "I'd given up hope that we should be alone."

"Aye," Allegra breathed, clasping her hands in her lap to keep from stroking a thick lock of hair from his forehead.

His eyes, both fully opened now, greedily looked over his former lover. She knew she was still a very beautiful woman, and when he shifted in the tub, turning slightly to the side she was gratified that his response to her was as immediate as it had been eighteen years ago. "You have not changed much at all, Allegra," he said quietly.

"Nor have thee." She felt her chest swell so that it was difficult to breathe.

"Come, soap my back," he invited, and sat fully upright.

Allegra's hands trembled as she drew a fine linen cloth from the water and over the large expanse of his back. There were more scars that marred its golden surface, and the ridges of muscle that she remembered were not as pronounced; but 'twas Michael.

The strong lye soap that was usually used for bathing had been replaced by one of Maris's specialties: a rosemary-basil scented soap. Its minty smell pervaded the air, accented by the steam rising from the scented bathwater. Michael eased back into the tub so that Allegra could massage his hair with the same soap; and when he closed his eyes, she almost leaned over to press a kiss to his lips.

She did not speak to him until she was nearly done scrubbing his body. Then, she had to break the silence and ask what had been niggling at her mind all along.

"Michael, did you—did you not know that Merle is my husband? Did you not know whence you came that I would be here?"

He stood at that moment, water cascading down the length of his slim, wiry body. Allegra's breath caught in her throat, and she turned quickly to retrieve a cloth that had been warming by the fire. As he stepped onto a thick wool rug in front of the fireplace, he spoke. "Aye, my love, I'd hoped to see you again."

Her hands, wrapped in the towel, smoothed over his legs and upward to his buttocks. She could not think; could not make sense of what he was doing here....

When she reached his chest, she caressed his shoulders with the towel. "Allegra," he said softly.

She tilted her head up and his arms suddenly wrapped around her waist, pulling her up against his body as he lowered his mouth to hers. With a groan of release, she dropped the towel and found herself swept up in a heady embrace. His damp body pressed into her bliaut and left marks at her breasts and thighs, and his arms were a taut band around her waist.

She'd felt nothing like this in her years of marriage to Merle. Aye, he'd been patient and slow when he thought she was a virgin; and, aye, he'd been tender with her and passionate during the nights they coupled...but he'd not been able to spark her insides as Michael had ever done.

His hands were on her breasts now, and his mouth left a

moist trail on her neck. She felt his need pulsing against her thigh, and her hand slipped to touch him. Suddenly, they were on the floor in front of the fireplace, and she felt his hands smoothing up her legs. Michael's weight pressed her head back onto the floor as he kissed her thoroughly. She was raising her hips to him even as he pushed her bliaut up to take two handfuls of bare breast and bring a nipple to his mouth. Allegra nearly screamed at the pleasure of it, her breath coming in small little pants.

At the urging of his hand, she spread her legs and suddenly he filled her as he'd done eighteen years earlier. He breathed her name as his fingers threaded through the mass of curls that was her hair; she raked her fingers down the length of his back, gouging his skin when she felt him climax.

Tears shimmered in her eyes when they opened as he pulled away to sit up moments later. "Michael…I have missed thee so," she told him.

He did not have a chance to answer, for at that moment Maella burst into the room, stopping short at the sight that greeted her. Allegra had rolled to her knees as Michael left her body; but her hair and clothing were disheveled and there were wet marks on her bliaut.

"Aye, Maella?" Allegra asked sharply to hide her guilt. She struggled to her feet. Knowing that her maidservant was loyal to her above all gave her the courage to act as if nothing had happened.

"My lord Merle wishes to see you in the hall," her servant told her pointedly. "He bade me finish bathing Lord d'Arcy and send you to speak with him."

"My lord Michael's tunic and hose rest by the fire," Allegra said with as much grace as she could muster as she fled the room.

Maella, in turn, gave Michael a hard look as she proceeded to clothe him in silence.

Nine ↣

*M*aris returned from the village in just enough time to change from an herb-stained overtunic to a well-laced bliaut of cinnamon-colored wool with gold embroidery.

Her day had been a fine one—the sun shone gloriously, melting the snow into wet, sticky masses. She'd spent the morning in the herbalry, preparing tonics and poultices for her first trip into the village since her near-drowning. Then, her leather bag filled with dried herbs and small bottles of medicines and tonics, she slipped out of the dark keep into the sharp, clean air.

Drawing a deep breath, Maris started across the bailey with brisk steps. She noticed her father's men gathered to practice their art of warfare and would have passed them by with naught but a bare glance, except that her gaze was drawn to one mock battle.

Maris stopped, curious, and recognized Dirick matched against Raymond of Vermille. Her attention focused on Dirick, admiring his grace and relentless power as he drove her father's best swordsman back into the crowd of bystanders. He'd tossed his dark tunic aside, and wore only a sleeveless linen pelisson and close-fitting woolen chausses. The swords flashed, catching the rays of the sun with each twist and thrust, arms and legs moving in perfect accord.

She watched, studying every fluid motion as Dirick's breeches clung and loosened, embraced and released his massive legs. When the chausses tightened over his thighs during one forceful lunge, she swallowed deeply, her hand clutching the leather sack. They were the size of tree trunks!

Sweat gleamed on his tanned arms, trickling over the ridges of muscle and tendon to fling into the air as he parried Raymond's skillful sword. Sun and shadow played over his huge arms and hair-sprinkled forearms and Maris's throat grated when she tried to swallow. He was beautiful, godlike, graceful…masculine.

She could not pull her attention away, even when she felt her father's gaze shift briefly to her. The dark-haired warrior fought on, ignoring the bystanders, unaware of Maris's own presence—even disregarding the thick hank of hair that dripped sweat into his eyes. Intensity furrowed his face; his eyes, hooded from the sun, did not waver from his opponent. Dirick's full lips—those same ones that had so sweetly kissed her—were tight with concentration, perfectly sculpted in his granite face. Chin thrust forward, he pushed a grunt of exertion from his chest, and veins and tendons coursed his neck as he rounded ferociously upon Raymond in one powerful pass.

A sword thunked to the snow and with a bellow of triumph, Dirick raised his own weapon aloft, then dropped his arms to his sides and stood, breathing heavily. A victorious grin lit his face and he swiped the hair out of his eyes amid the whoops and hollers of the spectators.

As he turned to acknowledge the ring of men clustered around him, Maris spun on her heel, hurrying away before he could notice her goggling at him. She rushed out of the bailey, barely greeting the guards at the portcullis, and hastened into the village.

Though she busied herself for the rest of the day by visiting the ill and making suggestions to the village goodwives, Maris's thoughts returned again and again to the powerful, agile knight. She'd spent time with him, teasing and conversing as if he were little but a squire or an ordinary man-at-arms…and now…now she could see him as naught but a fierce warrior, harsh and ruthless, relentless…formidable…manly.

Her breath became shallow. A warrior had kissed her with gentleness. 'Twas impossible to reconcile the tenderness and warmth of that kiss after seeing what great strength he owned.

Maris brushed her fingers over her own lips, remembering the surprise of desire welling inside her on that crisp, cold day. Even the memory of it made her fingers tremble. And she knew he would kiss her again, given the chance. That truth had been evident in his gaze yesterday, when she sat to play chess with him. She swallowed, remembering the heat smoldering in those thick-lashed, silver-black eyes.

Another truth became known to her: should he try to kiss her again, she would not deny him. Maris shivered.

A noise behind her jerked Maris's thoughts back to the present. Verna stood beside her, offering a wimple and looking at her with an odd intensity. Pulling to her feet, she took the wisp of cloth and started from her chamber.

Hurrying down the dark stone stairs, she tucked her thick hair into the sheer wimple, and entered the hall just as the meal began. As she pushed her way among the serfs that served the food, and between the rows of trestle tables, Maris saw the two strange men sitting with her father, Allegra, and Dirick on the dais. Her heart leapt into her throat and she almost stopped in the center of the hall. Could the man her father intended for her have arrived so soon?

Merle rose as Maris approached the table. "Ah, my daughter, at last!"

"I am sorry to be late, Papa." She made a neat curtsey, nervously avoiding a glance at Dirick, though she felt the weight of his stare upon her.

"Come you, let me make known to you my dear friend, Lord Michael d'Arcy of Gladwythe," and he continued, "…and his son, Sir Victor."

The emphasis Merle placed on those last words was enough to convey his intent: that Victor should be her husband. When she glanced at her father before turning to greet the men, she saw a hint of warning in his eyes, an expectation that she should act accordingly.

Turning, Maris masked her reluctance and extended her hand to father and son. Michael seemed to hold her fingers longer than necessary before pressing a kiss to her palm. Victor clasped her hand lightly, and his lips brushed the inside of her wrist.

"My lady, I have already prepared the most tender pieces of capon and removed all bones from the fish," Victor invited, patting the seat between himself and her father.

Maris leaned over before taking her seat to greet the other guest at table. "Good evening, Sir Dirick." She smiled, trying to hide her discomfiture.

He did not look up, and his response was a short, "My lady," before he swilled another sip of ale.

Stung by his curtness, Maris sank onto her seat next to Victor and forced herself to smile at him. Steeling all of her composure, she gathered her wits and courage and dutifully began to play the part in which she'd been cast.

Throughout the meal, Dirick found himself refilling his ale more oft than was usual; and catching a string of words here and there as the two about-to-be-betrothed chatted amiably. Maris batted her eyelashes and dropped coy smiles at her suitor and

Dirick found himself grinding his teeth at her silliness.

When the evening meal was finished, and the last of the courses had been delivered to the high table, most of its occupants were more than ready to vacate, Dirick being among the first. He pulled himself stiffly to his feet and made a short bow to Maris and Allegra, clapping Merle on the shoulder.

As he made his way—rather unsteadily, thanks to the amount of ale he'd downed—between the rows of tables and diners in varying degrees of drunkenness, he heard a loud trill of laughter from Maris.

His shoulders tensed and he hurried his pace, eager to get out into the chill air and away from all people. As he left the hall for the solace of the cold, starry night, he heard the minstrel pick up his lute and pluck a rainfall of notes.

Maris's laughter was the last sound Dirick heard as he stepped out into the cold air.

᠀

Merle strode across the parapets of Langumont Keep.

His breath blew like white smoke from the bristling hair that lined his mouth, and a winter breeze brushed his thinning hair. The men-at-arms that stood at the north and south ends of the roof of the keep stoked small fires to warm their hands, nodding to their lord as he walked past them.

A sliver of moon cut the deep blue sky, and hundreds of stars twinkled above. Merle stopped at the southeast corner of the parapet, looking out over darkness that covered the lands that fell under his rule. They stretched as far as one could see from this vantage point. He drew in a deep breath that was so cold it hurt the deepest part of his lungs, then exhaled strongly. Somewhere, out in that darkness, was the great water he'd crossed once to France. If he listened closely, he'd hear the crashing waves upon the cliffs.... He stopped breathing, just to hear the sound.

A movement near him drew Merle's attention. Turning, he found that Sir Dirick had come pell-mell around the corner, then jerked to a stop when he caught sight of the older man.

"My lord," Dirick said, easing back.

"Nay, Dirick, you do not disturb me. Come," he smiled at a sudden thought, "unless 'tis you who does not wish to be disturbed."

"Nay, my lord. 'Tis just that I did not expect to come upon you. I...wished...thought to be alone. But 'tis glad I am for your company."

Merle beckoned him closer, gesturing out into the darkness. "See you here, Dirick.... See you all that has been bestowed upon me."

Dirick stared out over the dark, though Merle knew he was unable to see far in the dim, starry night. "You are worthy of your blessings, my lord," he said quietly.

"Listen, and you will hear the sea...'t has been the cause of the wealth that has come to me. My father's grandfather was a Saxon thegn, betrothed to the daughter of a Norman lord in great favor with The Conqueror. My great-grandfather's land, here near the sea, was a most important fief. Since the day my great-grandfather wed with Lord Humprey's daughter, Margaret, this keep and this fief have served the King of England with no regret, and no hesitation—even when Stephen of Blois ruled, and ruined, this land."

Merle was silent for a moment, suddenly aware that he'd thrust his pensive mood and meandering thoughts upon his companion. Then he gave a short, bitter laugh. "Forgive me, Dirick, but my solemnity comes from the knowledge that my beloved Maris will soon belong to another man...and these lands will someday be ruled by another." He took a deep breath, shaking himself from his melancholy. His decision was right; the best he could wish for Maris. He was compelled to ask, "What think you of my guests?"

Dirick was surprised at the question, as his own thoughts had been running along those same lines, but he replied carefully, "They seem pleasant dinner companions...full of much news...confident and brave." His hands closed over the roughness of the stone half-wall, trying to ignore the memory of Maris's sunny smiles aimed at Victor. What was it to him that she should smile at her betrothed?

"Yet you do not sound convinced. Has my daughter complained to you?"

If it had been lighter, Merle might have noticed the faint flush that brushed Dirick's face...or he may have written it off to the brisk breeze that reddened his cheeks. "My lady does not seem overfond of the idea of marriage," Dirick admitted.

"And you, ever the chivalrous knight, do not wish to see a damsel in distress." Merle grinned. "Aye, Maris has a way of manipulating even her father with her sad stories. 'Tis the best for her, I trow, Dirick. The world can be an unfriendly place, and I'll not have her alone and vulnerable should aught happen to me." His voice softened at the last, and Dirick peered closely at him in the darkness.

"She may not understand my decision," Merle continued, "but 'twill stand. I owe a great debt to Michael d'Arcy...for 'twas his own fault that allowed me to return to my own once again." His eyes were piercing in the dim light. "I was grievously wounded and nearly did not live to see my beloved lands and family again. Michael saved my life, and for that I will bestow upon his son the greatest gift I have to give."

Dirick was silent. 'T made the most sense...yet there was something that disturbed him about the man who was to be the next Lord of Langumont.

The men stood in the dark night for a while, not speaking. A cold, brisk breeze ruffled their hair and the cloaks that huddled about their shoulders; yet each was lost in thought and 'twas as if the other were not present.

The world was quiet but for the breeze, and when he heard the sound of voices below, Dirick looked down into the courtyard, standing near the edge of the crenellation and peering over the waist-high stone.

Voices drifted up to him, and he watched as two figures trod through the snow to the stables. The brilliant blue of the cloak on the more diminuitive figure caught his eye and he recognized the daughter of the man standing next to him. 'Twas Maris; and with her, Sir Victor. They disappeared into the stables and Dirick turned abruptly from the view to find Merle watching him closely.

"My lord, I feel my pallet beckoning to me," Dirick said shortly, and bowed slightly—not one to forget his courtly manners even when there were other things that preyed on his mind. "I beg leave of you, now, Lord Merle.… And I shall thank you for your hospitality now, for I will leave early in the morn for Dreakskil. I've dallied too long here, enjoying your hospitality and your pallet."

He could see Merle's eyebrows raise even in that dim light. "'Tis sorry I am to see you go, then," he said slowly.

"I am well pleased to have spent the time here; but I must be on my way," Dirick said, as if to reaffirm for himself the need to leave.

He had come to realize nearly a se'ennight past that King Henry and his brother were right—Lord Merle was not the man who'd murdered his father. He'd delayed his duty to move on to find Bon de Savrille long enough, merely to stay in the presence of the beautiful Lady Maris…and, in sooth, to be near a man who reminded him of his father, now gone. Sadness swept over him, pushing away the resentment he felt toward Sir Victor, and mayhaps a bit of self-pity. Dirick could not covet a woman such as Maris, and he had known that since he'd been old enough to know what a woman was. 'Twas a hard truth, but one he had lived with forever.

Now, he must return to his duty, and he must redirect his energies from a woman who was beyond him to finding the man who'd taken his father from him. His fingers closed around the broken dagger that he carried deep in the pouch attached to his tunic. He squeezed its handle, allowing the rage at his father's murderer to resurface...to replace his self-pity and sadness.

"You do not wish to bid my lady Allegra...or Maris farewell?" Merle asked, jerking Dirick from his thoughts.

"Nay. I have enjoyed the ladies' company, yet I wish for an early start on the morrow." 'Twould be best if he were to leave without seeing her again.

"Then fare thee well, my son," Merle said feelingly. He clapped a hand upon the younger man's shoulder warmly. Then, for just a moment, it was as if some unusual, strong currents flowed between them. "I bid you well wishes in your quest, and if ever I can be of assistance, please let me know."

"Aye. You have been much help as of now," Dirick said, feeling unaccountably sad at leaving Merle; 'twas a mere portion of what he felt at losing his father...yet it was all over again.

ॐ

The sky had not the merest tint of light to it when Dirick rolled up his pallet. He stood, waiting for his eyes to adjust to the dark, then walked hurriedly over the other prone bodies in the chamber that housed other itinerant men-at-arms.

The few belongings he'd brought with him—including the broken dagger—were wrapped and stuffed in a leather bag that he would secure onto Nick. He shifted the weight of this baggage and pulled his fur-lined cloak about his shoulders. The edges of the cloak rustled against the sweet herbs and rushes that covered the floor of the Great Hall, stirring them amidst his booted feet. All was silent—even the boy who tended the fire overnight dozed nearby. Only an orange tomcat prowled among the other prone bodies, doubtless hoping to catch an unwary mouse among the rushes.

Dirick felt an odd sense of sadness as he stepped from the hall for the last time, and found himself under the dark blue, starred sky. He had enjoyed his stay here at Langumont, and the unhappiness he felt at leaving pushed into him like an annoying toothache. Mayhaps, he thought as he trudged through the powdery snow to the stables, 'twas because Lord Merle seemed to be the closest link he had to his father and his father's murderer.

The whuffling of the horses greeted him as he pressed the door into the stables. Nick was near the front, and he nickered as he sensed his master's scent. "Aye, boy, 'tis nigh time we were away from here," he said, leading the destrier from his stall. Nick pranced spiritedly within the small enclosure, and Dirick patted his nose to calm him. "'Tis happy I'll be to see this place behind," he said aloud, trying to convince himself of this point.

He heard the noise behind him and whirled, hand clapping to his sword, just as her words reached his ears, "Then 'tis happy we shall be to see you go."

Maris stood there, holding a tallow candle, looking ethereal in the shining beacon…or mayhaps 'twas only that he'd imagined her many times before as an angel. The anger glaring in her eyes did not, however, bespeak of celestial bearing. Her hair had been covered with a wrap, but as the woolen veil slipped, her dark hair showed and gleamed in the candlelight. Her little chin was pointed in annoyance and her full lips were firmed into a thin line. The blue cloak trailed in the rushes on the stable floor, effectively covering her from shoulder to toe.

Dirick recovered from his surprise and dropped his hand from the sword upon which it rested. "Maris...My lady," he amended quickly, "what do you here?"

Her frown did not dissipate. "Father told me that you planned to leave early this morrow, and I did not...I thought you must not go without something for your journey. But I see that my consideration is unwanted." He noticed now that she held a packet under her cloak. "So happy are you to see Langumont behind you that you would likely not wish to take any remembrance of this place."

She turned to go, her back straight as a sword and her shoulders thrown back. Hurt emanated from her stance.

"Nay, my lady." Dirick, feeling quite foolish having been caught speaking such nonsense to his stallion, spurred to action and grabbed at her arm. "Nay, 'tis not that I wish to leave Langumont...believe you me."

She turned back, her eyes still a hard, flat brown. "I am not hard of hearing, Sir Dirick."

He pulled her back toward him, taking both shoulders and turning her so that she faced him fully. She felt small and soft within his fingers, fragile and easily broken. "My lady, I am grieved that you should have heard the nonsense I spoke to Nick. 'Twas merely that I must leave, and that I had no desire to do so that I spoke the words."

She looked up at him as if trying to determine whether he was merely being gallant or whether the words actually were truth. "I could not fathom that you would leave without a word of farewell...."

"I bid your father good bye," he told her, realizing how close they were standing. The smell of lemon and rosemary from her hair caught at his nostrils and he had to stop himself from reaching to touch it. Dirick took a step backward and turned into the stall to gather Nick's bridle. "But I must leave now, my lady. I have spent—I have used your father's hospitality much too long."

Maris worked the candle into a cup appended to the wall of the stable, leaving it to light their way, and stepped toward him, unwittingly blocking him into the stall. She proffered the leather-wrapped packet from under the folds of her cloak. "I have brought you cheese and bread, and there is a bit of salted venison here. I…did not know how long your journey would be."

He took the packet, warmed by her thoughtfulness and her presence. "Thank you my lady. I was not able to break my fast and this will be a good meal for the road."

"Where are you going?" she asked.

Dirick started to tell her, but stopped in the nick of time. "I am a traveling knight, my lady, and I go where I can find work," he said. "I do not know where my next place of rest will be."

Maris frowned, a line crinkling around her nose. "Why do you leave then? Papa has work for you…I am certain he would hire you for as long as you wished."

A sudden flare of anger curled his lip and twisted his insides…verily she saw him only as a charity case; a man that could not make his own way! Despite the fact that he'd led her to believe just that, it rankled that she saw him in such a lowly light. "Nay." He turned his back to her, taking his time to loop up the reins and bit, hoping she would leave before he mortified himself again.

She had no idea why he'd become angry and she planted her hands on her hips in annoyance. "Sir Dirick, you are as befuddled as—as a chicken with his head chopped off! You make little sense of anything…I trow 'twill be good to have you gone!"

"Aye," he turned, his hands brimming with the leather bridle. "I am sure you will not miss my company now that your betrothed has arrived!" It wasn't until the words were out of his mouth that it dawned on him how much he truly disliked Victor d'Arcy…and that the reason was only that the woman before him would soon belong to Victor. The realization stunned him, then he shoved it away immediately. He needed to leave before he did something he would regret.

"He is not my betrothed!" she flared back.

"He will be anon. And when that happens, I am quite sure Victor will be pleased to follow you on your treks through the wood, digging in the snow for berries and watching as you nurse to the ill!" His grey eyes were silver anger in the dim light and his jaw clenched. "I saw you come in here with him last night," Dirick said, still holding the leather straps.

"Aye," she nodded, "he wished to meet Hickory."

Dirick quirked one eyebrow and managed to look sardonic. "Oh? And was there nothing more that he wanted? Did he not wish to taste the lips of the woman he is to wive?" He heard the angry words coming from his mouth but could do nothing to stop them from tumbling forth. "Do you not know to have a chaperon with you at all times? 'Tis not meet for a lady to have assignations alone with a man in the stable of all places!"

Maris's eyes snapped. "And here I stand with you, then! Alone in a stable, with no chaperon…and my virtue has never been safer!"

He dropped the bridle, grabbing for her as his patience broke. "I would not say that your virtue is safe with me, my dear lady," he said, pulling her to his long body. "In fact, Maris, I should say that you are treading upon very thin ice…once again." He looked down at her and saw no fear in her eyes, only surprise, and he felt the warmth of her breath touch his face. His hands on her shoulders, he eased her backward until she felt the wall behind her and he imprisoned her there, holding her with his muscled legs.

Maris's eyes sank closed as she felt two warm hands smooth

up the sides of her neck to cup the line of her chin. His thumb traced over her lips and her heart pounded madly, pulsing in her long neck against his touch. His hands moved to lift her hair from the nape of her neck, carefully pulling the long, long tresses from the confines of her cloak. It was warm and silky and it twined like vines around his wrists and about her arms.

Dirick let his breath out slowly as his hands ran through her hair. She was not afraid, he noted, although if she had any sense, she would be. It was all he could do to keep from tearing off her clothes and tossing her onto the bed of hay in the next room. It was madness! ...Nay, 'twas just that he'd been without a woman for too long.

Maris felt her body come alive as Dirick combed his fingers through her hair, along her arms and down her back. Her breaths were coming shorter, she was finding it hard to breathe...and she felt a need, a something undefinable, growing within her. His fingers brushed over her lips and she almost pursed them to kiss him.

When his hands stilled on her shoulders, and he eased back on the pressure from his thighs, she opened her eyes to look up at him. His face was set and there was a closed look about his countenance. "Maris," he said softly as their gazes met. He would never see her again; and she was not yet betrothed. "I cannot leave without kissing you once more." He did not wait for a response, but dragged her up against him.

When his mouth closed on hers, she felt the same tide of pleasure wash over her as the day in the woods. Her lips opened to his and suddenly his tongue was in her mouth, exploring and tasting her. She was as hungry to sample him and responded with fervor, tasting the faint mint of his mouth, sliding her own lips over his soft, slick ones. He dragged himself away from her, kissing the corner of her mouth, nibbling at her lips and chin. She sighed, her arms creeping around his neck as she leaned into him, and she felt a rush plunging through her body, and the responding shudder that came through him. Hurried fingers worked the clasp at her throat as he covered her mouth again as if to stifle any cry of protest she might make. The fur-lined cloak fell into a heap at their feet and his hands smoothed down the sides of her body in its trail, resting on the curve of her hips.

Maris was barely aware of the divestment of her cloak, but the pressure from his warm hands as they brushed the sides of her breasts caused her to draw a sharp breath. Her nipples surged hard and she felt a heaviness descend upon her lower abdomen. She dug her fingers into his hair, surprised at its silkiness. He pulled her hips flush with his and she was startled to feel a hard length pushing against her, arousing her in the same area. A tiny groan erupted from the back of her throat and she tilted her head back, exposing her neck to his mouth. Dirick's hands smoothed over the curves that had been hidden in the bulky cloak, and he held the swelling of her breasts and the roundness of her hips.

Suddenly, he jerked away, nearly sending her spinning to the floor. "'Sblood!" he cursed, staring at his trembling hands. His breath rasped harshly, as if he'd just felled a man in battle, and his heart thudded painfully in his chest as he realized how very near he'd come to taking her right there.

Maris had pulled back as if she too had just become aware of herself and her comport, and she stooped quickly to retrieve her cloak. Shock at her behavior and lack of control reverberated through her body, yet arousal still pulsed through her veins.

Dirick found his voice, hoarse as it was, and attempted an apology. "My lady, I cannot—"

"Enough, my lord," she cut in sarcastically to hide her discomfiture. "Have we not been through this scene before?"

Rushing a hand through his tousled hair, he stood, attempting to regain some semblance of order within. He could not understand why he made a living fool out of himself in front of this woman; he, the suave courtier from the courts of Paris who had women tumbling into his bed at the mere flash of a smile. "Again, my lady, my conduct was inexcusable and I do apologize. Mayhaps 'tis best that I do be on my way."

She looked up at him, an undefinable emotion flickering in her gold and green eyes. "Aye. 'Tis best that you do."

He brushed past her, accidentally catching her hair on a nail in the wall, and paused to free the curl. His fingers slid down the shiny dark length and he brought it to his mouth to press a light kiss on it. Then he turned away and bridled the neglected Nick as she watched in silence. Feeling her gaze on him made his fingers clumsy beyond belief, causing him to hurry and thus tangle it up even more. At last, he led the destrier from the stable, aware that she followed behind, watching in an unusual silence.

Outside, where their breaths showed white puffs under the starlit morn, he swung upon Nick and looked down at her. She'd covered her hair once again, drawing the veil closely about her neck. Dirick reined in and touched a hand to pull at his forelock.

"Go with God, Dirick," she whispered.

"Fare thyself well, my lady. Victor d'Arcy will be a fine husband to you," he forced the words from between bitter lips, making them sound sincere. "Your father wishes only the best for you, know you this, my lady."

"Aye."

"May the Lord keep you," he said, turning Nick to ride away. "*Adieu*, my lady." And then he was off, giving Nick his head to unleash his stored power, feeling the green-gold gaze that followed him into the darkness.

Ten ॐ

reakskil possessed a forbidding-looking keep, set near the top of a low-lying mountain. It was much smaller than both Derkland and Langumont Keeps, and it was not in the same pristine condition that those lands and buildings were in—Dirick could see parts of the walls crumbling from far away.

The village, again smaller, was filled with peasants that veered from Nick's path and peeked out from behind closed doors as he rode through. Most of the roofs seemed to be in decent condition, but the silence of the village ate right through to Dirick's bones.

The journey had not been long; he'd spent the full day riding hard, spending Nick's pent up energy, and now that he approached the portcullis, and the sun was sinking, he was well ready for his pallet. Cold wind was bitter upon his face, and the food that Maris sent with him was long gone.

Maris.

She had been much on his mind the day through. Too much.

Dirick reined in abruptly at the huge iron gates looming above him.

"Who goes there?" called a voice from above.

"Dirick de Arlande, begging for succor," he called back, tilting his head to see.

There was a long moment, then the voice returned, "From whence come you, Sir de Arlande?"

"I am late come from Paris," he replied. "I have traveled for days, looking for work. I am quite skilled in arms."

Again, there was a long pause. Then, "You are French?"

"Aye. I hail from near Brest," Dirick replied, trying to keep the annoyance out of his voice. Most often, unless there were unusual circumstances, questions such as these were saved for after a lone knight was allowed entrance. The reticence in gaining him entrance bespoke of naught good.

At long last, the portcullis began to creak and shake violently as the gate was raised. Dirck urged Nick forward, uncertain that the ailing gate was in good enough repair to ensure his safe passage. Once inside the bailey, he was greeted by a stocky, pock-marked man who held himself in high importance.

"You are well come to Dreakskil, Sir de Arlande," he said. A man hovered in the background until he was urged forward: "Take this man's mount, Severn."

Dirick relinquished Nick with some hesitation; yet the man seemed to know what he was doing and led the destrier away with little effort. "Many thanks for allowing me entrance," he told the first man.

"I am Sir Robert, castellan of Dreakskil. My lord, Bon de Savrille, awaits your presence within." That was it; no smile, no friendly greeting—just a barely disguised order that he draw himself within.

Dirick grimaced inwardly and followed Robert across the small, cluttered bailey. He noted that the keep was in need of some repair, but it was by no means falling down about him. There weren't many serfs, nor were there many men-at-arms about. It was a much quieter, sullen place than his home.

Sir Robert led the way across the smoky hall strewn with

rushes so old and rotted that they ground away under their mailed feet. Several dogs greeted them, sniffing annoyingly at their heels until Sir Robert lifted a foot to kick them away; then they slunk off to a spot under one of the tables. Smoke hovered in the air, along with the stench of old grease and rotting food. Breathing carefully through his nose, Dirick hoped that he would not be a guest of Dreakskil overlong!

Bon de Savrille, Dirick assumed, was the stocky, bearded man sitting in a heavy chair near the fire. The blaze, at the least, was in marvelous condition! De Savrille's dark eyes bored into him as he approached, slitted with mistrust. Immediately, Dirick allowed his features to relax and slip into a vacant expression.

"My Lord de Savrille," he greeted upon reaching the warmth of the fire. He made a fine bow, and upon the upsweep, was gracious enough to add, "Many thanks to you for a spot to sleep for the night."

"Aye," Bon returned, sipping from a goblet of ale.

Dirick inclined his head to the other man at the fire, a shorter, well-freckled one with a shock of red hair. His paunch was nearly the size of Lord de Savrille's, and his eyes not nearly as sharp, but there was a hint of suspicion within his countenance as well. "My lord," he greeted the other man.

"Meet Edwin Baegot," Bon explained carelessly.

"Well met, sieur," Dirick replied, then settled himself easily on a roughly-hewn stool near Bon de Savrille.

"Agnes!" barked Bon, taking a huge swallow of ale. "Bring this man some food and more drink for me!"

A shadow moved from a nearby corner, transforming into a skittish, gown-draped woman, and hurried out of the room. As Dirick's eyes followed her, he noticed that the Great Hall was nearly empty of men-at-arms, serfs, and any other form of life with the exception of the mangy dogs that had followed them into the room. Feeling the weight of Edwin's suspicious gaze on him, Dirick kept his face blank.

"You come recently from Paris, you say?" Edwin asked with steely grey eyes. "I am of the acquaintance of Pierre d'Enclaque, Lord Mertinique. How fares my old friend?"

Dirick saw the trap in his query and allowed his face to lapse into an uncertain frown. "D'Enclaque, you say? I cannot recall...nay, I am most certain that I met Lord Mertinique...and...of course, 'twas Francois Bartolle as holds the title at this time, my friend. I did not have the pleasure, then, of meeting your old friend." He stared unconcernedly into the roaring blaze.

"Ah, at last you have returned, you worthless creature!" Bon greeted Agnes, who nearly stumbled over one of the dogs. "Clumsy bitch," he muttered as she carefully poured a healthy portion of ale into his goblet, spilling nary a drop in the process.

When she turned to offer Dirick a piece of hard bread and pale yellow cheese, he saw the long purple scar that marred an otherwise pretty face. His countenance softened as he took the food. "Thank'ee milady."

"Lady!" scoffed Bon, nearly spewing ale in Dirick's face. He sneered. "If ye take a liking to her, she'll spread her legs fast enough to knock you over! Lady, indeed!"

Agnes ducked her head and turned away to her corner, drawing the folds of her gown so that she did not stumble again.

Ale dribbling into his neatly cropped beard, Bon slugged a hand across his mouth and asked, "How fares the Earl of Chantresse? Is it true that his daughter was to marry Enrique du Mathilde?"

Dirick idly scraped a bit of mold off the last bite of cheese. He was chuckling inside at these obvious, elementary attempts to validate his claim of being from France. "Aye, my lord, they were wed midsummer last. 'Twas said that the daughter, Elisabet, was near dragged to the altar and that her papa said her ayes!" He allowed his internal amusement to come forth in a short bark of laughter.

"God willing 'twill not be such a trial on my wedding day," Bon mused behind the hand that wiped again at his beard. The words were soft and not meant for his ears; but Dirick discerned the comment with little trouble.

"'Tis fair unlike to happen any different here," muttered Edwin more loudly.

Bon shot him a glare, but that did not suppress Dirick's ingenuous question, "Is there to be a wedding here then?" He made it a point to not look around the quiet hall.

"Aye, if the wench'll have me," Bon replied. He and Edwin exchanged pointed looks followed by deep guffaws of laughter.

"And the lucky wench? Does she bring a great dowry, then?"

Bon's eyes narrowed to slits as if he suddenly realized that the turn of the conversation was not to his liking. "'Tis a love match," he snapped. Edwin choked on his ale and was forced to spit onto the floor. Bon stood abruptly. "There is a place for your pallet there. I will expect that you will join us in a hunt on the morrow."

With that, he turned and, barking at the lump in the corner, "Agnes! Come!" left the hall.

Dirick watched them leave, then, under Edwin's sharp stare, gathered his belongings and trudged to the corner indicated by de Savrille. There were no more than five other men snoring in what he took to be the knights' quarters; and as he shook out his blanket, a small furry creature darted from between the folds. Rats. His stomach turned and he almost cursed his sovereign for sending him to spy on what seemed to be no more than two bumbling idiots who lived amongst rats...but cursing his God-given sovereign, his brother the monk would warn, would result in either hanging for treason if done aloud, or damnation if done in private.

Instead, Dirick eased his travel-worn body onto the only clean surface in the entire keep and closed his eyes.

~

Maris sat primly in her saddle, golden skirts fluttering lightly. The brilliant blue cloak that Dirick de Arlande had so admired covered her from shoulder to toe, and much of Hickory's rump as well. Maris's chestnut hair was modestly covered by a heavy golden wrap, edged in mink, and her hands wrapped in the folds of the rabbit-lined cloak.

She looked every inch the proper, controlled lady of the manor.

Inwardly, she was seething.

"Are you certain that you do not yet tire, milady?" asked Sir Victor for perhaps the dozenth time since they'd left Langumont Keep's portcullis behind.

"Nay," she replied, for the dozenth time, from between clenched teeth. In sooth, she was more weary from holding Hickory back from the spirited canter—or even full gallop—that the mare, as well as her mistress, desired. Maris slanted a glance to the man who rode comfortably next to her. He sat tall and straight in the saddle, loosely holding the reins, allowing his gaze to cast about over the villagers and the town buildings.

Victor's straight cap of hair, as pale as the wheat grown in Langumont's fields, barely shifted as he was jounced along in his saddle. He was not an unhandsome man, she admitted to herself—in fact, he was not at all hard on the eyes. He seemed to have an even temper, Maris reminded herself, although he tended—like her mother—to protect her as if she were a child. It was Victor who had suggested the ride; and Maris, anticipating a great race across the northwest field toward the forest, had agreed with alacrity. Alas, when she'd given Hickory her head and they moved into a canter just outside the wall of the keep, her companion had actually reached over and reined the mare into a trot!

It had taken every ounce of control that she as Lady of Langumont possessed not to loosen a torment of fury upon him. Instead, Maris, thinking of her father's wishes, swallowed her angry words at his presumption and meekly settled into a trot. Mayhaps, she thought as they wound their way carefully down the main street of the village, he did not know of any woman as comfortable on a mount as she.

"Good day, Mistress Beth," she called in English to the smith's wife with a wave.

"Good day, milady," the other woman responded with a bright smile. She had her youngest child by the hand, and nudged the toddler to wave also to the grand lady who rode past.

"You are much too familiar with the peasants, my lady," murmured Victor with distaste. "And why on earth would you learn to speak their coarse language?"

Maris stared at him in shock. "And how else would I communicate with them if I did not speak their language?" she sputtered.

Victor turned to her in surprise. "As I—and all other nobility—do: through an interpreter. 'Twould be in your interest when you go to court that you forget your knowledge of English…else you will make of yourself, and me, a laughing stock."

Maris turned an angry glare upon him. "Then my papa must not be nobility in your eyes, as he is the same one who encouraged me to learn the language; and he himself does better than I!"

Victor flushed ever so slightly—in fact, it may have been just a stinging wind that caused his cheeks to pinken—and looked taken aback. "My lady, I—"

"'Tis in my best interest, Sir Victor, to rely on no one but

myself as to what is spoken to me. Interpreters have been known
to twist words into their own!"

"Lady Maris—"

She would not let him finish; her temper had snapped and
her father's wishes thrown to the birds for the now. "And *I am
Lady of Langumont.*" She drew herself up in the saddle to her
full, diminutive height, her eyes steely now. "I care not what the
ladies—or even the men—at court think of me. And I particularly should not care if you are a laughing stock because I *choose*
to communicate with my people! And," she leaned out of her
saddle toward the now-silent Victor to drive her point home,
"you, sir, presume overmuch, as a betrothal has not yet been
announced nor signed!" She sat back and drew a deep breath,
ready to do more battle.

"Ah, but my lady, 'tis there you err," Victor's voice was
silky…too silky, and a surprise shiver creased her spine. Along
with his voice, he had found the way to silence her. "Even as we
trot along at such a sedate pace, our fathers are finalizing the
betrothal arrangements. 'Twill be announced at dinner; and we
shall seal the contract two days hence."

As Victor's words sunk in and Maris realized that her
betrothal was truly going to happen, she gave in to the urge to
run away. With a swift movement she'd perfected years ago, she
gathered her skirts and brought her right leg over the saddle so
that she was straddling the mare in a most unladylike—but prac-
tical—fashion. Giving a sharp kick and loosening the reins, she
let Hickory go and they shot forward. She heard Victor's shout of
surprise behind her, and, looking over her shoulder, saw that he'd
started after her.

Containing a cry of joy at the freedom of tearing across a
pristine field of white snow, she urged Hickory on, fully enjoying the risk she took of angering her soon-to-be-betrothed.
'Twould be worth the inevitable lecture; she grinned into

Hickory's mane.

They easily cleared the stone fence that marked the end of the Lord of Langumont's grain field, heading straight for the dense forest. Maris's headcovering was jounced loose and landed on a low bush. Her long braid flew free, the end bouncing off Hickory's rump with the rhythm of the mare's strides.

Glancing over her shoulder, she saw Victor, bent over his mount's neck, racing across the field. With a mental sigh of capitulation, she slowed Hickory just as they reached the beginnings of the forest. Turning about, Maris watched as Victor roared up beside her, nearly trampling them both. Either he was overcome with rage and did not care if he injured her, or he did not handle his mount well.

Before she had a thought to speak, he grabbed the reins from her hand and drew Hickory's head around toward the rear of his stallion so that he and Maris were very close and facing each other. His eyes were a flat grey and his mouth compressed in a firm line. "Are you a madwoman?" were his first words. "Am I to wed a madwoman?"

"Nay, I—"

"Silence!" he thundered so furiously that she reconsidered finishing her sentence. His eyes closed into slits, and, still holding tightly to her reins, he slid off his horse, landing in snow to his mid-calf. Looping his own reins over an arm, he reached up and grabbed her wrist. "Let me help you down, milady," he said in a voice that brooked no disobedience, nearly yanking her off the saddle. She came down gracefully, landing in the circle of his arms. Dropping the reins, he pulled her closer, and the other hand reached up to close over her chin.

For the first time, Maris had a sense of real trepidation and she reflexively stepped back. "Oh, nay," he whispered, jerking her close. "Do you not step away from me, *wife*."

"I am not your—"

Her words were stifled as he crushed his mouth to hers. At her involuntary gasp, his hand went to the back of her head, holding her immobile, as his lips and tongue brutally invaded her mouth. The hand on her wrist loosened to move around her waist and pull her close to his hips while the fingers of his other hand pressed into the back of her skull.

Maris fought the nausea that rose in her throat at his angry onslaught. Her eyes closed and she pushed against him fiercely. She should have known better than to anger him thus! she thought in panic.

He pulled away from her mouth, breathing heavily and eyes glazed with desire. "Aye, you'll be a fine wife," he breathed frost into her face, "once you have learned that I am to be obeyed in all things." As she stood frozen, he reached up to fumble with the ties of her cloak.

"What—"

"I believe I told you to remain *silent*!" His hand shot up to pinch her chin. "I would learn what other treasures I win along with the lands of Langumont." Before she could protest, her cloak fell to the snow in a pool of blue. With horror, she realized what he was about. Surely he did not mean to disrobe her...here!

"Nay," she cried, clutching her overtunic to her neck.

He grabbed her wrists, forcing them behind her back, and reached up to take hold of her chin again. She felt the rough bark of a tree behind her, rasping over her hands, as he forced his mouth onto hers. As the kiss deepened, his hand slipped from her chin to cover one of her breasts. She jerked in shock, pulling her mouth away with a violent twist.

Victor smiled in satisfaction as he kneaded her breast through three layers of wool. "Ah, my lady, 'tis well that you are not used to this kind of touch." He pressed an almost tender kiss to her bruised lips. "We shall suit well, my lady." His fingers found and teased the nipple that had stiffened with cold, pinching it enough to bring a gasp from her throat. Bending his knee, he pressed his groin into her thigh as he forced her mouth open once again with his teeth. A low moan escaped from him as he ground his throbbing erection into the joint between her torso and thigh. "Ah, Maris...." he breathed heavily.

He pulled back, recovering himself, and looked down at her. Still holding her wrists, he used his other hand to comb through her loosened braid. "Beautiful," he breathed with satisfaction. "When we are at court, you shall not cover this with aught but a net of jewels." With a sudden twist of the wrist, he grabbed a fistful of hair and yanked hard enough to pull her head back so that she looked into his face.

Victor met her wide eyes. "You angered me, my lady. You angered me with your sharp tongue, and your disregard for your person—tearing across the fields as you did. Take care not to anger me in the future, Maris, and we shall do well together."

With that, he turned and clomped away through the snow. Gathering up the reins of his mount, he swung himself into the saddle, and, without a backward glance, urged the horse into a loping canter back toward the keep.

Shaken, Maris stiffly gathered up her cloak and draped it around her trembling shoulders and tried to hold back the tears. The Lady of Langumont would not cry! Turning to look about, she saw Hickory and whistled for her mare.

A heavy weight settled over her as she climbed into the saddle, her trembling hands fumbling with the reins. He would be her betrothed two days hence. As her wedded husband, he owned her—*owned* her—and could do as he wished. He could beat her, rape her, even kill her if he chose.

With a fearful, shuddering sigh, she urged Hickory into a slow trot. Tears stung the corners of her eyes as she held onto the reins so tightly that her nails bit into the palm of her hand.

Never in her life had Maris been subjected to violent anger

such as Victor's. Her father had never raised a hand to either her or Allegra—though the rage in his voice threatened to bring the timbers of the roof down upon them at times. But she knew of how brutal a husband—or any man—could be from her friend Lady Joanna, who had been freed from an abusive marriage by the man she later wed. She'd been nearly killed by her first husband, and Maris had had to nurse her well. Maris had never thought to be married, let alone married to a man as violent as Joanna's husband…but now she realized that even she was not free of that threat.

Her heart was slowing its crazy pace, and now Maris began to get over her fright and become angry. Much of the anger was directed at herself; for, though she might be impulsive and headstrong, Maris knew that she owned faults enough to make a man mad. She was furious with herself partly because she'd chosen to enrage a man before knowing his limitations…but she was mostly disappointed in herself for submitting to his actions without fighting back. She'd been stunned at Victor's anger and the humiliating form it had taken…and had not had the presence of mind to bite the hand that held her chin, or raise her knee into his pulsing groin.

The memory of that hard length pressing into her thigh caused bitterness to well up into her throat, and she gagged, swallowing it back. How could she allow him to touch her again? How ever would she submit to his husbandly demands?

༄

Michael d'Arcy stifled a belch and wiped his hand over his mouth, his gaze scanning the hall. 'Twas empty of all but a few serfs preparing for the evening meal, and he took this moment to savor the knowledge that 'twould all soon be his…his and his son's.

Merle had agreed to the betrothal contract only that morning, and would make the anticipated announcement at dinner that evening. They would sign the contract after a ceremony two days hence, and all would be his.

Taking another gulp of ale, Michael fought to keep a complacent smile from curving his face as he contemplated the power that Langumont would bring him. A movement near the stairwell caught his eye, and Lady Allegra walked into view. As always, his body responded to the mere sight of her and he shifted langorously in Merle's chair. *Jesù*, but the woman was a spitfire!

He'd never forgotten her over the years, for she'd warmed his bed and tended to his needs better than any whore, noblewoman, or even his own wife. He supposed he loved her—for even now, after seventeen years, he could not get enough of her body. Just this morrow, they'd met in the far corner of the stables as Victor and Maris saddled their mounts for a ride...and Michael had had a pleasant ride of his own!

He wasn't able to keep the self-satisfied smirk from his lips now, but hid it behind the goblet of ale.

Since their arrival at Langumont, he'd not had any of the raging aches in his head, and that, too, was cause for satisfaction. Those aches frightened him with their intensity, and with the black memories and images that came with them—those evil dreams of his parents and their brutal death...the gripping blindness that seized his consciousness and caused his breath to labor. He sought ways to expel the fury within himself when incapacitated by those spells, but it became more and more difficult to do so as time passed.

Michael pushed such minor nuisances away as he saw Allegra passing nearby. He wanted her again. "My lady," he called, raising his goblet, "come you and serve me."

૭

It was an interesting group that was assembled at the high table that evening: an evening of utmost importance to all involved.

Lady Allegra's face, to anyone who passed even the most cursory glance over her, was drawn and tight. Her eyes were ringed with the purple of sleepless nights, and her usually-neat coiffure was loose, leaving several straggling strands of hair about her face.

Lord Michael, seated next to Allegra, looked obsessively pleased with himself. He was particularly attentive to the woman beside him—but she seemed oblivious to everything and spent most of the meal staring off into space with a haunted look in her eyes.

Sir Victor could barely keep his burning gaze from his soon-to-be-betrothed. There was a proprietary air of complacency about him as well.

Maris was subdued. She concentrated on her meal, accepting the choice tidbits of capon and goose from Victor without comment. She sensed that he was congratulating himself on establishing control over her…and she was frantically trying to devise a way to dispel that notion.

When the meal was nearly finished—just before the final, sweet course was brought from the kitchens—Merle stood, stepping carefully behind the long bench on which he and his guests were seated. He shouted for attention, although gossip had spread throughout the keep and all had been waiting for the announcement of their lady's betrothal.

"Two days hence," he began jovially, with a full cup of ale in his hand, "we shall celebrate a most auspicious event. It has taken many years for this decision to be made, and tonight I wish to make known to you the betrothed husband of my daughter,

Maris of Langumont." Beaming behind his silvering beard, Merle helped his daughter to her feet as the room erupted in loud cheers—at the prospect of a day of celebration as much as the announcement of a wedding. "Two days hence," he repeated, smiling down at his daughter—who managed a tremulous curving of the lips in response, "the castellans from Cleonis, Firmain, Shawdon, Edena, and Damona, shall arrive to once again pledge their fealty to me, and to my heir, Lady Maris. At that time, they shall also witness the betrothal covenant of my daughter to Lord Victor d'Arcy of Gladwythe."

The room erupted with joy, and Lady Allegra slid to the floor in a dead faint.

Eleven ✧

*D*irick was seated comfortably in the corner of Dreakskil Hall that was the darkest and most unobtrusive, but close enough to the roaring fire that warmth emanated to his very toes. It was after the evening meal—if one could call the fare that had been set before him food—and there were fewer people than usual in the hall. His mail hauberk, one that was of such quality that it would certainly be remarked upon as to how an itinerant mercenary knight had come to own it, had one taken a close look at it, lay draped over his crossed knees. He sat in rushes that were so old that he dared not contemplate what might be living among them, polishing the mail, and silently observing the lord of the hall.

There wasn't much to observe.

Dirick had been at Dreakskil for nearly three days, and he had come to the conclusion that de Savrille and his comrade Edwin Baegot were merely sloppy, stupid men who had no business calling themselves knights. There was, he intended to remind his sovereign, no law against having a lack of common sense…and although Henry Plantagenet had good reason to feel slighted that Bon had not graced his presence, Dirick intended to inform the king that it was no great insult. In fact, he planned to leave on the morrow to make a full report to his king, along with the recommendation that Bon de Savrille be disseissened from Dreakskil. There could not be another fief in all of Henry's kingdom that was in such disrepair. He would not need to remind Henry that a fief in this condition was surely putting little or no funds into its overlord's coffers.

Tsking to himself, Dirick was about to find his pallet when a shout reverberated throughout the hall.

"My lord, Berkle has arrived! He has news of great import!" cried Sir Robert as he burst into the hall.

Even from his shadowy corner, Dirick could see Bon's head snap up from the ale he drank. "Send him in immediately," was the reply.

Moments later, a tall, thin man dressed in a heavy black cloak was ushered into the hall. He hurried over to Bon and Edwin, and muttered something that, try though he might, Dirick could not understand. He caught the words "betrothal" and "two days hence" before Bon erupted from his huge chair with a roar.

"*The bitch!*" he snarled. "How dare that cock-licking whore ignore me!" He threw the tankard of ale across the room with full force. It splattered all over before it hit the stone wall with a loud clang. "I will have her! I will have her if—"

Bon suddenly stilled as if he realized there were other ears in the room. He glanced over his shoulder at the new arrival, Dirick de Arlande, whom he wasn't quite sure he yet trusted. But Dirick was propped in a far corner, head back against the wall, jaw relaxed…and even Bon could hear the snores that rose from an obviously drunken man-at-arms.

Still red-faced with rage, he sat back down on his stool and gestured Edwin and Berkle to pull their seats closer. And then he began to give orders in a low, urgent voice.

༺༻

The day after her betrothal was announced, Maris sought out her father.

Lord Merle was in his receiving room, going over the accounts with Gustave, Langumont's seneschal. It was a large chamber on the same floor as the women's solar, but much smaller than that woman's chamber. It was, however, comfortably furnished, with two heavy chairs, a table for the scribe, and several stools. A large abacus graced the table, along with sheets of vellum, writing utensils, and wax candles for sealing documents. Bright tapestries hung on the walls and candles lit every corner of the room. He looked up from the table where he and Gustave were perusing the account books when his daughter walked in, noting how very elegant and ladylike she looked in a pale blue overtunic that trailed behind her. Her eyes were wide and dark in her set face, and immediately he knew that this would not be a pleasant conversation.

"Gustave, please excuse us. I believe my daughter would like words with me." Ever since the evening before, when he'd stood and announced that she would marry Victor d'Arcy, Merle had been expecting this moment. In fact, he'd been surprised it had taken nearly a whole day for his daughter to approach him. After all, he'd finalized the contract and made the announcement without warning her in advance.

She'd taken it stoically the night before, he admitted to himself. Almost as if she'd known.

"How fares your mama?" he asked, gesturing for his beloved daughter to sit on a cushioned chair next to him.

Maris's face creased in a frown. "She has been awake since last eve, but she mumbles and raves on about things I do not understand. She speaks of a 'great sin,' and of 'damnation,' and in great despair of 'halting this mistake.' I do not make anything from her words, and she will not explain to me. Her body is fine, 'tis her mind that worries me."

"I do not understand this." Merle stroked his beard as he was wont to do when confronted with such a problem. "My lady has never been as energetic and strong as you, daughter, yet she has not been prone to such fainting spells either."

"Perhaps she is with child?" Maris suggested, then shook her head before Merle was able to react. "Nay, Papa, for you have just returned home. I do not know it myself."

"But that is not why you have cornered me in my chambers, is it, my sweeting?" Merle asked. "Methinks you have come to share with me your displeasure for the announcement I so rudely surprised you with last eve." His gaze was soft, but his words were firm. "I shall tell you now, daughter, that I will brook no arguments from you in this."

"'Twas not as much of a surprise as you may have anticipated, my lord," she told him primly.

"Oh, aye?" His brows rose into the thick waves of hair on his creased forehead.

"Lord Victor made it very clear to me that I was soon to *belong* to him," Maris told him without trying to hide the bitterness in her voice. "As we rode through the village, first he deplored my knowledge of English, telling me I will be a laughing stock when *he* takes *me* to court…and then he—he attacked me." Tears welled in her eyes and she wiped them furiously away.

Merle's face darkened at the presumption of the young man; yet, at the same time, he knew how provoking his daughter could be. "He attacked you for no reason?"

Maris had the grace to drop her eyes from his steely gaze. "N-nay, Papa. I could not bear to listen to his pompous words and hold Hickory to a mere trot, so I let her go and we raced across the north field. We stopped at the wood, and he caught up to us there. He was not in good humor." Her face paled.

"Did he strike you? I see no bruises," Merle asked, more disturbed at the expression of revulsion on her face than her words.

"Nay. He did not strike me—"

"'Tis a man's right to strike his wife," Merle reminded her. "Although I do not believe 'tis seemly for a stronger one to exert his power over a weaker one in such a way." He sighed, "Mayhaps I have not done right by you, Maris, in keeping you not only from court and its ilk; but also in protecting you from the harshness of this world. You have not been raised to expect anger or violence from your hoydenish ways...yet outside of Langumont, many would be appalled at your actions, and your disregard for propriety." Although his words were harsh, the tone of his voice was gentle and bespoke of his own hurt and despair for her situation.

Maris's eyes filled with tears. "Papa—"

He stopped her by pulling her to him in a tight embrace. "Maris, love, you must know that it is above all important to me to provide for you, and ensure that you are cared for. I know that you do not wish to marry, and mayhaps 'twas not right of me to surprise you in this manner...but you must know that I love you, above all things on this earth, and that it is only the recent reminder of my mortality that prompts me to finalize your betrothal. I know that I will not always be here to protect you, sweeting, and that is the only reason that I would send you away to wive with *any* man. Lord Victor will care for you, and for Langumont."

"But Papa," her voice was choked with tears, "he hurt me, Papa, and I fear what he will do when we are wed."

Merle's face settled as if in stone. "Did he violate you?"

Maris swallowed heavily. "N-nay, Papa. He was rough, and he groped about...." She shuddered.

Merle forced a kindly smile for his daughter; though he was more disturbed than he let on, his words were jovial. "My love, you are a beautiful woman...and I am certain 'twas merely that he was overcome with passion for you, as you are soon to become his wife. Do you not fret, love, he will be good to you." Or I shall peel every piece of skin from his body, he added fiercely to himself. "Now, go you and see to your mother."

When Merle was left alone in his chamber, he found himself unable to concentrate on the tasks at hand. His daughter's fearful, yet resigned face haunted him. Truly, was he doing right by her? Had he made the right decision?

His mind went back to the evening he'd spent wandering the battlements of his beloved Langumont…and the conversation he'd exchanged with Dirick Derkland. Harold must have been very proud of his son, Merle thought to himself.

Merle thought for a long time, all that day and for the remainder of the evening. He watched with a hawk's eye the others at table with him: his wife and daughter, Michael and Victor d'Arcy.

༄

Maris braved the evening meal as she imagined her father would stand in battle. She was polite, if a little reserved, to their guests; solicitous to her mother, who had insisted upon rising from her bed; and warm to her father.

The time to retire did not come too soon for her. She was anxious to be away from Victor's proprietary gaze; anxious to have time to plan her next strategy. The betrothal ceremony would take place the next afternoon, and at that time, she would truly belong to Victor d'Arcy as completely as if she'd wed him. Maris was realistic enough to know that while she couldn't stop the betrothal, or change her father's mind, she may be able to delay it. Or, if she truly had no other choice, she gnawed at her lower lip as she gathered her skirts to climb over the bench, she would find a way to make peace with Victor.

She stopped behind her father's chair at the fireside. "Good night, Papa."

He looked at her with sad grey eyes. "Daughter, I vow, all will be well. Know that I love you above all."

Tears skimmed the corners of her eyes: she loved and trusted her father. "Aye, Papa," she said brokenly, trying to regain her composure. "I love you."

He pulled her nearly onto his lap in a bear hug, making her feel as if she were but three years of age. "I want only the best for you," he told her yet again. "Believe you this. Good morrow, my daughter."

"Good morrow, Papa." She pressed a kiss to his bristling cheek and swept from the room, dashing back the tears that once again threatened.

In the privacy of her chambers, Maris found Verna strangely jumpy. "Go on," she told her maid tiredly, "get you to the man who waits you."

"Thank you, milady," her servant told her, slipping from the room with undue haste.

Maris collapsed on her bed, drawing thick furs up to cover her from head to toe. The fire that had been laid was burning merrily, and the chamber was not cold at all—still, she felt the need to hide from the world.

She must have slept, for suddenly she was being shaken awake.

"Milady," whispered Verna urgently, shaking her shoulders rather too roughly. "Milady, you must come—Ernest of the hillock has been grievously injured."

Maris's mind cleared of sleep instantly. She nearly leapt from the bed. "Please, Verna, my green overtunic," she said, fumbling to draw her shoes on.

"Be quick, milady, there is little time," Verna told her, pulling the requested gown from a trunk. "Widow Maggie says you must come at once."

Maris pulled the tunic on and tied her long hair into a knot, stuffing it into a long scarf, then allowed her servant to wrap her in her blue cloak. Quickly, she pulled the basket with her herbs from the nearby trunk and whisked from the room in Verna's wake.

The keep was fairly silent, and very dark. Even the boy who tended the fire in the hall was nodding off at his post. Maris did not have the heart to waken him on such a chill, dark night—although upon her return, she knew she'd have a few words with him.

"Come, milady," Verna urged, reaching for her arm to pull her through the hall.

Maris did not care for the strength of the other woman's grip—nor her familiarity—and she shook the tight fingers from her wrist. Her servant scarcely noticed, so quickly was she skirting through the hall, and then out into the bailey.

At the gates to the portcullis, Maris hailed the guards—who were not, fortunately, following the example of the fire-tender—and explained her mission. They waved her on through, misliking her intent to wander through at the darkest part of the night, but following her commands to remain at their post. "You need not rouse a guard for me," she told them. "I have Verna, and we are going only to Ernest Hillock's home."

Verna, for her part, barely stopped as Maris greeted the guards. "Come, milady," she urged again. "He is not well." She led her mistress through the dark streets of the village, through the center square and to the south side.

"Widow Maggie awaits within," Verna told her, opening the door to a dark hut and gesturing Maris to go within.

Maris stepped incautiously through the doorway and instantly, two strong hands grabbed her. One covered her mouth tightly, and the other banded around her arm. There was at least one other person, Maris sensed, as she kicked and fought and struggled to free herself. Her cloak fell from her shoulders, leaving her only clothing the light chemise she'd worn in bed.

One man grunted as he felt a well-placed kick, and he retaliated with a blow to her face. Maris whimpered in pain, but her silent struggle continued as a thick cloth was shoved into her mouth, gagging her. She tried to bite at the fingers that pressed it in there, and succeeded in tasting dirty flesh. Before she knew what was happening, another slap to the face stunned her, and her knees buckled when someone rammed them from behind. She collapsed to the floor of the dwelling, her arms yanked behind her back.

"Take care, ye idiot," came a rough voice. "He wants her alive and well!"

Her hands were bound behind her back with heavy rope, and, lying on a cold dirt floor, she was suddenly overcome with violent shivering.

"Make haste!" someone whispered.

A heavy cloth was thrown over her head, and she felt herself rolled loosely in the burlap from head to toe.

"I'll take the cloak," came a voice she recognized as Verna's, and Maris's struggles began anew at the realization that her own maid had betrayed her.

"Oh, aye?" sneered a man's voice.

Maris, shocked, but still able to hear, focused on the sounds that followed. There was a surprised gasp from her maidservant, then the sounds of thuds and and grunts. Verna gave a stifled shriek, moaning throughout the struggle. There were at least three men, Maris's fogged mind decided, and through the sounds that ensued, she had an ugly suspicion as to what they were doing to her.

"What a piece!" groaned one of the men after a particularly harsh whimper from Verna.

Finally, there was silence but for the sounds of harsh breathing. Maris, truly terrified, held her breath, wondering if she was next. Rough hands plucked at the enveloping burlap, and she felt herself being lifted into the air, over someone's shoulder.

"Hide her," said the voice closest to her. "I'll take this on ahead. Make haste, for the alarm may be sounded at any time."

Maris felt herself being carried, and then tossed into some type of vehicle, for it began to move thereafter. The cold was beginning to seep through the cloth, and her fingers and toes felt the worst of it. Though the burlap was thick, she had not been rolled too tightly, so that although her breathing was labored, she was able to draw it in.

After a time, she either lost consciousness or slept, for it must have been later that she felt herself being jostled from the cart. Her head pounded and the side of her face throbbed where she'd been struck. Still wrapped in the burlap, she shivered as she was placed over what must have been the back of a horse. Something warmer covered her then, and then she felt a rope over her back, securing her to the mount. Fear gripped her again as the horse was urged to a canter and then a hearty gallop, for she had no way to hold on, and if the rope gave, she would be trampled beneath the horse's hooves.

Up until now, her kidnappers had been relatively silent, except for short, terse directions from the one who gave the orders.

Who could have done this? she asked herself, willing her mind to focus. Earlier, someone had mentioned a "he," and obviously this "he" didn't want her to be harmed. Furthermore—she forced her mind to remain clear and work through the events slowly—Verna was involved, although, from the sounds of the struggle that had taken place, she was also somewhat expendable since she'd been left behind. In what condition she'd been left behind, Maris didn't know—and she shuddered at the thought.

Whoever it was, then, wanted her alive and for his own purposes. Ransom was a probable cause; or, mayhaps someone wished her powerful father to bend to his will in a political matter. At any rate, Maris tried to put her fears of being harmed to rest: obviously, if 'twere a ransom, she would be returned unharmed.

They traveled for an interminable length of time, it seemed to her. In reality, she had no idea of day or night. Once, she was yanked off the horse and roughly unrolled from her covering then allowed to relieve herself in the nearby brush. Her arms were kept tied and her captor, whom she did not recognize, stood with his back to her. Embarrassed but desperate, Maris tried not to think of his proximity as she crouched in the snow.

Then she was made to sit near a small fire with the three men, and they fed her a hunk of cheese and a small crust of bread. One of them poured ale into her mouth, heedless of the streams that ran down her chin and throat. At one point, Maris tried to ask them who they were and what their purpose was, but she was silenced by the threat of a gag.

She was rolled back up into the burlap and loaded on the back of the horse again, and the journey continued.

Twelve ↦

*D*irick sopped up the last of the juices from his trencher of bread with a hard crust. The Great Hall of Dreakskil was as loud and dirty as usual, and the food had not improved in the five days he'd spent there. He'd intended to leave the day before, but after witnessing the scene in which Berkle delivered his bad news to Bon, Dirick changed his mind. He sensed something was afoot, and decided to remain under Bon's roof for another day or two.

He'd chosen an unfortunate day to remain at Dreakskil, however, for 'twas cold and snowing outside of the keep, and there were few amusements other than sitting near the stilted fire, or trading stories with the other men-at-arms. Dirick ached to be outside, exercising his swordplay and perhaps riding Nick, who was as eager as his master to be away from Dreakskil. As it was, it was barely past midday, and the time stretched before him.

Shoving away from the crude table, he ambled through the rotting rushes. One of the other mercenary knights who was in Bon's employ hailed him to a chess table, and Dirick gratefully accepted. They'd just arranged their pieces when a great commotion erupted in the bailey.

Bon leapt to his feet from the bench on which he'd partaken of the midday meal. Dirick could see the glitter of excitement in his dark eyes, even from the corner where he sat. Excusing himself from the chess game, he stood slowly and unobtrusively made his way to stand near the high table. A group of men led by Berkle burst through the large oaken door carrying what looked like a long, rolled tapestry. As Dirick watched in amazement, a dozen of the men-at-arms gathered around. The serfs hovered in the background, staring with wide eyes.

With a quick flick of the wrist, Berkle yanked the tapestry roll, dropping it to the floor. It unrolled and a person—a woman—tumbled out, landing in the putrid rushes in a swirl of white gown and long, dark hair. Her hands were tied behind her back and she lay in the midst of her thick hair and the rushes, wincing as one of the dogs loped up to sniff at her. She wore a light chemise that had ruched up past the knees when she landed in her ignominious heap.

The gathered men reacted loudly with hoots and whistles, but the woman didn't move. "Silence!" shouted Bon angrily at his men. "You shall show respect to my bride!" The jeers and laughter quieted momentarily.

Her long hair hid her face, but when Bon leaned forward to brush it back, thus revealing a pert nose and sensual lips, Dirick's heart leapt into his throat. Maris of Langumont! Stunned, Dirick barely refrained from leaping forward to shield her from the men that gathered around. The moment that he paused, and thus remained anonymous, likely saved his life. There was naught he could do now, one man against many…but he vowed he would find a way to free Maris.

As Dirick struggled to master his horror—while at the same time, praising God that he had decided to stay longer at Dreakskil—Bon solicitiously helped her to her feet and sliced through the rope that bound her wrists.

"You are well come to my home, my lady." He made a short bow.

Maris stood as straight as her stiff, trembling legs would

allow. She was frightened and exhausted, her heart thumping so loudly she was sure it echoed throughout the hall. Shivers wracking her limbs made it nearly impossible to maintain what little composure she could draw to her defense. The chemise she wore was of the lightest linen and did not afford much protection from either cold or prying eyes, so she was thankful for her long hair. "Why have you brought me here?" she asked in a hoarse voice. She recognized him from his visit to Langumont, remembering his refusal to share his name. "Who are you?"

As of yet, she had not turned her attention from Bon de Savrille, and had not looked closely at the crowd of gawking men. Instead, though she was overwhelmed by fear, she forced herself to hold the dark gaze of the bearded man towering before her.

"My lady, I have brought you here to do you the honor of making you mistress of Dreakskil," Bon told her as he reached for her hand. He froze, pushing back a thick lock of hair to reveal a large, purplish bruise on her left cheek. Dirick's hand fell to his dagger and he would have stepped forward, thus endangering his purpose at Dreakskil, had Bon's reaction not been as forceful. At the sight of the bruise, a loud roar erupted from the Lord of Dreakskil, and he whirled on Berkle. "You have allowed my wife to be ill-used!" he screamed, spittle flying from his mouth. "'You are not to harm a hair on her head' were my very words to you, you low-lying, cat-sucking whoreson! Throw him in the dungeon!" he screamed at a nearby guard.

A violently protesting Berkle was dragged from the hall, and immediately after issuing that command, a calmer Bon returned his attention to Maris. "Accept my apologies, my lady, for your abuse at the hands of my loyal knights." His smile was as greasy as the capon they'd eaten for dinner. He leered at Maris, leaning forward to capture one of her hands in his and raising it to his mouth for a damp kiss.

Her mind had been struggling to focus, to make sense of her predicament. Just as her thoughts began to separate and to clear, her gaze swept the group of men surrounding her. They rested on a face that was familiar, but out of place…and as the realization that Dirick de Arlande stood in the crowd with her enemy, all went blank and she slid to the floor in the first swoon of her life.

༄

"My lord!" exclaimed Ernest of the hillock as he was ushered to the dais in the Great Hall. Merle, along with his guests and wife, was breaking his fast after attending mass that morning.

"My lord Merle," began Gustave, who approached with the horrified serf, "Ernest begs an audience."

Ernest fairly trod upon the seneschal in his excitement to reach his lord's table. Executing a brief, but respectful bow, he stammered in his guttural English that he'd found not only the body of Lady Maris's maidservant, Verna, but also his lady's blue cloak crumpled in the snow.

"What say you?" Merle nearly stood in his alarm. His words, too, were in English; and thus the meaning was lost upon the other nobility at the high table.

"Aye, my lord, 'twas a fright to me, my lord, whenst I came upon the bloodied, ravaged body of Verna of Langumont. Her's not breathing or moving and sure as I stand, the wench is dead. And my lady Maris," his eyes grew round, "'twas nawt sign of her'n but for her cloak, 'round the bend from mine own home."

"Gustave, send for the guards of last eve," Merle roared in French to the hovering seneschal.

"What is it?" cried Allegra, alarmed at the expression on her husband's face. Victor and Michael d'Arcy had stopped eating as well.

"Know you where Maris is this morn?" asked Merle fiercely

of his meal companions. "Have ye seen her yet this morn?"

They each in turn shook their heads, Allegra's eyes growing wide with fear.

The guards from the watch of the night before rushed into the hall, startled out of their sleep, half-dressed and with mussed hair.

"My lord," greeted the captain of the night watch with a bow. "What is amiss?"

"Did my daughter leave in the company of her maidservant during your watch?" Merle fired the question before the man rose from his bow.

"Aye, my lord, she said on as she were called to the side of Ernest of the Hillock," explained the captain. His eyes swiveled to Ernest and realization washed over him. He looked back at his lord. "She is gone missing?"

"Aye," grated Merle. His voice rose in supplication. "Has no one seen my daughter?"

Silence greeted him.

"*À Langumont!*" he cried, standing and nearly toppling the large table in his haste. "We must search while the trail of her abductors is fresh! *À moi!*"

"My lord husband," Allegra's voice wavered, barely heard above the roar of men calling to arms. "My lord!"

"I shall return her to you safely, fear not," Merle told his wife, worry creasing his face even as he gave orders to his men.

"But my lord, I—I believe I may know whence she has been taken." Allegra plucked at the sleeve of his tunic. "'Tis my—my brother—my half-brother, Bon de Savrille." She was barely able to choke the words out. Merle froze and turned, giving her his full attention as she stammered a wary description of his visit, including his threat to have Maris to wive.

꧁

Maris regained consciousness as she was carried up a long staircase.

Having never swooned before, she felt a momentary pang of shame that she'd succumbed to such a feminine weakness…and then dismissed the misbegotten feeling immediately in light of her predicament. And what a predicament it was!

The buffoon who carried her none-too-gently up the stairs misjudged a corner, and one of her hands—still ice-cold—slammed into the heavy stone wall. She could not hold back a moan of pain, but, mercifully, no one was behind to notice that her eyes had flown open at the shock. She would feign unconsciousness long enough to gain her bearings and make some sense of her situation. Assess the situation, her father told his pages and squires during their long training in the art of war, before developing a strategy.

It was, however, more difficult than she'd anticipated to fake an extended faint…especially when she was dumped unceremoniously onto a bed of some sort. Through slitted eyes, she recognized that the clumsy oaf who'd carried her jerkily up the stairs was none other than her intended husband—at least, it was *his* intention that he be her husband.

"Agnes!" he bellowed suddenly, and Maris nearly jumped.

Then there was a voice, squeaky with fear. "Aye, my lord."

"See to my betrothed," ordered Bon in a rough voice. "She is weak after her long journey. I would that she were bathed and dressed and prepared to sup with me at the evening meal." There was a short silence, then, "And see to it that she is cared for as befits her station. Do you not forget she is to be my wife."

Maris held her breath as she felt his presence near her face. A large hand took hers and raised it to dry lips. "Until later, my lady," he murmured. She felt the air stir as he whirled and left the room, bellowing for hot tubs of water for her bath.

She was to be his wife. Maris held back a shudder at the thought. Not bloody likely!

She listened carefully, eyes still closed, as the unfortunate Agnes bustled about the room. Calm orders were given to the servants who brought sloshing buckets of water, along with linens and other rustling items, into the chamber.

As she lay in repose, listening, her mind whirled, uncontained. Dirick de Arlande was here—in the home of her abductor! The pit of her stomach—mostly empty, for the fare on her unexpected journey had been little more than hard bread and old cheese—twisted in fear and anger. Had he merely wooed her—and her father, too—in order to plot her kidnapping for Bon de Savrille?

Many things made sense now, she thought, trying to keep her lips from twisting bitterly. His destrier was much too fine and expensive to belong to a mere mercenary knight…and his knowledge about Henry's court had been so pat that she'd wondered how a traveling knight from France knew such detail. And her father—and she—had taken him at his word, invited him into their home, and treated him as an honored guest all the while he plotted to snatch her for his master!

Maris swallowed, holding back tears.

At the last, there was silence. Maris heard the door close, and the unmistakable sound of a bar sliding into place across it. She was just about to open her eyes when the barest of sounds told her that someone was still in the room.

"My lady, you may open your eyes," came a quiet voice. "All have gone save myself. But be yourself ware, my lord has stationed a guard outside your chamber."

Maris's eyes snapped open in surprise. They rested on a woman, similar in age to herself, with thick honey-colored hair and a long purple scar that ran from the corner of one eye to the edge of her jaw. "How did you know?" she asked in a voice rough from disuse.

Agnes tilted her head shyly. "'Tis oft I have feigned the same faint, my lady." She drew near the bed as Maris's gaze traveled the chamber for the first time.

'Twas larger than she'd expected, and while not as luxurious as her own chamber at Langumont, the bed was fairly comfortable and there were tapestries—threadbare though they were—over the slitted windows to keep out the drafts. The fire, at least, was enthusiastic; although the rest of the chamber left little to comment upon.

"Would you like to bathe, my lady?" asked Agnes. "The warm water will ease your hurts."

Indeed, Maris could smell the comforting scent of rosemary wafting from the tub that had been placed before the fire. "Aye, I think that I should do that, at the least." She struggled up from her repose on the bed, and Agnes, though less quick than her own maid Verna, was just as efficient in pulling off her shift and helping her into the tub.

Verna!

The thought of her maid shot into her mind and a well of fear and anger erupted within. How dare her own maid betray her in this manner! For there was no doubt that Verna had lured her from the comforts of her own bed to the waiting arms of her kidnappers! She was doomed—betrayed by two people she trusted!

Then Maris shuddered as she recalled the violent sounds of Verna's own fate. Swallowing back a lump in her throat, she tried not to think about what those sounds had meant.

Agnes, though awkward, was gentle as she washed the tangled mass of Maris's long hair and bathed her with a faintly-scented rosemary soap. In fact, Maris felt lulled by these familiar comforts as she struggled to determine a plan. She definitely had to have a plan, for she had no intention of wedding the coarse, greasy Bon de Savrille!

Verily, her father had noted her disappearance by now. That realization sent a wave of comfort through her. If anyone could rescue her, her father could. All Maris had to do, she realized, was delay Bon's intent—for it didn't make sense that he'd plan to hurt his intended bride—until her father could get there.

Agnes helped her out of the tub and to a stool that sat before the fire. Maris, wrapped in a woolen blanket, stared into the flames as the maid tugged a wooden comb through her hopelessly snarled hair.

"Yer hair is beautiful, my lady," said Agnes, breaking the silence almost fearfully. "'T hath been long since I've had such a pleasure."

Although Maris did not feel inclined toward conversation, she responded, "Many thanks, Agnes. 'Tis your name, aye, Agnes?"

The other woman nodded. "Aye." She combed her hair in silence, gently, and for the tangled mass that it was, Maris felt no pain on her scalp. "My lord wishes for you to sup with him this even," Agnes told her. "Do you wish for me to say you are still ill?"

Maris was silent for a moment. How she would love to remain ensconced in this chamber, away from the prying, greedy eyes of her kidnapper…yet, the start of a plan had already begun to formulate in her mind, and she needed more information to know if 'twould work. "Nay, Agnes," she replied after a moment. "I shall sup with Lord Bon, as he wishes. It does not seem prudent to anger him, aye?" Hoping to learn more about her captor, and as yet unsure whether Agnes would be a help or a hindrance to her, she craned her head to look back at the maid.

"Oh, aye, my lady, my lord has a brutal temper," agreed Agnes. "An' one ne'er knows when 'twill break." She could not suppress a shudder. "Yet, my lady, he seems overly fond of you…in fact, I have heard stories that when he is in his cups, he sings love ballads in your honor."

"Indeed?" Maris could not hide the shocked expression on her face.

"My lady," began Agnes, hesitating. She took a deep breath and began again, "My lady, you do not come here of your own will, I trow."

Maris gave a short, humorless bark of laughter, "Nay, Agnes, of course I do not. I would wed with no man under my own will. Yet, I have a betrothed of my father's wishes that I have been snatched from…and he is no prize any more than Lord Bon is."

"My lady, I would—I would do all I may to help you…an'…." Agnes swallowed, trembling, her eyes fearful as she looked up at Maris. "I would ask a boon, my lady. I know 'tis unseemly to ask, my lady," her words now tumbled out as if she could not stop them, "but I would wish to leave here in exchange for—for helping you."

Maris turned a cool gaze on the frightened maid before her. "How might I help you leave as I am my own prisoner here?" she asked.

"My lady, you are the daughter of a powerful lord, 'tis certes that he or your betrothed will come for you," Agnes whispered, nearly cowering as if waiting for a hand to strike her face. "An' I would go with you when they come."

"You are mistreated?" Maris asked, thinking of her friend Joanna.

"My lady," Agnes swallowed heavily, "I am a freewoman, my father a merchant near York when I was taken from him. I wish only to be free from my lord Bon." She unconsciously touched the purple scar. "'Tis but a reminder of his anger." Tears welled in her eyes, and Maris felt sympathy washing over her.

"As you shall help me, I vow repayment in kind," she told the other woman, who, by mere misdirection of the Fates, was serving her rather than living the life of a merchant's wife. Ofttimes, the family of a merchant was more wealthy than those of the nobility—whose wealth lay in the land, rather than commercial goods. She could not leave Agnes here.

"Thank you, my lady!" Agnes fell to her knees, the tears tumbling forth. "Praise God and thank you!"

"Now, then," Maris became business-like and drew the maid to her feet, "we must have a plan. You must tell me all that you know about my lord and his plans, and we shall decide how to proceed from there."

As the women plotted in the abovestairs chamber, taking care to keep their voices at a low level, a different scene unfolded below.

Dirick de Arlande had not missed the look of shock, and then loathing, that had flitted across Maris's face before she slumped to the floor. While no one else seemed to notice her reaction, he felt her anger slice through him at the same time as a stifling fear when Bon de Savrille gathered her up in his arms to carry her above. Dirick almost started after them, determined to do whatever he had to in order to protect the lady's virtue. He would have, in fact, done so if he'd not noticed Edwin Baegot watching him carefully. Prudently, Dirick decided that he would be no help to Maris of Langumont if Bon learned his true reason for being there.

When Dirick heard the lord of the keep bellowing for hot water to be brought to the abovestairs chamber, and then the heavy footsteps of Bon himself returning to the hall, he realized he had some time yet before Maris was in danger. Sinking onto a short stool, Dirick stared into the fire that snapped viciously in its enclosure.

The first thing he must do is get a message to Merle of Langumont. Finding someone in the village that could be trusted would be a battle in itself. Then, he mused, plucking at a string on his tunic, he must find a way to delay the imminent wedding while protecting Maris's virtue: all without arousing suspicion.

సా

Dirick was just returning from his sojourn to the village—ostensibly to visit a whore—when the keep's inhabitants were shoving and jostling for place for the evening meal. He'd paid a heavy coin to a young man to carry the message to Langumont, as well as promising him that Merle would place him in his household as reward for defying Bon de Savrille.

Pushing his way between two men-at-arms who were arguing about the most dèsirable quality in a destrier—its weight or its thirst for blood—Dirick was able to find a place on the third bench from the dais. Hoisting a leg over the crude bench, he nudged at one of the hounds that slept beneath the table, moving the dog so he could take his seat.

Glancing at the high table, he saw Bon sitting in his large, throne-like chair. The bearded man sent expectant looks toward the stairs between strains of his conversation with Edwin, who sat at his left. Dirick was surprised to note that Bon seemed to have tidied his appearance. His beard was trimmed for the first time in three days, and the tunic he wore was not despoiled with any stains or tears. Even the man's dark hair had been subdued, brushed back from his high forehead and leaving wings of gray at his temples.

There was a murmur at the back of the hall, and, nape prickling, Dirick turned to see Maris descending the stairs. Voices quieted and Bon's attention snapped to the woman who wended her way between the benches and tables. A tall, fierce-looking man with a hooked nose followed in her wake.

Dirick found that 'twas not only his gaze that was fastened upon her; but the hall seemed to have frozen in time, all conversation dying, as Maris passed through. She did not at all look like a maiden who had been kidnapped from her beloved father, wrapped in a tapestry for a day, dumped into a room of gawking men, and threatened with an unwanted marriage. She looked regal, confident, and incredibly beautiful.

Someone—Dirick assumed that it was the scar-faced Agnes—had combed through the length of rich brown hair, coiling a huge mass of it intricately at the back of her head. A great length of it fell from the coil, brushing the backs of her thighs as she walked. The gown she wore, though not as rich as one she might have worn at Langumont, was more than appropriate for this ramshackle hall. The blue of the gown was so deep it shone like the midnight sky, and bright yellow embroidery trailed along the edges of the long sleeves that nearly brushed the floor. A girdle encircled her waist, and a sheer veil covered her head.

Dirick took a deep steadying breath. His heart was pounding in his throat, and his insides were in turmoil. How could she look so beautiful and unconcerned when she was in so much danger?

Maris took her time making her way to the high table where Bon awaited her. The hook-nosed man that trod upon the train of her gown was Sensel, the guard appointed to watch over her. She took a deep breath, keeping her pace slow, as she fought to maintain her composure. Papa is on his way, she told herself firmly. She could hold out for a few days until he arrived.

When she reached the high table, Maris almost lost her nerve. But then, steeling herself, she took the last step and swept into a beautiful curtsey at Bon's feet. "My lord," she murmured, looking at the battered boots he wore.

There was a moment of stunned silence, and then she heard a rumbling voice. "And see you, Edwin, the honor my wife pays me." Bon stepped down from the dais, taking Maris's hand and raising her to her full height. She modestly kept her eyes downcast until he said, "My lady, 'tis honored I am at your presence. Come you and sup with me."

Maris barely restrained a nervous giggle. Honored at her presence, indeed! As if she'd found her own way to Dreakskil—wherever that was! "Thank you, my lord."

Bon was solicitous as he assisted her onto the bench next to his place. "I had half-expected to drag you kicking and screaming down to sup with me," he said, filling her goblet with thin wine. "Sensel had my orders. 'Tis glad I am that you chose to obey my wishes." His steely blue stare fastened upon her.

Maris looked at him from under her long lashes, refusing to be intimidated by his glare. "Aye, my lord, your wish that I join you for supper—and otherwise—was quite evident," she said demurely. "Yet, I beg that any future travel arrangements you make for me have more care to my comfort than these last!"

Surprised, Bon burst into a loud guffaw, turning every head in the hall back to the dais. He cocked his head to one side, taking a large gulp of wine. "And have you any other requests regarding your comfort, my lady?" he chortled.

One of the serfs approached with a wooden platter of food, followed by another with several bread trenchers. Bon, as gallantly as any courtier, chose bits of meat and potatoes for them, placing the choicest pieces of rabbit on her side of the trencher.

Maris favored him with a brilliant smile, and its brightness was enough to stun even the sour Edwin. "My lord, how kind of you to ask," she said sweetly, dragging a crust of hard bread through the meat's juices. "There are a few suggestions I might make, my lord, as I am to be your chatelaine, am I not? I should not wish your hall to seem lacking to any visitors."

Bon froze, turning to look at her. She could almost see the suspicion darted through his mind like a rabbit through its warren. "You are to be my chatelaine, and my wife," he said darkly. "You seem to be much too well accustomed to this notion, my lady. What game do you play?"

Maris wondered if perhaps she'd gone too far, but 'twas too late now and she must dodge his blow, thrusting with her own. "My lord," she looked at him unwaveringly, "it appears that I have no choice in the matter, and, in truth, as I must wed, methinks I'd sooner wed with a man whose desires for me are such that he should whisk me away under my own father's nose than the sop-eyed man chosen by my papa!"

Bon looked surprised for a moment, and then a pleased smile slid across his face. "I do believe I have received my first compliment from the lady," he said to Edwin.

"Aye, my lord," Maris agreed, "and now, may I ask a boon of you?"

"Ask, my lady."

"May I be given charge of your steward and your cook?"

The expression on his face would have been comical if she'd been in the mood to appreciate it. "My steward and my cook?"

"Aye, my lord. The state of this hall is deplorable...and this...this food is not fit for the dogs that crowd about my feet!" Her words, for the first time that evening, were truly in earnest. Maris did not think she could survive until her father arrived to rescue her if she had to partake of what passed for food in this keep. "When was the last time these rushes were changed?" she asked, kicking at them under the table and landing her pointed toe in the ribs of a well-fed hound. "And though my chamber is comfortable enough, it could use a good cleaning as well! It must be done, certes before we are wed, my lord." She turned a limpid gaze upon him.

"We are to be wed on the morrow, my lady."

"On the morrow?" Maris managed to turn an expression of shock into one of joy before he noted the difference. "My lord, how you honor me!" She ducked her head quickly, pricking the corner of her eye with a fingernail, then, raising her head, fixed him with a wide-eyed look pooled with tears. "But, Lord Bon, I have naught to wear…and you could not wish to dishonor me by inviting our guests to the hall in this state! Why, I cannot have the time to prepare a proper meal for your vassals and your men! I do not know what the stores hold and the talents of your cook!"

He fixed her with a shrewd look. "Methinks you are inventing excuses, my lady. I shall not be dissuaded from wedding with you."

"Nay, my lord, I am most aware that we shall wed upon your word…yet, I implore you…please do you not dishonor me in this way! I should at the least want the bedchamber prepared for our wedding night," she offered convincingly, hardly believing that those words could issue from her mouth without nauseating her. She caught his gaze shyly from under her lashes, then turned away, lest he think her too bold.

"Ah…aye, our wedding night," he responded thoughtfully. A lascivious smile curved his face. "Mayhaps I shall make tonight our wedding night, my lady, and delay our nuptials as you ask."

Maris felt the blood drain from her face. "My lord, you would not dishonor me such!" she replied carefully, trying to sound only frightened and not as desperate as she was. "If we do not have the blooded sheets to display after the eve of our wedding, there will no doubt be questions as to whether we are truly wed. All will cast aspersion on our vows, and mayhaps I shall be taken from you and returned to my betrothed."

Bon did not reply immediately. He knew she was right, though he may be loath to admit it. Taking a bride by force was one thing, and being able to prove the validity of the wedding and its consummation was the crux of its success. "Aye, my lady, as you argue so prettily, I shall grant your wishes and allow you to order my kitchen and steward. I will not delay the wedding more than one day hence, my lady, so mark me well. On the day after the morrow, we shall be wed." His face leered close to hers.

"And I shall anticipate that evening greatly."

Maris took a large swallow of wine. Folding her hands in her lap, she asked demurely, "May I then beg your leave, my lord, as I have much with which to occupy myself on the morrow."

"Aye, Lady Maris, hie yourself to your chamber. Sensel will guard your door this night so you may sleep in peace."

Head held high, Maris gathered her skirts and stepped over the bench, and off the dais. She made her way carefully through the hall, aware not only of the man dogging her footsteps, but also of the many pairs of eyes that followed her.

Only one face did she recognize, and upon that face, she turned a look of such loathing and disgust that Dirick de Arlande could barely hold her gaze before returning to his goblet of ale.

Thirteen ⁊

Maris found her chamber a welcome refuge after such a nerve-wracking meal. Agnes was waiting for her when Sensel swung the door open, gesturing for Maris to enter.

As the great oaken door closed ominously behind her, Maris resisted the urge to flop weakly on the bed. Instead, she stood in front of the fire that roared in the grate and tried to calm the tremors that shook her hands. Although she'd hid it well, her heart had been lodged in her throat during the entire meal, making it nigh impossible to choke down the smallest bits of food. She seemed to have fooled Bon, however, and for that she was thankful.

"Agnes, know you whither herbs are kept here at Dreakskil?" she asked, sinking onto a three-legged stool next to the blazing fire. She shivered.

"Aye, my lady, there are some still in the kitchens. Methinks the midwife in the village may have some as well."

"I am in need of as much pennyroyal as you can locate," Maris told her wearily. "Can you gather it without arousing suspicion?"

"Aye. I shall say 'tis a tonic for myself."

"Good." Maris stared into the fire for a long moment, watching as the orange flames curled about the logs. "We must not give Lord Bon or Sensel any reason to believe you will assist me. Come you, sit near the fire—here, Agnes, turn your face so that your cheek reddens. I shall make as if you have displeased me, and then you must leave quickly to fetch the pennyroyal. Be certain to show Sensel your reddened cheek so that he believes I have struck you."

"Aye, my lady," Agnes agreed. She turned her unscarred cheek as directed, and as the warmth spread to her face, she watched in shock as the lady began to play-act.

"Stupid wench!" cried Maris suddenly, knocking over a tankard of ale. "Do you not have any more sense than a dog?" With a loud shriek, she dropped a piece of wood near the fire. Just as the door swung open, Maris slapped her hands smartly together, creating the same sound as hand meeting cheek, and in a swift movement, grabbed Agnes's arm and jerked her away from the fire. "Go you and do not come back until you have learned not to be so clumsy!" Giving the startled maid a shove toward Sensel, who glowered at the door, she added, "I must have my tonic immediately!"

Then Maris whirled angrily on Sensel, for he had no business bursting into her chamber unannounced. "How dare you enter my chamber without my leave?" She planted her hands on her hips and stared up at him.

By this time, the altercation had caught the attention of residents of the hall. Great clomping footsteps hurried up the stairs, and Bon, followed by several other men-at-arms, including Dirick de Arlande, crowded into the doorway of the chamber to see the interesting sight.

Maris stood with her hands on her hips, knowing that her eyes flashed with feigned anger. Her face was warm with emotion and exertion, and her heavy hair swirled like silk about her. The train of her gown tangled among her feet, and the overturned goblet lay across the floor as a silent echo of the scene she had created.

Unaware of the witnesses behind him, Sensel's face darkened and he leaned threateningly toward Maris. "My lord has commanded that I guard you day and night, my lady, and I answer only to my lord Bon."

"You may guard my door all you like, Sensel," Maris continued imperiously, "but you will not enter unless you are bid." Then, as if she had just caught sight of her intended husband, who stood watching the scene, she swept into a curtsey. "My lord, I am sorry if I interrupted your meal. 'Tis only that clumsy girl pulled on my hair and overturned a goblet of ale! I'd as lief take a switch to her if she does not attain some grace!"

"If Agnes does not please you, my lady, I shall find another maid to serve you," Bon told her, taking her hand to his lips. He stared at her as if bewitched—and for good reason. The heightened color in her cheeks and the bristling anger had aroused her passionate nature, and the snapping eyes and pouting lips were enough to lead his thoughts astray.

Maris paused as if to think on it. "Nay, my lord, as I have already begun her training. I should not wish to start again. I shall try her for a time."

Assured that his lady was satisfied, Bon turned on Sensel, his face darkening. "Never did I bid you leave to enter my lady's chamber. You are dismissed. You shall take the night watch at the south tower until you are bid otherwise." His gaze scanned the gawking group of men and rested on Dirick. "You, sir, will replace Sensel. And know that if you should displease my lady, you will find yourself in a less desirable duty."

Dirick nodded smartly. "Aye, my lord." His eyes flickered to Maris, noting the reaction of her narrowed eyes, then back to his lord just as the chamber door closed in his face.

The door slammed shut, leaving Bon in the chamber with

Maris. He turned to her. "At last, my lady, we are alone."

She eyed him with trepidation. "Aye, my lord, that we are. And what will be your pleasure? Wine, my lord?"

"Bon. I wish for you to call me Bon when we are private." He was still looking at her as if besotted.

She used that opportunity to pour him a goblet of warm wine, wishing that she had her store of herbs in her chamber. "Did you have aught you wished to speak with me on, my lord—Bon?"

His dark eyes glinted at her in the dim light as he sipped from the goblet. "Nay, my dear Maris. 'Tis only your company that I wished." That gaze did not waver from her person, and Maris was beginning to feel discomfited. She carefully took a seat on the three-legged stool closest to the fire, watching him warily.

"My lord," she began, wanting to keep conversation going so that his thoughts would not trail to the fact that she was alone with him and helpless, "'twould please me greatly to have use of the large chamber betwixt this and the garderobe. I will need such a chamber for a solar, where I and my women might work."

Bon's eyes, which had drifted to her bosom, snapped back to her face. "Your women?"

"Aye, my lord. How else shall I keep you in tunics, and tapestries on the walls?" She looked guilelessly at him. "You are in need of a new tunic for our wedding…and do you not think me shallow, my lo—Bon, yet I should like other than this to wear for that day." She gestured to the gown that fit rather too snugly through the bosom, and whose sleeves were the merest too short to be considered a perfect fit.

His dark eyes gleamed. "And for such a boon as that, my love, I should wish a token of your affection. Come hither, dearling." He gestured to the floor near where he sat.

Maris hesitated, then, gathering her skirts, sank into a kneel next to his stool. Keeping her head lowered, for now she was truly fearful for her virtue, she made a great play of arranging her skirts about her ankles. Bon reached down and grasped one of her fine hands, pulling it firmly to his lips. She concealed a shudder as moist lips smoothed over the back of her hand, then, as he turned her fingers, over the tender, inner side of her wrist. His tongue flicked out, like that of a snake, tracing the pale blue vein of her wrist.

"My lord," she murmured, trying to pull away. His fingers tightened and he chuckled quietly. The lips continued to trail along her wrist, sliding her sleeve back, as they pressed moist kisses on the inside of her elbow. "Bon, please," she looked up at him. "Please do not...tempt me so." Maris swallowed the clot of fear in her throat and managed a tremulous smile. "'Tis only one more day and we shall be truly wed."

"Aye, 'tis one more day...an' two more nights," Bon agreed, his voice rough. "I would have a taste of what it is I'll wed, Maris." His fingers like iron bands, he pulled her to the front of his stool. Placing a hand under each elbow, he half lifted her so that she was between the crux of his legs and half risen on her knees. One hand reached to hold the back of her head, his thick fingers sinking into the intricate coils of hair, as his bearded face leaned toward hers, blocking out the light from the candle behind him.

The hair on his face was rough over her smooth skin, and his lips were damp and sloppy. She tried in vain to twist her head away, but Bon's strength prevailed, and he succeeded in lifting her onto his lap even as his mouth smothered hers. Heavy, rough breathing rasped into her mouth as his kiss coaxed and demanded in turn.

Maris clenched her fingers into his tunic to keep from scratching his face. Then she tried to push him away, and, at last, was able to free her mouth from his. His arms were around her waist pinning her onto his lap and, gasping for air, he looked down at her own heaving chest. "Do you not be affrighted, my love," he said in what he must have thought was a seductive voice. "I'll not hurt you."

Just then, there was a loud knocking at the chamber door. Maris leapt to her feet, but was jerked back onto a solid lap. "Nay, sweeting. I'll not be interrupted."

"But, my lord, 'tis no doubt Agnes with my tonic."

"Your tonic can wait," he growled, seeking her lips once more.

With a cry, she managed to slide her face from his mouth, gaining a good scrape of beard across her cheek. "Nay, please my lord, if we do not answer the door, there will be much talk of what is happening herein, and then we shall be in quite a fix if there is any question as to our marriage."

The knocking became louder, sounding almost as desperate as she felt.

Bon's hand slipped down the front of her bodice, closing around her breast through the thin chemise under her bliaut. The other hand plucked at the lacings that held her bodice together.

Suddenly, the door swung open. Bon's head snapped up from Maris's bosom.

"Begging your pardon, my lord, my lady…. Methought I heard you bid entrance." Dirick strode boldly into the chamber. "It looks as if the fire needs to be stoked."

"My fire does not need to be stoked," Bon said meaningfully to Maris, stroking her back.

She squirmed in his lap. Then she saw Agnes hovering in the doorway. Smothering a sigh of relief, she pulled firmly from Bon's hands. "There you are, you lazy fool!" she exclaimed. "Have you brought my tonic?"

"A-aye, my lady." Agnes was so accustomed to being spoken to in that manner that it was not difficult for her to feign fear. "A tea of pennyroyal and chamomile, to help you sleep, my lady…and peppermint leaves to chase the ache from your head."

"And about time it is!" Maris snapped, taking the pitcher from Agnes more roughly than necessary. She turned, curtseying to Bon. "My lord, as we have been interrupted, I pray you will allow my maid to prepare me for bed. I have much to accomplish on the morrow to prepare for our wedding, as I wish to do you proud."

Bon swaggered to his feet and she gave a silent sigh of relief. "As you wish, my dearling," he said, as if granting her the moon. "But know that the taste I have had will barely suffice until we are well and truly wedded." With a last press of a kiss to her hand, he turned to make his way from the chamber, then stopped in his tracks, realizing that Dirick was still meddling with the fire. "Dirick, you belong on the outside of this chamber, and do you not forget that. Come now—the fire is blazing."

"Aye, you are dismissed." Maris turned regally away from him.

Dirick froze. Then he pulled himself to his feet with careful, deliberate movements, towering behind her. The hair on the back of her neck prickled, and she fancied she felt the spear of his stare driving into her back. Refusing to acknowledge him, she walked over to the bed, untying the curtains that would keep the drafts out during the night.

There was silence, and then Dirick pivoted and stalked silently from the chamber. The door shut behind him and Bon, leaving the women to themselves, and at last Maris was able to breathe a sigh of relief.

"Oh, my lady, are you—are you untouched?" Agnes asked, pouring the pennyroyal tea into a goblet. "Did my lord—did he hurt you?"

"Nay." Maris took a long drink of the lukewarm tea, then refilled the goblet and drank again. "Though 'twas a near thing."

"My lady, what is the purpose of the pennyroyal? Methought

'twas for Lord Bon, that you planned to poison him in some way."

Maris shook her head and forced herself to drink more of the bitter tea. "Nay, for were he to be poisoned, would I not be the first to be pointed to? 'Tis to bring on my monthly flux. Certes Bon will not touch me while I am unclean, and I pray my Papa will arrive before 'tis through. I must drink a good portion to ensure that it begins before the eve of my wedding. On the morrow, I must needs find some other way to keep him from me, as 'twill surely not start ere then."

"Mayhaps there is something to put his lordship to sleep early," Agnes suggested.

"Mayhaps, yet that is bound to be discovered. Is it not common for a bridegroom to spend the eve before his wedding fasting and doing penance?" Maris asked with a hint of humor in her eyes.

"I've not heard of such a thing, my lady," Agnes shook her head.

"Methinks I'll make such a suggestion to my lord Bon, and I'll pray he swallows it." Maris took a final draught of pennyroyal tea, then, looking ruefully under the bed, added, "I'm certain to be up in the night to use this," she pulled a chamber pot from under the high bed, "after drinking this tea, but it cannot be helped. Here, Agnes, climb you into bed, and we shall keep the other warm."

⌇

Outside the chamber door, Dirick seethed. How dare she take that tone of voice to him—dismissing him as if he were a mere servant!

He slumped against the rough stone wall, trying to blank from his mind the picture of Maris sprawled on Bon's lap, her breasts spilling from her gown. He clenched a fist, sorely tempted to drive it into the wall to ease the frustration at his helplessness.

Nay, he thought. 'Twould leave him with naught but bruised and bloody knuckles, and the helpless maiden still in the clutches of the evil lord. Helpless! Dirick snorted. Maris of Langumont was anything but helpless. She already had her abductor wrapped neatly around her little finger: Bon would probably set her free if she begged prettily enough.

Yet, he thought perhaps he'd noticed more than a trace of fear in her eyes when he burst unannounced into her chamber. Maris was definitely not out of danger yet.

Dirick did some quick calculations: he'd sent the messenger to Langumont just before the evening meal. The man would not reach his destination until late on the morrow...and then 'twould no doubt take Merle some time to gather his forces before they were on their way to Dreakskil. 'Twould be two days at best, more likely three, until Dirick would have help from that quarter.

Maris and Bon were to be married in less than two days. And there was only he to stop them.

Dirick shook his head, raking a hand through his overly long hair. 'Twasn't the marriage itself that was so much the problem: a forced marriage could easily be annulled; 'twas the fear of the harm that may be done Maris in the meanwhile. The loss of a maidenhead, so crucial to a profitable marriage, could not be rectified. His hand shook at the thought of the stocky, hirsute Bon poised over the innocent Maris.... Bile rose in his throat at the realization that there was little he could do to prevent it.

Unless he could find a way to get her out of Dreakskil. But first, he had to get her to trust him.

ళ

Maris awoke with a start to find her mouth muffled by a large hand, and a great weight pushing her into the bed. She panicked, thrashing frantically beneath the figure above her, ignoring his urgent whispers. Her eyes bulged wide open above the firm hand, trying to see her tormenter.

The chamber was still dim, although the fire, which had quieted during the night, gave off a low light, and a hint of dawn peered around the tapestries that covered the windows. She kicked and clawed viciously, forcing him to capture a wrist with his free hand.

"Maris, Maris, my lady, calm yourself," the voice urged, coming altogether too close to her ear.

She was as startled as he when, with one lucky thud, she placed a heavy kick in his groin and in the ensuing confusion tumbled him off the bed. Then she let loose a blood-curdling scream.

"God's blood, Maris!" Dirick scrambled to his feet, tangling in the rumpled bedclothes. "Do you want me killed that badly?" He stood, staring down at her, hands on his hips, breathing heavily.

"Sir Dirick!" she exclaimed in relief; then fury lashed across her face. "How dare you—Where's Agnes?"

"Shut up, my lady, and listen to me." He spoke rapidly and urgently. "I mean you no harm. I will help you escape if you will only trust me—"

"Trust you!" she spat, pulling the bedclothes up to cover her bare thighs. "Pah! You were there to welcome me to this—this serpent's lair!"

"Maris!" Dirick resisted the urge to throttle her in the interest of time. In fact, he could hear the stomping of feet drawing near. "Dammit, wench, I mean you no harm! I am sent by the ki—"

The door flew open and Bon burst in, followed by Edwin

and two other men-at-arms.

"What goes on here?" Dressed only in a loose shirt, he brandished a sword which was immediately thrust at Dirick's neck. "I shall kill you as you stand for daring to enter my lady's chambers!" The other men surrounded Dirick as he froze in place. Dirick swallowed hard, fighting to keep a blank expression on his face.

"Nay!" Maris's commanding voice stopped the final thrust of the sword. "My lord, this man—er, Sir Drake?—but entered the chamber in response to my scream." She had the grace to look uncomfortable. "I am sorry, my lord, I—I could not sleep, and as I prepared to rise to stoke the fire, I saw a mouse skitter across the floor." She ducked her head in embarrassment as one of the men-at-arms snickered.

Dirick held his breath, feeling the sharp point of the sword pricking his adam's apple. By God, he *would* throttle her—if they got out of here alive!

Before Bon could question why he had needed to open her chamber door if, indeed, Dirick had rushed in to her rescue, Maris put a pout of indignation on her face and said, "An' I see, my lord, that the rodents are yet another matter to which I must attend in this keep! Do you not think I could find a cat in the village and keep her in my chamber—*our* chamber—until we are well rid of these mice?" She widened her eyes innocently and even Dirick had to grudgingly respect her portrayal of guilelessness.

Slowly, Bon dropped his sword point and made the slightest bow to Dirick. "My apologies, sir. I am well-pleased that you have taken my lady's well-being to heart." He turned to Maris. "My lady, I do not care for cats…however, I shall think on your request." He said these words with such sincere formality that she had to choke on a nervous giggle.

"An' now, if you please," the imperiousness had returned to

her voice, "I fear I am much exhausted from all of this excitement and should seek my bed." Her eyes fastened on Bon. "Until the morrow, my lord."

"Until the morrow, my wife." And for the second time that night, Bon de Savrille meekly led his men from her chamber.

Fourteen ✍

llegra had not risen from her bed since Merle led his army of men-at-arms to Maris's rescue. Maella fussed worriedly over her mistress, but the frail woman did nothing but clutch at a worn wooden crucifix and pray.

"Milady, 't has been nearly two days. You must needs eat!" The maidservant thrust a bowl of broth under her lady's nose. "Lord Merle will bring the lady home safely."

"Nay," Allegra's voice was hoarse from overuse in cantations to the saints. "I have not much chance for life when he returns to Langumont. My lord Merle will kill me."

Maella's face grew soft at her mistress's confession. Pulling a stool near the bed, she smoothed a worn hand over the furrowed forehead of the woman she had served since birth, noticing the new white streaks throughout her soft brown hair. "My lord is just and fair. He holds no anger toward you for the actions of your brother, my lady."

"Nay." Allegra's hand curled around the hand that stroked her forehead. "Nay, Maella, 'tis not for that that I fear my life. 'Tis that I—I have told Michael that he is Maris's true father, and begged him to release her from the betrothal."

The maidservant drew back sharply. "My lady, you did not!"

"My daughter cannot wed with his son!" Allegra's voice was

stronger.

"Aye, my lady, but you did not tell the lord of the truth—yet you told Lord Michael?"

Allegra moved her head in affirmation. "I dared not tell Lord Merle, Maella. I dared not," her voice trailed off weakly. "God forgive me."

ﾐ

Maris had a plan.

She spent the day ordering the serfs about in the Great Hall, poking into the foodstuffs in the kitchen, and finalizing her plans to escape. Sir Dirick trod, it seemed, in her every footstep so that she was unable to turn without barreling into his large frame. Lord Bon sat for much of the day in his throne-like chair, watching in astonishment as Maris took the reluctant serfs to task. If either man noticed the absence of Maris's maid, Agnes, they did not comment on it.

At the midday meal, the preparation of which had been supervised by Maris, Bon dug heartily into the excellent fare—as did the other diners. "Ahh," he belched, patting the hand of his intended wife. "I'd not realized the lacking of my cook! If you continue to feed me thus, I'll not be able to sit a horse!" He laughed as if 'twas impossible to imagine this coming to pass.

Maris, noticing his already considerable girth, chose not to comment. Instead, taking a last drink of ale, she poked the venison in her trencher to the side. "My lord, there was a stink to some of the meat hung in your kitchens," she told him. "I do not believe any of it was prepared for the meal, yet I cannot be certain. Much of the venison had been stewing before I came upon it. In any case, I rid the kitchens of what was left of the bad meat, but, my lord, there is naught for our wedding feast on the morrow."

"Do you not fret, my lady." Bon stroked her fingers, heedless of the grease that slicked his own. "'Twill not be the first I've eaten bad meat…an' I have already planned a hunt on the morrow for our wedding feast."

"My lord, you have astonished me yet again with your foresight!" Maris fluttered her eyelashes at him as she pulled her hand away. Wiping it surreptitiously on her gown, she clambered over the bench, noting with satisfaction that there was nary a crumb of food left for even the dogs to nibble on. "I must see to the evening meal, now, my lord." She hurried away.

"'Twas an excellent meal, my lady," Dirick's deep voice came behind her as she crossed the hall.

Her back stiffened even as her heart leapt. Would he never stop dogging her footsteps? Maris ignored the man as she entered the kitchens. After giving rapid direction to the cook, she gathered her skirts and returned to the hall to order the rotting rushes to be removed.

By the time new rushes were being spread upon the floor, Maris's stomach was churning. 'Twould not be long now, she thought nervously. "My lord, I will withdraw to my chamber," she approached the dais. "I do not feel well." The queasiness that stole over her was not entirely fabricated. "I will nap and join you for supper."

Bon nodded graciously. "Of course, my lady. I shall send Agnes to you ere I see her."

"Thank you, my lord." Maris turned and walked steadily toward the stairs, aware of Dirick's dark gaze boring into her back. He must not suspect anything! she thought, pulling herself slowly up the steps. Desperate, knowing that his gaze had held a hint of suspicion at her excuse, Maris jammed a finger down her throat as she rounded the corner at the top of the steps.

She managed to gasp a convincing, "Sir D—" before she turned and retched up her dinner—right onto Dirick's leather boots. Sagging against the rough stone wall, she struggled for breath against what was actually a laugh at the horrified look on his face. "I'm sorry." She managed to make her voice sound embarrassed and contrite. "I must needs lie down." She fled from his presence and into her chamber as quickly as her "illness" would allow.

Once behind the closed door, she allowed her mirth to escape, smothering her giggles with the heavy pillows on her bed. It was several moments before she heard Dirick take up his post outside her door—just enough time for him to have wiped off his boots and called for someone to clean up her mess.

ॐ

Maris did doze whilst she waited for Agnes to join her…and for hell to break loose belowstairs. She would need all of her faculties about her later that night.

When the maid arrived at the bedchamber, she was in good spirits. "My lady, 'tis happening," Agnes announced as the door shut heavily behind her. "Just as you said!"

"Excellent!" Maris smiled complacently. "How does our guard seem to be faring? 'Tis he that concerns me the most…besides my lord Bon."

"Sir Dirick has not become ill yet, though from the very look on his face, verily he will be reaching for a chamberpot soon!"

"Or rushing for the garderobe!" Maris stifled a giggle.

"What did you put in the food, my lady?"

"'Tis a plant called broom," she explained. "'Twas luck, really, Agnes, for one of the old brooms in the kitchen had bristles made from the plant. The dried branches, with leaves and flowers, may be steeped and used for medicinal purposes. Yet, my mentor, Good Venny, always warned that 'tis an herb that must be used with care, for 'tis very powerful. 'T causes the body to—

ah—dispose of its contents in a violent manner. Though 't will-n't kill them, 'twill likely cause more than one to wish for death! 'Tis a much better choice than elder bark, which I had thought to use until I espied the broom."

"Do you not think Lord Bon will suspect 'twas you that poisoned the meal?" asked Agnes.

Maris rose from her prone position on the bed. "Nay, for I told him that the meat stank, and that mayhaps some of it was prepared for supper. Then, I made myself sick upon Sir Dirick's fine leather boots!" She drew the tattered tapestry back from the window slit, noting with satisfaction that the sun had nearly set. "Is all in readiness?"

"Aye. I have hidden the foodstuffs I purchased in the village with your ring, my lady, and a mount awaits us near the hidden entrance to the keep."

Maris turned in surprise, delight spanning her face. "A mount, you say? Agnes, how on earth…?"

"The stable master bears no love for Lord Bon, my lady, and 'twas no great feat to convince him that I plan to escape with a lover now that my lord has found a bride!"

Her eyebrows cocked in amazement, Maris stared at the woman before her. "Very well, then. 'Tis nigh time that we should leave." She scrabbled through a trunk and pulled a large leather pouch from its depths. Inside were two heavy cloaks she'd found in the piles of clothing Bon had made available to her, as well as a dagger she'd sneaked into her sleeve earlier that day.

As the two women moved toward the heavy door, they heard a loud groan from without. Maris looked at Agnes and carefully opened the door.

Dirick was doubled up on the floor, his tan face pasty with pain and glistening with sweat. When he heard the oaken door creak open, he struggled to sit, but the pain that wracked his abdomen had weakened him. There was a pool of vomit nearby, proving that he had not chosen to leave his post when the sickness struck.

Maris tried to slip past him, but Dirick gathered enough strength to snatch under the hem of her gown and grasp her ankle. "You are not ill!" he grated, understanding spreading across his face. "By God, woman, you have done this!"

Agnes hurried past, but Maris, still caught by the ankle and not wishing to make a great disturbance, struggled to free herself. "I had no choice," she told him, confident that he was too weak to stop them. Indeed, his strong arm trembled with the effort to hold her and she saw a ripple of pain cross his face. "Papa would not be here soon enough." With her other foot, she kicked at his hand, but his grip did not loosen. "Release me," she hissed, bending to claw at the arm that held her firm.

Dirick's other hand shot up to grab her wrist. "Have you poisoned me, then?" His eyes glittered. "Have you poisoned the whole keep in your haste to escape?" He could barely force the words forth and he yanked her down to her knees next to his prone body.

Her face was nearly in his, and her long, sweet-smelling hair caught in the sweat on his cheek. For a moment, a brief instant, regret washed over her that he should be in such pain because of her doing. Then sanity reigned, and she pulled with all of her strength. Dirick, weakened beyond measure, could not hold her and she came free, tumbling backward onto the floor. Scrambling to her feet, taking care to pull her skirts out of reach from his fingers, she stared down at him as a spasm shook his body. He groaned aloud, breathing a foul curse as his arms crossed over his belly as if to hold the pain at bay.

"Witch...." The word was more a breath than a curse.

Gathering her skirts and the leather pouch, Maris forced herself to turn from the agonized man and hurry to the steps in Agnes's wake. She stopped, whirling at the top. "You are not poisoned," she told him. "I am a healer, do you not forget. All will be well ere the morn. *Adieu*, Sir Dirick, and mark you well: though I doubt to see your deceitful face again, ere I do, I shall see you pay for this treatment of my person!"

With that, she whirled again and hurried down the narrow stone steps, leaving him in a heap behind her.

༯

The last thing Dirick remembered before he succumbed to the pain was Maris's caustic words.

That defiant threat was the first thing to come to mind when he regained his faculties many hours later. He knew it was much later because a stream of light came up the stairs, indicating that it was daylight.

Struggling to his feet with the rough wall as his prop, Dirick tried to swallow to moisten his bone-dry throat. He'd lost count of how many times he'd vomited and otherwise expelled the contents of his body through the night. From the stench that greeted him as he made his way to the steps, others afflicted with Maris's poison had not found their way to a garderobe either.

Smothering a curse for the woman who'd caused this havoc, Dirick carefully picked his way down the stairs, leaning heavily against the wall. If he could sit a horse, he and Nick would be out of this bloody place and on the trail of Maris and her maid as soon as he could walk to the stable.

In the Great Hall, collapsed bodies strewn about bespoke of the effects of whatever Maris had done to the food. Even the dogs were in heaps amongst the men. Dirick tried to swallow again and managed to choke up enough saliva for his throat to convulse. It made a harsh, grating sound.

Nary a soul stirred as he picked his way toward the outside entrance to the hall, bent on reaching the fresh air. Dirick wondered, fleetingly, if Maris and Agnes had actually made it safely past the guards at the draw bridge…and then he dismissed the question. Of course the wench had succeeded—every man in the place had been incapacitated, thanks to her meddling!

His empty stomach roiled painfully, and he cursed Maris. Again.

Out in the crisp, cold air, the fog lifted from his head and he felt strengthened. The bailey was relatively quiet—some of the men-at-arms were stirring, groaning and complaining about their sickness of the night before—and even the guards posted at the drawbridge sat slumped against the crennellated walls.

God's blood, he thirsted!

Dirick bent heavily to scoop a mass of clean snow to his mouth. The wet coldness felt like life to his cracked lips and swollen tongue. Another handful followed, and then another, and then he realized that he was hungry.

Maris had been right—she had said all would be well ere morning. There had been a time—many times—during the night when he'd doubted her words, certain that he'd be standing before God before long.

His stomach roiled again, this time indicating its emptiness. He turned to make his way back to the hall—'twould be best not to leave with an aching belly—but froze in his tracks at the sound of a bellow from within. Weak though the shout was, Dirick recognized Bon and what must be his fury at the disappearance of his bride.

Making a swift, prudent decision, he swung back to his path toward the stables, hobbling as quickly as possible to their refuge. Once inside, he wasted no time finding Nick, and, slipping the bit into the destrier's willing mouth, Dirick vaulted onto his back, sans saddle.

The shouts from the hall were getting louder, spilling out into the bailey, and he knew he'd be hard-pressed to make his escape now. A flash of weakness swept over him, and he fought it back, fought to keep his mind clear and to find a way to get out of Dreakskil.

Nick was eager to go, and Dirick gave him his head out of the stable. The scene in the bailey was one of chaos: men stumbling to their feet, sluggish and bewildered. Bon stood in the doorway of the hall, screaming orders, even as he leaned heavily against a feeble Edwin.

As the only man ahorse, Dirick immediately caught Bon's attention and was the recipient of an enraged bellow. Wheeling Nick, Dirick gathered all of his bravado and urged the stallion to the Lord of Dreaskil.

"My lord," he gasped as if in a hurry, "I caught sight of them over the hill yonder!" He gestured in a northeasterly direction, realizing in the back of his mind that he actually had no idea in which direction they'd gone, and hoping that he wasn't sending the forces onto their trail. "I'll catch them! Send after me!"

Without waiting for an acknowledgement—praying that Bon would accept his actions and not order arrows to be loosed at his back—Dirick kicked Nick and let him go. Men jumped from their path, rightfully wary of the fierce destrier, who, true to his nature, sensed a battle to come. Bon screamed in his wake—what words, Dirick did not care to find out—and some of the men tried to spring their weakened bodies to action. None dared grab at the stallion, however, and man and horse easily plowed through them. The men at the drawbridge were just reaching for the winches to lower the portcullis when Nick and Dirick tore past them, kicking up snow and narrowly missing a clumsy man.

Dirick bent low over his mount's neck, urging him on. The hair stood at his nape as he waited for a shower of arrows to engulf them. The ragged drawbridge began to rise slowly as they thundered across, but Nick made a beautiful, flying leap and soared easily to the ground on the far side of the moat.

The first arrow landed in the crusty snow not far from them and Dirick cursed. Glancing back, he saw the drawbridge lowering again and was just in time to duck when a cross bolt whizzed past his head. "Aye, Nick, boy, go! Go!"

The destrier heard him and picked up more speed. The arrows were falling further behind, and the men swarming over the bridge were not moving with enough energy to pose a threat. Dirick saw the haven of the forest ahead and knew he'd succeeded in putting Dreakskil behind him.

Now, God willing, he'd have luck and would find Maris and take her to safety.

Fifteen ⁊

Merle had been driving his small army of knights at a ferocious pace; still, it was nearly two days since Maris had been taken before they approached Dreakskil.

Though they'd stopped both nights, Merle had slept little. The grinding fear in his middle kept him staring at the stars for the few hours he'd allotted his men for rest. On the second night, when they were within hours of Dreakskil, a dream had pulled him from the restless sleep that his body finally accepted; and the content of that dream brought him fully awake.

Terrible foreboding lingered as he struggled to still his pounding heart. He sat upright. The rest of the camp lay still, many of the men snoring, as Merle reached for a leather sack. He pulled parchment, writing utensils and ink, and his wax and seal from the sack's depths.

The moon was bright, and its reflection on the snow-covered hills lent enough light to find what he needed for a letter, but 'twas not enough to write. Merle lit a candle, his insides having settled slightly, but the horrible apprehension that had seized him in his dream did not abate.

He wrote for a long while.

When he had at last finished the missive, and having no sand to sprinkle on the wet ink, he waved the parchment in the cool air, praying that the words would not run. He hadn't the time to write another.

Satisfied that the words were dry and affixed to the paper, he folded it, sealed it with the seal of Langumont, and crept between the sleeping men until he found the one whom he sought.

"Raymond, wake thee!" Merle pulled firmly at the shoulder of the man.

With barely a groan, the knight came wide awake, his eyes unglazed though moments earlier he'd been fast asleep. "Aye, my lord!" He nearly leapt to his feet, hand reaching for his sword.

Merle drew Raymond of Vermille away from the men clustered about the fires to give him terse instructions about the delivery of the missive. "Well I know that you are the greatest asset I may have should we be forced to battle at Dreakskil," he concluded, "yet 'tis this which I place the greatest import upon. Ride fast and hard and place this in my liege's hands if you do no other task for me on this earth."

"Aye, my lord." Raymond nodded solemnly at the trust that was being placed upon him.

"God speed to you." Merle placed a heavy hand on his man's shoulder, then watched in satisfaction as he mounted a powerful destrier and charged through the crisp snow.

'Twas dawning then, and the lord returned his attention to the sleeping army. "*À moi!*" he shouted. "To me, to Langumont!"

The well-trained knights sprang to their feet, instantly awake and wary. Lord Michael and Sir Victor were among the first to mount their horses, and all drew near Merle as he barked out orders.

"On to Dreakskil!" he announced after splitting the group into two smaller parties, placing Michael as leader to one and pulling Maris's betrothed to follow in his steps. "God willing, we'll have my daughter in our hands by noon tide!"

⁓

'Twas good fortune, Dirick thought hazily, that Nick had been well-sated with food and had rested comfortably ere they began their journey, else he may have found himself in more dire straits than he did now.

True, he and his mount had been following what appeared to be the trail of Maris and her companion Agnes for much of the day, but they'd not come upon the two women as of yet…and the sun was beginning to sink into the far trees. Upon leaving Dreakskil in his haste, Dirick had presumed to catch up with them by mid-morn; yet he'd not anticipated that they'd be ahorse. Ahorse! Even his befuddled mind grasped the incredulity of that fact. How, on God's earth, had they managed to sneak a mount from the keep?

There was no doubt that the trail he was following was that of Maris and Agnes: his mind had been functioning well enough at the start to recognize the unmistakeable sweep of two skirts in the snow before the women had mounted the horse.

A wave of weakness coursed through him, and his abused stomach tightened painfully. His only sustenance had been handfuls of snow when he'd cared to stop, and once, a few red berries he'd spied in the crusty white. Fervently praying that they were not poisonous, Dirick had munched on what he could find. They tasted minty and did little to fill his stomach, but were enough to take the staleness from his mouth.

He thought he was hallucinating when he saw smoke curling through the trees; but, urging Nick closer, Dirick caught sight of some type of structure. It was a small building with a neatly thatched roof and well-fitting door. Ignoring the fact that the trail he was following veered well away from the building, Dirick coaxed Nick toward the hut, hoping at the least for a bit to eat.

Nearly falling from his horse's bare back, he stumbled to the door, taken by surprise at the violence of his weakness. The world tilted as he banged a fist upon the sturdy oak.

'Twasn't until that door opened, and the elderly woman's presence registered in his mind, that Dirick allowed his ravaged body to succumb to its infirmity and he sank to the ground.

⁓

Maris drank deeply of the rich venison broth set before her. Its warmth flowed through her body and she sighed with a smile. "'Tis wondrous, Mother Abbess," she told the bewimpled nun.

"An' you have your fill," the woman with the stern, wrinkled face told her. "'Tis glad I am that the Lord saw fit to lead you here, my lady. We've enough passersby that certes aught will come to lead you back to Langumont in safety." The face wrinkled more to express a smile. "I've heard of Langumont, my lady, and of the beauty of the ocean that can be seen from its highest towers. And of its richness, and the skill of its tradesmen."

Maris stifled a smile. Her welcome had been warm, of course, but the intensity of the abbess's friendliness, and her personal attention, indicated her hopes for a generous donation to the sisters and their work. The older woman was as shrewd as Lord Merle when it came to bettering her estate and caring for her charges. "'Tis certain my papa will express his gratitude for your hospitality on my return to Langumont," Maris told her. Then she turned her attention to more pressing matters. "My maid, Agnes—where have you settled her for the night, then?" Of the two of them, 't had been Agnes who'd succumbed more readily to the elements, and she'd been nearly frozen when they were lucky enough to come upon the abbey just before sunset.

"Sister Gracia made a pallet for your woman in the infirmary. She'll be cared for there until we are certain the dangers of frost-bite are past. I've had a chamber prepared for you, my lady, and you may bathe before retiring. You may wish to join us in the chapel for the evening vigil. 'Tis announced by the tolling of the bells."

"Many thanks, Mother, yet I'd prefer to say my confession in my chamber and bathe before I sleep. I fear I'm more exhausted than I realized!"

"Of course, my dear." The abbess patted her hand. "I'll call for Father Alphonse to see to your confession now, if you've eaten enough, while your bath is prepared."

Maris rose and followed the black-gowned woman as she wound her way through the corridors of the abbey. Though not much lighter than the keep at Dreakskil, the building was warmer and more inviting than that dreary place. And, indeed, Maris's chamber, though not richly furnished, held more welcome than hers at Bon de Savrille's home—mainly because no guard was stationed outside of the door. The bed was smaller, and not as plush, but the bedding was clean and thick and promised heavenly warmth after a long, frigid day of wandering through the countryside. A fire nearly burst through the grated fireplace, easily heating the room, and Maris sighed as she sank onto a stool nearby.

Father Alphonse, summoned by the abbess's servant, arrived to hear her confession. When that was done, and her penance given—Maris did not blink at the large number of paternosters that was her penance; in light of the many lies to Lord Bon and the pain she'd inflicted upon the folk of Dreakskil 'twas a small enough penalty—a tub and buckets of steaming water paraded into the room, carried by quiet and efficient servants.

When the priest had left and one of the servants had assisted Maris with disrobing, she sank gratefully into the generous wooden tub. One of the women sprinkled chamomile flowers over the warm water and Maris inhaled the sweet, calming scent as they steeped in her bath.

As she rested her head back, she felt a folded cloth being inserted between her head and the rough stone wall. The vapor from the tub swirled about her face and she could feel the fear and tension of the last few days easing away as tiny rivulets of sweat trickled down her cheeks. She was safe at last. She sighed and closed her eyes.

They popped open as an image of the agonized face of Dirick de Arlande intruded into her thoughts.

She firmly turned her mind toward the relief of seeing her father again, refusing to let the face of the man who'd betrayed her encroach upon her peace.

Dirick's face, and the fury in his voice as he'd named her "witch," would not be banished, however. Maris shivered, remembering the glint of anger in his grey eyes as she'd yanked free of his grip and swept past him to the steps. She'd felt something akin to remorse as she left him behind, knowing the pain her herb was capable of inflicting. He'd always appeared so large and strong that it disturbed her, for some reason, to see him laid low.

He'd been grey with fatigue and breathing heavily against the agony in his middle. Thick hair clung to the sweat on his face and neck, and Maris remembered how his hand, though gripping her ankle tightly, trembled with the effort. She could not dismiss the memory of the lines of pain that radiated from his eyes and mouth. His lips had been thin and taut…not at all like the full, soft ones that had closed upon her mouth in the stables.

For a moment, she was back there, his arms around her and that mouth devouring hers. She remembered the feel of his fingers grasping handfuls of her hair, pushing up through her scalp…the warmth of his hard body in the chill of the early morning…and the spiraling pleasure curling up into her belly.

Maris jerked her thoughts from their pathway so violently that her body moved in the tub, splashing water onto the floor and startling the servant who sat silently in the corner. *Nay,* she thought to herself, *I cannot have these thoughts of my enemy!*

Pulling upright in the tub, she gestured for the maid to attend her. As the sure fingers of the servant massaged her scalp, spreading a rose-scented soap in her damp hair, Maris allowed her eyes to ease shut again.

Lulled by the fingertips stroking her head, she found herself back in Dirick's arms. His eyes were a silvery grey, flecked with black and fringed with dark lashes, half-closed with desire, his soft, smooth lips moving closer to hers…she could not block the image from her mind.

Abruptly, she was reminded of the anger that emanated from him upon her flight earlier that day. Had he not been so weakened, she would have been frightened of the look of loathing on his handsome face.

Absently, Maris bent her head so that the soap could be rinsed into the tub in front of her. The water trickled down her neck and the sides of her face, spilling into the water. Fear struck her then, nearly causing her to jerk her head back. Had she given too much of the broom? Mayhaps he'd not survived, as she'd promised. Mayhaps she'd risked overmuch in using the potent plant…and even now, Dirick and other innocents could be lying in their death pools.

She shuddered, pushing the thought away. Nay, she'd taken care so as not to make the dose too strong. But the look of agony…and the hatred in his eyes.… Maris swallowed deeply as she was made to stand in the shallow tub. Careful hands soaped her body as she struggled to dismiss the fears and regrets that plagued her mind now that 'twas not occupied with thoughts of escape.

Nay, she decided firmly, she'd not worry over it. Her papa may not have arrived in time, and she could not give pause to regret. What she'd done, she'd done. She'd escaped Dreakskil and would return home to her family.

Banishing the lingering thoughts of Sir Dirick, Maris stepped from the tub and allowed the maid to towel her dry. The fire still roared in the grate, keeping her warm, until a borrowed night shift was slipped over her head. The maid braided the long dark hair then helped Maris climb into the high bed.

Just as she began to slip into sleep, a menacing thought prodded her wide awake. Returning home to Langumont meant returning home to her betrothed.

For an instant—a brief one—Maris contemplated returning to Dreakskil and accepting Lord Bon's offer of marriage. At the least, he was malleable and would do her bidding! Sir Victor was naught but a rough bully.

But, nay, she'd return to Langumont and find some way to dissuade her father from finalizing the betrothal.

Sixteen ❧

Dirick's head swam.

He closed his eyes, then reopened them carefully. Aye, the room was still moving, tilting to one side.

At his movement, a face bent over his. It was a woman's face, aged and covered with the fine, soft hair of the elderly. "Ah, milord, you've come back to this world at last." The voice was gentle and its accompanying smile the same. "Ye gave me quite a scare, lord, for how was I to explain how a dead knight came to be in me home?" Old eyes sparked with humor, but Dirick was too weak to acknowledge it with more than a grunt. "Drink this." She firmly shoved a crude wooden mug of something warm and heavenly-smelling at his mouth and he accepted it gratefully.

She held the cup long enough for him to take several sips, then eased it back.

"My horse?" he was able to ask now that his mouth was moistened.

The woman nodded. "Aye. He's well-tended. He's had more to eat than ye have in the day past."

"A day?" Dirick croaked, struggling to a seated position on his low pallet.

"Aye. Ye came to me yestereve, lord, an' 'twas a struggle to get ye in here when ye chose my doorway to collapse in." Again, the eyes glinted with humor. "But I coulden leave ye there, now could I? 'Twould get to be horrible cold in here for me auld bones if the door weren't shut!"

"Maris!" Dirick followed her name with a grating curse. He'd surely lost her now.

"Ah, aye, ye called for her last even, lord. There weren't no one with ye, that I could see." The head tilted to one side as she looked down upon him. "But she weren't with ye, were she, lord? Ye were after her, for what I know not, but the leaves will tell me. Here ye, drink all of this now, as yer sittin' up." She pushed the mug into his face and brought his hand up to hold it.

Dirick drank the rest of the brew, thankful that the room had righted itself. The old woman, whom he now saw wore a long, heavy gown that dragged the floor, took the cup and peered into its depths. "Ah, aye, I'll look at these in a moment."

He watched as she trundled over to the fire in the grate and stirred something in a large pot. She ladled the pot's contents into a bowl modeled in the same crude fashion as the mug and brought it to him, accompanied with a piece of hard bread and a wooden spoon. Dirick smelled rabbit stew, and his mouth watered instantly when the food came into his presence.

Knowing that he was in need of sustenance before continuing his search for Maris, he fell upon the stew like the starved man that he was. He barely noticed that the old woman was clucking over his empty mug, peering with a tallow candle into its depths, until she began to speak.

"Ahh, aye.… Ye've some grief of late, milord…'tis sad I am to see it." She glanced up at him, then back at the mug. "Yer Papa, 'twas, aye?"

Dirick swallowed a chunk of rabbit meat and stared at the woman. "Aye."

Her white head shook sadly. "Much blood, I see 't…an' evil

'round…spreadin' 'round this land…'tis a madman, I warrant."

"I'll find him," Dirick told her fiercely.

She nodded. "Aye, an' afore more bloodshed, I pray." She turned her attention back to the herb leaves that plastered the bottom of the mug. "An' what of this Maris ye called fer?" The woman spoke more to herself than to Dirick as she frowned into the mug. "Ahh… mmm…. The lady's bound fer some hardship herself, 'though it doesn't 'pear that ye'll be the one to bring it to her."

"Hardship?" Dirick asked. "She's hurt? Lost?" He struggled to pull himself from the bed, hardly daring to credit the fact that he was believing the words from the old crone's mouth.

"Sit yerself, if ye please, milord…yer jarrin' the tea leaves an' I cannot read them," grumbled the woman. "She 'pears to have no evil 'bout her now; fact is, I see naught but calm amongst her leaves. Fer now. She'll soon have a bad time, milord, but 'tis naught ye, or any man, can shield her from. An' ye won' be seein' her to prevent it, so don' be harin' yerself off when yer so weak ye can barely move yerself. It's all over and done with, lord, an' ye won' be seein' 'er," she repeated, waving her hand as if to dismiss him into the bed. "Mmmm…an' I see that she'll soon be safe in the company of many armed men…so ye've naught to worry yerself 'bout, milord."

"I—will I not see her again?" he asked, wondering why he cared.

The woman frowned at the mug, angling the tallow candle over its depths. "Pah!" she spat suddenly.

"What see you?" Dirick demanded.

"Ahh, nay, 'tis only that I dripped a bit of wax onto the leaves," she waved the offending candle in disgust, nearly splattering Dirick himself with hot tallow. "Ye'll see the lady again, milord, but not fer many moons an' 't may not be to yer likin' when ye do. But if ye go easy with the lady, mayhaps…mayhaps ye'll win her."

Dirick snorted and shoved the tattered blanket from his thighs. Go easy with her, he thought nastily, dropping his bare feet to the dirt floor. He had every intention of throttling the life from the wench at the next he saw her…which, if he could stand enough to mount Nick, would be very shortly.

"Milord," chirped the woman in surprise, "ye cannot be well enough betimes to be up an' about!"

"Good woman," Dirick dismissed her fluttering concern as he groped for the boots that rested near his pallet, "I am much thankful for your kindness, but I must be on my way. 'Tis nigh at the time I must see to Lady Maris and get her to safety." He stopped short at the doorway, realizing that he had little to thank her with. "Good woman, I've little to leave you with for gratitude." He dug into the small leather pouch that always hung from his tunic. There was only the cloth-wrapped dagger—the clue to his father's murderer—and a very few small coins. Pinching one from the bottom of the pouch, he pressed it into her hand, promising, "I'll send to you with more as soon as I'm able. I give you many thanks, woman, for caring for me. I'll see that 'tis not forgotten."

The woman took the coin, admonishing, "Milord, ye need-n't be in any such hurry. Ye'll not see the lady in the murderous mood yer in…and 'tis just as well, else ye'd be prone to do or say as ye shouldn't!"

"Again, good woman, I thank you, and I thank you even for your dire predictions," Dirick flashed a brief grin, "but I'll be on my way."

Tsking to herself, the woman followed in his unsteady foot-steps to the doorway, and leaned against the wall as he let him-self into the cold air. "Have a care, milord," she called as he mounted upon Nick. "An' most especially, be yourself ware of the dagger!"

Though it had been nearly a full day since Dirick collapsed at the old woman's hut, it wasn't difficult to pick up the trail left by a tired horse carrying two women. Since there'd been no snow, and the winds were low, he was able to see faint hoofprints and, more than once, the sweep of a skirt in the powdery white.

Thus it was not long before he came upon an abbey. He rode to the entrance gate, hailing for entry. A robed sister accompanied a male serf to the gate and invited him in betimes.

"Sister, I seek a noble woman and her maidservant with only a mount between them," Dirick told her, declining to dismount until he learned if Maris was within.

The nun bowed her head. "You must speak with the Mother Abbess, my lord, an' you seek information about any of our guests. Please come within."

Gritting his teeth, Dirick slid from Nick and handed the reins to the serf. He forced himself to retain a grip on his patience as he followed the calm sister. She trudged so slowly he was tempted to take her arm and yank her along in his wake, but that would certainly not endear him to the Abbess.

In fact, once in front of the stern-looking woman, he managed to state his query in a calm, unhurried manner. He felt the Abbess's look keenly upon him. She did not appear to be fooled by his seeming nonchalance.

"A lady such like you describe did just leave our gates early this morrow," the woman told him. "A party of traveling monks and their escort did pledge to see the lady safely to her lands, as they rode in that direction."

Dirick felt a keen sense of disappointment. Maris was in good hands to be returned to Langumont ,and he no longer had reason to be involved. As it was, Lord Merle's lands lay in the opposite direction as his own liege, and 'twas well past time for Dirick to report on his findings about Bon de Savrille.

Alas, he'd not see Maris of Langumont again…and 'twas only

as he was drifting off to sleep on a pallet in the abbey that he remembered that the words of the old crone had predicted just that.

Nearly a sevennight after she'd been abducted from Langumont, Maris and her escort rode up to the gates of the imposing keep.

"Hail, guard!" she called, urging her mount to the lowered portcullis and separating herself from the rest of the travelers. "Do you raise the gate for me!"

She heard the shout of surprise from the watchman and the sudden scrambling to comply with her wishes. The portcullis rose quickly and easily as the drawbridge came down, and Maris, not waiting for the monks behind her, eagerly cantered across the slanted bridge.

"My lady! My lady!" The shouts and men-at-arms surrounded her so that her horse could go no further.

"We thought you dead, my lady!" cried one of the knights she recognized from her father's retinue.

"My lady, 'tis horrible bad!" another man called, grabbing the bridle of her horse.

Maris slid from the saddle unassisted, smiling profusely, and patting the shoulders of the men she recognized. "But I am here and now all is well," she told them, looking toward the keep. Verily her mama had been informed of her arrival; but there was no sign of anyone coming to greet her except the men in the bailey.

"Nay, nay, my lady!" Bern of Tristoff, the captain of the men-at-arms, urged her forward. "Nay, my lady, all is not well. You must see to your mama, as she is distraught and will not rise from her bed."

"Aye, Bern, I'll see her and she will regain her life as I am safe." She smiled gaily, so glad to be returned home…but none of the men and serfs seemed to share in the joy of her home-coming. "Send to me a messenger and I'll see to Mama." She hurried toward the keep, noting that it seemed oddly quiet for the normal bustle of Langumont. She'd need to send a messenger to find her papa to relay the news that she was returned. But first, she'd kiss her mama and show her that all was well.

"Lady Maris!" Bern dogged her heels, an urgent frown creasing her face. "Lady Maris, 'tis the lord!"

"Aye, I must needs send to him that I am returned—"

"My lady!" The frustration in his voice was not to be ignored and he was at last gratified by his lady's full attention. "Lady Maris, 'tis because of Lord Merle that the lady rises not!"

"Papa? He is here?" Maris's heart leapt for joy and a beatific smile crossed her face. "I'll not need the messenger, then."

"My lady, the lord is dead."

Part II ✤

Seventeen ॐ

"*T*is only right that the king requires my presence at court," Maris told her mother wearily.

"But your papa has been gone for a mere three moons," Allegra wailed, her ever-present handkerchief fluttering to the face that seemed much more weary and old since her husband's death. "Can his majesty not leave us in peace until the mourning period passes?"

Maris shook her head in frustration as she pulled a bolt of finely-woven linen from a trunk. "Mama, you know I must go to the king to pledge mine own fealty to him as heir to Langumont. 'T has been more than time enough since Papa's passing in King Henry's eyes, and, aye, I've no complaint to see my liege anon."

"I'll not go," Allegra told her.

"Aye, Mama, you'll not. 'Tis I who must pledge to my lord. You'll stay here." Maris did not think that her frail mother would last the journey to London. In the last few moons, her grey-streaked hair had become almost pure white and the lines that creased her face bespoke of a great weariness and worry.

"Aye. An' I'll offer a score rosaries a day for your papa's soul." The words came out in a moan.

"Agnes, this green linen I'll have for an overtunic," Maris announced, turning from her mother with relief. She handed the cloth to the woman who'd become an invaluable support since her return to Langumont and the death of its lord.

Taking the bolt, the maid added it to a growing pile of other fine cloths. If the Lady of Langumont was to be summoned to court, she'd be dressed in all the finery and fashion that her position warranted. The seamstresses had been working night and day since the missive from Henry arrived two days earlier, and still Maris delved into the stores of imported fabrics held in Langumont's solar. Since most of her gowns would be made whilst she was at court, to be certain that they were of the latest style, she thought to bring her own fabrics rather than pay the higher price most certainly demanded in London Town.

As Agnes took the cloth, a corner fell and something clattered to the floor. "*Peste!*" Maris exclaimed, reaching under the stool for the object. It was a dagger, and she examined it with interest.

Allegra, brought from her trance of woe by her daughter's unladylike language, sat upright. "I'd forgotten...." she murmured, reaching to take the ornate dagger from Maris.

"How did this come to be in a trunk of cloth?" Maris had not taken her eyes from the silvery dagger, replete with carved roses on its handle.

"'Twas your papa's," Allegra said dreamily, turning the wicked-looking knife around in her hands.

"Papa's?"

"Nay, 'twas a gift of his to me," she explained. Then her eyes became focused again. "You'll take it with you, Maris. He'd want you to have it. An'," she looked piercingly at her daughter, "you may be in need of protection betimes. Ofttimes, court is less safe than a battle field...with its dark, dank hallways and ears that listen betwixt the walls."

"Aye, Mama." Maris took the dagger gingerly. 'Twould be no hardship to have such a means of protection hidden under her skirts. She, at the least, was under no illusion as to the dangers of the king's court. Too, she was surprised and relieved to see aught other than pain and sorrow in her mother's eyes for nearly the first time since her return to Langumont. She leaned over and pressed a light kiss to her mother's worn face. "God willing, I'll see his majesty and return to your side before two moons," she told Allegra.

જી

London!

Maris straightened in her saddle, straining to take in all she could of the bustling city. The streets were narrow, beaten paths, lined with buildings and strewn with refuse. Hawkers selling their wares crowded between the people on foot and darted out from under the hooves of well-reined mounts.

'Twas even louder than she'd expected, and much dirtier. But, to Maris's innocent eyes, there was beauty in the variety of people that filled the streets. Since she rode Hickory, she had no concern of treading in the garbage that was everywhere. Instead, she gawked like the country girl that she was as Raymond of Vermille led the entourage from Langumont to the king's palace.

When he rode up beside her, she beamed upon him a smile rare since her father's death. "'Tis wondrous loud," Maris commented.

"Aye, my lady, loud and filthy," Sir Raymond responded. "And unsafe, Lady Maris. You'll not venture out without several guards." His words were the merest tentative as he well knew that she was used to coming and going as she pleased. Thus, he was gratified when Maris nodded in agreement. "I've sent Sir Garrek with the news of your arrival to his majesty. 'Twill certes be some days before the king will see you."

"Aye. 'Twill be time to settle and learn my way of the palace. Methinks I'll have chambers within and near the other ladies." Maris's attention was drawn to a vendor dressed in unusual garb: dusty, draping clothing and a headdress of cloth wound around his head and face. The man's wares did not interest her; but the small furry creature that perched on his shoulder caused her to rein in Hickory for a closer look. "Sir Raymond, look you at that creature!"

The knight paused beside his mistress, "Aye, my lady. 'Tis called a monkey and comes from afar, mayhaps from Jerusalem itself."

The other men-at-arms drew themselves near Maris and Raymond, causing a large blockage of the street with their mounts and the cart which carried Agnes and all of the trunks brought from Langumont. "My lady," Raymond attempted to pull her attention from the creature that held her fascination, "let us on to the castle. We can return to the market when you wish, and, I trow, you'll see more than a mere monkey!"

Gathering her dignity about her, Maris nodded regally. She could gawk and stare at the sights of London Town at another time; now, alas, she would heed Sir Raymond and proceed onward.

The party gained entrance within the bailey walls of Westminster and Sir Raymond helped Maris alight from her mount. Inside the castle, the Great Hall of which had been built by William the Conquerer himself, the steward greeted the Lady of Langumont and directed her to the chambers she would inhabit near the other wards of the king.

"Ward of the king!" Maris muttered to herself, her full lips twisting into a frown. 'Twas the first she'd realized her new position, and its implications shook her composure as she followed a page through the intricate hallways of the palace. The king's ward was his to do with as he wished, to marry to whomever he desired a political alliance with, or give as a reward to a faithful vassal. He could even, Maris gasped to herself, require that she remain a permanent member of the royal court until such time as he chose to bestow her person—nay, her lands—upon some greedy lord that was not of her choosing.

Yet—her heart's pounding slowed its breakneck pace—she was betrothed; she was safe—was she not? If her papa had signed the betrothal contract, 'twould be no easy task for even the King of England to go against the Church and annul a betrothal agreement, even though no betrothal vows had been spoken.

Maris came from her private musings as the page stopped at a large oaken door and bowed her entrance. She realized she had no idea how they'd come through the twisting halls of the castle to these chambers and turned questioningly to the page.

Before she could speak, the young boy said, "Your maid and trunks will be brought to you, my lady. When you wish to go to the hall for dinner, you have only to send for me or another of the pages and we will happily guide you within." And then, with a little bow, he was gone.

᠅

Maris smoothed the cloth-of-gold fabric of her wimple and swallowed hard. She hadn't realized she'd feel so nervous before seeing the king—and her trepidation was heightened by the fact that she'd barely received the trunks in her chambers when Henry summoned her to his presence.

The page who brought the message was not the one who'd escorted her only an hour earlier. He was slightly older than his predecessor—mayhaps nine or ten years—and he wore his dignity about him like a bishop. Maris bade him wait in the hallway whilst she and Agnes tried frantically to make her presentable enough to appear in the royal presence without benefit of a bath to wash the dirt from travel, nor the opportunity to press the wrinkles from her gowns. As it was, the boredom and disdain of the page—who, despite his minimal height, seemed to look down upon her—spurred Maris to leave the chambers with her hair still merely braided and her traveling shoes still upon her feet.

Now, waiting just on the other side of the door leading to Henry's court, she regretted her haste. The wimple covered her simple braid—only a few wisps of hair straggled about her face—but the toes of her shoes were stained and worn and peeped from beneath the skirts of her best gown. The gown itself would do—although the brief glimpses Maris had seen of other ladies of the court told her that it was seriously out of fashion—for 'twas a brilliant gold that shimmered as she moved, with long sleeves that opened nearly to the ground at her wrists. A dark red overtunic—matching the garnets that she wore in a heavy neck-let—fitted over the gown and displayed the talents of the seam-stresses at Langumont, who'd labored over its gold and green embroidery for days. The gown had been intended for her betrothal ceremony and, in spite of its out of date style, was certainly fit for meeting her sovereign.

She was just beginning to fidget nervously when the doors opened and yet another page gestured for her to enter. Standing regally, although her heart was pounding, Maris followed him into the room, swallowing heavily.

Henry stood directly to her left near a large, gilt chair. He was a handsome man, she thought to herself, with his reddish hair and muscular build. Maris drew near, noting that the chamber was empty of people other than her king and the page who'd summoned her.

"My liege," she murmured, sweeping into a full curtsey before him with her forehead nearly to the ground. Her skirts pooled around her and she covertly adjusted them to cover her shoes.

"Maris of Langumont." The king's voice was booming but kind. She could almost hear a smile in its timbre as he continued, "Rise, child, I've long waited to meet the daughter of the loyal

Merle of Langumont."

Though he was a mere four years her elder, somehow it was appropriate that the stunning, powerful man before her call her 'child.' "Thank you, your grace," Maris told him as she pulled lightly to her feet. "I've long wished to meet you as well, sire," she said, emboldened by the warmth in his blue eyes.

"We were aggrieved to hear of your father's demise," Henry told her in his regal voice. "'Twas unfortunate that one of my most loyal vassals should die in an attempt to retrieve his kidnapped daughter."

"Aye, your grace." Maris's voice cracked with pain. "My father was well-loved and 'tis a tragedy that he should be felled by an arrow during my rescue, most especially since I had already made my escape."

"Ah, yes." Henry nodded. "Most unfortunate, my dear lady Maris. Yet, 'twas quite enterprising of you to have made your own escape." Before she could respond, he beckoned to the shadows. "Well, Dirick, now you have seen that indeed the lady lives. Are you well satisfied?"

Maris froze. A tall figure stepped from a dark corner behind the king, metamorphosing into the familiar person of Dirick de Arlande. The blood drained from her face and she felt a pounding in her temple take its place. Clenching her fists into the folds of her skirt, she turned to the king.

"With respect, my lord," she said, keeping her eyes from the man who drew near the throne, "you harbor a traitor in these chambers!"

"Traitor?" Henry's fine red eyebrows rose in question. "Treason is a very serious charge, my lady. Are you certain?"

"Aye, your grace." Maris darted an angry glance at Dirick, then returned to the king. "'Tis this man who plotted with my kidnapper after lulling my father into complacence during his stay at Langumont!"

The barest hint of a smile playing about his lips, Henry turned. "Dirick, what say you to these accusations?"

"My liege," Dirick kept his voice steady. How dare she accuse him of treachery in the presence of the king—and how dare the king play this game with him! "You are as well aware as I that I was at Dreakskil at your behest and became accidentally entangled in this nightmare!"

Maris gasped. Whirling to face him, she countered, "Sir Dirick, how then do you explain your stay at Langumont if 'twere not to plot against myself and my father?"

"Lady Maris," Dirick drew his imposing self face to face with his accusor, "'t may come as an enlightenment to you that the entire kingdom does not revolve about you in its every working, and that I may have had other reasons for availing myself of your father's hospitality!"

"And what was I to think, then, when you were one of the gawkers at whose feet I was cast by my kidnappers? You, who made no move to assist me, even to the extent of breaking into my chamber—"

"Lady Maris, I do not believe this conversation need continue here." Dirick's mellow voice carried a hint of warning.

She drew herself up, suddenly aware that she stood shrieking like a harpy in the king's chambers. "Well said, Sir Dirick." She lowered her eyes as mortification swept over her. "*I* have no wish to continue this conversation at any other time," she muttered to herself.

"I beg your pardon, my lady?" asked Henry, the trace of a smile still cinching his face.

"'Twas of no import, my liege." She gave a small curtsey.

Henry glanced at Dirick, who stood tall and stiff next to him, then turned his regal gaze back onto Maris. "About this charge of treason, my lady. You do realize that the sentence for this crime is hanging?"

She swallowed, refusing to look at the dark-haired man who stared at her with brooding eyes. "Your grace, I—I may have misspoke myself and—and may not have fully considered the situation. I withdraw my accusation—for the time being," she added with bravery, still keeping her gaze averted from Dirick.

The king nodded. "Aye, my lady, I think that a wise decision." He stroked his beard with thick fingers as if deep in thought. "You'll pledge your fealty to me three days hence, Maris of Langumont."

The king would have continued speaking had there not been an urgent knocking upon the chamber door. The sole page left in the room hurried to answer it, and Henry looked on curiously.

"Your grace!" A royal messenger entered and swept toward the king, his bow fluid and elegant.

"Rise, Merren, and tell what brings you in such haste."

"Your highness, I bring terrible news!" The lanky messenger scraped another quick bow, waiting for permission to continue.

Henry's gaze flickered over Maris, who watched in interest, and met Dirick's stare. "My lady, you may return to your chambers. I will expect to see you at supper this eventide—in fact, why do you not find your place as my guest anight?"

"I—I thank you, my liege," she managed to stammer, stunned by his invitation and disappointed that she would not hear what terrible news the messenger brought. Picking up her skirts, she turned, keeping her look averted from Dirick, who now leaned casually against the king's chair.

'Twas that posture, and his hard, dark contemplation that followed her movements, that confirmed a fear settling in her mind. She made a curtsey to the king and walked unhurriedly to the chamber door, acting for all the world as if she had not conducted herself the complete fool in front of her liege lord. Maris felt rather than heard the heavy door close behind her and she released her breath in a forceful whoosh of relief.

"My lady?"

The voice from behind startled Maris. She whirled, embarrassed at being observed in such an informal state. A woman, mayhaps some years younger than her, hovered near one of the torches that lit the hall. "Yes?" Maris recovered and looked imperiously at her.

"I am sorry to have disturbed you." The woman smiled, and a huge dimple cut her round cheek. "'T can oft be unnerving in the presence of our lord, aye?"

Maris nodded, uncertain whether this cheery-looking woman was trying to be friendly or looking for gossip to spread amongst the other ladies of the court.

The other woman gave a little curtsey. "I am Lady Laurette of Ungton, ward of the king and lady in waiting to Queen Eleanor. Her highness bade me bring you to her, Maris of Langumont, upon your dismissal by the king." She gestured toward one of the hallways leading from the entrance to the royal chambers.

"Queen Eleanor?" Somehow, the thought of meeting that great lady was far more imposing than meeting her husband. "What would the queen wish of me?" Maris found herself falling into step alongside the other woman. "I've only just arrived at Winchester this day."

Laurette gave a dainty shrug. "I am not privy to her majesty's intentions, but had I to make a guess, I'd expect she should like to determine if you'll do in her court. Come, now, she awaits—and her highness is not known for her patience."

Eighteen ❧

*T*he harsh wind whipped, stinging Dirick's cheeks and nose. He pulled the fur lining of his cloak closer, burying his mouth into its warmth. Merren, the royal messenger, rode just ahead of him, setting the urgent pace.

There was a need for haste, else he'd still be at court and, at this time, most likely be partaking of a warm, filling meal in the Great Hall. Course upon course of food prepared for the purpose of impressing the king would be served to his court. Jesters and troubadours would take their turn at entertaining the ladies and lords who gathered at the king's behest—including, he reminded himself, the lately arrived Maris of Langumont.

Even in the frigid winter air, the thought of that woman made his blood boil! She had more brash than a stallion in heat, and more feminine guile than his royal queen Eleanor. The manner in which Maris had turned those wide golden-brown eyes toward his sovereign and blithely declared Dirick a traitor…and then, mere moments later, simpering that 't had been an error…. God's nails, the daft woman was out to see him hanged!

It had been most fortuitous that he'd been in Henry's presence when news of Maris's arrival was brought to the royal chamber. Dirick had apprised his liege of the events that took place at Langumont and at Dreakskil, leaving out the description of her last revenge upon him. Henry had called for Maris to attend him, to Dirick's surprise, and had invited him to stay whence she came.

Mayhaps 't hadn't been the most prudent decision to obscure himself in the shadows…but, truth to tell, he'd wanted to see her…to look upon her to assure himself she was as he remembered.

Beautiful…aye, she was still the beauty his mind had conjured and conjured again over the past several moons. Even travel-weary and worn as she must have been, and dressed in fashions that the court had not seen since King Stephen, Maris of Langumont would have outshone any other lady at court had one been there to see her. Mayhaps the exception would be Her Highness Eleanor…but his Maris would indeed cause all to look twice or thrice at her, even in the presence of the queen.

His Maris? Dirick wrenched his head as if to shake off the thought. From where had such a notion sprouted? Aye, the woman was beautiful…and spirited…and resourceful…and, aye, intelligent—though most men would not consider that an asset—but she did not—*could* not—belong to him. 'Twas best that he disabuse himself of that notion at the outset. Nor could he allow her to overset him as she nearly did in the king's chambers. He'd had to keep a firm rein on himself to keep from throttling the wench.

It occurred to Dirick, just then, how many times he'd privately vowed to strangle Maris of Langumont and he gave a little laugh. 'Twas just the remedy he needed to cure himself of her beauty: the reminder of his constant temptation to murder the wench!

"My lord," Merren's voice came to him over his thoughts. "Draw near me now and I'll show you the scene."

All thoughts of Maris driven from his mind, Dirick urged Nick abreast of the messenger's mount. "The bodies are here?"

"Aye, lord, there." Merren pointed to two lumps that were covered with a smattering of snow.

Dirick approached the bodies of Sir Harris of Bristol and his squire, the news of whose deaths had interrupted the king's audience with Maris. When Henry learned that they had been found in a state similar to that of Harold of Derkland, and the other lord whose death scene had been described to Dirick by a messenger from Derkland, he'd sent his man posthaste to the scene of the murders.

Now, Dirick dismounted, commanding Nick to stay, and gingerly moved toward the larger body. The new snow that covered the man was not heavy enough to obliterate the splashes of blood that colored the old, crusty snow. Nor was the posture of the man, and that of his squire, to be mistaken.

'Twas just as it had been described in the earlier events: both men were face-down, sprawled on the ground, with their arms bent awkwardly above their heads, each hand meeting that of the other man. It looked as though they'd fallen from some great height while clasping each other's wrists. Sir Harris's neck was broken, and slit so that his head flopped back eerily onto his shoulders, blank eyes gaping up into the falling snow.

~

"Here, my lady." Agnes knelt at Maris's feet, holding a finely-crafted leather slipper.

Maris slid a foot into the embroidered shoe, then the other into a second. "'Tis a good fit," she mused. "I was not so certain in light of the haste of my order, but Lady Laurette assured me the shoemaker would meet my needs."

"Aye, and the tailor as well," nodded her maid as she stood to survey her mistress. "The gown becomes you, lady."

"At the least 'tis more stylish," Maris replied with a shrug;

but she was more pleased than her words indicated. Upon Lady Laurette's suggestion, she'd retained a tailor and his seamstresses to create a gown from the store of material she'd brought from Langumont. Now, only a day after her arrival, she looked more like the other ladies that clustered about the queen in her chambers: the undertunic and bliaut were cut to fit more closely than her old gowns. The girdle of gold links wrapped thrice about her waist and hips, and its ends dangled nearly to the floor. And the sleeves of her pine-hued bliaut were so long and wide that Agnes had tied knots in the ends of them so that Maris would not tread upon the yellow and orange embroidery that decorated their cuffs.

A heavy necklet of rubies and one large emerald sat about her neck, and three rings adorned her hands. 'Though Maris declined to wear such amounts of jewelry at Langumont, Allegra had warned that she must decorate herself so at court, else the strength and wealth of her title be questioned. Agnes had plaited her long walnut-colored hair into four braids and closed them into heavy gold cases, then covered her head with a fine gold veil.

A knock came at the door and the maid opened it to find Lady Laurette, Lady Monique of Trysdon, and a young page. Maris hurried from the room to join her companions on the trek to the Great Hall.

A trek it was, Maris smiled to herself, as she stepped into stride with Lady Laurette. She wondered how long it had taken the page—a young boy not more than eight years of age—to learn his way from the various chambers through the warren of dark, dank halls to the public areas of the castle.

Upon entering the Great Hall, Maris, Laurette and Monique left their guide and made their way to the trestle tables where Eleanor's other ladies-in-waiting were seated. After her brief audience with the beautiful but austere queen, Maris had been given a firm royal invitation—which amounted to nothing less than an order—to join Eleanor's court until further notice.

The ladies had to pass in front of the royal dais as they wended their way through the rows of tables and hoards of self-seeking courtiers. Intent upon her feet and their placement, Maris did not look up at the royal couple and their supper guests until Lady Laurette swept a curtsey in front of the queen.

"Your Majesty," Maris murmured, curtseying first to Eleanor and then to Henry. As she straightened, her gaze fell upon a tall figure looming just behind the king.

Dirick's stare bored into her and she wondered that she hadn't felt its weight before now. Lashes sweeping down to shutter her eyes, Maris turned coolly away.

As her heart thumped in her throat, she gathered her skirts and followed Laurette and Monique when they turned from the dais. This was the first she'd seen of Dirick since their meeting in the king's chambers, and the intense look in his eyes caused her middle to clench.

Even as she took her seat, gracefully swinging her gown over the hewn-log bench, the image of his solemn, brooding face was foremost in her mind. He looked tired, she noted to herself as she took the bread trencher Laurette passed to her. His face was drawn and lines creased his lean, tan cheeks. Thick, dark hair was pulled unstylishly from his face and tied with a thong at the nape of his neck. Under the pretext of turning to fill her cup with wine, Maris sneaked another look at him and was startled to find his piercing look still trained upon her. Again, she turned away, but not before she swept her gaze along the length of his long body. One sleeve of his undertunic had fallen back to the elbow, revealing the hardness of his well-toned, tanned forearm. The memory of those hard muscles wrapped around her in the stables at Langumont snapped into her mind and she drowned the thought with a hasty quaff of wine.

'Twas her misfortune that the swallow of sweet red wine

choked her, and she was forced to turn, coughing, from the table. Once she'd regained her composure, a quick peek at the dais revealed that a complacent smirk had settled on his face as he looked down haughtily on her.

Feeling the warmth of a flush spread through her cheeks, Maris leaned toward Monique and Laurette, forcing herself to concentrate on their conversation.

"Aye, an' not too telling upon the eyes," Monique was giggling.

"Are you acquainted with him?" asked Laurette of Maris. "The tall man near the king seems to find our table of interest."

Her blush renewing, Maris shook her head and took a nibble of roasted pheasant. "He and I have met but briefly, and did not find each other to our liking."

"Methinks there is little *not* to like!" Monique sent a warm smile toward the dais. "Who is he? Pray, should you arrange an introduction, I'd be well-pleased."

"Dirick of Arlande," Maris told them tartly, still smarting from his cocky grin, "is naught but an arrogant, rude, man-at-arms with little to his name but a fine destrier, which he no doubt won in some lucky moment of combat. He's naught to bring you, Monique, but lies and tricks!"

"And a trick from him would be no hardship, I trow!" The other woman fluttered disgustingly-long lashes and a slow wink at the man in question.

Maris rolled her eyes and helped herself to a soft-roasted turnip, ignoring the pang in her middle. The man was insufferable—and she still had no reason to believe that he hadn't participated gladly in her abduction—confidante of the king or nay! Yet, her gaze continued to wander toward the dais of its own accord.

She was just beginning to rejoin the conversation and enjoy her meal when a heavy hand was placed on her shoulder.

"My Lady Maris," purred a familiar voice. "'Tis glad I am to see you in full possession of your health."

Startled, she looked up to see Victor d'Arcy with a cold smile on his face.

కా

Dirick stuffed a large chunk of bread into his mouth, watching through slitted eyes as Victor d'Arcy approached Maris. An unaccountable surge of dislike oozed through him at the sight of the man with the beacon-colored hair. There was something about the way he moved...the way he laid a hand so familiarly upon her shoulder...that made Dirick uneasy.

The sound of the queen's husky, pleasant laugh rang next to him, and she leaned closely enough to speak in his ear. An exotic scent wrapped around his consciousness, drawing him reluctantly from his thoughts. "What ails you, Dirick?" Eleanor asked. "You act as though you'd eaten a lemon!"

He turned to her, smiling. Eleanor was not one to mince words! "Naught, your grace, of any import. 'Tis only that I hoped to be closer to finding the man who has murdered my father—and the other men."

The queen's smile faded. "Aye, 'tis worrisome to my husband as well. But he has great faith in you, sir, and I trow 'tisn't misplaced." The creases in her white forehead smoothed as she looked down at the table where her ladies sat. "Why do you not take your mind from such evil thoughts and join my women? They should always enjoy a knight with your penchant for poetry, and I have seen you cast your eyes that way more than once this even!"

Unease curled in his stomach at the thought of facing Maris with the trite, empty phrases praising the lips and hair and forms of other women. He'd become quite popular with the ladies of the queen's famous Court of Love years earlier, when his liege traveled to Aquitaine to woo Eleanor. Somehow, he could not picture Maris receiving such superficial praises without making him feel a fool. "Pray, your grace, excuse me from fulfilling your request anight. I am rather weary, and fear that my skills may desert me under such duress."

Eleanor looked at him shrewdly. "Dirick de Arlande," a smirk curved her well-shaped mouth, "do you not feed me such a lie! The day that your skill with women deserts you is the day I cannot hold a man to me, should I wish to do so!" Despite her confident words, they both knew that her loyalty to the king was unequivocal. Her eyes twinkled as she made a little moue with her lips and pressed a long-nailed finger onto his forearm. "Your disinterest can only mean one thing, I trow."

As he was well and truly a man, Dirick could not help but respond to the feminity of his queen. "Aye, your grace, and it 'twould be only this: that as you, my lady, are well beyond my reach, I have no stomach to play meaningless games with women who can be naught to me." His charming smile may have fooled a less artful woman, but Eleanor was well known not only for her beauty, but her cunning and intelligence as well.

"Ah, Dirick, such pretty words trip from your beautiful mouth! I do envy the woman who finally steals your heart!" She took a sip of wine from her native lands, her thick-lashed eyes watching him steadily over the rim of the cup. When she replaced the goblet, the expression on her face had changed from that of a coquette to one of certain knowledge. "An', by the rood, 't has happened at last." Before he could open his mouth, she placed a hand over his, "Save your protestations, Dirick. Though the Courts of Love over which I've ruled consist of worshipful love from afar and knights honorably laving attention upon ladies out of their realm, I believe there is a place for a more earthy, reachable love—such as I have with my lord." A smile hovered over her face. "Aye, Dirick, even love can be found in such an alliance as that of the Angevin and the Aquitaine."

"Your grace—"

"You have long been loyal to my husband, and, through him, to me. Though Henry oft does not see what is before his eyes, and may neglect to reward those who are true to him, I do not." Her glance flicked to the table of her ladies, casting over them as if to measure the possibility of whom he loved. "You'll have her, Dirick. I will see to it."

"But I did not say that I love her! I do not love her!" he stammered, feeling overwhelmed by Eleanor's all-knowing demeanor. "And I have not sought only one of your ladies out—how can you know this?"

She laughed her husky laugh again. "If 'tis true love, you shall not be able to hide it from me—or anyone who cares enough to watch. You'll have her, Dirick, unless she is promised to another." And with that, she turned from him to rejoin her husband's conversation.

Nineteen ॐ

Wall sconces were the only light, and they cast flickering shadows upon the rough stone walls.

Despite the lack of natural illumination, the hallway was well-enough lit for Maris to see the glint in Victor's eyes. Her hand rested reluctantly on his forearm, as it had since he'd led her from the Great Hall, and she walked sedately beside him.

Maris couldn't help but remember the last time she'd been alone with Victor—the time she'd raced her horse across the fields of Langumont in a rash challenge to his manhood. A little shiver raced up her spine as she relived the humiliating moments when his mouth invaded hers, and his hands groped her breasts.

"Have you taken a chill, my lady?" His voice was smooth and mellow with concern. "Take my mantle." They paused beneath one of the sconces as he slid the cloak from his shoulders.

His hands, cold and rough, brushed her chin as he pulled the fur-lined wool about her, taking much too long with the fastening at her throat. A finger brushed the line of her jaw, then slid underneath her chin, lifting firmly into the softness to raise her face. "You've yet to cast your eyes upon me this night, my wife." With a slight movement, he shifted his finger and the nail pressed into her skin. "If I did not know better, I should say you are disappointed at my presence."

Maris swallowed and attempted to keep her voice steady in her reply. "Aye, I confess, 'twas a surprise to see you here. As you've made no chance to contact me since Papa's…demise," her voice became scratchy with pain, "I had no choice but to presume you'd decided against our betrothal."

A smile that was by no means meant to be soothing crossed his face. "Ah, you'd like that, would you not, Lady Maris? You'd like nothing more than to see me walk away from the riches and power that Langumont would bring me!" His hand opened and slid down to cup her throat. She swallowed again and felt the constricting band of his fingers.

"Nay," she whispered, then gave a little cry as the hand tightened—not enough to cut off her breath, but enough to threaten her. When she reached up to pull those fingers away, he was quick enough to snatch her wrists and force them down between their bodies.

"If you were not to be my wife," he murmured, bending closer to her face, "I'd not have this at my pleasure." His lips were cool and dry, but his tongue thrust hot and wet into her mouth.

Maris gave a soft groan and struggled to turn her face aside. His hand tightened, holding her head immobile as his mouth continued to delve into hers. She allowed her body to slacken in his grip, then rammed a knee into his groin. Taking advantage of his shock and pain, she jerked away and groped beneath her overtunic for her dagger.

As he straightened from his doubled over position, Victor was met with a glinting blade that rose with the level of his eyes. "Bitch!" he hissed, clumsily swiping at her wrist.

Maris easily avoided his lunge, but did not turn her attention from him as she began to back away. "If I am so unfortunate as to be forced to wed with you, you will never touch me in that manner again. Else," she slowed her gasping breaths, "you'll find a third party joining us in the bridal bed." She brandished the dagger.

Victor would have grabbed for her wrist again had the sound of voices not reached their ears. As it was, he pinned her with a look filled with hatred before swiveling on his heel and starting off in the direction from whence they'd come.

Miraculously, the approaching voices faded away, leaving Maris alone in the dank hallway. She ripped Victor's mantle from her shoulders, flinging it into a corner. A tapestry fluttered against the wall above her head, but all else was still. She slumped against the cold stone, relieved, and struggled to stop the trembling that had suddenly attacked her.

"Bis!" came a voice from the shadows. "Well done, my lady."

Maris whirled to see Dirick materializing from darkness yet again. "You!" she gasped, fury lighting her face.

He stood, lazily leaning against the wall, arms folded nonchalantly across his middle. "'Twas a close one, that, Maris. I was nearly ready to step in to assist you." The hardness in his grey eyes belied his seeming ease, and his look covered her as if to assure himself she was unharmed.

"What do you here?" she demanded, stepping back and finding the rough wall behind her. She angled the blade of the dagger as if to ward him off.

Dirick stepped closer, blocking the light from the torch behind him. Maris's heart bumped in her throat and her breath became shallow. "I suspected you might find yourself in danger when you left the hall in his presence."

"I do not need your help," she hissed. "I want nothing from you!"

"Ah. But I want something from you, Lady Maris."

Her heart leapt, and sweat sprang from her palms. His eyes were so very dark and hard, gleaming with something intent, undefinable; and the hard set of his mouth bespoke of little patience. His calm intensity frightened her as Victor's rough anger had not. She edged the dagger in warning. "What—what is it you want?"

"A great many things, Maris...." He stepped into the pool of light, drawing close enough that the dagger's blade wavered near his shoulder. "But my greatest desire is to hear an apology on your lovely lips." Suddenly, his hand shot out and closed around her wrist. Knowing the futility of struggle, she allowed the dagger to fall from nerveless fingers and it clattered to the floor.

She looked up at him, unable to speak...overwhelmed by the effect his nearness was having upon her.

"Come now, Maris, it cannot be that words have failed *you*!" His smile was arrogant, then faded into harshness. "On the last we met, you accused me of treason in the presence of my sovereign...and, on the time before that, you left me to die in a pool of my own leavings."

"I did not leave you to die!" she burst out, heedless of his anger. "I am a healer and I knew what I did!"

He quirked an eyebrow, "Oh, aye, 'tis what you say when faced with the other option of admitting you tried to kill me!" He leaned forward, engulfing her in his commanding presence. "And did I not pull your body from an icy river? And you repay me by attempting murder...and, failing that, by trying to see me hanged for treason?" His fingers tightened around her wrist. "I should be praised for not choking the life out of you, woman!"

"Leave me be!" She wrenched away from him.

But he was quicker and snared her arm, jerking her back so that she slammed against his broad chest. When Maris's body connected with his, the fury in his eyes drained away to be replaced with an odd light. "Oh, nay, my sweeting, you'll not get away that easily!" His other hand closed over her shoulder, firmly but without pain. "I've been waiting quite some time to exact my vengeance for the dirty trick you played on me at Dreakskil...and since an apology does not seem to be forthcoming, I may have to demand a...a boon, my lady, a boon." His lips softened as he searched her eyes with his own.

"Dirick—"

"Ahh, 'tis sweet to hear my name on your lips." Then, he was devouring her mouth, tasting it as if he'd been without food for moons. And as she slackened in his arms, and began to kiss him back, he felt as though he had been starved without the essence of her.

Her body was slim and fragile in his hands—hands that quickly relearned the smooth curve of her hips and the silkiness of her skin, rough hands that rasped over the tender line of her jaw, brushing their knuckles against her ear, trailing a fingertip down the sleek line of her neck. They plucked at the veil that covered her thick, wavy tresses, freeing them from their confines and loosing them from the intricate braids that held them prisoner.

Maris sighed against his mouth and pressed against him, drawing a lost moan from the depths of his throat. He smelled of wine and smoke from the fire, of horses and leather, of wool and a tinge of sweat, of…maleness. She could not help herself, but reached to touch the thick, dark hair that had come loose from its leather thong, dipping like the smooth wing of a raven into his face, and found that it was heavy and soft. With light fingertips, she tucked the lock behind his ear and allowed her hand to fall along his neck and rest on the hard plateau of his chest. She felt the roughness of the cold stone wall against her back, and the heat building from his body against her breasts, hips, and thighs. The heat became more intense when one large hand slid, cupped, to hold one of her breasts, closing over its firmness, to thumb over her thrusting nipple, to gently massage its heaviness.

"God in heaven," he breathed into her ear, forcing his hands to return to the relative safety of cradling her head. "Maris, you make me lose my anger, you do…. Try as I may, I cannot forget you." He pulled away enough to look down into her green- and gold-flecked eyes. They were wide, dazed, and hot, and he forgot the decorum of the apology he'd meant to offer, instead, pulling her to his mouth yet again.

This time it was she who pulled away as the force of her passion overwhelmed her, and Maris stood motionless as her breathing began to slow. "You say you came to save me," her voice was husky, "yet I do not know that the danger has passed even now." She turned, bending to pick up the veil lying crushed on the floor, stunned by the desire she'd felt…and afraid of what it meant. Even if 'twere aught more than passion, they could never act on it. Maris forced her voice to steadiness, hardness. "'Twas not so great a boon you asked, Sir Dirick, as I have been groped by no less than two other men…both of which, verily, had more claim to do so than yourself."

He stepped back as if slapped. Then his face darkened, ominous in the half-light. "I am well aware that I have no claim to you…nor, do you not misunderstand, do I wish to." Dirick stepped aside, rigid in his stance. "I'll not bother you with my presence any longer than to see you safely to your chamber." He bent to pick up the dagger lying harmlessly in the pool of light.

When he straightened, the fierce look in his eyes was enough to make her back away. Those grey eyes glittered with anger and hatred such that she knew it would haunt her dreams. "What is it?" she breathed, her hand going to her throat as his hand shot out to grab her arm.

"Where did you get this?" His face filled her vision, his breath rasping in short drags. "Tell me, where did you get this dagger?"

"I—'twas Papa's," she stammered, drawing as far away as his grasp would allow. "Release me!"

"How did he come by it?" Dirick ignored her demand, staring at the silver-handled dagger as if he'd seen a ghost.

Maris tried to jerk away, but her puny strength was naught

against his ferocity. "I do not know! What is it to you?" she cried, becoming truly afraid. "You are bruising me, Dirick!"

With a sudden oath, as if he'd realized his actions, he released her arm. She backed off, rubbing the spot he'd gripped and staring at him as if he were a stranger. In truth, she didn't know him at that moment.

"Where did you get this dagger?" he asked again, controlled but still intent upon the small weapon.

"As I said, 'twas my papa's! I found it in a trunk when I packed to come to court," Maris explained. Still wary of his sudden temper, she sidled along the wall.

"Do not fear; I'll not harm you again," he told her wearily. He looked at her. "If I replace it for you, may I keep this?"

She shook her head, "Nay, please do not ask that of me. 'Tis one of few things I have left from Papa." They both knew that he would keep it if he liked, so when he handed it back to her, she breathed a sigh of relief.

"I did not ever express my sorrow at your father's death," Dirick said, his face grave. "He was a good man."

Maris nodded, sudden tears choking her throat. She'd become adept at stopping the tears of grief, now, more than three moons since Papa's death…but the pain had not lessened. "I miss him terribly," she admitted, even as she wondered why she shared that with Dirick.

"As I do my father."

Maris looked at him in surprise, realizing she knew nothing of his family, and struck that they should share the commonality of the loss of a parent.

"A knife such as this—the likes of which I've never seen before or since—was found at the scene of a murder…and that murder scene was identical to the one at which my father was found." Dirick's eyes held a sober pain. "At the king's behest, I am searching for the man who has now killed seven people, leaving behind three scenes of the most senseless slaughter in England."

"I've heard naught of such killings," she told him.

He nodded. "An' I trow you'll hear little else. Do you not speak of this to anyone until the man is found...I do not wish him to know that I am on his trail. Come," he was suddenly abrupt, "I will take you to your chamber."

Ignoring Victor's cloak, which still lay in its ignoble heap on the cold floor, Maris turned, sweeping her skirts, and without further conversation, allowed him to return her to her chamber.

Twenty ✍

"**M**y Lady Maris, her majesty requests that you attend her." A page stood in the doorway of the ladies' solar, giving a slight bow. "She asks that you bring your bag of herbal medicines as she is in need of your talents."

Maris sprang to her feet, at once nervous that she would be asked to attend the queen, and grateful that she would have something to do other than embroidering in a room filled with chattering women. "Please tell her grace that I will be at her service anon."

The page gave another bow. "I will take you to her, lady."

With a quick smile to the other women, who looked on with interest, Maris dropped her embroidery in a heap on a stool next to her chair, hoping to not see it again before the day was over. "I shall meet you at supper," she told Lady Laurette, who was busily stitching a surcoat for her brother. Without waiting for a reply, she swept from the room and followed the page to her chamber.

Within, she unlocked one of the trunks she'd brought from Langumont, retrieving a well-worn leather sack with dried herbs packed in wrappings of linen, wool, or leather. Digging deeper, she pulled a wooden box, tied shut with a silken tie, from the bottom of the trunk. The box held a mortar and pestle, tinctures and oils, knives and spoons and small wooden bowls for mixing. Though 'twas likely that the queen had such at her behest, Maris felt more comfortable with her own equipment and was determined to be prepared for any request Eleanor should make.

The trip to the queen's presence was not long, but it was complicated, and Maris soon lost her way. Not for the first time did she wonder that a young boy could find his way with such ease! At last, they reached a large oaken door with heavy metal slats bracing it, and ornate carvings on the wood framing the doorway.

The page knocked on the heavy oak, then, although Maris heard nothing from within, bowed yet again, and gestured for her to enter.

She opened the door and stepped in.

Eleanor sat in a large, well-cushioned chair lodged in a far corner. A small table next to her held a pitcher, two goblets, and a silver platter loaded with cheese and bread. The fireplace, near enough the chair to cast shadows from its flames but far enough that there was no danger of skirts catching afire, contained a crackling blaze. Another chair, positioned to face that which the queen used, was not so well-cushioned; though the pillow on its seat was generous enough. A heavy tapestry covered the floor, Maris noted in surprise, having never seen such a luxury before, and more tapestries hung from the walls and over the arrow slits in the stone.

"Come in, Lady Maris," came the mellow voice of the queen.

Maris did as she was urged, closing the door in her wake, and taking in more of the room. A large, curtained bed hugged another wall, and was warmed by its own fireplace—it, too, filled with a roaring fire. A table littered with parchments, quills, and a pot of ink sat near the two chairs, and trunks bursting with gowns, cloaks, cups, plates, cloths, leather bags, and all types of trinkets lined the walls throughout.

"Your grace," Maris curtsied when she reached the edge of the floor covering.

Eleanor waved a graceful hand to the empty chair. "Sit."

Maris's quick glance about the room revealed that she was alone with the queen, and she wondered whether her grace's affliction was that of a private nature. Trundling her leather sack and wooden box, she did as ordered and sat, waiting.

"You may pour some wine, Lady Maris."

Accepting this as an invitation to serve both herself and the queen, Maris filled two of the goblets with a heavy red wine. "How may I assist you?" she asked, placing a cup within Eleanor's easy reach.

"You are well-versed in healing and the use of physic herbs I am told."

Maris bowed her head in acknowledgement. "I have studied such medicines since I was ten summers."

Reaching for her drink with long white fingers, the queen asked, "Tell me how you were taught."

Sipping her own wine, Maris explained, "My mother, Allegra Lareux, began to teach me the simple uses of herbs. As I became more skilled and yearned to know beyond her knowledge, I studied with a midwife of Langumont. Some years ago, a man well-taught in the healing of the Holy Lands lived at Langumont and shared his great mastery with me." Emboldened by the queen's interest, she asked, "How did you come to hear of my skills?"

A faint smile quirked Eleanor's lips as she drank. "I am told by a trusted friend that your skill is so great that you can bring a man—nay, a whole keep, the tale goes—near enough to death that he wishes to die, yet not so close that he does expire."

Maris felt her face pinken. "I am abashed that you should hear of my expertise in such a sorry way. 'Tis not the way I was taught—"

Eleanor laughed. "Do you not apologize, Maris, as I am of the mind to reward a woman—not reprimand her—when she rises to an occasion to save herself! Does the Church not say that God helps those who help themselves?" She reached for a piece of cheese. "I am one to espouse such actions if the end justifies the means!" She chuckled again. "'Twould have been an interesting sight to see an entire keep laid low whilst yourself and your maidservant tripped blithely over the drawbridge!"

"'Twas a more memorable moment in my history," Maris admitted with a wry smile, "'though I would never choose the words 'tripping blithely' to describe our hasty departure!" She took a sip of wine, wondering that Dirick had such familiarity with the queen that he should tell her of his own misfortune. 'Twas a testament to his own cocksureness that he should freely share of an event in which he was bested by a woman. "Your grace, how may I assist you?"

"'Tis a minor affliction, Lady Maris—naught but an ache to my ear. I often have the same complaint during the winter months, and most often, the leeches or physicians direct me to soak my feet in a bath of hot water with ground mustard seeds." She settled back into her chair, her gaze direct upon Maris whilst her fingers stroked the tassel of her girdle. "'Tis not the most…convenient treatment and I but search for another answer to this illness."

Maris nodded her head in understanding. Aye, 'twas of no surprise that the beautiful and regal Eleanor of Aquitaine would not wish to do something as ungainly as to soak her bare feet! "Tell me, does the pain in your ear act like the beat of a drum, or more like a sharp pinch of pain?"

"'Tis most like the beat of a drum, far inside my ear."

"Is it accompanied with a sound like the peal of a bell as well?"

"Nay."

"And, tell me, your grace, have you any other complaints at the time you have this ache of the ear?"

"Nay."

Maris rose. "With your permission, I'll prepare a remedy that will be easily and discreetly administered, and mayhaps even decrease the frequency of the affliction."

Eleanor nodded, watching with hawk eyes as Maris delved into her leather satchel, and then into the smooth wooden box. She withdrew a small knife, a small, empty bottle with a tight cork stopper, a second, larger bottle, and a fruit that looked like a small, bulging onion. Watching Maris peel the crisp, white skin from the onion, Eleanor asked, "Is that not a garlic?"

"Aye," Maris looked up in surprise. "'Tis not a common fruit here in England, though 'tis popular near the Holy Lands. Other healers I have spoken with complain of its rank smell, though I rather like it. It has many uses aside of which I will show you today."

"I have seen it on my own Crusade to the Holy Land," the queen told her as Maris used the little knife to chop a clove of garlic. A pungent smell pervaded the room.

Maris adjusted her long sleeve and reached for the large bottle. "Your majesty, I'll pour a small amount of this oil over the chopped garlic in a small vial. You should pour a tiny drop of this oil into the ear which pains you one time in the morning, and one time in the evening until the ache is gone." She scraped the chopped garlic into the smaller bottle, then added a generous amount of oil. Using the cork to stop the vial, she shook it briskly, then offered it to the queen.

"Thank you, my dear." Eleanor took the bottle, studied it, then set it upon the table next to her.

Expecting to be dismissed, Maris gathered up her equipment and packed it away.

Thus, the queen's words took her by surprise. "Dirick of

Derkland speaks well of you, Lady Maris."

Unable to control the color that rose in her face, Maris kept her attention on the silken cord she wrapped around her wooden box. Her fingers became clumsy and would not cooperate as she sought to tie the knot. She did not know how to respond to the queen; indeed, she was not altogether sure that Eleanor required a response.

It seemed that she did not. "Are you promised, Lady Maris?"

Maris looked up into an intent gaze. "My father arranged a betrothal but he was killed before the ceremony could take place. I do not know—I do not believe that the contracts were signed."

Eleanor steepled her fingers. "Very good. I thank you for your service. Payment shall be rendered to you." She smiled. "You may go."

∼

Maris pushed back her hood, letting the spring breeze caress her face. She tilted her head up to the sun, eyes closed. It felt heavenly to be out of the dark castle and away from the busy, smelly streets of London!

Hickory nickered next to her, as if to agree with her mistress's unspoken thoughts. They were wading through the tall grass of a meadow just outside of the city, harvesting herbs to replenish the ones Maris had used throughout the winter. Sir Raymond of Vermille, along with three other men-at-arms from Langumont, stood in the road at the edge of the meadow, idly watching over his mistress.

Pleased to see that the bright blue chicory was already blooming, Maris pulled several plants from the soil, shaking dirt from the heavy roots. They were sturdy plants with bristly leaves and finely-haired stems and were good for many uses. She cut the roots and wrapped them in thick cotton sleeves, to be brewed later into a light tonic, and stuffed the leaves into a different cotton bag. The leaves were useless when dried, so fresh ones were always of value when available.

She strolled further across the meadow, toward a smattering of trees where she suspected raspberry bushes might grow. Those leaves created the best tea, along with peppermint, for breeding women: the tea eased nausea and helped the babe root itself firmly inside its mother. As she reached the line of shade from tall oak trees with branches that spread across the sky, she noticed the shiny, dark green leaves and pale pink buds of a familiar herb.

Maris stopped, crouching in the cluster of the ground-covering plant, and stilled her hands. 'Twas bearberry, the leaves of which she and Dirick had gathered one chill winter afternoon. The scene, with all of its vibrant color, had imprinted itself upon her memory: she'd been clutching those thick, padded leaves, and he'd tossed the bright red berries over the snow before drawing her to his mouth for the warmth of a first kiss.

A pang of heat hummed through her as she remembered the sweetness and fire of that meeting of mouths…and how on later occasions the demands of his lips had coaxed a more compelling response, when her limbs became liquid and her heart thudded heavily in her breast. Drawing a shaky breath, Maris plucked a few leaves, running her callused finger over their smoothness.

Try as she might; as furious as she might be with him, Sir Dirick's face and presence had not been far from her mind since…aye, since the eve he'd nearly trampled her with his prized destrier. She lowered her rump to the ground, sitting surrounded by tall grasses and shaded by the oak trees. Her fingers were busy, tearing the leaves into halves and pulling the petals from the flower buds, even as her thoughts rambled through the range of emotions he evoked in her: anger at his seeming complicity with Bon de Savrille…warmth and passion from his kisses…tenderness upon her recovery from the near-drowning…laughter and smiles from their bantering in the stables…and, increasingly, a settling fear of the depth of her emotions, from her inability to forget Dirick for more than a short time.

Was it possible? Could she love him?

Maris closed her eyes tightly, trying to block away the unwelcome thought. Even if she did—God in heaven!—love him, even if 'twere true, there was naught she could do about it. Her life and lands belonged to Henry to do with as he would, and he'd not bestow the well-landed heiress of Langumont upon a mere knight—no matter how much Dirick amused him!

Something obstructed the glare of the sun, and her eyes sprang open. A figure, a man, sat on a horse just in front of her, casting his shadow over her. Blinded by the blazing sun, at first she did not recognize him—but then he spoke.

"Lady Maris," his voice was familiar, purring—and unwelcome. "May I assist you to your feet?"

'Twas Bon de Savrille!

Strangling a cry of surprise, Maris started to her feet, caught herself in her skirts, and tumbled back into the tall grasses. Lord Bon loomed over her, but she still could not see his features for the glare of the sun behind him. A large, blunt-fingered hand reached down from the saddle and clasped her arm, pulling her easily to stand.

"Where did you come from?" she spoke at last, looking surreptitiously about for Sir Raymond.

"Do you not fear," Bon said as his mount danced aside, blocking the sun so that she could see him. "Your men-at-arms are near—I did not come from the road, but through the forest whence I saw you start across the meadow."

"What do you here in London?" Maris was not able to comprehend his sudden appearance.

"My lady, you are never far from my thoughts…an' in turn, I did not wish to be far from your person."

"What do you want?"

"Only you, my lady."

"Bon, I—"

A far-off shout reached their ears, and both turned to see Sir

Raymond and his companions galloping across the field toward them.

"Ah, your saviors come." Before she could react, Bon took one of her hands and, bending, brought her fingers swiftly to his lips. "I'll have you, my lady, if 'tis the last action I make on this earth. I find I cannot live without you—though you nearly murdered me with your poisons, you are the water this thirsty man must sip, the meat this starving man must partake...and, make no mistake, you will be mine—lands or no."

And with that, just as her escort came thundering up, Bon wheeled his mount and cantered off into the forest.

"My lady, are you hurt? Shall we go after him?" Raymond reined in next to her.

"Nay, I am well," Maris replied, still stunned at Bon's sudden appearance and disappearance.

"Did you know that man?"

She nodded. "Aye, 'twas none other than Bon de Savrille of Dreakskill."

"What?" Raymond would have started after him had Maris not raised her hand to halt him.

"Nay, Raymond, do you not trouble yourself. He did not harm me, or even threaten me—except with his desire to have my person." She giggled. "I do believe Lord Bon is quite harmless, as he could easily have swept me up and away with him. And, in truth, I prefer him to wed over Lord Victor." Her smile faded at the ugly memory of his advances two nights earlier.

"Will Lord Victor press his suit with the king?" Sir Raymond asked, alighting from his steed. He stood close to Maris, protectively, and they stepped away from the other three men.

She drew in a deep breath. "Pray God he does not, else I'd as lief be a traitor or a murderess before I'll share his bed!"

Raymond dashed a glance about, as if to be aware of unseen ears. "Nay, Lady, ne'er should you compromise yourself thus.

'Tis I 'twould free you from such an unwelcome match, know you this." His gaze did not waver. "I should be branded murderer in your stead."

"Sir Raymond—"

"'Twas your father's wish, lady."

She looked up at him, confused. "What say you, sir? 'Twas my father who arranged for my contract with Victor d'Arcy."

Raymond shielded his eyes from the sun that glared from behind her. His rugged face settled into serious lines and he drew her further from the rest of her escort. "Lady, your papa saw his error in promising you to Victor and had taken steps to reverse his offer whence we came to free you from Dreakskil. He sent me with a missive to his majesty on the chance that he'd not live through the battle ahead to retract the betrothal himself."

"An' he did not." Maris's words were pained. Tears welled in her eyes for the loss of the person she'd loved most in the world.

"Nay, he did not…an' I am thus torn that I was not there to cover his back in the battle—brief though 'twas—but instead that I brought the message to the king. I was your father's man, and I am now your man for my life."

She rested a hand on his steely arm. "Thank you, Raymond. I thank you for your words. I could not bear to think that I would go against my father's wishes if I were to fight the betrothal contract; an' now I know that his spirit is with me ere I do."

He squinted into the lowering sun. "Let us back to the castle, my lady. Eventide draws near."

She nodded, suddenly elated at the thought of returning to the city. Doubtless, she would share the evening meal with her friends Lady Monique and Lady Laurette…and, mayhaps, chance to speak with Dirick of Derkland.

Twenty-One ✑

"S ir Dirick, would you not play the lute for us?" Lady
Monique simpered, looking at him over the rim of her goblet. "Her Majesty but praises your talent."

He forced his attention from the entrance to the Great Hall.
Why had Maris not come to dinner? "An', my lady, how could
one not have great talent when faced with such inspiration?" His
lips curved into a smile that he did not feel as he pulled a leg
from the goose offered by a page. The leg twisted easily from the
roasted fowl, juices running down into the trencher he shared
with Monique. "Do you wish some, my lady?" he asked, avoiding a commitment to honor her request.

"Aye, my lord, as you prepare it so prettily." She ducked her
head, giving him a coy glance that failed to stir even the slightest
response from him, and tore a small piece of bread from the
trencher.

Even as he passed the meat to her, Dirick's gaze scanned the
room, searching yet again for the absent Maris. He sought, and
found, Lord Victor and his father, who sat several tables further
from the royal dais than he did. Their presence, at the least,
soothed some of his concern as to why she was not at dinner.
But, just as he brought his wine to his mouth, he noticed a man
seated near the rear of the hall, where naught but the meanest
men-at-arms were seated. Dirick froze and returned the goblet to

the table, rising to his full height in surprise. Aye, 'twas him! 'Twas Bon de Savrille! Dirick's heart slammed in his chest and a sudden chill rushed through his body.

"What is it, Sir Dirick?" Lady Laurette asked from across the table.

He barely heard her as he stepped over the trestle bench with the barest glance at her. "Pardon, my ladies," he muttered, pushing hastily around a page holding a pitcher of wine.

Dirick made his way to Bon de Savrille's side in moments, ignoring the surprised murmurs of the other man's table companions when he barged along behind them. "What do you here?" he demanded, placing a firm hand on Bon's meaty shoulder.

The other man craned his head around, then nearly fell back off the bench in surprise. "You!"

Dirick did not remove his hand, instead, he slid his grip down to Bon's upper arm and propelled him away from his dinner seat. He bent full-faced into his visage, close enough that the untrimmed wiriness of Bon's moustache grazed his chin. "What have you done with her?"

"Take your hands from my person," growled Bon, making a great show of brushing crumbs of bread from his tunic. When he finished arranging his clothing, he held a dagger in one hand.

Dirick stilled. Blood rushed through his limbs and he became aware that the attention of several men-at-arms from the table was focused upon them. A glint of steel winked in the torchlight, barely flickering as Bon held the blade steadily under his nose. Dirick forced himself to breathe normally, gathering his wits enough to look at the handle of the knife gripped tightly in the hand of the combative man before him.

"An' what say you sir?" sneered Bon. "You demand answers from me when 'tis you who availed yourself of my hospitality under false pretenses!"

Dirick jerked his gaze to a point behind Bon, reaching to the side as if to catch something. The ruse worked and the other man lost concentration, letting his glance shift away from Dirick for the barest of moments. 'Twas enough to suit Dirick's purpose as he lifted his knee in a powerful thrust, ramming Bon's wrist and sending the dagger scuttling to the floor. He stepped closer to him, setting his jaw and muttering between clenched teeth, "What have you done with her?"

Bon grasped the front of Dirick's tunic and shoved him aside. "Leave me to finish my meal."

Before Bon could return to his seat, Dirick clamped a hand on his shoulder and yanked him back. "Where is Lady Maris?"

"I do not know what you are talking about!" He shook off Dirick's hand and swung a fast fist.

Dirick ducked quickly, aware that more attention had turned to them. He grabbed Bon's tunic and dragged him so that they were chest to chest. He could smell a large quantity of ale on his breath and even see a piece of meat stuck between Bon's two front teeth. "By God's bones, man, do you tell me what you've done with Lady Maris!"

Bon shoved hard and succeeded in pushing Dirick back. "I've naught to say to you, sirrah, that cannot be said with the steel of my knife! An' I'll gladly speak to you with that!"

"An' I vow, if you've laid a finger on her person, my blade will address yours! I'll carve you into little pieces—"

"'Tis just as well my person is fine and fit," came a musical voice from behind him, "else His Majesty's meal would most certainly be ruined by the bloodshed!"

Dirick dropped his hand from Bon and whirled to find Maris, flanked by Sir Raymond and another man-at-arms, with an amused, quirked mouth. She was unharmed, he noted immediately, and she was also laughing at him with those beautiful green and gold eyes. Laughing! He felt a flush rise to his cheeks and realized that more spectators had been drawn to the vicinity of the altercation, and that even the attention of his sovereign and the queen had come to rest upon them. The hall, most usually so loud that the barking of a dog or the dropping of a platter went unnoticed, breathed as close to silence as a crowded chamber could.

"My lady," he gave a stiff bow, attempting to recover his poise. "I am well-pleased that you are unharmed." He bent to retrieve Bon's dagger, noting its unexceptional wooden handle, and returned it to the other man.

As he spoke those words, the attention of the diners returned to their meals as if the entertainment had never occurred. With one more glance at Maris, who watched him with a brooding gaze, Dirick turned to make his way back to his place at the front of the hall.

Somehow, amid the din that had started back up to accompany the meal, he heard her gasp. He spun about in time to see Bon's dagger slashing down upon him. Dirick instinctively raised his arm, and the blade, which had been meant for his back, sliced through the woolen tunic, along the back of his shoulder. A howl of rage tore through his throat, and he leaped at Bon, knocking him to the floor.

Kneeling over the stocky man, he pinned one thick arm in the sweet rushes and grappled with the other that held the dagger. "I did not ever," he grunted, "have the occasion to repay the hospitality which—" Dirick's breath was cut off by a knee shoved into his ribs, but that effort cost Bon the battle for the knife. "—the hospitality which you provided to Lady Maris." The struggle ended with the point of the blade very near Bon's throat, and a crowd of men pressing in upon the scene. Dirick pulled himself to his feet, slightly winded but enlivened from the sudden intensity of the quarrel. "Get you out of my sight, else I will well and truly repay your graciousness to the lady. An' you need have no fear of turning your back to me, Bon de Savrille, for when I mean to strike you, there will be no need for stealth."

His face distorted with rage, Bon pulled himself to his feet and pushed through the cluster of spectators. Again, as the altercation dissipated, so did the viewers, returning to their interrupted meals with the aplomb of long-acceptance of such scenes.

"You'll have a care in the dark hallways, anon," murmured a voice behind Dirick.

He turned to Maris. Her smirk had been replaced by a frown that creased her forehead. "The man is a buffoon," he said carelessly. She stood close to him, her long cuff brushing against the hem of his tunic, and he did not move away.

"Ah, buffoon though he is, 'tis he who walked away unscathed and you who have the wound." Concern lurked under her nonchalance as she rose on her toes to look at his shoulder. Dirick became aware of the spreading dampness of warm blood and a throbbing pain beneath it. "Come, I'll see to your ill, as you made the fool of yourself on my behalf."

Her brisk voice dampened any tenderness that may have been in her eyes and Dirick was strangely annoyed. "Nay, lady, I'll not keep you from your meal."

Maris tilted an eyebrow, looking up at him. "I have little hunger left, as your talk of bloodshed sapped my desire for food. Come, if I am skilled enough to treat the queen, verily I can do you little harm. Hasten now, for you are soiling your tunic!"

He muttered that she could indeed inflict harm upon him, as he had the memory of an agonizing night on a cold floor to prove it, but in the end, he followed her from the hall. Sir Raymond dogged their footsteps as Maris led the way toward the main hallway to the other side of Winchester Castle.

"I will watch over your mistress, Raymond, you may return to the hall for your meal." The other man ignored Dirick's comment while Maris stopped short.

"My men take orders from no one but me, Dirick Derkland, know you this, but you are in the right. Raymond, you may return and join the others for dinner. Though he has a wounded shoulder, I vow Dirick will allow no harm to come to me."

"My lady," Raymond began hesitantly, then tried again. "But Lady Maris, you cannot take him to your chamber! 'Twould be but more fuel to the fire already started back there!"

Maris shook her head. "Agnes awaits me—we'll not be alone. I'll give him a poultice and send him on his way before anyone is the wiser. Now, go you."

They were silent for the remainder of the long walk to her chamber. When they reached the heavy oaken door, Dirick opened it and preceded her in.

Maris stood in the entrance, watching as he scouted the room with a sharp gaze. His attention went from the smoldering fire to the trunks lined neatly along one short wall, to the narrow bed piled with pillows from her own bedchamber at Langumont. He gestured for her to enter, and she hid a smile. How often had she walked into the chamber with no thought to her safety!

"Your maidservant is not here." He'd moved back to the door and stood half in and half out of the room.

"I did not expect her to be," she dismissed the thought. "Come within." She pushed the door closed, nudging him out of the way. Maris knelt beside a trunk, untying its leather straps and flinging its lid open. As she rummaged through cloths and small bags, the hem of her veil fell forward and tangled in the contents of the trunk. With a mutter of frustration, she yanked it off her head, uncovering the four thick braids that were looped up at her crown. Tossing the wimple aside, she delved once more into the depths of the trunk and at last retrieved the small pouch for which she searched. She set it aside, rummaged further, and withdrew a small square of folded cloth.

She pulled to her feet and turned to find Dirick poking at the fire, his back to her. The dark red stain on his shoulder had seeped further, but not alarmingly so. Maris reached to shift the cloth away from the wound, but he moved just as she touched him. "You must remove your tunic and shirt," she told him.

He hesitated as his gaze rested on her unveiled head, then dropped to her hands holding the leather pouch. "Aye."

She waited for a moment, but when he did not move, she stepped toward him. "Does it pain you to move? Let me help you."

"Nay." He stopped her. "It does not pain me overmuch. Mayhaps—" He craned his head at an odd angle, twisting to see the blood stain. "Mayhaps 't has stopped bleeding and I do not need nursing."

"Dirick, do not be foolish. 'Twas a deep enough cut and I've seen many lesser wounds fester. Take off your tunic and I will see to it." She gestured to a three-legged stool in front of the fireplace. "You must sit, as I'll not be able to see well at your height."

Maris frowned at him until he acquiesced and began to struggle out of the tunic. As he sat on the stool, clad only in a thin linen shirt and breeches, she turned to find another candle. Lighting the tallow, she placed it on one of the trunks where it would cast a ready light on his shoulder. Then she added water to a small pot hanging over the fire. At last, she returned her attention to him just as he slowly pulled off the linen shirt.

Her breath slowed, shallowed, and caught when she saw his sleek, muscled back and broad bare shoulders. She must have gasped, for he turned from his contemplation of the fire to look at her with half-hooded eyes.

For a moment, she could not speak. The fire played golden and rust shadows over the planes of his arms, caressing the dip in his shoulder and the hollow of his collarbone. It tipped the curling ends of his thick hair with sunlight, smoothing over the jut of angular cheekbones and square chin. Shadows mingled with the thick covering of hair that grew from the widest part of his chest down…down to a place she could not see…to where heavy, muscled arms rested between his knees.

Maris forced herself to recover. "Ah, the stab—'tis worse than I'd thought." She moved toward him and he turned back to look at the crackling fire. Reminding herself that she'd treated numerous injuries of this type, and that the only cause of her sudden nervousness was that they were alone in her chamber, she bent to examine the laceration.

His skin was warm and taut, with a few wiry hairs scattered over the curve of his shoulder. There were many, many other scars healed into pale puckers of skin…and some that were purple or red, ugly and jagged. Maris wanted to touch them all, to smooth over the remnants of the dangers he'd faced in the service of the king, to be certain they were as healed as possible. Her fingers trembled as they brushed over Dirick's shoulder blade and little bumps erupted over his skin. One of her braids fell from its mooring and thunked onto his shoulder, and Dirick started so that it slid down his back and rested along his spine.

She felt him draw a breath when she dabbed a damp cloth over the cut, then poked gently at it. 'Twas a clean cut from a very sharp dagger, not deep enough to slice through the tendons, but enough that 'twould take some time to heal. Some threads from his shirt had caught in the coagulating blood and Maris used a bit of the heating water to wash them free. As she became more engrossed in her work, he seemed to sense it and released a long, slow breath.

When she left his side to prepare the poultice, Dirick shifted on the stool to watch. Her fingers seemed to have grown twice as long and thrice as fat, as they first dropped the leather pouch, and then could not undo its knot, and finally, when she pulled a handful of dried woad leaves forth, her fingers did not hold them tightly enough and the leaves scattered over the floor and table.

Muttering to herself, Maris stooped to scrape up the dried herb, taking care not to crumble the fragile leaves further. By the time she gathered them into a small wooden bowl, the water on the fire was bubbling and steaming. When she glanced over to check it, Dirick noticed, offering, "I'll get that for you."

She nodded gratefully and returned to her work. The dried woad, at one time a pretty blue-green, but now dried into a dull black, crumbled in the bowl. She took a handful of dried chamomile flowers from a different leather pouch and added them to the woad. Dirick stood at her side, holding the hot water, and she gestured for him to add some to the herbs. He poured gently, taking care not to splash it, and when the water embraced the flowers and leaves, a pungent but pleasing scent filled the air.

Maris brushed past him, lightly touching his bare arm as she reached for the square of cloth. He stiffened, stepping out of her way, and returned to the stool. She stirred the contents of the bowl, unfolded the cloth into a long strip, then turned back to her patient. The bleeding had slowed to a mere ooze, and she washed the cut once more.

Then, using a flat wooden utensil, she scooped up the mass of herbs and water and murmured, "'Twill be warm." Dirick did indeed start when she smoothed the poultice onto his injury, but she felt him relax as the treatment began to work to soothe the pain and cleanse the cut. Maris placed the cloth over his shoulder, lifting his heavy arm to wrap the bandage under it.

Once it was in place, she patted the poultice gently, checked that none of the herbs were leaking from beneath, and tied the cloth firmly.

Then, her hands did not want to leave him: they brushed his thick hair from the nape of his neck, pulled a few strands from under the bandage, and smoothed over the uninjured shoulder. Dirick's chest rose as he drew in a deep, ragged breath, and he stilled.

"You have many hurts," Maris said, tracing a finger over one scar, and then another, and another.... His skin tautened, the little bumps erupting wherever she touched him.

"And not one tended as carefully as this one." His voice was rough. Reaching over his good shoulder, he captured her hand and pulled it forward, turning his head to place a kiss on her knuckle, and pressing her palm to the center of his chest.

The front of him was hot from the proximity of the fire. She smoothed her hand through wiry hair over the hard swell of muscle, brushing a flat nipple and tracing the ridge of bone down his center. The tingling that began in her fingers shot through her body, culminating in a pool in her middle that warmed and stirred her entire being. Her chest rose, breasts pushing against his back, and her breathing became shallow and labored. Dear God, she wanted him!

With a cry of surprise at this realization, Maris jerked her hand away and stepped back. Dirick whirled off the stool, turning onto her with dark, glittering eyes and a taut mouth. He was beautiful, masculine: all muscle and thick, dark hair, haloed by the dancing fire, towering over her.

"*Jesù*, Maris," he breathed, reaching for her.

She did not resist when he pulled her flush to the long, hard length of his body. Sinking against him, fingers closing over his shoulders, she tilted her head back to receive his kiss. His mouth demanded a response equal to his own desire, and Maris felt herself swept into a maelstrom of heat and energy. With a harsh groan, Dirick fitted his hips to hers, and slid his mouth along her chin to the softness of her neck. When she eased a hand up into his thick hair, and the other back down over his chest, he pulled away enough to look down at her.

The intensity in his eyes, the deep need there, caused a great tightening in her middle. She met his gaze, reaching up to touch his parted lips with trembling fingers. "'Tis not right," Maris whispered.

He wrapped his fingers around her hand, pressing his mouth

to its sensitive wrist. His mouth closed over the thick pad of her palm, biting gently, sliding full lips over the inside of her hand. His tongue darted out to thrust slick and wet between two fingers, and Maris closed her eyes, sagging against him. A low cry keened in the back of her throat, and when she opened her eyes, he still looked down at her, still wanting and needing, still dark and beautiful.

His fingers closed over her shoulders. "I want you," his words were forced, harsh, as if wrung from his very depths. "I have no claim to you, but God above, I must have you."

She shook her head, remaining in his grasp. "Nay. I cannot give what belongs to the king."

He did not understand her meaning, for his eyes darkened to black and his face settled into stone, livid with shock. "Henry?"

Maris realized his mistake. "Nay, Dirick, you mistook my meaning." She pulled firmly from him. "I am the king's ward, to do with what he will."

The fury drained from his face. "Aye." His eyes still glittered with desire as his gaze swept over her hungrily. He reached for her again, but she moved out of reach, not trusting her own self-control.

"'Tis my fate to be used as a pawn, dangled as a prize, no doubt, for some well-landed baron close to the king," she said bitterly. "And of all men in this kingdom, 'twould not be you as you've naught to bring to the great lands of Langumont."

Dirick stepped back as if slapped. "Aye, 'tis true, I've naught to bring to your great lands," he said caustically. "You'd not lower your momentous self to be given to one as mean as I even if you did not answer to the king."

Grabbing an arm, he jerked her to him so hard that when she collided with his chest, the breath was knocked out of her. His mouth crashed onto hers, furious, as one hand held the mass of braids at the back of her head. Abruptly, he released her, setting her away so hard that she stumbled backward onto the bed. "For one determined not to be associated with one so mean as I, you easily give up your kisses."

He stalked to the door, pausing to give a mocking bow before he opened it. "Good night, my Lady Maris."

Twenty-Two ﹏

Dirick tore off his tunic and dropped it into a heap next to his pallet. His body still hummed with frustration and anger. Sinking onto a stool, he unwound the cross-garters that kept his chausses from bagging around the ankles, gathering them into a mass and tossing them onto the tunic. His shirt followed, and then his breeches, and he crawled, naked, onto his pallet.

Stretching his arms and legs, cracking his long spine as he did so, Dirick struggled to contain his anger and bring his tight body under control.

Damn the wench!

He gritted his teeth, grinding them so that his jaw hurt, and flopped over onto his side. The wool blanket and hay-stuffed pallet were rough on his bare skin, so he pressed into it, hoping the prickles would take his mind off the throbbing source of discomfort between his legs. But, nay, it did not.

Dirick rolled onto his back and stared up into the darkness. A whore could ease him. He started to pull himself upright, then dropped back down. 'Twouldn't help anymore than it had in the past, he thought, his mouth twisting bitterly.

He willed himself to relax, to ban Maris from his mind.

Lady Monique seemed willing, he reflected. She'd made sure

he'd learned that she'd buried her second husband less than four moons past, which meant he'd be spared the guilt of despoiling one of the king's wards. He tried to picture her honey-colored hair spread over a plump red pillow, but the image was ruined by the memory of thick, chestnut-colored tresses wrapping about his wrist…and green and gold-flecked eyes, rimmed with thick lashes…full lips, moist with his kisses.…

Stifling a groan, he flipped over so that his face was buried in what passed for a pillow in Westminster's knights' quarters. He breathed deeply, inhaling its musty smell…so different than the clean, minty smell of the rosemary and lemon that clung to her hair.

She haunted him. Her laughter, her smile, even her tart tongue and short temper. He seemed to be unable to keep from making a fool of himself in her presence. He, the practiced courtier, with the quick tongue and charming wit, could do little in her presence but pant like a bitch in heat. How had he come to be in this state?

He had to have her. He needed her, wanted her…could not forget her.

Dirick swallowed and slowly eased himself over. A piece of hay poked through the pallet, jabbing him in the base of his back. He shifted, stabbed a hand through his heavy hair, and bent one knee up to the ceiling.

He could not have her. She was a ward of the king and her maidenhead was as important as her lands. She'd belong only to her husband and 'twould not be he.

The woman had spoken the truth anight: he'd naught to bring to the lands of Langumont. Henry would not squander the opportunity to make a political match between Maris and one of his barons in favor of betrothing her to a landless, mercenary knight. In truth, though he'd been a good and loyal man to the king, and more than a mere knight fighting the king's battles,

Dirick knew 'twas an impossibility to hope his reward could be aught of that nature.

When he awoke the next morning, Dirick's head pounded. His eyes were bleary and a dull, angry mood had settled over him.

He stumbled to a pail of water, splashing it over his face in an attempt to wash away the grit of dirt and frustration. He was expected to attend the fealty ceremony at which Maris, among others, would pledge loyalty to Henry and his Crown.

His sour mood lasted as he dressed in a clean, richly-embroidered tunic appropriate for wear to a royal ceremony and flipped his pallet into a small square. Wet hair dripping onto his nose, he made his way to Westminster Abbey, where Mass would be held, followed by the swearing of fealty to the King of England.

ॐ

Maris knelt in front of Henry, holding an old, dried bit of bone which was purported to be a finger of Saint Peter. The king closed his hands over hers, drawing them under his mantle, as he looked down at her with steely grey eyes.

"I become thy woman of such tenement to be holden of thee." Maris spoke clearly so as to be heard above all the rustling of the crowded abbey. "To bear thee and thine heirs faith of life, and member, and earthly worship against all men who can live and die on this earth, in the name of God, the Father, the Son, and the Holy Spirit." She bent her head to kiss his hands.

"We renew upon thee thy vassalage to the lands of Langumont, Cleonis, Firmain, and all such properties encompassed by the baronage of Langumont." Henry pulled her to her feet, pressing a dry kiss to her cheek.

Maris gave a short curtsey and moved aside and off the dais, turning to watch as the Lord of Southampton took her place opposite the king. The bishop took Saint Peter's finger bone from her with reverence, and she shifted so that she could see the crowd filling the abbey.

Her gaze wandered the many faces, looking for whom or what she did not know, and rested at last upon two silver-beaconed heads near the front of the chamber. The Lords Victor and Michael d'Arcy looked back at her with twin pairs of shimmering eyes, purposeful and glinting with anger.

Suppressing a shudder, she turned her attention away. Clenching her fingers so hard that her ragged nails bit into her palms, Maris closed her eyes for a moment. She feared those two men as she'd never feared before…but she could not understand why they should strike such loathing in her heart. Lord Victor was her intended betrothed, but surely he was not an evil man!

Then the memory of his brutal lips and grasping hands returned, and she felt nauseated. If he wasn't truly evil, at the least, he was greatly reprehensible and she renewed her private vow that if she were unfortunate enough to be bound to him, he'd not live past their first moon of wedded bliss.

When she opened her eyes, Maris's gaze fell upon a tall, dark-haired man no more than a few rows from the dais. Dirick's handsome, unshaven face was set as if carved of stone, and his stare was trained upon her. Abruptly, he turned away, bowing his head slightly.

A tremor of heat rushed up her spine even as her lips pursed in anger. Aye, the man could melt her with his kisses and the strength of his large, powerful hands…but he was rude and offensive! How dare he criticize her for kissing him! 'Twas his own doing that caused her to become breathless with desire, and he'd had no cause for such anger when she'd but spoken the truth the night before!

"Maris of Langumont."

The sound of her name ringing out jerked Maris's attention

back to the altar, where the king stood, looking expectantly at her. The bishop gave her a none-too-gentle push and she caught her balance before she stumbled onto the dais. Gathering up her skirts, for 'twas certain that she was meant to join his majesty, she took two steps onto the altar.

"Monique of Trysdon." Another name was solemnly intoned by the king's secretary. "Bertilde of Hyannes."

Bewildered, but taking great care to keep her face devoid of emotion, Maris stood near the king, joined by Lady Monique and Lady Bertilde. She clasped her hands over her abdomen, tangling her fingers in the heavy golden girdle that wrapped about her waist.

There was silence after the three women were assembled, and then the king spoke. "'T pleases us to decree the betrothals of three of our wards on this day, to such lords of the realm who have since pledged their loyalty—and who have maintained it in instances of great adversity."

Maris's heart plunged to her stomach and she felt light-headed. Betrothals! She'd not expected this; had had no time to prepare herself for this eventuality. She'd been certain that the king would simply collect the tithes from her lands as his ward for many years before giving her to one of his barons. Unless…her heart skittered and she flashed a glance at Michael and Victor. Had they pressed their suit to the king and did he now intend to honor the betrothal her father had made? Her stomach clenched.

She dared not look at Dirick, but from the corner of her eye, she could see his tall form. Instead, she returned her attention to the king, who'd just announced the name of Lady Bertilde's betrothed—one of the powerful barons whose holdings fell upon the Welsh border.

"Lady Monique of Trysdon."

The lady in question stepped forward, and Maris saw her

gaze flicker to Dirick. Her stomach dropped in surprise and she clenched her fingers, digging her nails into the palms of her hands.

Nay, not to him! Her silent plea to God was instinctive, and Maris took a small step backward in her confusion, jostling the priest.

"Lady Monique of Trysdon is hereby promised to Lord Bartholemew d'Ausignan."

A wave of relief swept over Maris, but was instantly usurped by a light-headed faintness when her name was called. She steeled her features to show no emotion as she stepped toward the king, her gaze brushing over Queen Eleanor, who sat with a satisfied smile behind him. Maris gave a little curtsey, then straightened, swallowing the lump in her throat as she awaited her fate.

"Lady Maris of Langumont is hereby promised to the Baron of Ludingdon and Fairhold."

There was a pause as the audience digested the announcement, and then, as exclamations of confusion and surprise erupted, a loud voice shouted, "The lady is already promised!"

Voices quieted as Michael d'Arcy pushed his way through the crowd, followed closely by his son. "The lady is promised!" his voice rang loudly into the sudden stillness.

Maris's heart thudded in her chest and her limbs prickled with tension. Though she had no knowledge of the Baron of Ludingdon, verily he was a more desirable groom than the one who now stood at the base of the dais in his father's shadow.

Henry looked down at the two men, raising his eyebrows. "What say you, man? The lady is promised?"

"Your grace, the lady's father, Merle of Langumont, entered into a betrothal contract between his daughter and my son, Lord Victor d'Arcy."

The king stroked his beard. "And can you produce the contracts to verify your claim?"

From his place in the crowd, Dirick could see a glitter of humor in the king's grey eyes. Through his numbness, he wondered what game Henry played, even as he chafed to learn who this Baron of Ludingdon should be. Having little knowledge of the English court through the fault of his years in Paris, Dirick did not keep abreast of who held which title at any time…thus, he found himself craning his head to spy the man who would have his Maris.

"Nay, my liege, the contracts were drawn up but the lady was spirited away before they could be finalized," Michael explained. "An' Lord Merle was slain during her rescue. But there are many witnesses to the lord's intent, as 'twas announced to the people of Langumont."

"And 'tis your claim that the contract should be honored though 'twas not signed?" Henry glared down at the man before him.

Maris had been still throughout the exchange, and now Dirick saw her move as if to speak. Henry must have sensed the same, and he turned to her. "Lady Maris, what have you to say of this? Do you wish to pursue his claim of betrothal?"

"Your grace, I did not see the betrothal contracts of which Lord d'Arcy speaks," her voice was steady, "but 'tis true that my father announced such an intention." A grin of satisfaction creased Michael's face, broadening with her next words. "An', my liege, 'tis my intent to abide by *my father's last wishes before his untimely demise.*"

Coldness swept over Dirick. She'd honor the betrothal! The bitter tang of disappointment touched his tongue, and he swallowed back a retort of frustration. He almost missed the small smile touching her lips as she bent her head demurely.

The king shot her a glance, giving a slight nod and a matching smile. Sensing some undercurrent between the two, Dirick renewed his attention as Henry spoke. "Ah, aye, my lady. We, too, intend to honor the *final* wishes of our faithful vassal."

Michael started to speak, confident that he'd won the battle. The king cut him off, producing a curling parchment sheet. "We have a missive writ in the hand of Lord Merle of Langumont, to ourselves, on the thirteenth day of this January. This letter, scribed as he prepared to besiege the castle where Lady Maris was held, repudiates the betrothal contract between his daughter, Maris, and Lord Victor d'Arcy."

"Nay!" shrieked Michael d'Arcy in surprise, echoing his son's shocked exclamation.

Henry looked down his nose at the furious man. "We assure you, 'tis true," he said regally. "The contracts were not signed, and the lord recants his decision to betrothe Lady Maris to Lord Victor."

The bishop nodded in agreement and Michael and Victor had no choice but to retreat.

Henry raised his gaze from the angry men, casting it about the chamber. The rising noise subsided when he lifted his hand. "Lady Maris of Langumont is hereby promised to the Baron of Ludingdon and Fairhold," he repeated his earlier decree. "An' that title has been undesignated since the baron's death without issue for some moons. This day, Dirick of Derkland shall swear fealty to us in that name of Baron of Ludingdon and Fairhold."

Dirick felt a rush of blood to his face as shock numbed his body. His head snapped up to meet the king's gaze and the twinkle of mischief in those pale grey eyes, and, dazed with his sudden good fortune, Dirick moved toward the dais. A barony! He'd been awarded a barony!

Stepping eagerly onto the altar, he could not keep back a grin. "Your grace, you honor me beyond my belief! 'Twould be my greatest pleasure to pledge my loyalty to you and your heirs." Though intent upon the king's presence, Dirick could not keep from flashing a glance at Maris. His look at her was scarce, but her pale, wide-eyed face, stony with horror, impaled its impression on his mind. She looked as though her death knell had been rung.

He could attend to that anon; but for now, he returned his attention to Henry. Kneeling on one knee before his sovereign, Dirick took the bone of St. Peter into his hands and swore his vassalage to the king with strong, steady words.

When he rose from his knees, Dirick found himself full-faced with Maris. Her gaze was so cold that he almost shivered. He kept his face devoid of emotion as the bishop stepped between them to administer the betrothal vows.

Maris's small, cold, scratched hand was placed in Dirick's larger one, her skin pale next to the brown roughness of his fingers. He repeated the vows with a clear, strong voice as he studied her inclined head. As he spoke, a rush of energy shot through him. She was to be his! He felt suddenly weak with the realization.

"And to thee I plight my troth." Maris's voice uttering the words that would make her his brought his attention back to the present. She withdrew her fingers from him as soon as she finished reciting her promise.

They stood side by side, arms brushing sleeve to sleeve, as the other couples cited their betrothal vows. Dirick felt Maris's unyielding stiffness next to him and he was overwhelmed with the sudden yearning to gather her into his arms and kiss her into a malleable handful of woman. He shifted on his feet as his thoughts brought about a surge of arousal.

Henry announced that the wedding ceremonies would take place on Sunday next—four days hence—and that the betrothal contracts would be prepared within two days. With that, he dismissed the crowd.

"Felicitations, Lord Dirick," purred a voice behind him.

He turned, recognizing the voice, to find the queen with a complacent smile on her face. "Your grace." He kissed her hand, suddenly aware of his debt to her.

"Look you here," she spoke, resting a possessive hand on his forearm, "in the space of one morn, you are entitled, enfeofed, and engaged to be married to a well-landed heiress!" Her eyes danced with pleasure and mischief.

"Your grace, I have never met a more fortunate man—with the great exception of your husband," he said with all sincerity.

The teasing left her eyes to be replaced by earnestness. "As you have served us well, 'tis well deserved. I wish happiness for you and your lady."

"I thank you with all of my heart." He kissed her hand again, and turned to confront Maris. She was gone. He whirled back to an amused Eleanor.

"Have you lost your wife so soon?" the queen teased, tucking her hand into the crook of her husband's elbow. "She'll be quite the challenge for you, Lord Dirick, I trow."

Henry chuckled in his booming way. "Aye, my love, I should say Dirick may have to raise his hand to her rump more than once in their life anon. And what a rump she has!" He added for Dirick's ears only.

"Your grace." Dirick bowed, his mouth tightening. "I beg excuse to leave."

"Aye, Dirick, go you in search of her. I wish you the best of luck in taming that lady!"

❦

Maris had made her escape from the abbey as soon as Dirick turned to greet the queen. Sir Raymond of Vermille met her as she slipped from the crowded chamber, dogging her footsteps as she hurried down a narrow hall back to the castle.

Betrothed! Betrothed to Dirick, Lord of Ludingdon!

Her heart had been choking her since the announcement.

How had he done it? How had he convinced the king to award him not only a title, but her hand as well? Her mind spun with the incredulity of it, with excitement and titillation.

Presently, she became aware that Raymond had followed her and she slowed her frenzied pace. They paused, ducking into an alcove not far from her chamber in the keep.

"My lady?" asked her faithful knight.

"Raymond," she said, leaning back against the stone wall. The hall was lit from the sun shining brightly through the arrow slits above her. She sighed wearily, passing a hand over her face. "I am to be married in four days!"

He nodded. "Aye, lady, an' not to Victor d'Arcy! Praise God!"

"Aye." She breathed more calmly now. "There is that."

He waited silently, as if knowing she must gather her thoughts.

"Dear God, Raymond, what am I to do?" Her voice sounded piteous even to her own ears, sounded as if she'd not a hope left in the world.

Raymond rested a light hand on her arm. "Lady, lady…I'll not let any harm come to you!" He hesitated, and his voice dropped. "As I vowed once before, I am willing to do your bidding—to rid you of your betrothed."

"What? Do you plot against me already?"

Maris jerked her attention to the spot behind Raymond where Dirick had appeared. Though his words were light, a darkness flashed in his eyes and she knew to beware of his anger. Raymond's face paled and he stepped in front of Maris as if to protect her, hand dropping to the dagger that rode at his waist.

"Do not be a fool, man," Dirick said when he saw his stance. "I am in the right, and I intend no harm to the lady anyway." He looked warningly at Maris, as if to quell any argument on her part, then ordered the other man, "Leave us."

Before Raymond could speak, she nodded, knowing that Dirick would have his way. "You may go," she agreed. With a quick look to assure her that he would be nearby if she was in need of him, Raymond left their presence.

"Come," Dirick took her hand, placing it firmly on his arm. She let it rest there, resisting the urge to close her fingers over the pronounced muscles and feel his warm strength.

They proceeded down the hallway and directly to an opening that led to a courtyard. He did not speak, but walked her out into the spring sunshine, leading her to a single bench at one end. Proffering her a seat, Dirick waited until she sank down before sitting next to her.

Maris busied herself by arranging her gown, grateful for an excuse to remove her hand from his arm. He'd sat upon the edge of her skirt, and when she looked up at him to ask him to move, she froze at the bright anger in his eyes. Suddenly, she knew why he'd brought her outside: so that they would be alone and no one could overhear.

"No sooner is our betrothal announced than you are plotting to rid yourself of me!" He leaned close to her face, close enough that she felt the warmth of his breath on her cheek. Dirick tipped up her chin, forcing her to look at him. "You'll not be rid of me that easily!"

Maris pulled back, disturbed by the fluttering in her stomach. "Dirick—"

He cut her off. "I've just been given everything I want in this world, and you'll not destroy that for me!"

"Nay," she whispered, wondering, hoping, that perhaps she had been part of what he wanted in the world...*she*, not her lands. But the hope was futile, as his next words proved.

"I've been given a title, and my own lands—and Langumont will bring even more leverage to the Barony of Ludingdon—'tis more than I'd ever thought possible." If Maris hadn't been so hurt by his words, she would have been warmed by the pride and happiness that lit his silver-grey eyes. "If you are so repulsed by the notion of wedding with me, so be it—but do you not squander my own life for your whim!" The warmth in his eyes was gone, replaced now by the flashing anger that had been there before.

She rose, looking down at him. "'Twas only the concern of my loyal man that you heard, as I'd made it clear to him in the past that I'd not suffer Victor d'Arcy in my bed!"

Dirick's face took on a serious cast. "Aye, lady, 'tis certain he is miffed by the dissolution of your betrothal to him. Have a care to yourself."

Mayhaps he did care for her…or, more likely, he feared aught would happen to halt their wedding before he gained her lands. Her lips tightened. "He would gain naught by harming me—'tis you who should watch your back." A cool smile flitted across her mouth. "In less than the space of one day, you've made two enemies on my behalf."

He pulled to his feet, tall and powerful in his great height. "My dearest Maris, I have many, many enemies—two more, especially for your sake, mean naught to me." His gaze caught hers, holding it steadily, then falling downcast as he took one of her hands. He raised it to his mouth, brushing full, warm lips over the sensitive skin of the back of her hand. She shivered and tried to pull it free, but he held her firmly, turning it palm-side-up and pressing a gentle kiss to the cup of her hand.

"Dirick.…" she breathed through a heavy, tight chest.

"I should require a kiss to seal our betrothal," he told her, gathering her to his chest. He was warm and solid, his arms a strong band holding her to him. Dirick looked down at her, not to seek permission to kiss her, she knew, but for her to see the determination in his gaze before his lips descended.

A new strength—a possessiveness—colored his kiss, confidence exuded from his person, as he skillfully plundered her mouth. She did not resist, but kissed him back, reaffirming the desire he'd kindled in her the night before.

His hands slipped from her back down over her rump, pulling her up against the ridge of his arousal. He sighed, dipped his head to gently bite her neck, and released her. They looked at each other for a moment, assessing the other, gathering their wits, realizing that in four days they would be wed.

"I shall tell you this only once, my lady," he said at last in a voice rough with desire, "though you may find marriage to me repulsive, you will suffer me in your bed...at the least until you have presented me with an heir." He stepped away, shooting a glance toward the building they'd left. "Call upon your faithful knight to see you to your chamber. I shall escort you to dinner this even."

Twemty-Three ❧

*T*he next morning, Maris broke her fast in her chamber, alone. She had no desire to rest her attention upon her betrothed husband any sooner than her wedding day demanded. She'd been so stunned by his kisses, and then broad-sided by his steely command that she bear him an heir, that she'd been able to do naught but gape after him as he left her standing in the courtyard.

Dirick had not escorted her to dinner as he'd promised, as the king had called his council of barons together to discuss the problems with his brother in Anjou. As a newly-confirmed lord who also had the ear of the king, Dirick was expected to participate in this activity, and, Maris thought, 'twas no hardship to her. Verily, she hoped he'd spend the rest of his time in the company of his liege lord!

Agnes assisted her to dress in a traveling gown for a trip into Town. Despite her anger with Dirick for his blunt, offensive orders to her the day before, Maris knew that she would be wed three days hence, and the womanly part of her desired to dress the part. And, though she loathed to admit it, she wanted to find a wedding gift for her husband.

Raymond and five other men-at-arms waited without her chamber, following as she and Agnes started down the hall.

Their horses were ready for them at the great royal stables.

Maris offered Hickory a scrubbed carrot in apology for not visiting the day before, then, using a tree stump reserved for that purpose, hoisted herself lightly into the saddle.

As they approached the market area of London Town, the six men-at-arms stayed close around the two women. Once they reached the stalls where the cloth-makers were, Maris and Agnes dismounted from their horses and, leaving their mounts with two of the burly men-at-arms, began to weave their way through the crowds of people.

Raymond and the rest of the men cleared a path for the women, stepping out of the way when they reached a vendor that interested Maris.

She spent a better part of the morning searching for cloth to make her wedding gown, fingering silks and wools and linens from France, Italy, even the Holy Lands. At last, she discovered a merchant with brilliantly-colored, tightly-woven fabrics of such quality that she'd not seen. Each bolt cost more than one peasant family subsisted upon in one year at Langumont, and Maris nearly went on to a different stall.

But the merchant knew his trade, and when he saw the interest in her eyes and noticed the fineness of her clothing, he pulled a special cloth from the bottom of a trunk. Maris's eyes widened when she saw it, and her mouth opened in a soft gasp. She'd never seen anything as beautiful as the shimmering pale gold cloth. 'Twas nearly sheer, and shot through with shiny gold threads in a spiderweb pattern, and it slithered over her fingers with a mere whisper. 'Twould make a stunning undergown. Maris fingered it thoughtfully for a moment, then acquiesced to its beauty and commenced with haggling over the cost of the bolt.

Her undisguised interest was her undoing, and, though she was normally skilled in the technique of bargaining, the merchant was able to wring rather more gold from her than she should have paid. Maris purchased a second bolt of darker gold silk for her overgown at a much lesser cost, and a light, cinnamon-colored wool for a cloak from the same merchant.

The party moved along from the cloth vendors, pausing to buy meat pies and cheese for a mid-day meal. The libation offered by a local alewife was strong and pleasingly bitter, sending a tingle of happiness along Maris's spine. They found sweet pastries at yet another stall and stood enjoying them at the side of the busy street.

Now came the difficult part: a wedding gift for her betrothed.

The men-at-arms wandered along the streets in Maris's wake as she perused stall after stall, vendor after vendor, and was able to find nothing she deemed suitable for Dirick.

At last they came to the market section that housed the jewelers and the goldsmiths. Wandering up and down the narrow aisles between stalls, Maris felt a growing sense of frustration as nothing seemed appropriate for her soon to be husband. And why this task of finding a gift should plague her, she didn't know…but it did.

Finally, she paused at a goldsmith that specialized in fashioning brooches and pins for the cloaks and mantles worn by men and women alike. The thought came to her of a sudden.

"How quickly could you create a pin with my lord's standard upon it?" she asked the smith.

The man frowned and ventured, "In six days, mayhaps, my lady."

She shook her head. "Half again as much if you can deliver it to me by Sunday morn."

Obviously unwilling to the let opportunity pass him by, the smith agreed. Maris dug out her leather pouch to give him an initial payment. When she pulled two silver coins from its depths, her dagger tumbled out onto the ground.

The smith stooped to retrieve it for her and gave a start of surprise. "I've not seen this work for many a year, my lady!"

Instantly, her attention left the coins and focused on him. "You know of this work?"

"Aye. 'Tis the skill of Judas of Gladwythe." He seemed surprised at her interest.

"Where might one find this Judas?" she asked, knowing that Dirick would demand the same.

The smith shrugged. "Ah, my lady, I've not seen the man for well nigh five, six summers. He may be dead for all I know, as I've not seen any of his creations for that long. He was not a young man."

Maris dug an extra coin from her purse. "If you recall anything more about him, or where he might be found, do you send word to me, Maris of Langumont, or my betrothed husband, Dirick of Ludingdon. 'Tis a matter of life and death."

He accepted the third coin with alacrity. "Aye, my lady. That I will do. And I will see that your husband's pin is delivered to you by Sunday matins."

"I thank you, good sir." She bid him a good day and returned to Raymond and her other companions with a new bounce in her step. On their wedding day, she would have two presents for her husband!

Because the streets were so crowded, the party did not mount their horses. They were ambling along, the urgency of the trip now gone, when a loud noise behind them drew their attention.

A heavy cart was speeding down the narrow street in their direction, bouncing pell-mell behind two heavy horses. Screams and shouts rang through the air, and passersby jumped out of the way.

The cart narrowly missed the stall where Maris's goldsmith was and trundled along without pause. As the crowd surged and ebbed, frantic to escape the runaway cart, Maris became separated from her party.

"Lady!" Raymond shouted when he saw the horses running straight at her.

She tried to duck out of the way, but the cart jerked its direction, following her as she dodged off the street. It rumbled along in her wake, tearing stalls from their moorings and knocking displays from their tables, gaining proximity as she stumbled down an alley.

Her lungs hurt and her leg ached where she tripped against the side of a stall, but Maris did not stop. The cart came closer, the noise barreling behind her like the rush of a huge wave, and she knew she would not come out of this alive.

Suddenly, as the alley opened onto a wide street, she spied the stone enclosure of a public well. Heading for it, she said a quick prayer. Maris grabbed the heavy wooden framework that supported a large bucket and jumped up and out of the way of the cart.

The cart stormed by, leaving dust in its wake, and disappeared down a side street.

Raymond ran up, his face tight with fear, exclaiming, "Lady, lady, are you all right?"

Shaken, Maris clambered down from her perch on the side of the well. Though she knew her eyes were huge, belaying her fright, she spoke calmly, "Aye, I am unhurt but for my leg." She looked down at her torn, dirty gown, and knew that her hair, which had come unveiled during the chase, hung in sagging braids and straggles down her back. Discreetly, she lifted her skirt to examine her bloody, bruised leg.

Rufus, one of the other men-at-arms, brought Hickory to her and assisted Maris into the saddle. Her leg pained her and her head felt light, but she determined to ride back to Westminster on her own accord.

They were nearly to the castle when they were met by a small company of men carrying the standard of Dirick of Ludingdon. Dirick himself rode at the forefront, and drew up his reins at the approach of the men from Langumont and its mistress.

"Ho!" he called, separating from his men to ride up to Maris's side. His eyes widened at her disheveled appearance. "Maris! What has befallen you?"

She brushed a grimy hand over her face. "Naught but a near miss by a cart. 'Twas a runaway that got loose in the market place and I fell while trying to evade it."

His lips tightened. "You did not tell me you were going to London. I would have been your escort, had I known."

Maris bristled even as she felt Raymond stiffen beside her. "My men are more than an adequate escort for me, my lord, and I will visit the market when I will, with or without your permission."

Dirick's face blanked and he reached over and took the reins from her hands, then led Hickory and her mistress away from the group of men. "I did not demand that you ask my permission to visit the market, Maris," he said with a steely note to his voice. "However, you will not speak to me in that manner in the presence of my men or your men. I was concerned only for your safety, as you are still unwed and a desirable match for any man—and from the look of your clothing, I can see that I was right to think so."

With that, he turned and rejoined the party of men-at-arms, leaving Maris to follow him.

"Sir Raymond," Dirick said, "ride with me if you please. The rest of you, see that my lady returns to Westminster without acquiring any more dirt on her face."

Raymond approached him with a set look on his freckled countenance. Dirick shielded his hand against the beaming sun so that he could look him full in the eye. "Do you not look at me with such fury, man. I did not mean an insult to you—'twas only that I wish to be told of my wife's whereabouts in the future." He raised his hand to stop the other man from speaking. "Nay, 'tis not your task to inform me—'tis a courtesy I request of my wife. Verily, Raymond, I can think of no other man that I'd want to escort my lady—with the exception of myself—than you. Truly."

The other man seemed to accept his apology. "My lord, I thank you for your trust in me. I have served Langumont for greater than a score winters, and I will serve my lady Maris until such time as she does not wish me around."

Dirick nodded. "Aye, Raymond, and as you serve her, you serve me as well. Now, I must tell you that I am greatly pleased that you should take your service so seriously that you would rid her of an unwanted husband—"

"Lord Dirick," the other man interrupted, a shameful look shadowing his face, "I meant naught—"

"Nay, do you not apologize. You meant only to protect your lady as any man should, particularly from the likes of Victor d'Arcy. However, as I am now her betrothed, I should take it as a personal affront should you attempt to rid her of my presence!" He grinned.

A smile of relief broke over Raymond's countenance. "Thank you, my lord, and you can be certain I shall take your words to heart as I know full well you can beat me at swordplay."

"Not without much effort and a little luck," he told him, remembering their mock battle at Langumont. "Now, tell me what passed this day in the market."

Ramond sobered. "'Twas not a runaway, my lord, I should stake my honor on it."

Dirick drew up in his saddle. "What say you, man?"

"'Twas not an accident, I trow. The cart did not slow, and the horses did not act as though they were crazed…it seemed as though the driver urged them on. And," he looked behind as if to see how far back was Maris, "it followed her when she ran down an alleyway." He described how she had escaped from the cart.

"God's blood!" Dirick swore, tension settling in his face. *Someone had tried to kill Maris*. She had nearly died. The blood drained from his head, rushing to throb at the ends of his limbs. "You did not see the driver to recognize him?"

Raymond shook his head. "Nay, my lord, he wore a helm pulled low and a mantle about his face. There were no markings on his clothing or on the cart."

Taking a deep breath, Dirick looked up at the sky. "I will investigate, and I would welcome any assistance you may give me. In the meanwhile, do you double your guard about her—especially when I am not near—and let us not tell her of our suspicions as yet. She will only argue or disregard them."

With a grim smile, Raymond nodded.

Twenty-Four ❧

T wo days.

Maris had two days until she was to wed Dirick of Ludingdon.

The thought had driven her from badgering the seamstresses who worked diligently on her gown into the courtyard near the queen's apartments. She was alone with her thoughts and sank onto a stone bench in the corner of the square garden.

An oak tree spread shady limbs over her perch, and a small forsythia bush burst with sprays of yellow flowers. Maris idly watched as a bee nipped into a blossom, then out, skipping over the expanse of the tree, buzzing happily all the while.

Dirick had not been far from her mind in the last days, though she'd only seen him briefly when they met upon the road from London. She'd angered and embarrassed him in front of his men and her men, yet he'd done naught but give her a brief, pointed warning.

She sighed and broke a twig from the forsythia. Fingering the soft, tender blossoms, she closed her eyes. In two days' time, she'd belong to him…and though she'd fought the idea of marriage long enough, somehow she'd come to accept—nay, welcome—that she would be Dirick's wife.

A shiver raced up her spine, coiling at the base of her neck, reminding her that she would be his wife in all ways. Her mouth became dry at the thought of his lips, his hands…his body on hers, touching her, joining with her. The heat she'd come to associate with Dirick pooled in her middle, surging to her womanly place, causing her breasts to tingle, and she drew a deep breath.

She suddenly became aware that she was not alone.

Her eyes flew open and she saw a page standing there, just off to the side, as if waiting for her to acknowledge him. He held a silver goblet encrusted with rubies and sapphires, and when her attention rested upon him, he gave a short bow, proffering the cup.

"My lady Maris, I am sent by your husband with this gift to quench your thirst."

Her face heated at the possibility that Dirick was nearby and had seen her mooning over him. When she looked about, however, she saw that no one else was in the vicinity, and she returned her gaze to the page. "Is he not to join me?" She tried to submerge the pang of disappointment.

The page shook his head. "Nay, lady. The lord said only that 'tis a gift to you, his bride, and that he looks to the day you shall become one."

Maris took the goblet, admiring its weight. "Thank you, and you may thank my lord for his thoughtfulness as well."

The page bowed, turned, and walked sedately from the courtyard, leaving Maris alone with the bees.

Ruby wine glistened in its silver cup, and she took a sip before resting it on the bench beside her. Mayhaps Dirick, too, was willing to put their differences behind them as their wedding day drew near. 'Twould be more than she could hope that he should welcome their marriage for more than the riches and lands she would bring him.

Another sigh escaped her lips. She could not deny it any longer: she loved him.

Though he caused her ire to rise at their every meeting, he was never far from her thoughts…and the memory of his touch lived in her dreams.

The soft rustle of someone's approach brought Maris's attention from the goblet beside her. Without looking up, she knew 'twas Dirick.

"My lady." He greeted her solemnly, almost warily.

She raised her face to him and was immediately ensnared in his piercing grey gaze. "My lord. I did not think you would join me."

He looked at her, tilting his head to one side. "The ladies told me you'd come for some air. I thought to sit with you for a time, as I've been otherwise occupied with the king for the last days."

Her heart leapt. He had sent her a gift, and then he'd sought her out. "Please have a seat."

"Our betrothal contracts have been finished," he began, sinking onto the bench next to her.

A sense of disappointment settled in her middle. He'd not come to be with her for any other reason than to talk of their contract, and of the lands she would bring him. "Verily they meet your approval," she replied coolly, refusing to look at him or his gift, "and that of the king, I trow."

She felt him nod next to her. "Aye. They are more than fair, and follow the wishes of your father."

"My father?"

"In the missive he sent to the king, he repudiated your betrothal with Victor. He also named you as his heir, though you are not of his blood, and—"

"What?" Maris turned to him, shock numbing her.

"You did not know?" Dirick's face showed his concern.

"That I am not of my father's blood? Nay! Nay, I did not!" She felt lightheaded, lost, paralyzed. "How can that be?"

He reached for her hand, and the warmth of his fingers over her suddenly icy ones was welcome. "I am sorry that this was unknown to you. Your father stated that he married your mother though he knew she was with child, but because he was unable to father a child, he chose to accept her babe as his heir. 'Twas the agreement he made with Stephen." The breeze ruffled his hair, tossing a wave onto his forehead as he gazed at her.

"Who is my father?"

He stroked her hand. "I do not know that, my lady. He did not say in the missive."

"*Jesù*," she breathed. "And that is why he and my mother never had another child." Tears dampened her eyes. "He was my father, though I am not of his loins. I do not care that another man sired me."

Dirick nodded. "Merle was a fine man and had I not my own father of which to admire, I'd be proud to be of his blood." He pressed her index finger to his lips. "The contracts are ready to be signed...." He hesitated. "I will have them brought to you, should you wish, before I place my seal upon them. If there is aught that you do not like, I will try to change it to your liking."

Maris could only stare at him. He asked for her agreement before he signed the contracts? "My lord, I do not know what to say." Indeed, her tongue stuck in her throat, her mind paused at the realization that he should care for her opinion. "I—I...I thank you, Dirick, for your consideration. If you believe they are fair, and if they allow me to retain mine own lands should you pre-decease me, I shall not contest them."

"Henry showed me the missive from your father, and his wishes were just that. Your dowry is generous and shall also be returned to you should I die, and even if we produce an heir, those lands shall revert to you upon my death. Our heir should accede to Ludingdon and Fairhill, unless 'tis a girl, and then, if you wish, she shall have Langumont."

"'Tis more than fair." She could barely form the words as she pictured the babe they would produce. Her throat was dry, and she reached for the wine. "Thank you, my lord, for this beautiful gift." She raised the cup to him, then to her mouth to drink.

The goblet never made it to her lips, as a sudden force sent it spinning to the ground. Maris shrank back from him in surprise as much from his action as the fierce look on his face.

"I did not give you such a gift!" His grey eyes had darkened ominously, turning into steel in his ferocity. "How did you come by that thought?"

She could not speak for a moment, so unexpected was his reaction. Then sanity reigned, and she replied, "But only moments before you came to me, a page delivered it, saying 'twas a gift from you."

"Did you drink of it?" He grabbed her shoulders, pulling her near him as he searched her eyes. "Did you?"

Maris pulled sharply away. "Aye, but no more than a small sip. What ails you, Dirick?"

"It could have been poisoned. It most likely was poisoned!"

"Why should anyone poison me?" She could not contain her shock.

"For the same reason they should try to run you down in the market place. I do not know." His face sagged into serious concern. "Maris, you must have a care! Someone here does not want you to live. Promise me, promise me, that you will go nowhere without me or Raymond until we leave this place."

Maris nodded, the lump in her throat lodging any words she may have wished to speak inside. Why should anyone wish to kill her?

"Did you recognize the page? What did he say?"

She shook her head and described what had happened when he'd brought the wine. There were no answers there, she knew, and even only the suspicion that the wine had been poisoned.

They would never know for certain.

"We will leave Westminster the day after we are wed," Dirick told her firmly, the possessive, protective look in his eyes sending a thrill down her spine. "I will take you to Derkland for a time, to meet my mother, and then we shall go on to Ludingdon. At any rate, I shall take you away from this place."

Maris was just about to speak when another page approached. "My lady Maris?" She nodded acquiescence and he bowed. "I have been asked to inform you that your mother, Lady Allegra of Langumont, has arrived."

"My mother?" she repeated dumbly.

"Aye. She has been shown to the ladies' chamber, and wishes you to attend her."

Maris rose. "Aye. I will go to her." She looked down at Dirick, who stared up at her with eyes that seemed to devour her. "I thank you for all you have told me this day, and I will look to see you at dinner this night."

"My lady, I look more to two days hence when we shall be wed." He grabbed her hand and pressed a kiss to the inner part of her wrist, then released her. "Until then."

⁂

Allegra had been summoned to Westminster in order to attend her daughter's wedding.

When Maris appeared to answer her bidding, she wore a surprised but pleased expression on her face. "Mama! How glad I am that you have come to see me wed!"

Allegra drew her daughter into a brief embrace, then set her back gently. "You are to marry Sir Dirick de Arlande?"

"Aye, only now he is called Lord Dirick of Ludingdon." Maris sat in a chair next to her. "Mama, why did you not tell me Papa is not my father?"

Allegra's heart skittered in her chest. "How did you come to learn this?"

A familiar expression of stubbornness crossed her daughter's face. "It does not matter how I came to learn of it, only whether 'tis true."

A chill swept over Allegra. "Aye, daughter, 'tis true. Your papa did not sire you." She clenched her hands tightly. "But how did you come to learn this? Tell me."

"Papa wrote it in a missive to the king," Maris explained.

"Your papa?" Suddenly, she couldn't breathe. "Your papa told the king?"

"Aye, Mama."

She swallowed tightly. "Your Papa did not know…I did not believe he knew. I did not tell him—'twas my greatest sin.…" Dear God, she was cursed, damned! If Merle knew that Maris was not of his loins, 'twould have been no hardship to tell him of Bon's threats…and why he could not betrothe her to Victor. Instead, she lived the lie and now he was dead…and she still had judgement to face. A sudden trembling overtook her and she stuffed her hands into the folds of her skirts. "I must go to confession." She stood abruptly, moving without hesitation and without a backward glance, to the door. She felt, but ignored, Maris's gawking stare upon her back as she swept from the chamber.

꒰ꕤ꒱

Later, when night had come, and when she'd said enough paternosters and supplications to the Virgin, she hoped, to salvage her soul, Allegra crept from the chapel, tucking her greying hair into her veil. She cast about, looking for a page, a maidservant, someone to guide her back to the ladies' chamber.

"Allegra."

The smooth voice from the shadows caused her heart to leap into her throat, and she whirled to face him. "Michael!"

"Sshhh," he admonished, stepping fully into the light. He pressed a finger against her dry lips with a soft caress. "'Tis not meet for us to be seen together."

"Why? Why should we care?" she said, just so she could feel her mouth moving against his beloved flesh.

"Come." He dropped his hand from her lips and grasped her own fingers, firmly tugging her along in his wake.

Allegra followed—she would do naught but as he bid—and he drew her along in the shadows of the dark hall. Reaching a small alcove, he pulled her inside and into a bare chamber, then into his embrace.

With a cry of delight, she pulled his face to hers, sampling his mouth with her starving lips. "Michael!" she sighed. "Oh, my beloved, how I have missed you! I thought to lose you yet again after you left Langumont!"

His hands were warm and possessive over the swell of her hips, pressing her into the need that pulsed at his groin. "You are my only love," he told her as his mouth slid to the hollow of her neck. "Marry me. Dearling, be my wife!" He pulled back so that she could see the glitter of hope and desire in his eyes.

"Oh, aye, Michael, aye! 'Tis half my life I have waited to hear those words of your lips!" Her hands were busy, pulling his tunic up so that she could feel his warm, solid chest against her fingers.

"'Tis long I have waited to utter them." He helped her by yanking off his tunic, then pushing his chausses down past his waist. Expertly, Michael slid her to the floor, pulling her gown up so that it bunched above her hips. When he thrust inside of her welcoming body, she cried at the pleasure of it, raising and lowering herself to meet his rhythm.

With a guttural groan, he met his end, and she with him, and they lay for a moment in a heap of tangled clothing, sweat, and lust.

"Let us marry on the morrow," he suggested, pressing a kiss behind her ear, at a place that never failed to cause her to shiver.

"But, Michael, what of the banns? We cannot find a priest to marry us so soon! And what of Maris?"

"I have already paid a priest to marry us without calling the banns…I planned to ask you tonight and could not bear to wait any longer than need be. He awaits us on the morrow. And," he flicked his tongue into the depths of her ear, sending a sharp, pleasant twinge down her spine, "let us not tell Maris as yet…she may look askance at us for marrying so soon after Merle's death."

Allegra pulled away as a thought struck her. "Did you tell Maris that you are her natural father?"

Michael peered down at her in the dim light as if trying to read her face. "What do you say?"

"Her betrothal to Victor was repudiated and now she is to marry Lord of Ludingdon…was it you who told the king of her relation to your son so that he would deny the betrothal?"

Michael nodded. "Aye, he was prepared to formalize the contracts between them, and I could do naught but step forward and share the truth with him. 'Twas all for the best. Dirick of Derkland seems a fine fellow."

Allegra nodded, pleased at his concern for their daughter, and overwhelmed by the comfort of his nearness. "I have never stopped loving you, Michael, and I cannot believe that we shall be husband and wife at last!"

She felt him smile against her cheek. "Aye. 'Tis all that I have ever hoped for."

Twenty-Five ☙

irick leaned heavily against Raymond's shoulder, his head reeling from the large amount of ale he'd imbibed at The Blue Goat, The Bow and the Apple, The King's Shield…and all of the other places his men had dragged him to.

"This way, m'lord," directed Raymond, his voice slightly slurred. The party of men stumbled along the street, their way lit as much by the full moon as by the lanterns that hung intermittently about.

"I know where I am," growled Dirick, struggling to hold his head upright. 'Twas not the best thing to do the night before one's wedding, but it had been impossible to deny his men their chance to celebrate his marriage. Verily, dawn could be no more than two or three hours away. Dirick groaned at the thought. Henry expected him, as well as the other two bridegrooms, to join him for a celebratory hunt not long after the sun rose…to be followed shortly after by the wedding ceremony. In a matter of hours, he would be married to Maris.

Even in his befuddled state of mind, Dirick grasped the clarity of that fact. At this time on the morrow, he'd be abed with his new wife. And despite the amount of ale his men had poured down his throat, Dirick's body reacted accordingly, filling and hardening with desire. A thrill of need rippled down his spine, causing him to catch a sharp intake of breath at its intensity.

He'd not seen Maris since the announcement that her mother had arrived from Langumont—between the king's demands on his time, and her own responsibilities to Allegra, neither of them had been in the Great Hall for meals at the same time. He'd not see her again, he realized, until they met at the altar on the morrow. Not for the first time, Dirick wondered if she'd become accepting of the fact that he was to be her husband. He did not want a battle in their bedchamber on the night of their wedding if she had not.

She'd ever welcomed his kisses in the past, he reflected, the heaviness between his legs growing…and if they were truly wed, she'd have no reason, and, he prayed, no desire, to refuse him.

Dirick stumbled over a rock in the street and would have pitched face-first onto the ground had Raymond not had a firm grip on his tunic. One of the men in their group—he blearily thought it might be Sir Gerald—guffawed loudly in the still night, commenting that his lord had nearly fallen into a pile of dung. Dirick responded with a slurred insult, which the rest of the men found so uproariously funny that they nearly failed to spot the shadow slouching along the wall near the castle's entrance.

"Ho!" Raymond stopped short. He was the least inebriated of the bunch, Dirick realized, and was thankful that 'twas he who'd offered to guide him home. "Who goes there?"

Dirick pulled himself upright, standing almost solidly under his own balance, as the shadow was pulled into the torchlight, metamorphosing into Bon de Savrille.

"What do you here?" Dirick demanded, separating himself from his men and approaching Bon. Through the haze of his drunkenness, he found the comforting handle of his dagger.

"Do not fear," sneered the other man. "I do not wait to accost you, but only to issue a warning."

"You seek to warn me? Against what?" Dirick choked back a deprecating laugh. Then, fury shot through him and he lashed out to grab the other man's arm. "Is it you who seeks to show Maris to an early grave?"

Bon shook off his grip with effort. "Nay, fool! Why would I wish to see the woman dead? 'Tis why I come to warn you!"

Dirick stared at him, uncomprehending. "Speak more clearly, then, man!"

Bon leaned toward him, his dark eyes glittering with intensity. "I do not wish to see her dead, but there is one who does…and the same one wishes harm to you as well."

"Why do you warn *me*, then, as I know you have no love for me!"

The other man shook his head. "Nay, I do not," he agreed, "but 'tis Maris for whom I care…and I would see her protected." He looked at Dirick with bleary eyes. "I love her."

"She is mine." He snapped the words, suddenly afraid that Bon might find a way to have her.

"I am aware that the king has promised her to you." Bon's reply was bitter. "But that is not the purpose of my warning to you. Ask yourself why did Merle of Langumont not return from Dreakskil, and you will know why someone desires her dead."

"Merle of Langumont died in the siege of Dreakskil, most like of your own hand," Dirick returned slowly, the ale still swimming in his mind.

"Nay. Merle of Langumont was alive to accept my surrender," Bon told him.

"You do not—"

Bon began to melt back into the shadows. "Nay, that is all I can tell you, sirrah, as I do not wish to be the next casualty…an', in faith, I wish to be the one left to hold and comfort my lady when all is said and the battles done." With that parting promise, he disappeared from sight.

"Who is it?" demanded Dirick of the shadows.

"Her father!" whispered a voice before its owner swept away into the night.

Her father. Dirick's mind swam as he lay on his pallet, Bon's words echoing in his memory, swirling among the ale that sopped his brain. Her father was dead, he reminded himself. What did the man mean? Nay, Merle was not her father, he remembered foggily. *Ask yourself why Merle of Langumont did not return from Dreakskil.* Why?

I love her. Those words taunted him with their sincerity. Another man loved his betrothed wife—truly loved her, if the pain in Bon's eyes was to be believed.

A heaviness settled over Dirick's chest. His breathing quickened, then slowed, then rose faster again. If another man loved her enough to warn his enemy of danger, just to ensure that Maris should be safe, what would he do to have her?

Could she love him?

Dirick frowned at his absurd thought, fighting to crystallize the murkiness of his mind. Damn that last jug of ale!

Her father. The words returned. *I love her.*

Ask yourself why Merle of Langumont did not return.

He slept, dreamt, slept.

Twnety-Six ♔

irick's head felt thrice as large as normal, his ears a hundred times more sensitive, and his belly like the ocean during a storm.

The barking of the dogs was enough to drive him mad, yet he gritted his teeth and managed to smile at Henry's jest.

"What ails you, Dirick?" the king asked, obviously noticing his pained grin.

"Naught but enough ale to drown a village," he admitted.

Henry chuckled. "'Twould be a travesty were you not at your best this even when you take your bride to bed!" Then he laughed outright. "Say the word if you cannot perform your duties and would wish some assistance!"

Dirick glared at the king, finding little humor in his liege's jest. "Nay, your grace, I assure you I have waited long enough for this night, and I will have no problem with performing as I should!"

The king laughed again, then turned his attention to the howling hounds. "They've scented a boar!" he cried in excitement. With a spur to his mount, he leaned forward and the stallion leapt into the wake of the frenzied dogs.

A party of twenty-some men and their horses trampled through the forest, bearing down upon the hounds. The fresh air whipping about his face dissolved the brunt of Dirick's nausea and he began to get into the spirit of the hunt. With a cry of delight, he brandished the spear he carried and urged Nick harder, so that they gained ground on the king.

At last, the howling of the dogs indicated that they'd cornered the boar. The hunters raced into the clearing, reining up on one side, readying themselves to take passes at the snorting animal.

The boar's red eyes blazed from its long-snouted face, and angry tusks curled with enough curve to rock a careless dog before tossing it into the air. Bristling, wiry hair sprang from the beast, and hot breath rasped from flaring nostrils as it cast frantically about for an escape route. All avenues of freedom were blocked by hound, horse, or man, and the boar grew more frenzied as it readied itself to rush through the blockades

"Now!" cried Henry, nodding at the three bridegrooms, who'd been given the honor of the first strokes.

Lord Bartholemew readied his spear and dug his heels into his mount's gut. They leaped forward, crashing through the clearing, passing by the boar in a flurry of hooves, flapping cloak, and a well-thrust spear. A spurt of blood sprang forth from the beast's shoulder, and a cheer erupted from the other hunters.

Lord Richard followed shortly after, missing his stab at the boar, but distracting the howling beast from the spear wielded by Dirick. His aim was true, and the boar received another telling wound in its belly.

As Dirick halted Nick to the side, watching as the boar pawed the ground, readying itself for a vicious pass through the ring of men that surrounded it, he had a moment to reflect upon his garbled memory of Bon's warning from the night before.

Why did Merle not return from Dreakskil? If he were alive when Bon saw him last, and he was not felled during the attack upon the keep, then he must have died by the hand of someone else.

Michael and Victor d'Arcy?

The thought sprang to his mind, followed quickly by the question of why.

A shout from one of the hunters distracted Dirick from his thoughts, and he saw that the boar was wavering on its feet.

Her father. Could Michael be Maris's father? That could explain Allegra's odd reaction when she greeted them back at Langumont. The hair prickled at the nape of his neck. Things were beginning to make sense.

Dirick turned to Lord Bartholemew, who watched the last thrust at the boar with rapt attention. "Bart, know you much of Lord Michael d'Arcy? Is he trustworthy?"

The other man turned, a look of satisfaction on his face as the boar crashed onto its side. "Lord of Gladwythe, you speak of? Verily, the man has an oddness about him. Mayhaps 'tis because of his parents' death…findin' them like that would have to touch anyone's mind."

"What of his parents' death?"

Bartholomew shook his head sadly, turning from the bloody scene of the boar's demise and giving Dirick his full attention now that the hunt was over. "He was naught more than a boy when his papa and mama jumped to their death from a tower at Gladwythe."

"He found them?"

"Aye. They'd jumped together, their hands joined, and landed thusly in the bailey at Gladwythe."

Dirick stared at him for a moment, a chill creeping down his back. The pieces slipped into place and he felt the blood drain from his head.

"Ludingdon, are you well?" asked Bartholomew as if from very far away.

"I must go." Dirick wheeled Nick around, his heart crashing

in his chest. He drove his heels into Nick's sides, leaning forward over the stallion's neck, urging the horse on. "Tell the king I've found him!" he shouted over his shoulder as horse and man thundered through the brush.

He felt the saddle slip as Nick leapt over a tree trunk, and before he could think, its girth loosened, then gave way and suddenly, he was falling, falling.

His last thought before he hit the ground was that he had been sabotaged.

کہ

Maris opened the heavy gold box and gasped, sinking onto her bed.

"'Tis beauteous!" she exclaimed, pulling a rope of fine gold links from the small chest. Topazes and emeralds dangled erratically from the necklet that would wrap around her neck at least thrice. Each jewel was set in an ornate, filigreed hasp, each one different and a work of art in its own right.

"'Tis a wondrous bride's gift," said Lady Laurette with a twinkle in her eye. "Lord Dirick is a generous groom."

"Aye." Maris looked down at the small chest that rested in her lap. The box itself was a lovely gift, and along with the bejeweled necklet it held bespoke of the value Dirick placed upon his bride. She could not hold back a smile of pure joy. Mayhaps he did care for her as much as he desired her lands!

She poured the gold rope back into the chest. Delivered by one of her own men from Langumont, the box had been tied with a golden ribbon and sprigs of rosemary, lemon verbena, and violets. Maris sniffed the small purple flowers and placed them, along with the herbs, on top of the necklet, and closed the chest. Her stomach tingled and she smiled again. Tonight, she would lie with Dirick, would feel his lips and hands over her body, would mate with him and feel his skin next to hers, would become his. Anticipation sent a shiver down her spine. Today, she would marry the man she loved.

The fear and hesitancy were gone, and in their place was comfort, love, and happiness that she would belong to Dirick, with Dirick, and would live with him and bear his children and rule their lands at his side. Maris took a deep breath, hardly able to credit the fact that she was welcoming, embracing the event of marriage, after having fought against it for so long.

An urgent knocking on the door drew her from her wool-gathering, and Maris and the other ladies watched expectantly as a maidservant went to answer it.

"My Lady Maris," Michael d'Arcy nearly burst into the room when the door opened. "There has been an accident! 'Tis your betrothed husband!"

Maris jumped from her stool. "Dirick!" she exclaimed. "What is it? Is he all right?" Her heart lodged in her throat, and she was dimly aware that Laurette was patting her arm comfortingly.

Michael shook his head soberly. "Maris, I do not know. He is with the physicians now. He fell from his horse during the hunt. You must come with me."

"Of course!" She moved quickly toward the door, trying to quiet the tension and fear thrumming through her veins. "I must fetch my medicines from my chamber," she told Michael as they started down the hall.

"Nay, there is no time. He has called for you to come to his side, and 'tis best that you come with me now…. Maris, 'tis serious, and he wishes to speak with you."

The fear in her middle grew and she found herself blinking back stinging tears. To lose love so soon after finding it would be more she could bear…especially coming so closely upon the heels of her father's death. Maris clenched her fist in the folds of her skirt as she was propelled along by Michael's very firm grip. She would not think about that possibility. She would not!

At the stables, she was faintly surprised to find Hickory saddled and ready, with Victor holding the reins. "Come, lady, before 'tis too late!" he urged, helping her into the saddle.

Michael mounted his own horse and nudged Maris and Victor ahead of him through the bailey. They trotted quickly through the entryway, over the drawbridge, and away from the keep.

꒜

Bon de Savrille emerged from a corner of the bailey just after Maris and her escort passed by. His face was creased with concern as he hurried into the stable and selected a horse under the watchful eye of the marshal.

"Hurry, man," he demanded, looking in the direction in which she'd disappeared.

At last, he was given the reins and he vaulted into the saddle. With a loud, "Hah!" he whipped the stallion and thundered through the bailey and across the drawbridge, following the path of the two men and the woman he loved.

Dirick forced his eyes open from the darkness that beckoned him with a soothing aura. There was something…something urgent….

Voices reached his ears, as if from far away. He thought he moved…aye, he must have, for pain ricocheted up his leg and curled in the low part of his back.

The urgency came to him again…then it was gone.

Firm hands pulled and pushed at him, and he wanted to slip into that blackness and sleep…but the urgency kept kneading at him…kneading…like the hands that interrupted his comfort.

Maris!

The name struck his consciousness like a lightening bolt and he jerked awake. Something about Maris.... His eyes were open, blearily focusing on the faces that stared down at him. Maris was not there, he realized dimly...Henry...Bart...Raymond....

Maris...his mind screamed the name, the urgency, but it took all of his effort to pinpoint his concentration. The urgency had aught to do with her.... Maris, his betrothed wife, his beloved....

D'Arcy!

Dirick croaked the name as he struggled to sit upright. God in heaven, he was going to take her! "Maris!" he managed to push from a dry, swollen throat.

Faintly, he heard Henry laugh, though the concern still ringed his eyes. "The man's worried that he won't be able to do his wife justice this night...he must be fine!" Nevertheless, the king himself bent toward Dirick. "Can you stand, man?"

Dirick gathered all of his wits and strength and nodded his head, reaching for the hand that was proffered to him. It was a beringed hand, and it belonged to Henry...but Dirick disregarded that fact as he lunged for the offered grip and pulled himself to his feet.

He was in the forest. The members of the hunt had gathered around with their mounts, and the hounds, and even the carcass of the boar. "I must go," was all he could say once he found Nick with his gaze.

"Ludingdon, what ails you? You must come back to the castle and be tended to!" Henry boomed the order. "Richard! Marcus! Take him and bring him back to the physicians, and do not listen to his arguments! He has delayed my hunt long enough!"

Twenty-Seven ✧

*H*ow much further are they?" asked Maris, looking about the forest for some sign of the hunting party. She'd ridden quite far out of London Town with Michael and Victor and expected to find the hunting party at any time.

Neither man replied to her question, but she noticed that they exchanged glances over her head.

"I do not see them anywhere," she said more forcefully. "Surely the hunt did not take the party this far from the castle." An uncomfortable twinge started in the base of her spine and she reined Hickory up. "Are you certain we are going in the right direction?"

Michael stopped his horse and turned back to her. "Come, Maris, do not question me." He grabbed the reins from her hands and began to propel Hickory behind his own mount.

The twinge blossomed into a full foreboding and Maris felt fear curdle in her middle. Aught was not right here and she must do something about it. "I must return to the castle for my wedding," she said, squinting up at the sun that was beginning to climb down the sky.

Victor laughed and the sound sent a chill up her spine. "Your bridegroom is in no condition to attend the ceremony. There is no need for you to return."

Those words held a finality that did not sit well with Maris. It had occurred to her earlier that she'd disobeyed Dirick's orders to go nowhere without him or Raymond…but her fear for his safety had been the overriding factor in her decision…and, in sooth, she'd forgotten of her promise in her terror that he'd been injured.

Michael urged his horse into a canter, and Maris was forced to lean forward and grab Hickory's mane. She forced herself to examine the situation and her conclusion was that this was no mere kidnapping. She swallowed the fear in her throat. She could not escape on foot, and Michael was in control of her horse. Victor rode so close to her that his mount's tail brushed against Hickory's shoulder.

"'Tis not far from here," he told his father, moving up so that their horses were neck and neck. Maris was now out of their sight, though being towed along on Hickory, and she used the opportunity to slip a hand under her skirt and pull forth her dagger. She sent up a prayer of thanks that her mother had warned her never to be without the knife and set to cutting away at the reins. If she were quick, and lucky, she could cut herself free and be off. Mayhaps, she and Hickory could outrun her kidnappers. If not…that, she thought calmly, was not worth thinking on.

In truth, Dirick should have learned of her absence by now and verily he would search for her. Then, as she continued to saw through the thick leather, a pang of fear shot through her. Michael and Victor talked so certainly of his injury…mayhaps there was a truth to it and he would not be able to come after her. Mayhaps he was dead!

Angry, frustrated tears welled in her eyes and she pushed the thought away. She'd think only of one thing now: escaping from Michael and Victor.

When the reins were nearly cut through, Maris gathered herself and readied her courage, gripping Hickory with her thighs and tightening her fistful of mane. With a final slice, she cut the last bit of leather and kicked her horse to veer suddenly away.

The shout of surprise erupted too close behind her and she leaned forward, urging Hickory as they raced for their freedom. The trampling of hooves in their trail was loud and gaining proximity and she felt tears sting her eyes. "Nay! Hickory, go!" she cried into the mare's ear, kicking her again.

'Twas of no use. One of them galloped up next to her and with a swift jerk, pulled her from her saddle across his own. She landed on her stomach with the air knocked out of her and saw the ground race by at a dizzying speed. She'd failed.

"Bitch!" Michael's voice was tight with fury as he slowed his horse to a walk. "Foolish woman!"

Victor barrelled up to them. "I'll take her, Father. 'Tis my right to enjoy what little time we've left together."

Maris struggled as she was passed none too gently to the younger man's mount, placed in front of him on the saddle. Michael gave her a hard slap to the face, stunning her, as Victor's arms tightened around her waist.

"What are you going to do?" she demanded, trying to ignore the pounding in her temple from the blow.

Victor laughed harshly. "You seem so concerned about your wedding, my dear, that I should hate to disappoint you and have you forego your wedding night." One of his hands slipped to close over her breast as he pushed his arousal into her bottom. "I would expect that to occupy us for some time, and then…well, my love, I do not see any purpose in returning damaged goods to your bridegroom…if indeed he still lives." His fingers pinched cruelly at her breast, closing over her nipple so that she could not suppress a sharp moan of pain. "And I have no use for damaged goods myself. After all, 'twould do no good for me to beget a child upon my sister, now would it?"

"What?" she gasped from pain as much as shock.

"What, Father, you did not tell her that we are blood?" Victor asked, his hand moving to cup the full weight of her breast, fondling it roughly.

Michael looked at Maris. "Your mother, whore that she is, begat my child before she married Merle of Langumont and birthed you."

"You are my father?" The pain from Victor's seeking fingers faded in light of this revelation. "Nay."

"Oh, I assure you, 'tis true."

"But...I was to marry...your son...my brother."

Michael shrugged. "I did not know you were my daughter at that time. I did not learn of it until your stupid mother told me as we set out for Dreakskil to save you. In truth, it did not matter to me or to Victor...but your papa—Merle—must have learned such as he told me he'd changed his mind over the betrothal." A cold smile of such evil spread his features that Maris felt nauseated. "I could not accept that decision."

The nausea turned to cold anger. "You killed my father," she whispered.

"Oh, nay, he did not," said Victor, leaning forward to thrust a tongue wet with slime into her ear. "'Twas I who sank the blade into his back, as I had already decided I must have you to wife."

Maris jerked away from his cold mouth and was just as harshly jerked back onto a solid chest. "Nay, lady, you'll not escape me this time. It is long I have waited for the opportunity to break your arrogance and impudence, and I'll have no more delays." He sank his fingers into the mass of braids at the back of her scalp, pulling her head back at an impossible angle, and kissed her forcefully.

Just then, the sound of galloping reached their ears. All three turned to see a single man on horseback careening through the trees.

Maris's heart leapt until the man drew closer and she recognized him. 'Twas Bon!

"Halt!" he cried as Michael and Victor started to wheel their horses about, ready to make their escape. "Unhand her!" Bon did not slow, and his momentum brought him to their sides. Maris saw that he brandished a sword that glittered in the afternoon light and she took the opportunity to jerk loose of Victor's hands.

With a quick elbow into his abdomen, Maris was off the saddle in a flash and tearing through the woods. There were shouts of anger behind her, and she heard a scream of pain from one of the horses, but she kept running.

There was no sound of horse's hooves following her, but she knew in her numb mind that when they finished their battle, whoever was left would chase her down.

⁓

Swallowing back the nausea that threatened, Dirick leaned forward over Nick's neck. His head still pounded and his entire body throbbed with pain...but his intent was single: to find Maris.

Fear sickened him, overwhelming him as he led the party of men through the forest. Fortunately, Michael and Victor had been spotted with Maris by several people and they'd had to waste little time in gleaning their trail. The odd part, he reflected, needing some puzzle to focus on so that he would not go crazy with worry, was the third man who had followed in their wake.

The sun was lowering and soon the forest would be dark. 'Twould be next to impossible to follow the trail in the dark, and this realization was the impetus that drove him on.

Dear God, he could not lose her! Dirick swallowed back the

unmanly urge to cry in frustration. She was his, she was to be his…tonight, he was to wed with the only woman he'd ever wanted with such agonizing need. He drove his heels into Nick's middle, pushing the destrier even harder than he did in battle. This was the most important battle he'd ever fought, he realized numbly. He could not lose it.

He almost missed seeing the shadow that rushed out from a deep thicket.

"Help me!"

"Maris!" Dirick jerked back on the reins, wheeling Nick on his hindlegs to land just next to her.

"Dirick?" she cried as he slid off his saddle and pulled her into his arms in one fluid motion.

She was sobbing and shaking and running her hands all over his face as he pulled her close to his chest. Nothing had ever felt so good. "Dear God, I thought I'd lost you," he murmured, burying his face in her neck, smelling the rosemary and lemon and touching the tangles of her hair. "Maris, Maris," he said her name over and over. "Beloved, have they hurt you? How did you escape?"

She sniffled in the first show of womanly weakness he'd ever witnessed. "I am not hurt," she told him, looking up with wide golden-green eyes. "But 'twas Bon de Savrille who saved me."

"What?" Dirick propelled her back to his horse as the others gathered around.

"Aye, he came after us and in the confusion, I managed to get away. 'Twas not far from here," she looked over her shoulder, gesturing in that direction, "and no one came after me. I do not know what happened."

With a curt nod, Dirick sent several of the men scattering to see what they could find. "Are you truly not hurt?" he asked, drawing them away from the rest of the party and angling Nick so that he stood between them and the gawking men. "My beloved, I cannot tell you what fears I had for you!"

She reached up and smoothed a cool hand over his face, touching a scrape from his fall. "They told me you'd been hurt, that you'd fallen from a horse."

He nodded. "Aye. And I trow 'twas Michael or Victor who slit the girth of my saddle, nearly causing me to be trampled among Nick's hooves. I am fine, now that you are safe."

She pulled him down, covering his lips with her own. "I nearly did not have the chance to tell you...." She looked steadily at him. "I—I am well-pleased to be your wife. I—I love you, Dirick." When he would speak, she pressed a finger to his lips. "Nay, do not speak. 'Tis enough for me that you came after me...I do not expect that you should feel that. And, in sooth, Dirick, I do not care."

He would have spoken, but a shout drew his attention. Gathering her into his arms, he gave her a well-placed kiss on her lips and lifted her into his saddle. Vaulting gracefully up, he settled behind her and they started off toward the shout.

A group of men gathered in a small clearing, and when they drew near, Raymond of Vermille caught Dirick's eye, shaking his head slightly. Maris should not see, was the message in his gaze. But 'twas too late.

She slid from the saddle and pushed her way through the gawking crowd of men, ignoring Dirick's shout. The scene that greeted her was one to leave nightmares, but she moved forward. She had to see it.

Victor d'Arcy lay on his stomach, head turned to one side, and his back soaked with blood. Bon de Savrille was arranged so that he lay in a similar position, with his hands reaching eerily for Victor's. His beard was wet with the blood that oozed from the spot where his nose had been, and his neck was bent at an awkward angle so that, although he lay on one cheek, his face was tilted back and his eyes looked at nothingness.

Nausea gathered in the back of her throat, but she was able to keep it at bay until she saw the horse. Then, she could control it no longer, and she turned to spew it into the bushes.

Dirick caught her in the middle of her wild retreat and held her while she emptied her belly in a thicket. Coughing and spitting, she raised her face and he offered her a corner of his tunic. There was a gentleness in his eyes, a tenderness and a light of such depth that she'd never seen in his countenance before as he turned her away from the bloody scene. Placing a comforting arm around her waist, he walked her back to Nick.

"Come, let me take you back to the castle." He placed a gentle kiss on her forehead and once again lifted her onto Nick.

"Our wedding day is ruined," she told him tearfully, suddenly overwhelmed with emotion.

"Nay, my lady, our wedding day is saved." He pulled her back against his broad chest, pulling his cloak about them to ward off the spring evening, and turned Nick back toward Westminster.

Twenty-Eight ✑

I do," Dirick said clearly, looking straight into Maris's eyes. The bishop joined their hands, intoning, "I pronounce you man and wife. Let no man tear asunder what God has thus joined."

Dirick's hands closed tightly over Maris's smaller, rough ones, and she could not help but smile up at him.

"Congratulations, Ludingdon," the king boomed from his stance off to the side of the chapel.

"My thanks, your grace." Dirick did not release Maris's hand as they walked over to bow to their king.

Though their return to Westminster had been late in the day, and the other two wedding ceremonies had been performed, Dirick had refused to wait any longer to finalize his marriage to Maris. Henry, when told of the events of the day, had agreed to witness the wedding and had managed to roust the bishop from his prayers in order to say yet another marriage. Thus, the guests and witnesses to the joining of the Lord of Ludingdon and the Lady of Langumont had been limited to Henry and Eleanor, several men-at-arms from Langumont, Lady Laurette, and a smattering of other nobility. Maris's mother, Allegra, had not been found in time for the ceremony.

Maris pressed close to her new husband after she curtsied to the royal couple, enjoying his warmth and solidness. Though she'd had time to bathe and dress for the ceremony while Dirick was making the arrangements, she'd been unable to shake off the horror of the scene in the wood…and the knowledge that Michael d'Arcy had not been found. Thus, she realized, lay the reasoning behind Dirick's insistence that they wed immediately.

She remained in a happy daze throughout the quick meal of cold pheasant, cheese, and bread that they ate in the Great Hall, and she imbibed a more generous amount of wine than usual. It made her warm and trembly, especially when she thought about being with Dirick in the marriage bed. Though she'd expected this wedding between two of the more powerful nobility to be a grand affair, with feasting, dancing, and entertainment, Maris was not altogether displeased at the outcome.

Taking another sip of the rich bordeaux from Aquitaine, she reflected that 'twas just as well that she did not have to make merry among a throng of guests and well-wishers until it was such a time as to go abovestairs, else she would surely go mad from the wait. Her heart skipped a beat every time Dirick looked at her with the hooded grey eyes that bespoke of his own impatience for the evening to end. He offered her a small bit of cheese and lightly caressed the center of her bottom lip as she opened her mouth to accept it. The lids of his eyes swept down, then rose, and the flare of desire in them was unmistakeable.

"Let us go abovestairs," he told her.

"Aye," she breathed, curving her mouth into a tremulous smile.

They stood and the chatter of their companions stilled. "Whither are you off to, Lord Dirick?" grinned the king.

"I do not believe 'tis too difficult to divine my destination, your grace," growled Dirick.

"Aye, then, be off with you." Henry waved them away.

Maris looked at Dirick in surprise as they backed away from

the king and the other well-wishers. There was to be no bedding ceremony?

"Come," Dirick hissed, taking her hand and pulling her quickly from the hall, "before they decide to follow us!"

She stumbled along as quickly as her long skirts would allow, thankful that she was not to be disrobed in front of a gaggle of women and gawking men before being urged into bed with her husband.

They reached their chamber safely and without escort.

Dirick ushered Maris within, closing the door firmly behind him. Agnes had stoked the fire into a low blaze to keep the night chill from the damp room, and now she dozed on the floor near their bed.

Maris shook her maid awake and dismissed her. "There is no need to attend me this night," she told Agnes, watching as Dirick sat to remove his boots. "My husband will assist me." She loved the sound of those words from her lips: my husband.

She barred the heavy door behind Agnes, then turned slowly to face her husband. He was naked from the waist up: a golden statue of muscle and glittering eyes and coarse dark hair in the firelight. He sat on a stool near the blaze, watching her as he had done the night she treated his stab wound. This night, she knew, would end much differently.

"Maris, my love, come here," he invited, holding out his hands to her.

Nervous, excited, anticipatory, she moved quickly to him and allowed him to pull her onto his lap. He drew the transparent veil from her head and thrust his fingers into the long thickness of her hair, combing through the braids and untangling the mass of waves and curls. "Your hair is so beautiful," he told her, pressing a kiss to the end of a thick lock.

He stroked the edge of her chin, then closed his lips over her mouth in a wonderful, sensual kiss that left her breathless. His hands, knowing and experienced, unfastened the golden girdle that rested on her hips and eased the long overtunic over her head with barely a pause in his kisses.

The warmth that had pooled in her belly surged to the very center of her being when he slid two hands over her breasts, gently teasing their nipples into miniature erections while he tasted the long cord of her neck. Maris felt the rasp of his breath in her ear sharpen and catch when she boldly traced his own flat nipples in the thick expanse of hair on his chest. His muscles tightened, shivered, as she smoothed the flats of her hands over his breast and down the sides of his ribs and abdomen. Lightly, lightly, she ran the raggedness of her fingernails over the back of his shoulders, down and around to the ridges of his belly. Tiny bumps followed their paths and he shivered.

Abruptly, Dirick stood and directed her toward the large bed where the curtains had been pulled back invitingly. Sprigs of rosemary and violets lay on their pillows, and he swept them to the side before easing Maris onto the plush bed. She watched, unafraid, as he slid his breeches down over lean hips and well-defined, muscular thighs. A sigh culled the back of her throat when he came to lie next to her, pulling her to the long, warm length of his body.

Her chest rose and fell, and he placed his hand over the swell of one breast, allowing it to rise and fall with it.

"Maris," he spoke, looking at her directly. "Do you…do you know what is to happen?" The gentleness in his grey eyes stirred her and she reached up to smack a playful kiss onto his lips.

"Aye, Dirick, 'tis no secret to me what a man and woman do when they mate. And…I am not afraid," she told him. "I am not afraid of you. I welcome you." Her fingers twisted in the thick hair that dropped from his forehead, then fell, drifting down his chest and boldly to the hardness between his legs. She brushed against him and he stiffened, catching his breath…and when she closed her fingers over that hard, soft, pulsing heat, the groan that came from the back of his throat was primal and needy.

"You are bold, my lady," he flashed a tense grin at her, pulling out of her greedy reach. "And I find myself at an unfair advantage as I am at your mercy and you are still armored by some manner of cloth. Allow me to rid you of your protection."

With a quick movement, he yanked the fragile cloth, rending it down the center of her body, leaving its ivory curves bare to his gaze. "Dirick," she admonished laughingly, "you've just ruined the dearest piece of cloth I've ever purchased."

"I don't care," he mumbled, burying his face between her breasts.

Maris gave a cry of delight that quickly changed to a moan of pleasure. When he closed his lips over one hard, thrusting nipple, she bucked her hips in surprise at the pang that shot to the place between her legs.

He raised his head, looking at her with glazed, intense eyes. A hand smoothed over her belly to that warm, moist place where all of her senses seemed to have collected, fingering, teasing the thatch of hair that grew there. The desire in his gaze deepened, darkening as he felt her respond to him as he stroked, tickled, and taunted that center of her.

When his fingers were sliding easily in, out, and around her, and her breaths were short and labored, he leaned forward to press a kiss under her ear. "Beloved, I would not hurt you, but I cannot prevent it and I must have you now!"

With a fluid motion, he moved between her legs, anchoring up on one elbow while he guided himself to her opening. And then, suddenly, she felt him fill her, full, oh…full…. and then the sharp pain…and then pleasure, heat, a spiraling feeling that reached to ends of her limbs.

She knew, hazily, that he reached his fulfillment when he threw his head back and froze like a beautiful god above her:

bronzed, muscled, corded neck, sweat streaming from his brow, and those beautiful lips parted in a sigh of perfection.

ꝓ

When Dirick awoke much later that night…or mayhaps 'twas nearing the morning…the first thing he saw was the unruly mass of thick, lemony-smelling hair that belonged to his wife.

Joy welled inside him and he smoothed a wrist-thick wave away from her face, baring the fair skin and rosy lips of Maris. She stirred and sleepily rolled over toward him. Her eyes fluttered, then opened wide as if surprised to see him. Then, they shuttered and a smile curved her mouth before she opened them again, now fully awake.

"Good morrow, dearling," she told him, reaching to touch his face.

"Good morrow, beloved." His voice was raspy with desire and sleep. "How do you feel?"

"Wonderful," she told him, stretching like a cat. "And 'tis all you to blame!"

He grinned sensually down at her. "I will not shirk that blame, my lady." Squinting at the sunlight filtering through a light tapestry, he said, "'Tis morn. They'll arrive anon to check that the sheets are blooded."

"Aye." Instead of ducking her head in embarrassment, Maris eagerly drew the blankets away from their naked bodies to show the white sheet and its dark red drops of blood.

Dirick rose from the bed to use the chamberpot, and Maris followed. They embraced in passing; one long, lean, haired body pressing to a smaller, softer, rounder one.

Though he felt himself harden in response to her proximity, Dirick pulled reluctantly away. Their chamber would soon be invaded by a delegate to ascertain whether the marriage had indeed been consummated, and that the lady had indeed been a virgin…and he did not relish the thought of being interrupted thus.

"We will leave London this day," he told her as he sprawled back on the bed. He felt her gaze caress his nakedness and a shiver rippled down his spine at the realization that she was well and truly his. He forced his mind to more pragmatic things. "Michael d'Arcy has not been found, and you will not be truly safe until he is."

Maris wrapped a light cloth around her shoulders and curled on the edge of the bed. "He is my father," she told him unsteadily.

Dirick pulled her to rest her head on his chest. "I learned that only yesterday. I am sorry, my dearling, that I did not know sooner."

"He killed my father—Merle."

"I know that, or suspected that, as well. He is the man who killed my father—the one that I spoke of to you." Dirick tightened his lips. "I will not rest until he is found."

Maris pulled away, sitting up to look down at him. "You will have a care, Dirick. You will not put yourself in danger. Michael has killed so many—"

"I cannot let him go unpunished." He searched her face with his gaze, seeing the love and respect that shone in her green and gold eyes. "You must know I love you, Maris. I never thought to feel this way, but I could not live without you…and I must ensure that the one who would see you dead is also gone. And then I can have no fear that you will be taken from me by a crazed madman."

Her fingers smoothed the hair back from his forehead. "How lucky I am that my papa chose to repudiate my betrothal to Victor…else I would surely be a murderess on this morn."

Dirick smiled. "Had that happened, I would have spirited

you away before the ceremony that bound you to him…or after you had done the deed, I'd have been your escape route." He frowned, "'Tis always bothered me: why would you think I could have been party to your kidnapping by Bon?"

"What else was I to think when I tumbled onto the floor and looked up to see you staring down upon me?" Maris asked indignantly.

"But…I thought you'd known me better than that…and, Maris, how could I have stolen you for someone else when I wanted you for myself? Did you not know that I wanted you? That was why I had to leave Langumont so suddenly—I could not bear to see you given to another!"

She looked at him with wondering eyes. "I did not know, truly. I could only think that you had wooed me to your side so as to make your abduction of me easier."

"Oh, nay, Maris. On the night we first met, I wanted you…and that desire grew, and so did the despair that I could never have you. I could not believe my good fortune when Henry betrothed us…and then he showed me the missive from your father.

"In that missive, not only did he repudiate your betrothal with Victor," Dirick could not hold back a grin, "but he also requested that, if the king agreed, I should be your husband and Lord of Langumont."

She gaped at him. "'Twas my papa's wish that we should wed?"

"Aye, my lady, and 'twas also the wish of my father that one of his sons should wed with you as well."

"Our fathers have exacted a sort of revenge upon Michael d'Arcy, then." She managed a wavering smile.

"Aye, they have. Yet, I still must see this through to its end," he told her firmly.

"Dirick, you must take care…please," she looked up at him

so earnestly and sweetly, with tears pooling in her eyes, that he felt his heart jerk at the emotion there.

"Aye, my love, I will take care. After all," he pulled her fingers to his lips, "I have everything to live for. I have everything I could ever want. And I have no intention of letting it go."

Epilogue ⌘

Come, my love," Michael grasped Allegra's hand and drew her up the tall, curving stairwell.

She followed him willingly, as she had ever done, and always would, until the end of time.

The tower was cool and damp. It was a part of the keep that she rarely accessed, and which normally sent chills down her spine…but today, it didn't matter. Today, she was with Michael.

Her skirt trailed in the dust as they clambered up more steps and more steps, holding hands, silent.

When they reached the top, he opened the door and allowed her to step out onto the balcony of the tower ahead of him. She felt his strong, sturdy body behind her, solid and fearless in its warmth. The wind was stronger at this height, and the view of the blue sea sparkling to the west was expansive. The sound of the surf was lost in the breeze, lending a hollow, windy sound and giving the impression that they were separated from the rest of the world.

They were.

She looked over the lands of Langumont, seeing the village, the bailey of the keep below, noticing the thickness of the forest to the east and the varying shades of green meadow to the north and south.

She'd been happy here. Though her heart had always been with Michael, she'd been happy. Merle had been a good husband to her. She had betrayed him in so many ways, and now he was dead…by the hand of the man she loved.

Michael had told her of his part in Merle's death…yet, she still loved him. It was her curse, her damnation, that she should love such an evil man with all her heart. She would follow him willingly, anywhere, until the end of time.

"Are you frightened?" he asked suddenly, his voice rumbling in her ear.

"When I am with you—nay, never," she told him, turning to face him. They could not be together here, she knew. This was their only chance.

"Come, Allegra, let us go."

He took her hands in his, facing her fully, and looking down at her with those blue eyes lit with an odd, unsettling light.

She moved willingly with him to the edge of the tower's railing, stepping up on it in tandem with him. "I love you," she told him.

"I love you."

And then it was over.

COLLEEN GLEASON lives near Ann Arbor with her husband and children. She works full-time in the managed care industry, has an interest in a small publishing company, and loves to cook...but what she really would rather be doing is writing about knights in shining armor, ghosts, and intelligent, take-charge heroines.

She's always loved Disney's version of *Sleeping Beauty*, but what really cinched her love for the medieval time period was seeing the movie *Becket* one rainy Sunday afternoon...then shortly thereafter discovering *Ivanhoe*, the stories of King Arthur...and, later, Roberta Gellis's Roselynde Chronicles.

This is her first published novel, and all of her royalties will be donated to the Cystic Fibrosis Foundation in honor of her son.

Journeys of the Heart

An anthology of stories by

Colleen Gleason
(including the prequel to *A Whisper of Rosemary*)
and
best-selling author
Denise Dietz

Linda Colwell
Sally Painter
Kelley Pounds

Sample some of Avid Press's favorite authors with our new historical romance anthology *Journeys of the Heart*

Each of the five novellas feature a map that helps bring two lovers together through adventure and intrigue.... And each novella will have a full-length sequel published by Avid Press in 2001!

ISBN: 1-929613-92-X $6.99 paperback

Available from:
Amazon.com
Avidpress.com
1-888-AVIDBKS

Includes a chance to win $100 worth of free books!